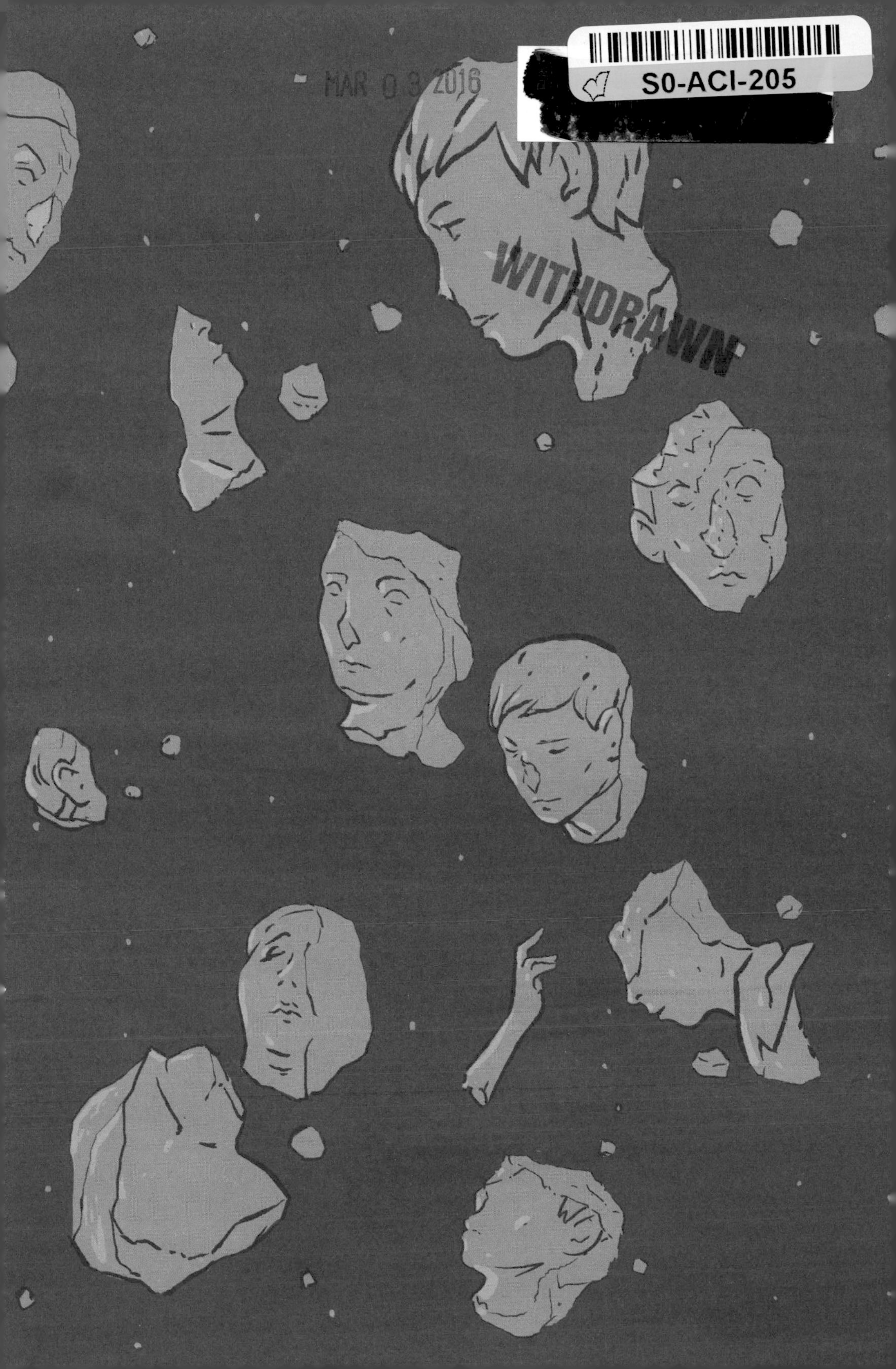

ISCARIOT ™

a Graphic Novel by
S. M. VIDAURRI

Published by
ARCHAIA ™

For my Mother

and all single mothers

raising two daughters

and one little boy

who did that high-pitched scream

much too often.

Written, illustrated & created by
S. M. VIDAURRI

Letters by
LEIGH LUNA

Designer **KELSEY DIETERICH**
Assistant Editor **CAMERON CHITTOCK**
Editor **SHANNON WATTERS**
Special Thanks to **REBECCA TAYLOR**

ARCHAIA.

Ross Richie CEO & Founder • Mark Smylie Founder of Archaia • Matt Gagnon Editor-in-Chief • Filip Sablik President of Publishing & Marketing
Stephen Christy President of Development • Lance Kreiter VP of Licensing & Merchandising • Phil Barbaro VP of Finance • Bryce Carlson Managing Editor
Mel Caylo Marketing Manager • Scott Newman Production Design Manager • Irene Bradish Operations Manager • Christine Dinh Brand Communications Manager
Dafna Pleban Editor • Shannon Watters Editor • Eric Harburn Editor • Ian Brill Editor • Whitney Leopard Associate Editor
Jasmine Amiri Associate Editor • Chris Rosa Assistant Editor • Alex Galer Assistant Editor • Cameron Chittock Assistant Editor • Mary Gumport Assistant Editor
Kelsey Dieterich Production Designer Jillian Crab Production Designer • Kara Leopard Production Designer • Michelle Ankley Production Design Assistant
Devin Funches E-Commerce & Inventory Coordinator • Aaron Ferrara Operations Coordinator • José Meza Sales Assistant • Elizabeth Loughridge Accounting Assistant
Stephanie Hocutt Marketing Assistant • Hillary Levi Executive Assistant • Kate Albin Administrative Assistant • James Arriola Mailroom Assistant

ISCARIOT, October 2015. Published by Archaia, a division of Boom Entertainment, Inc. Iscariot is ™ and © 2015 Shane-Michael
Merritt Vidaurri. All Rights Reserved. Archaia™ and the Archaia logo are trademarks of Boom Entertainment, Inc., registered in various
countries and categories. All characters, events, and institutions depicted herein are fictional. Any similarity between any of the names,
characters, persons, events, and/or institutions in this publication to actual names, characters, and persons, whether living or dead, events,
and/or institutions is unintended and purely coincidental.

BOOM! Studios, 5670 Wilshire Boulevard, Suite 450, Los Angeles, CA 90036-5679. Printed in China. First Printing.

ISBN: 978-1-60886-761-5, eISBN: 978-1-61398-432-1

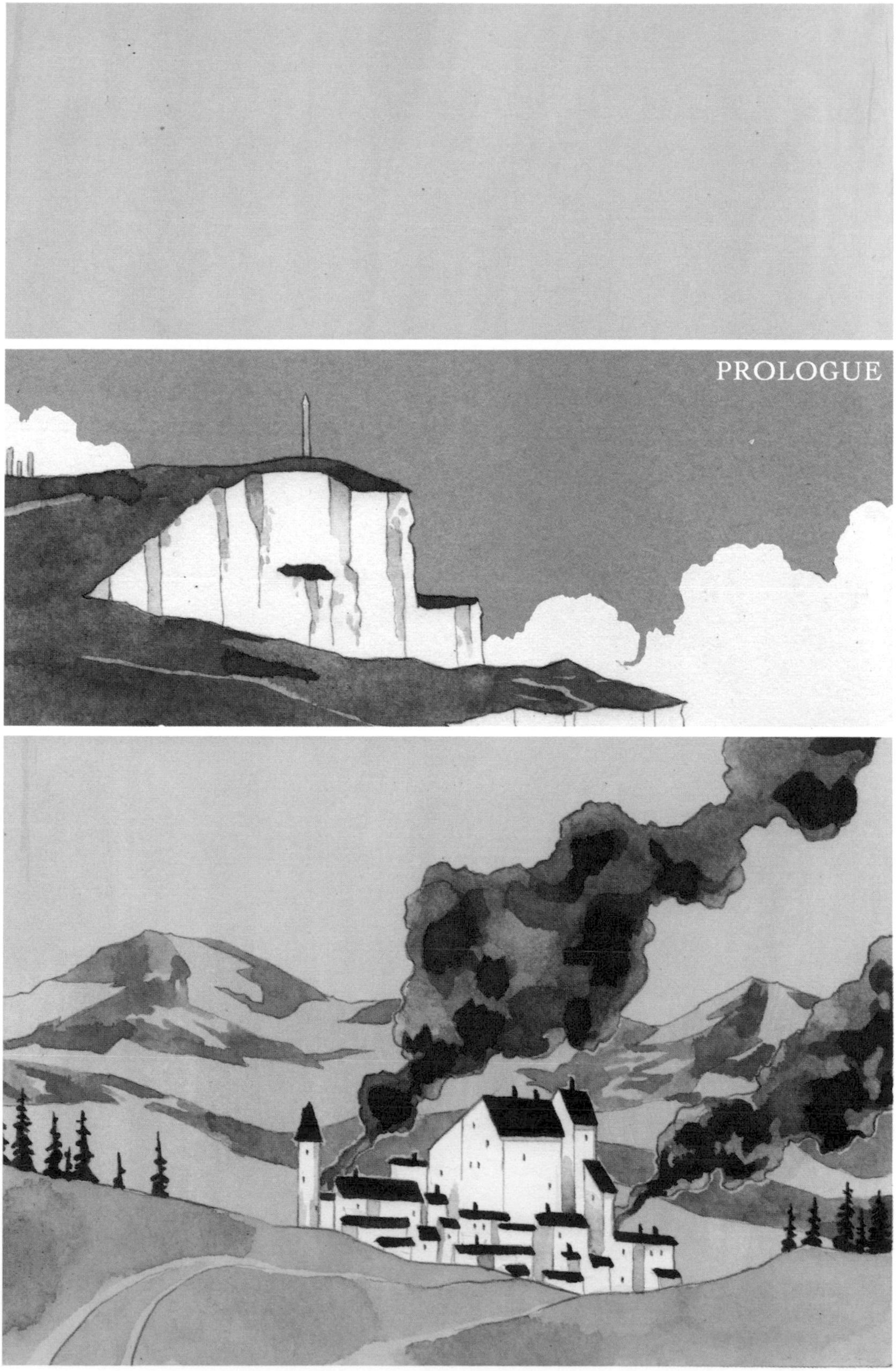
PROLOGUE

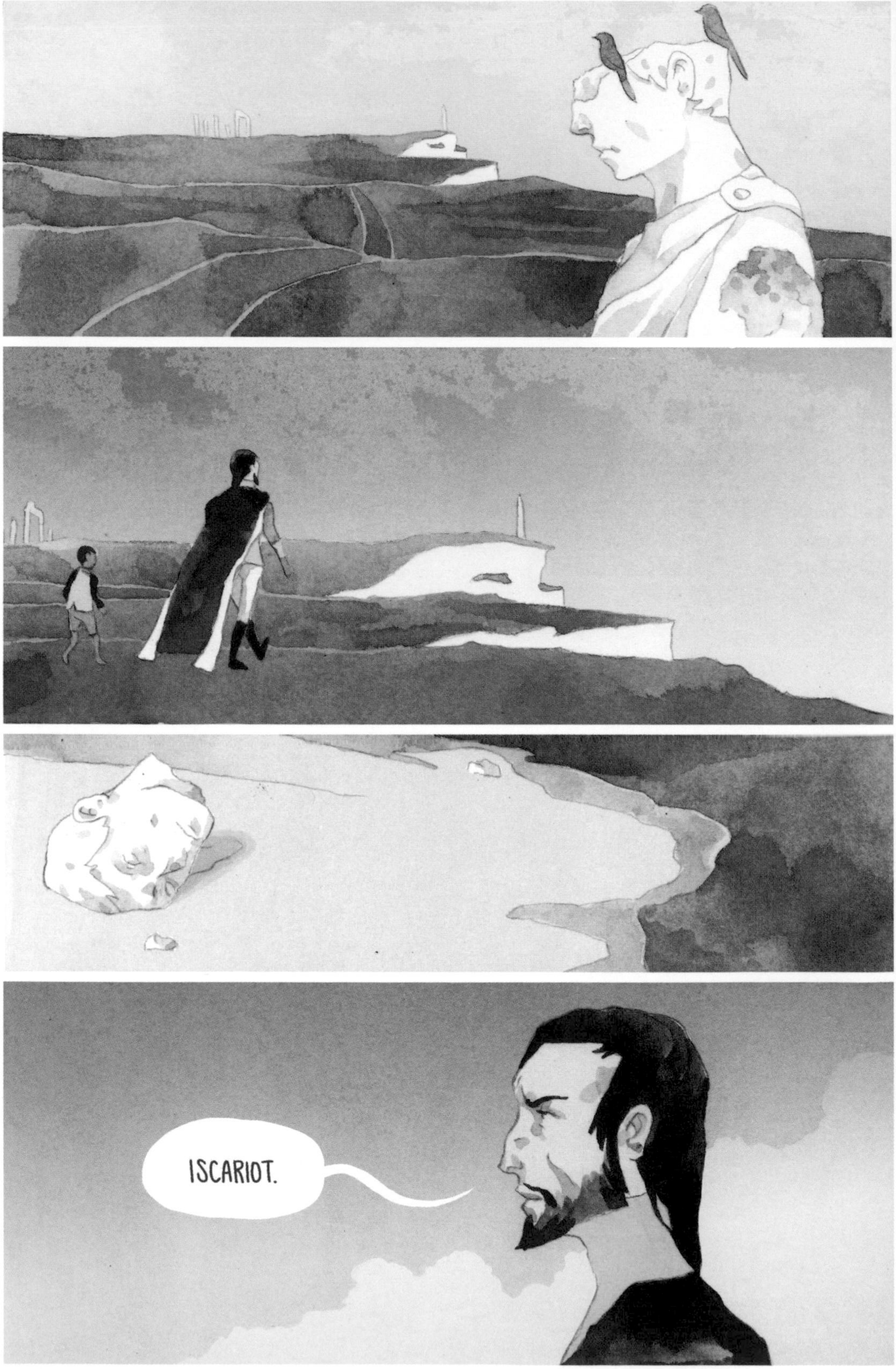
ISCARIOT.

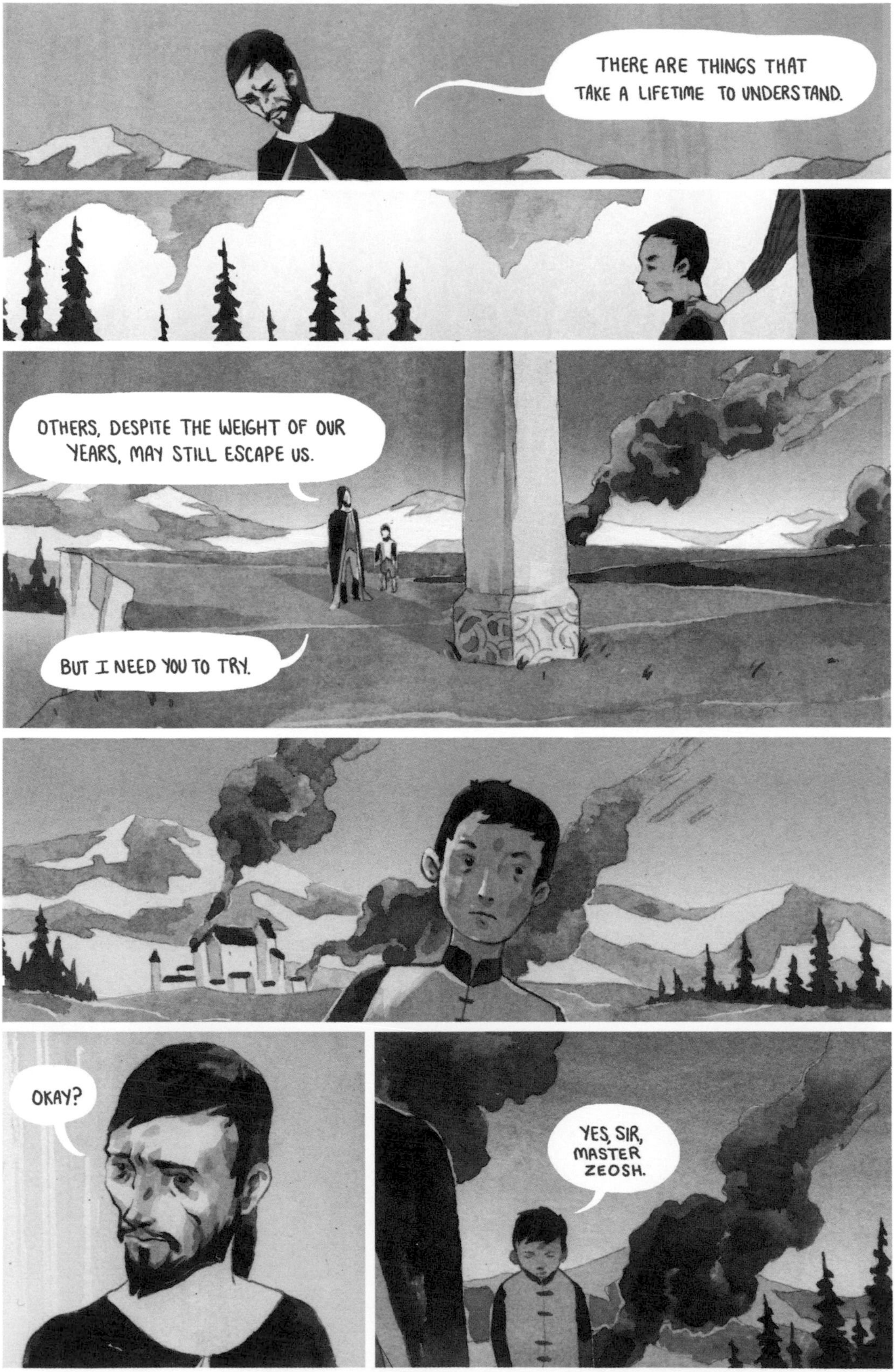
THERE ARE THINGS THAT TAKE A LIFETIME TO UNDERSTAND.
OTHERS, DESPITE THE WEIGHT OF OUR YEARS, MAY STILL ESCAPE US.
BUT I NEED YOU TO TRY.
OKAY?
YES, SIR, MASTER ZEOSH.

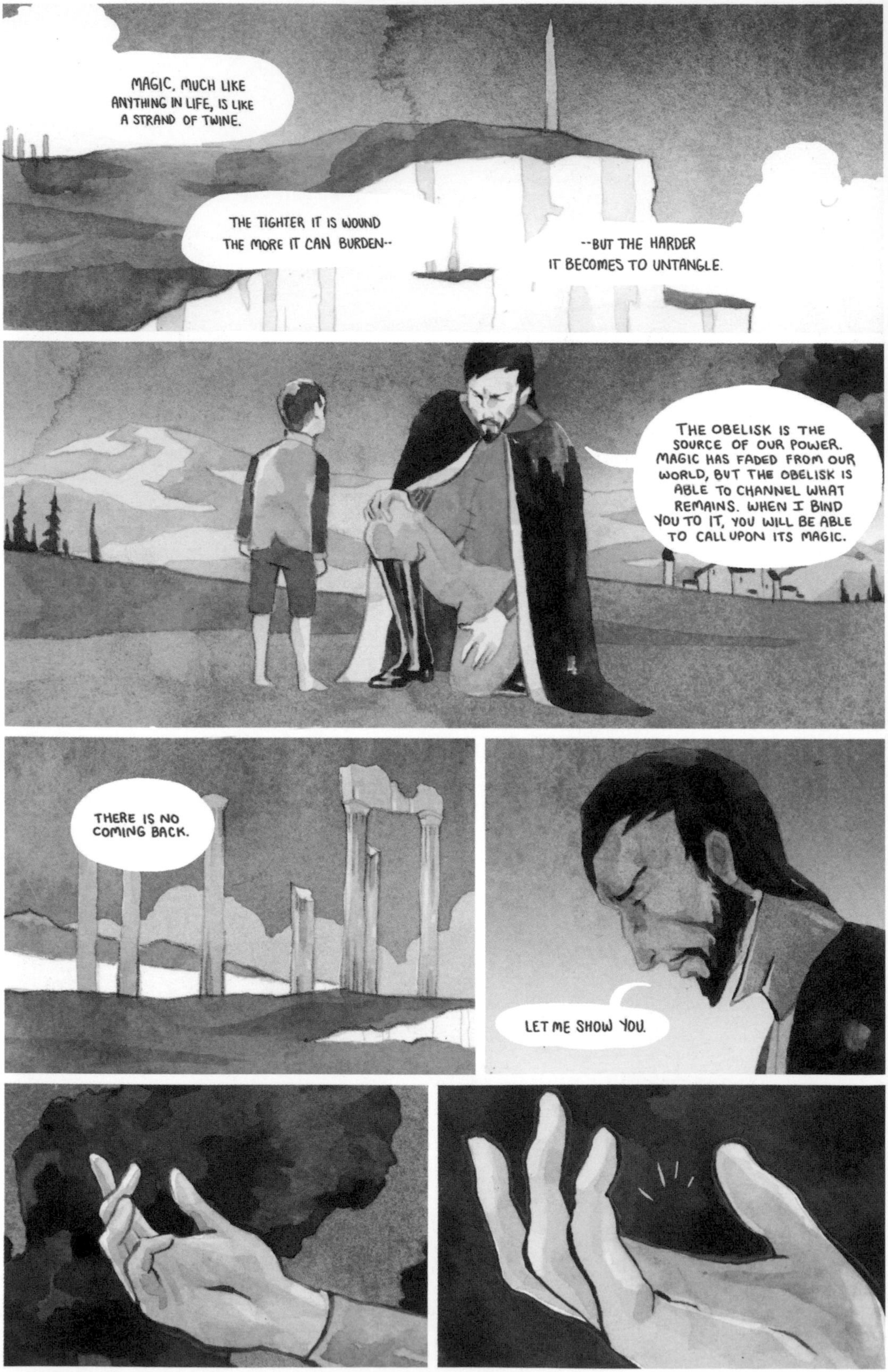
MAGIC, MUCH LIKE ANYTHING IN LIFE, IS LIKE A STRAND OF TWINE.
THE TIGHTER IT IS WOUND THE MORE IT CAN BURDEN--
--BUT THE HARDER IT BECOMES TO UNTANGLE.
THE OBELISK IS THE SOURCE OF OUR POWER. MAGIC HAS FADED FROM OUR WORLD, BUT THE OBELISK IS ABLE TO CHANNEL WHAT REMAINS. WHEN I BIND YOU TO IT, YOU WILL BE ABLE TO CALL UPON ITS MAGIC.
THERE IS NO COMING BACK.
LET ME SHOW YOU.

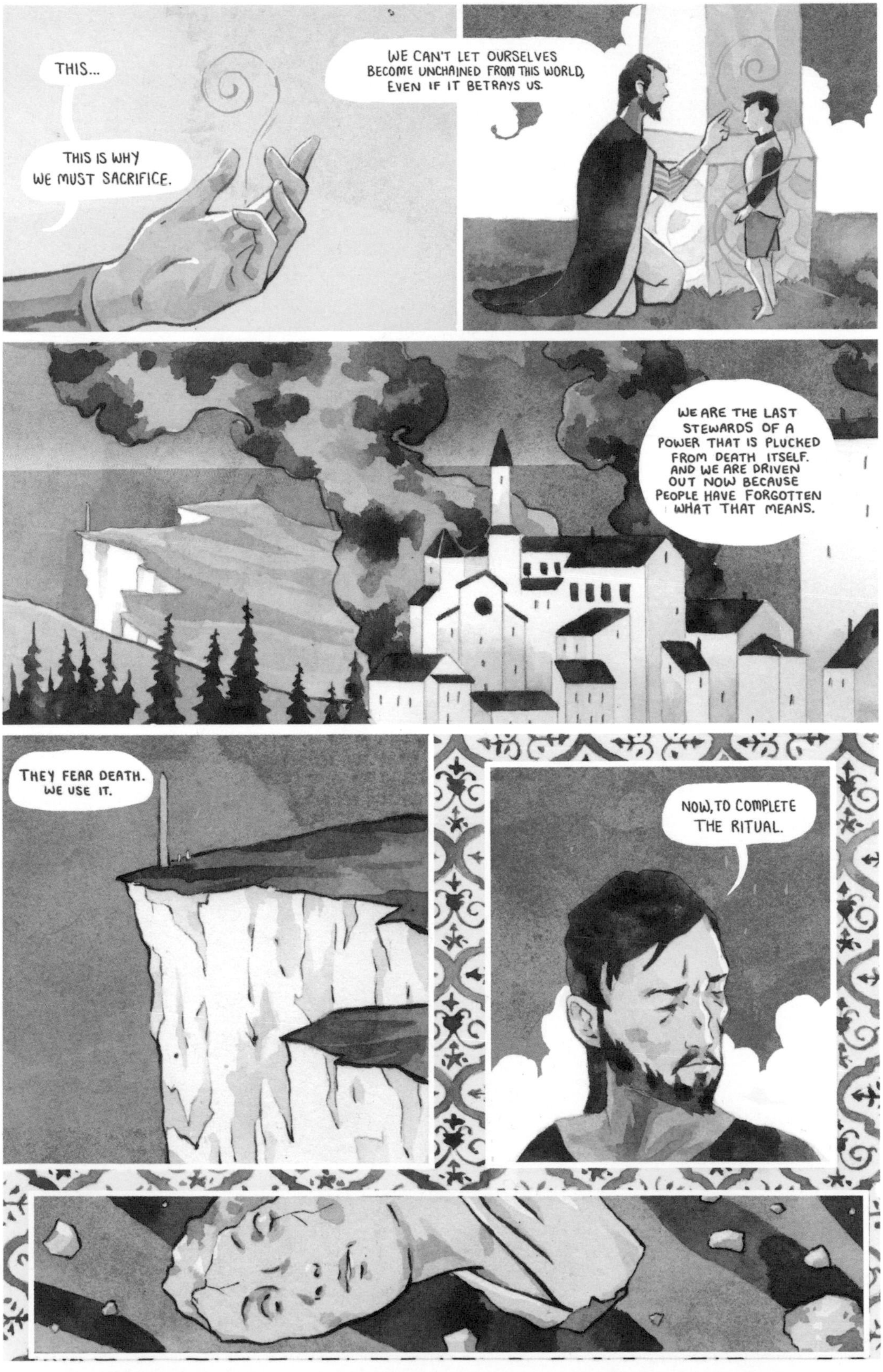
THIS...
THIS IS WHY WE MUST SACRIFICE.
WE CAN'T LET OURSELVES BECOME UNCHAINED FROM THIS WORLD, EVEN IF IT BETRAYS US.
WE ARE THE LAST STEWARDS OF A POWER THAT IS PLUCKED FROM DEATH ITSELF. AND WE ARE DRIVEN OUT NOW BECAUSE PEOPLE HAVE FORGOTTEN WHAT THAT MEANS.
THEY FEAR DEATH. WE USE IT.
NOW, TO COMPLETE THE RITUAL.

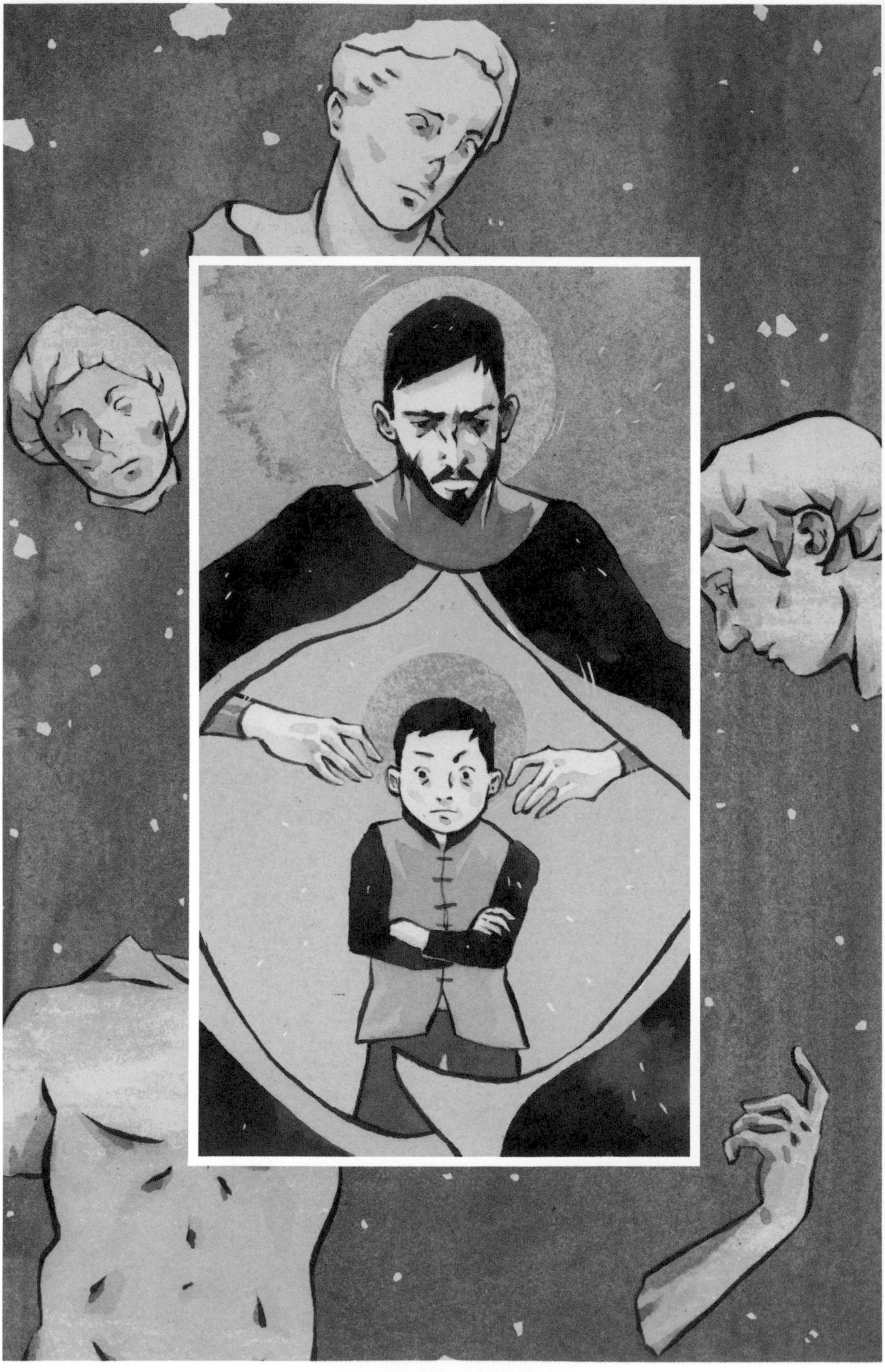

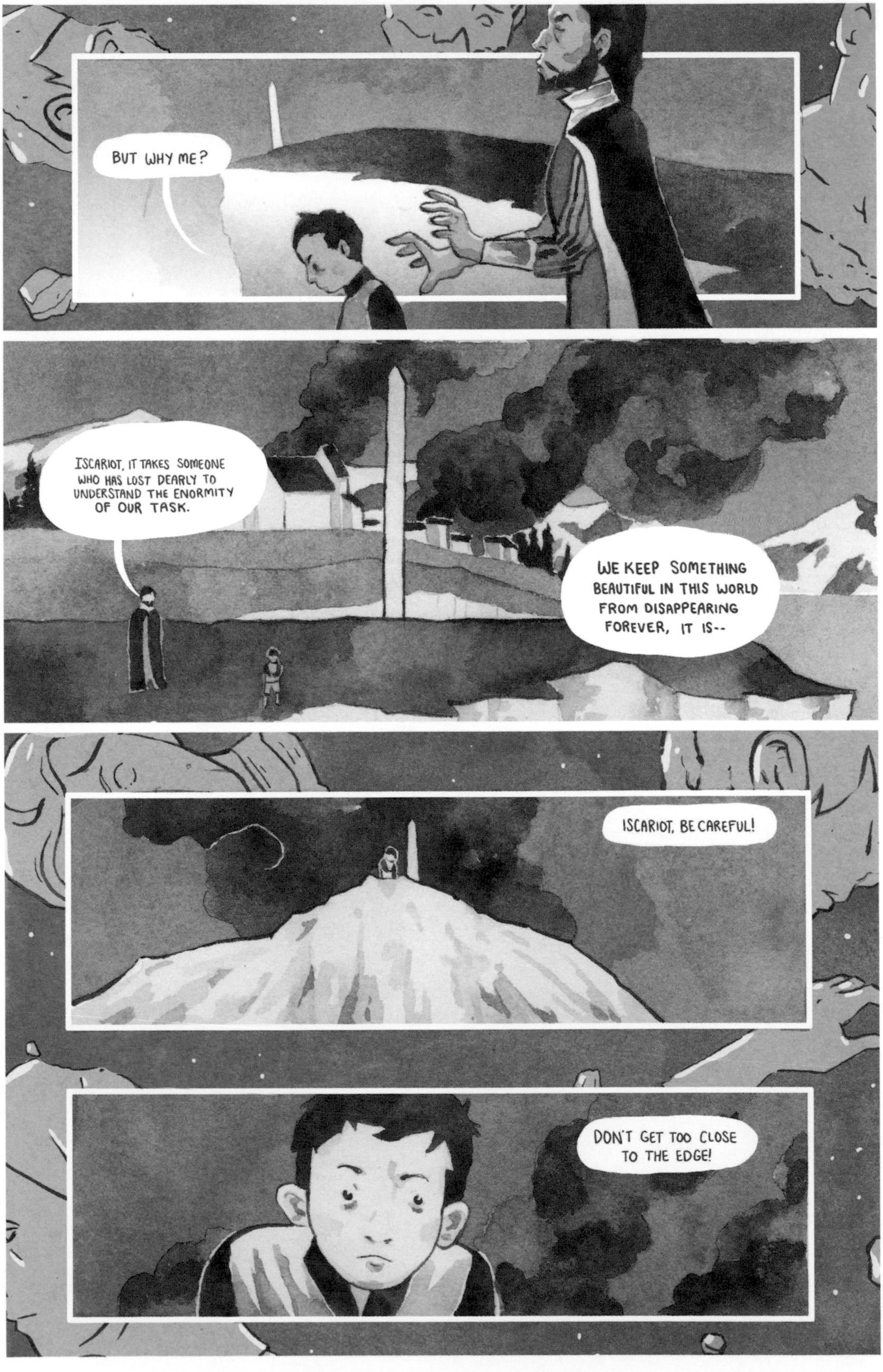
BUT WHY ME?
ISCARIOT, IT TAKES SOMEONE WHO HAS LOST DEARLY TO UNDERSTAND THE ENORMITY OF OUR TASK.
WE KEEP SOMETHING BEAUTIFUL IN THIS WORLD FROM DISAPPEARING FOREVER, IT IS--
ISCARIOT, BE CAREFUL!
DON'T GET TOO CLOSE TO THE EDGE!

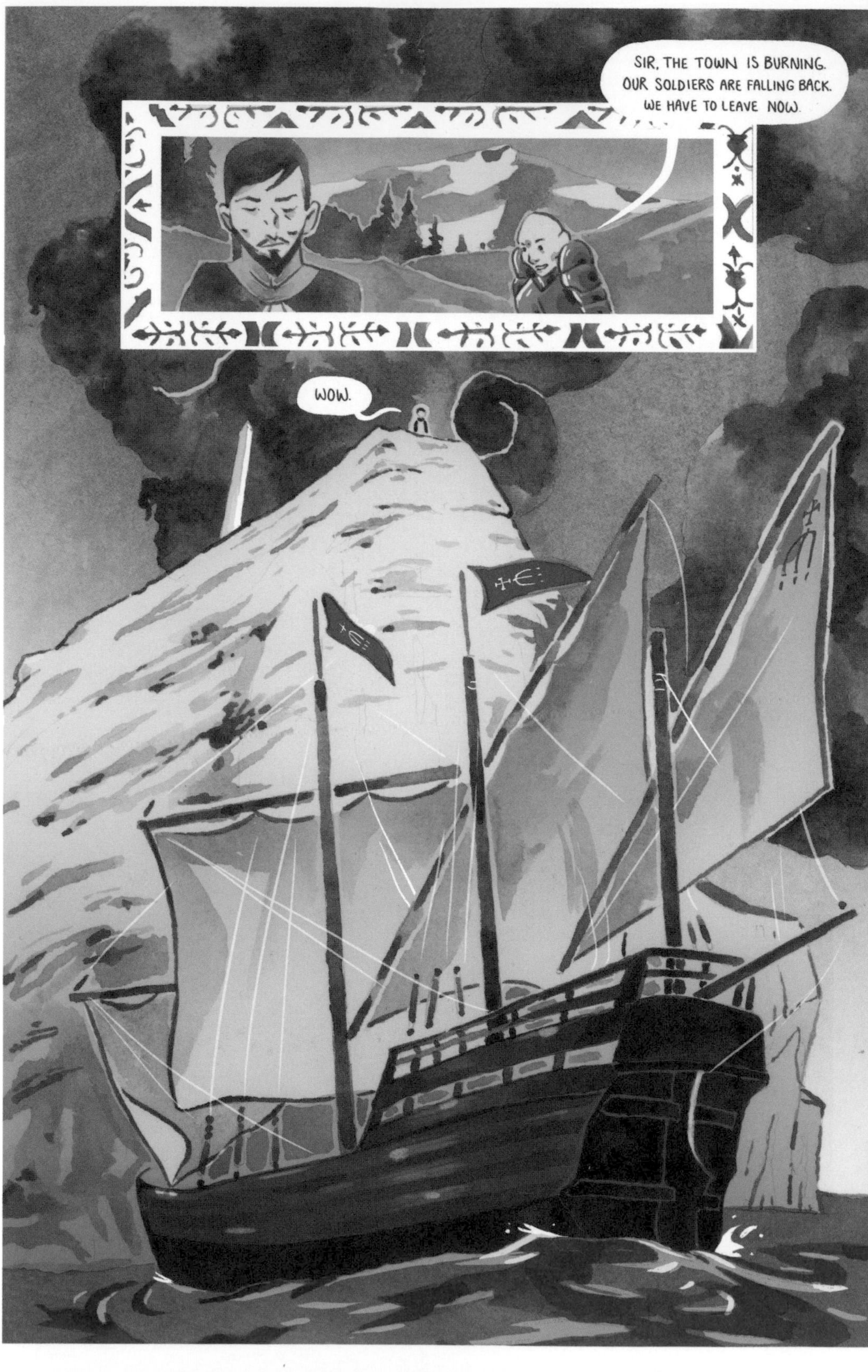
SIR, THE TOWN IS BURNING. OUR SOLDIERS ARE FALLING BACK. WE HAVE TO LEAVE NOW.
WOW.

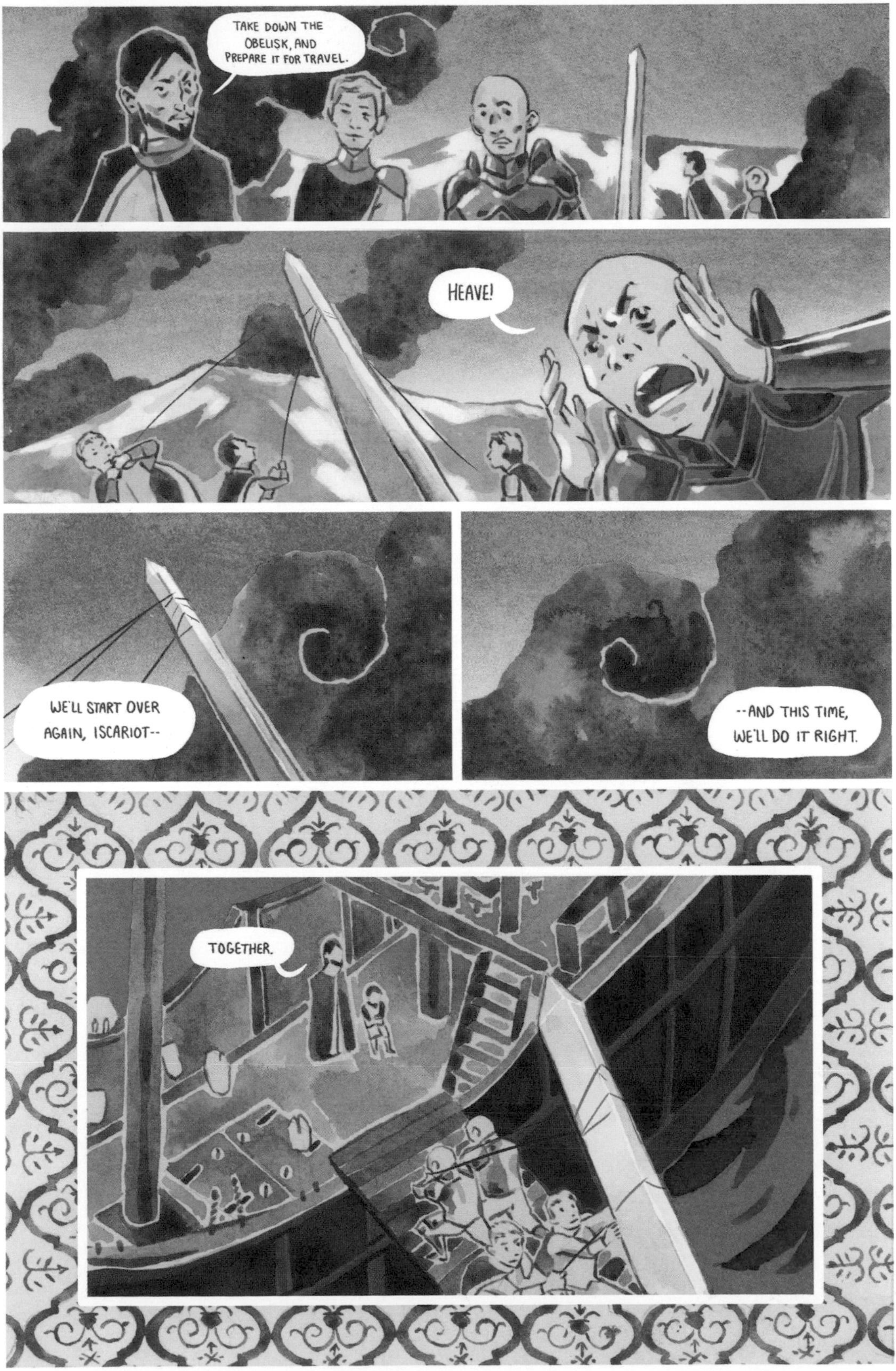
TAKE DOWN THE OBELISK, AND PREPARE IT FOR TRAVEL.
HEAVE!
WE'LL START OVER AGAIN, ISCARIOT--
--AND THIS TIME, WE'LL DO IT RIGHT.
TOGETHER.

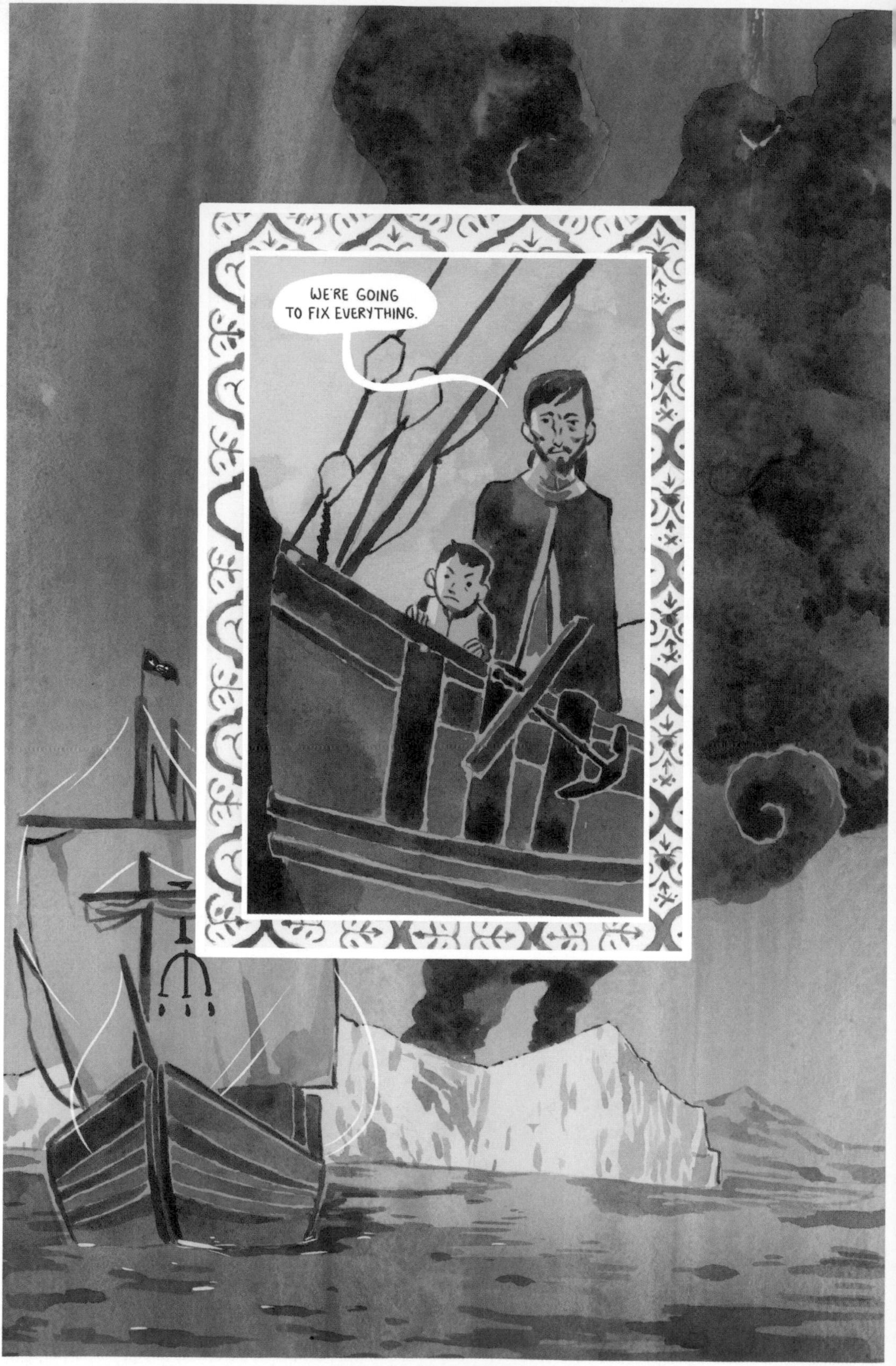
WE'RE GOING TO FIX EVERYTHING.

CHAPTER ONE

I want to say
But I don't want to ruin
Whatever there is to ruin.

Like a casket
Most people don't know
Breaks immediately
Under the weight of soil,

Roses.

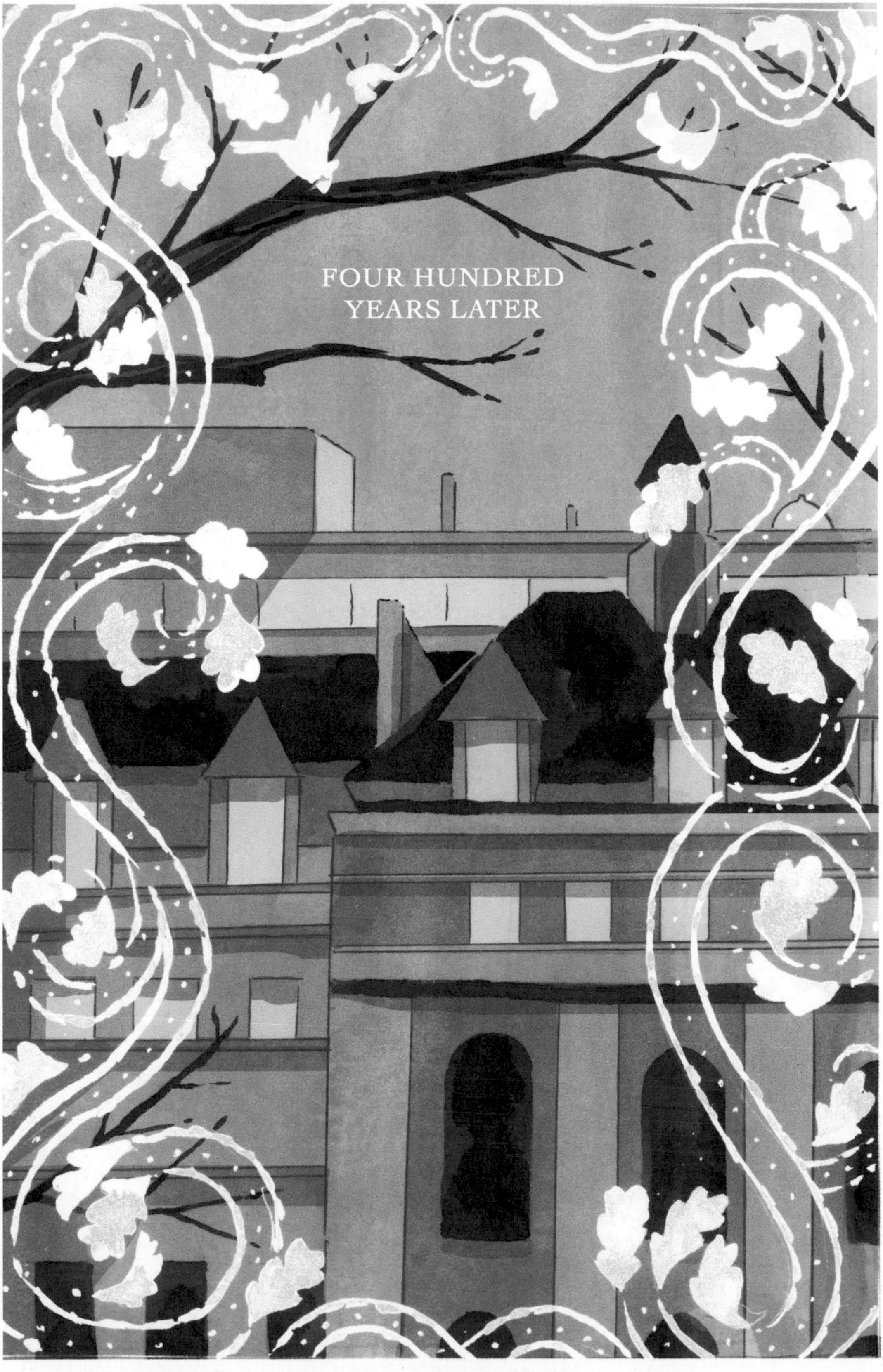
FOUR HUNDRED
YEARS LATER

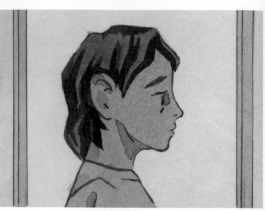

HEY, KIDDO.
SORRY, I'M LATE.

I BROUGHT
YOU A SNICKY BAR.

YEAH, BUT IF ADYAN
SEES ME EATING THAT,
HE'S GOING TO WANT ONE.

I BROUGHT
TWO!

THANKS.

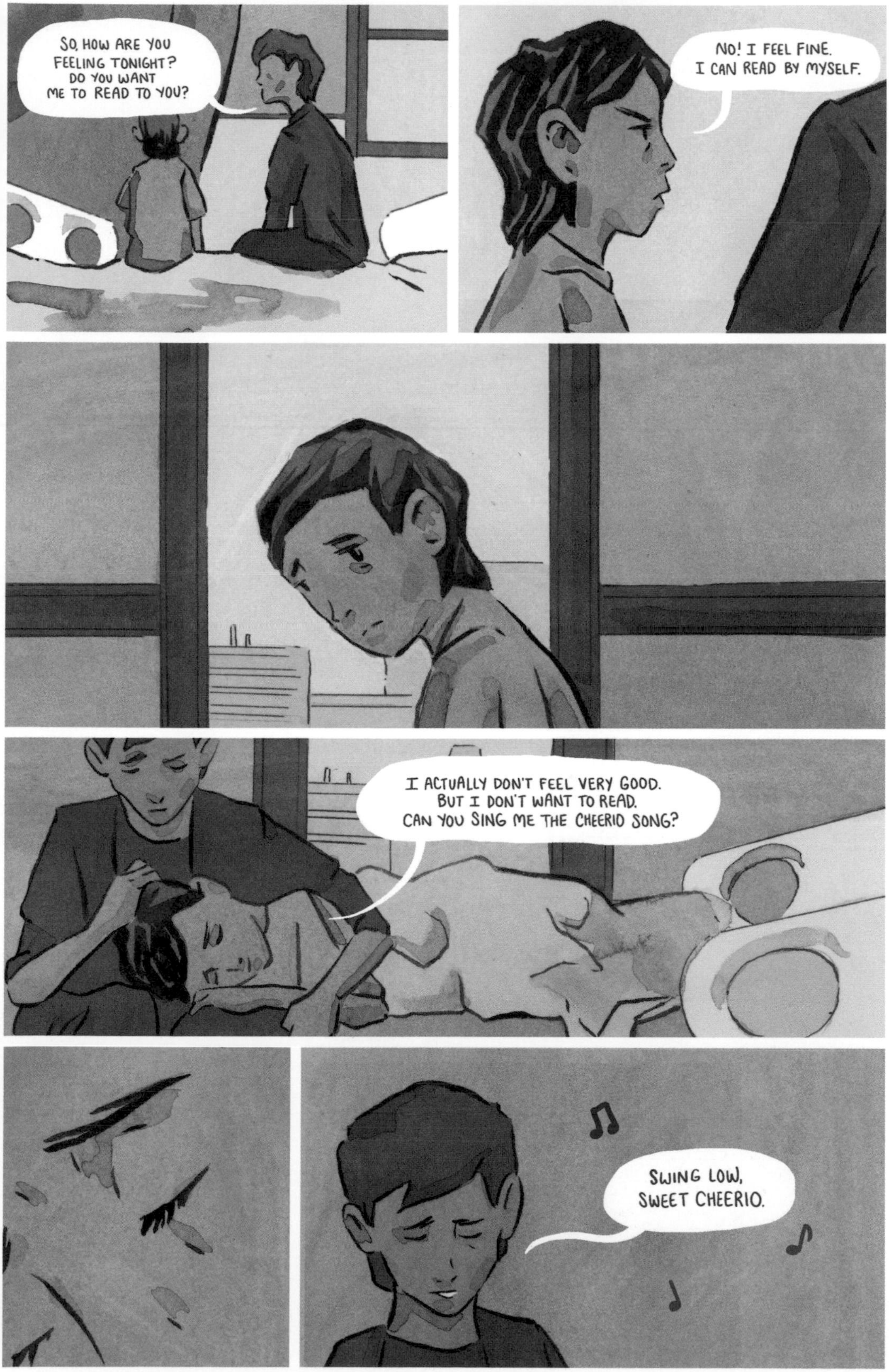
SO, HOW ARE YOU FEELING TONIGHT? DO YOU WANT ME TO READ TO YOU?
NO! I FEEL FINE. I CAN READ BY MYSELF.
I ACTUALLY DON'T FEEL VERY GOOD. BUT I DON'T WANT TO READ. CAN YOU SING ME THE CHEERIO SONG?
SWING LOW, SWEET CHEERIO.

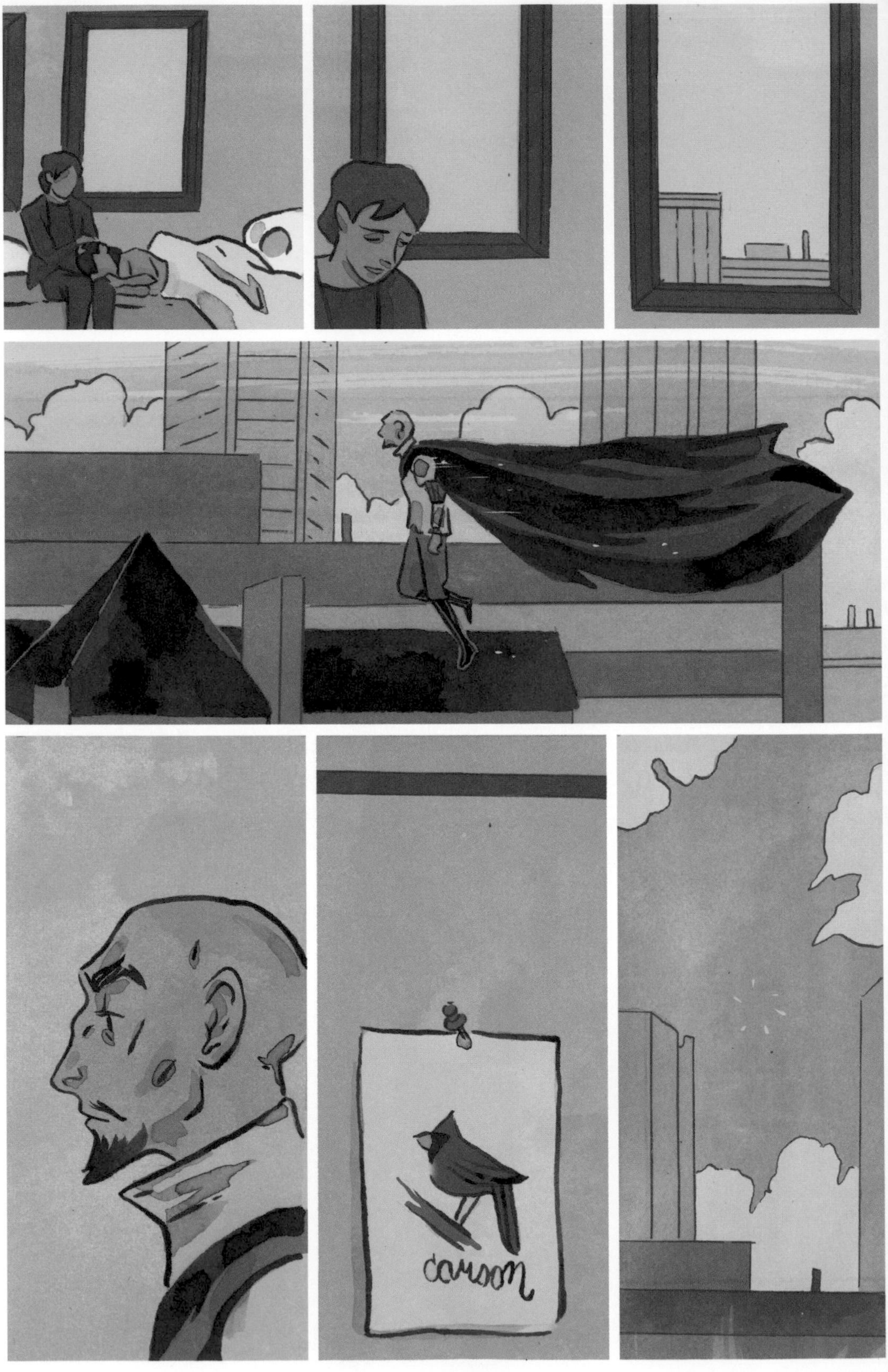
carson

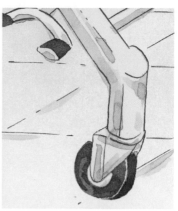

WHEN I WAS YOUNG, YOU COULD JUST USE THE DDT.

ME AND MY BROTHERS-- I LIVED IN HAWAII AT THAT TIME-- WELL, WE WOULD SPRAY EACH OTHER WITH SQUIRT GUNS FILLED WITH THE STUFF. YOU KNOW, BEFORE WE WENT OUT.

I HAVE TO GO, MIMI.

NOW IT'S ILLEGAL THEY SAY, CAN'T USE IT, HURTS BABIES OR SOME SUCH.

AND MAYBE THAT'S TRUE, BUT--

I'M REALLY SORRY, MIMI, BUT I HAVE TO GO. I'M GOING TO SEE THE MAGICIAN.

--BUT IT DID MORE GOOD THAN HARM, IF YOU ASK ME.

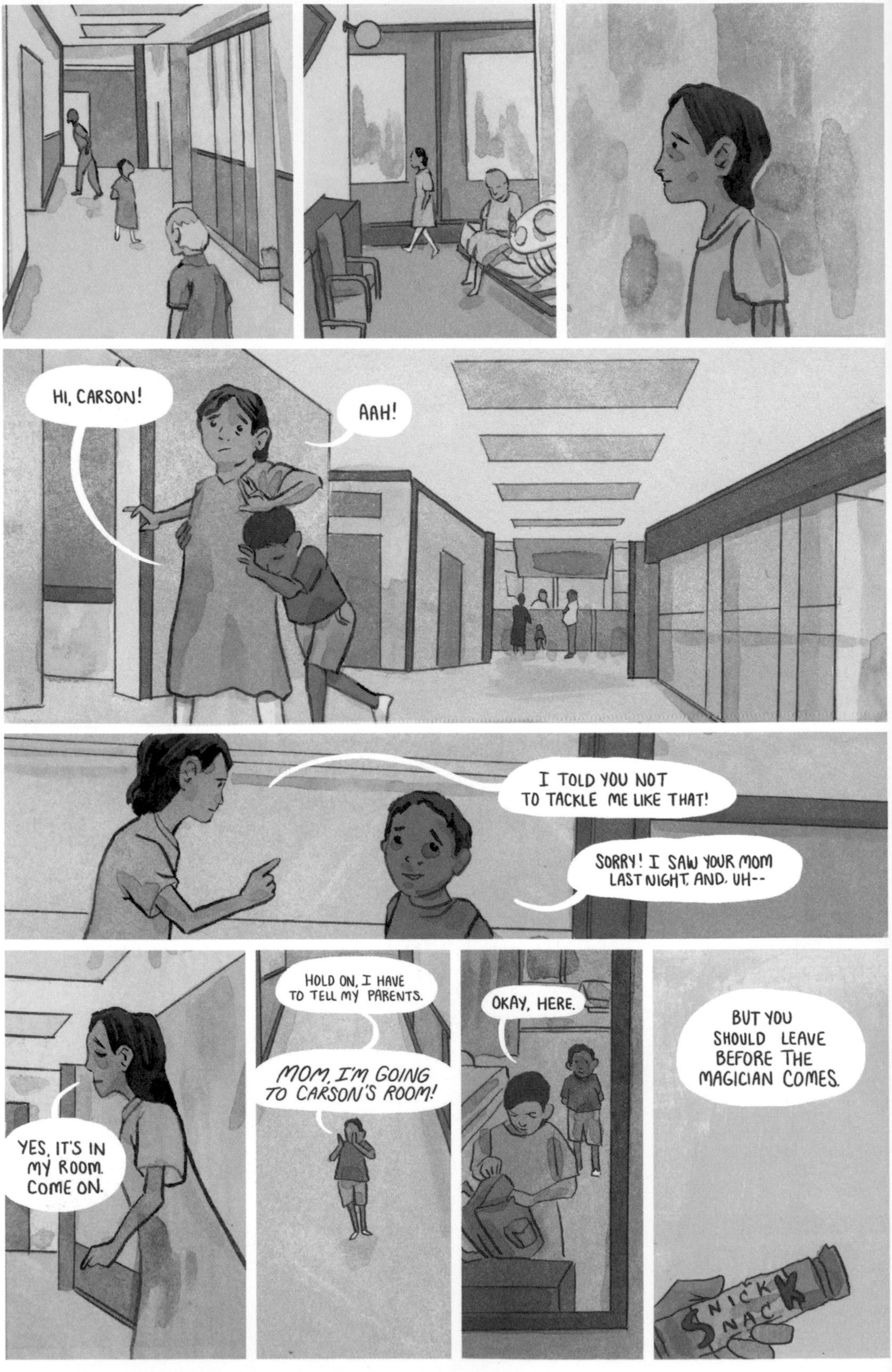
HI, CARSON!
AAH!
I TOLD YOU NOT TO TACKLE ME LIKE THAT!
SORRY! I SAW YOUR MOM LAST NIGHT, AND, UH--
YES, IT'S IN MY ROOM. COME ON.
HOLD ON, I HAVE TO TELL MY PARENTS.
MOM, I'M GOING TO CARSON'S ROOM!
OKAY, HERE.
BUT YOU SHOULD LEAVE BEFORE THE MAGICIAN COMES.
SNICK SNACK

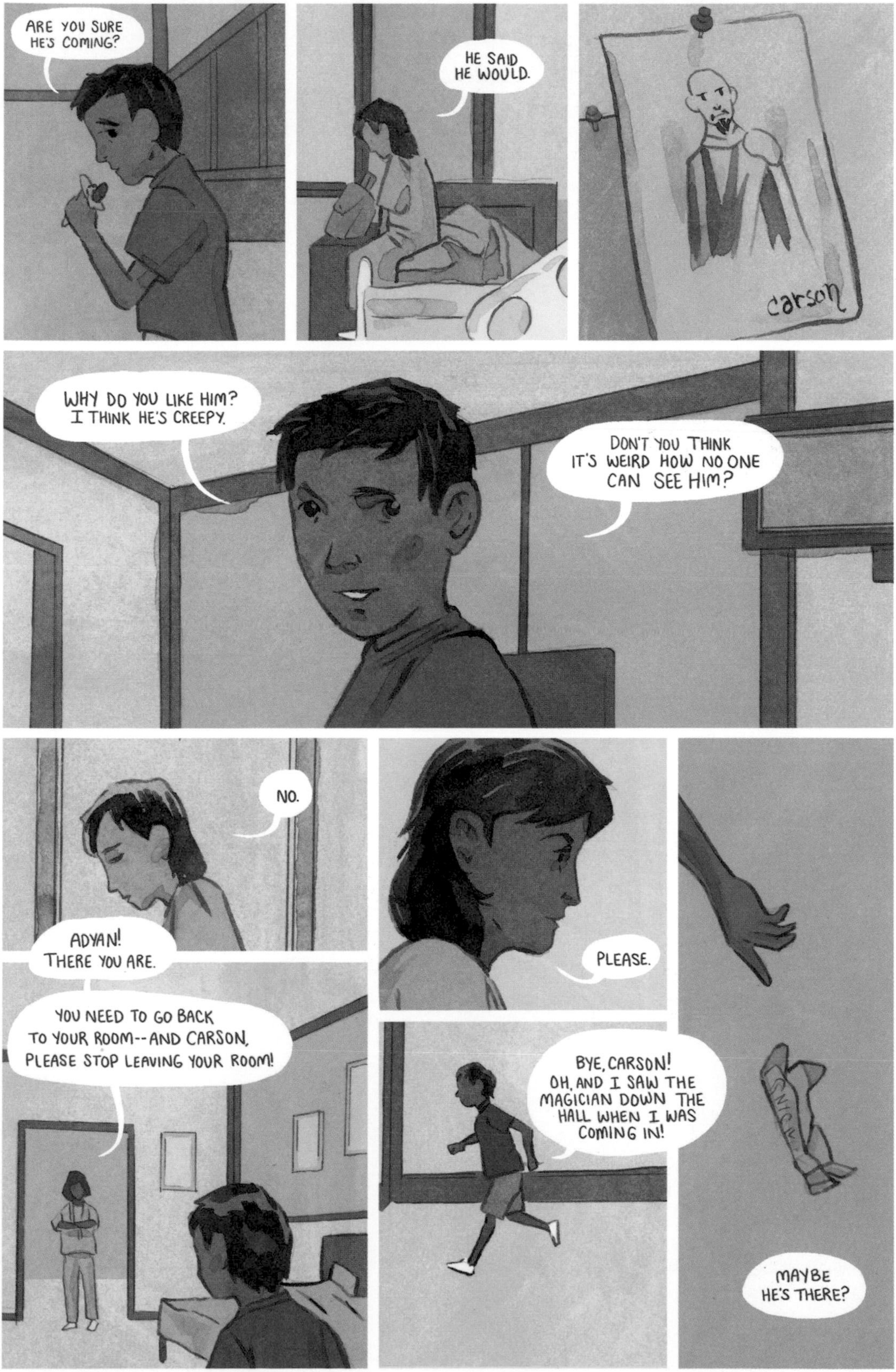
ARE YOU SURE HE'S COMING?
HE SAID HE WOULD.
carson
WHY DO YOU LIKE HIM? I THINK HE'S CREEPY.
DON'T YOU THINK IT'S WEIRD HOW NO ONE CAN SEE HIM?
NO.
PLEASE.
ADYAN! THERE YOU ARE.
YOU NEED TO GO BACK TO YOUR ROOM--AND CARSON, PLEASE STOP LEAVING YOUR ROOM!
BYE, CARSON! OH, AND I SAW THE MAGICIAN DOWN THE HALL WHEN I WAS COMING IN!
MAYBE HE'S THERE?

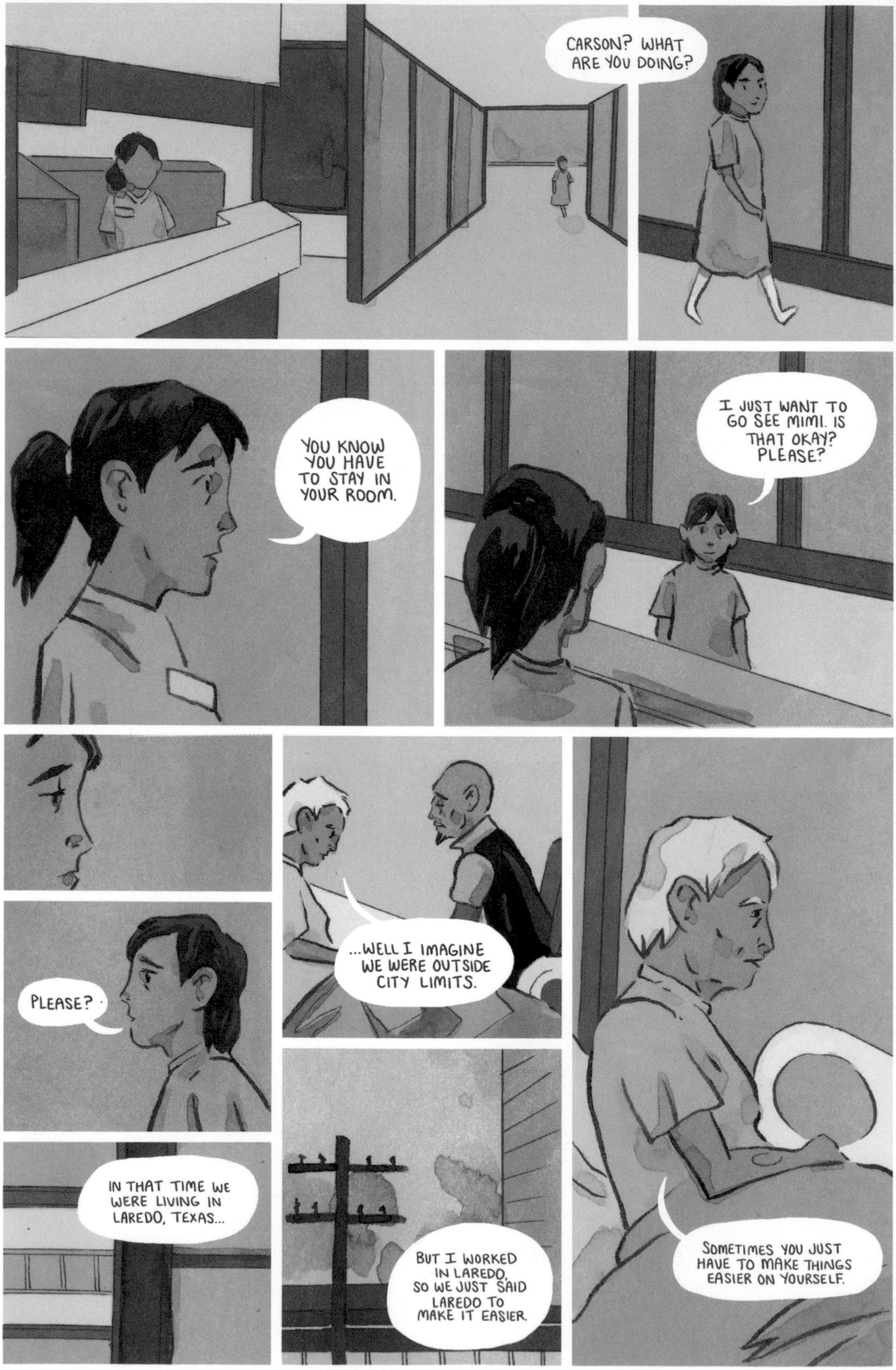
CARSON? WHAT ARE YOU DOING?
YOU KNOW YOU HAVE TO STAY IN YOUR ROOM.
I JUST WANT TO GO SEE MIMI. IS THAT OKAY? PLEASE?
PLEASE?
...WELL I IMAGINE WE WERE OUTSIDE CITY LIMITS.
IN THAT TIME WE WERE LIVING IN LAREDO, TEXAS...
BUT I WORKED IN LAREDO, SO WE JUST SAID LAREDO TO MAKE IT EASIER.
SOMETIMES YOU JUST HAVE TO MAKE THINGS EASIER ON YOURSELF.

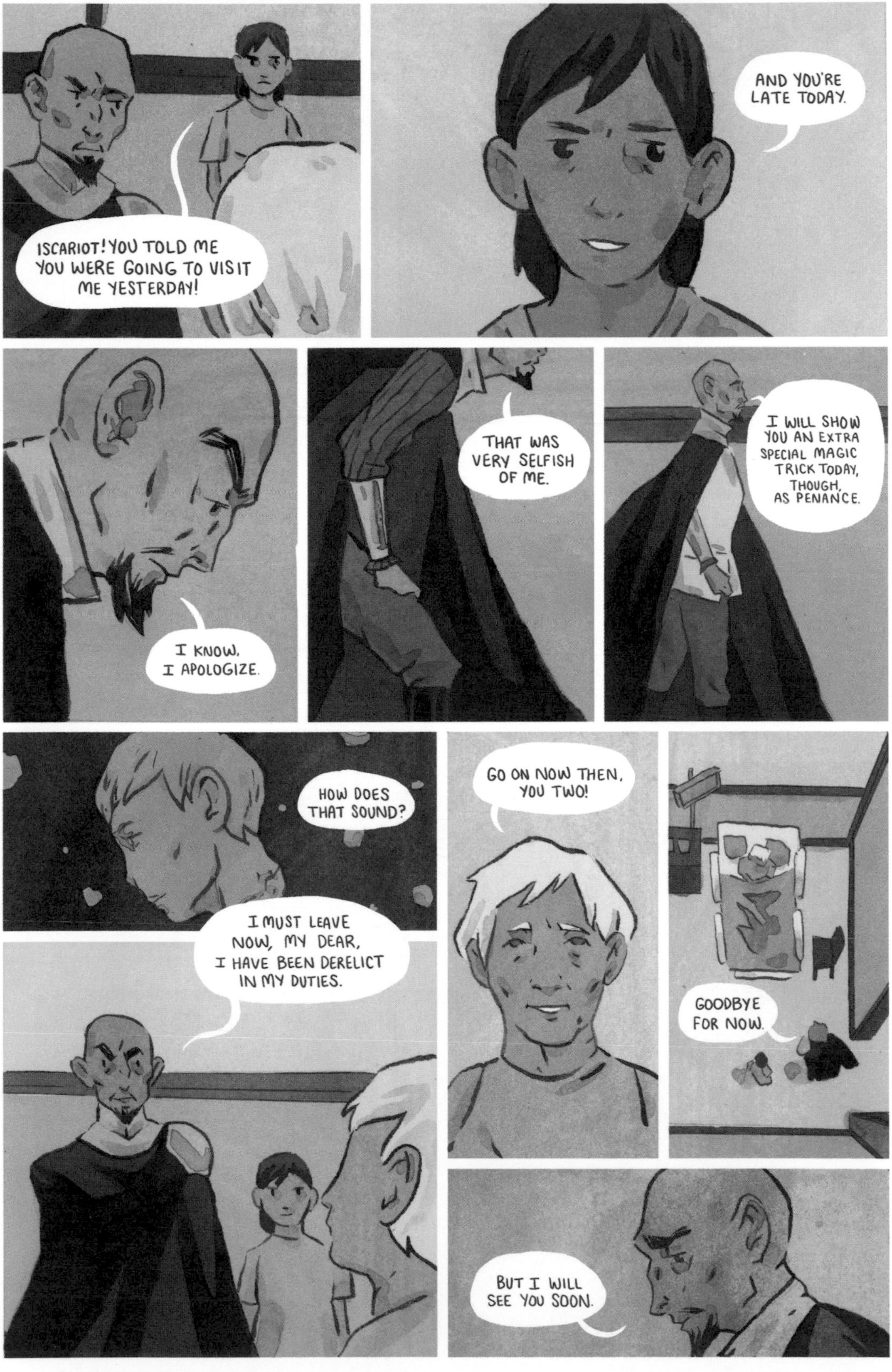
ISCARIOT! YOU TOLD ME YOU WERE GOING TO VISIT ME YESTERDAY!
AND YOU'RE LATE TODAY.
I KNOW. I APOLOGIZE.
THAT WAS VERY SELFISH OF ME.
I WILL SHOW YOU AN EXTRA SPECIAL MAGIC TRICK TODAY, THOUGH, AS PENANCE.
HOW DOES THAT SOUND?
I MUST LEAVE NOW, MY DEAR, I HAVE BEEN DERELICT IN MY DUTIES.
GO ON NOW THEN, YOU TWO!
GOODBYE FOR NOW.
BUT I WILL SEE YOU SOON.

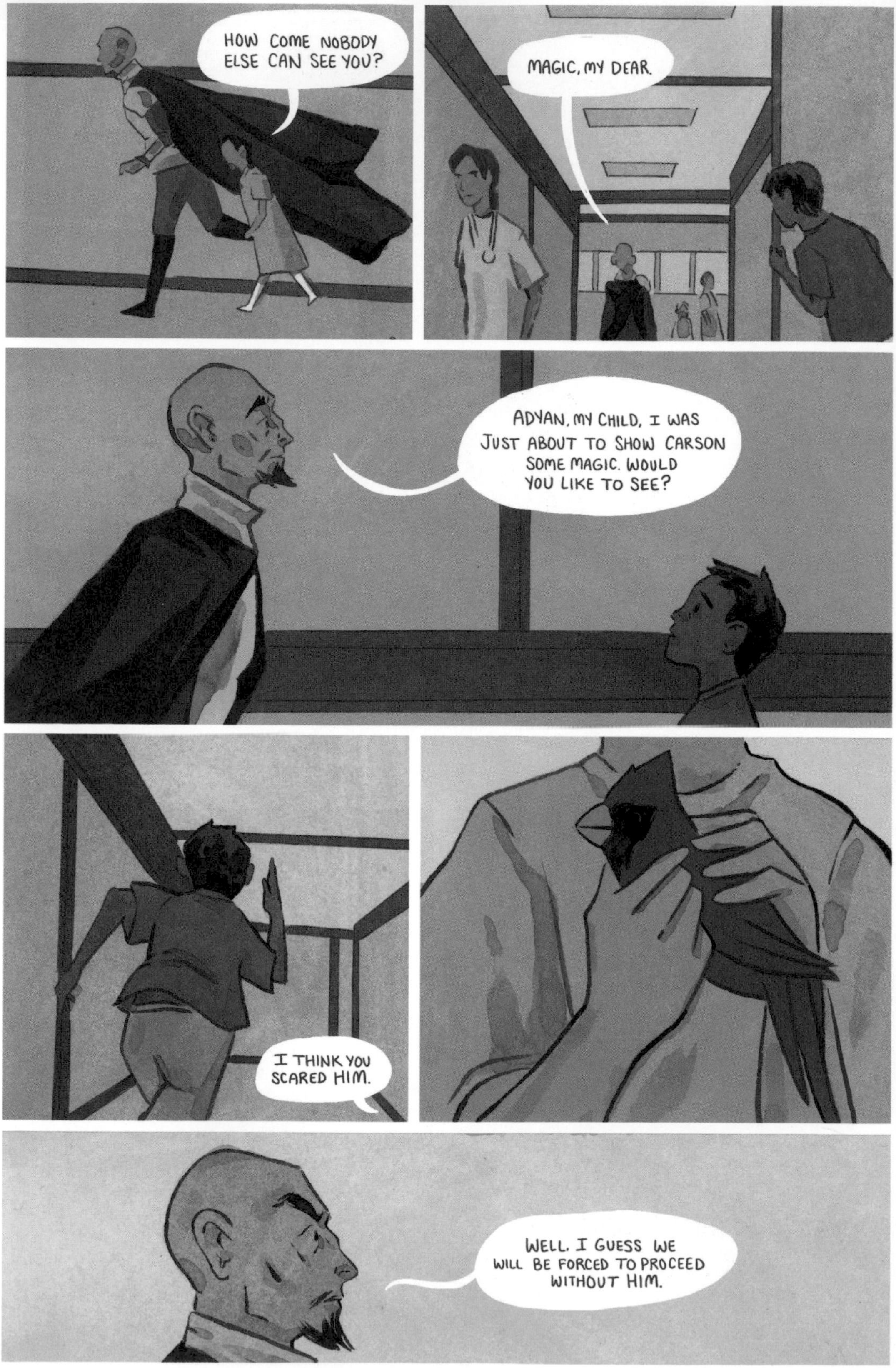
HOW COME NOBODY ELSE CAN SEE YOU?
MAGIC, MY DEAR.
ADYAN, MY CHILD, I WAS JUST ABOUT TO SHOW CARSON SOME MAGIC. WOULD YOU LIKE TO SEE?
I THINK YOU SCARED HIM.
WELL. I GUESS WE WILL BE FORCED TO PROCEED WITHOUT HIM.

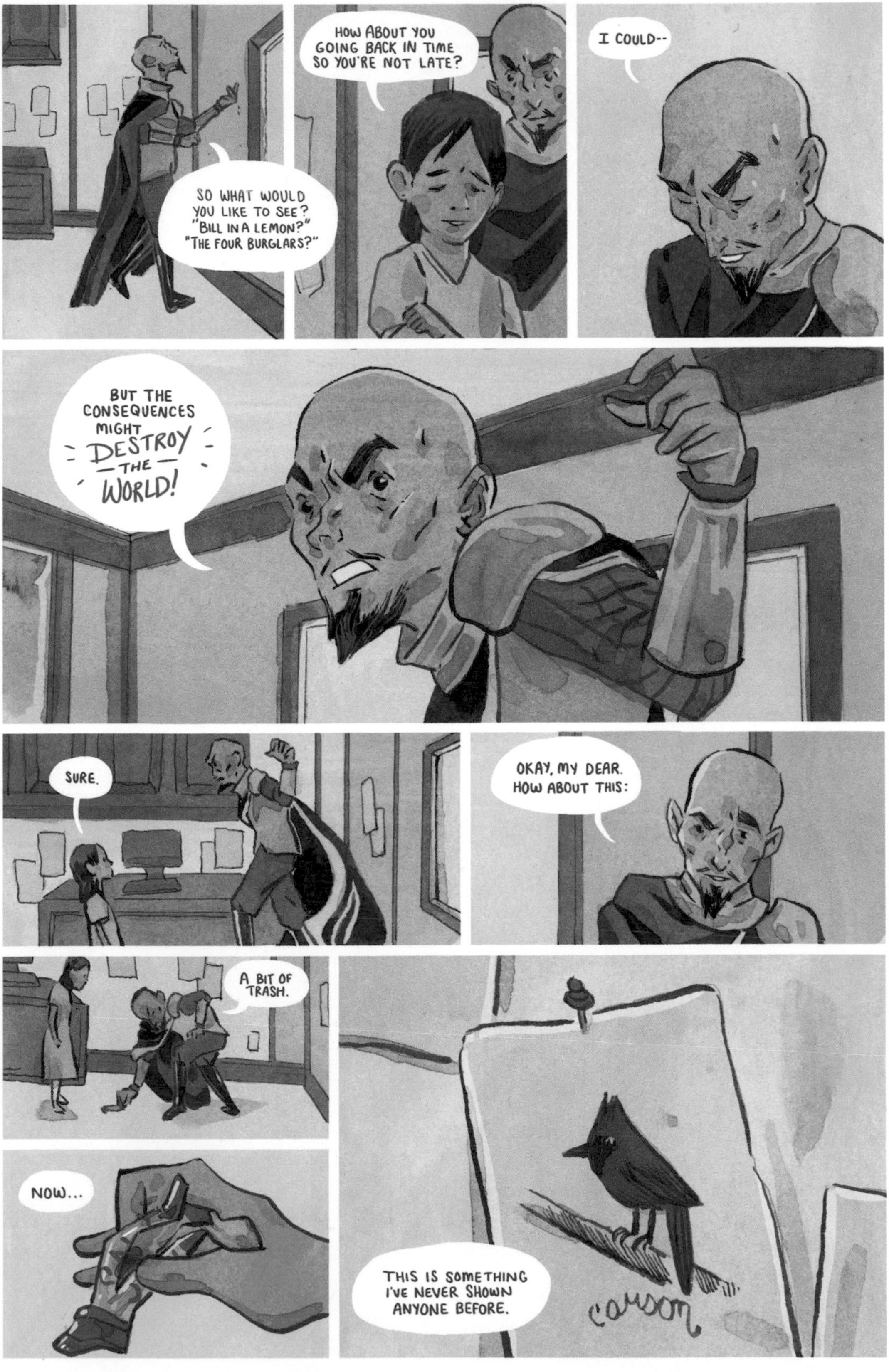
SO WHAT WOULD YOU LIKE TO SEE? "BILL IN A LEMON?" "THE FOUR BURGLARS?"
HOW ABOUT YOU GOING BACK IN TIME SO YOU'RE NOT LATE?
I COULD--
BUT THE CONSEQUENCES MIGHT DESTROY THE WORLD!
SURE.
OKAY, MY DEAR. HOW ABOUT THIS:
A BIT OF TRASH.
NOW...
THIS IS SOMETHING I'VE NEVER SHOWN ANYONE BEFORE.
CARSON

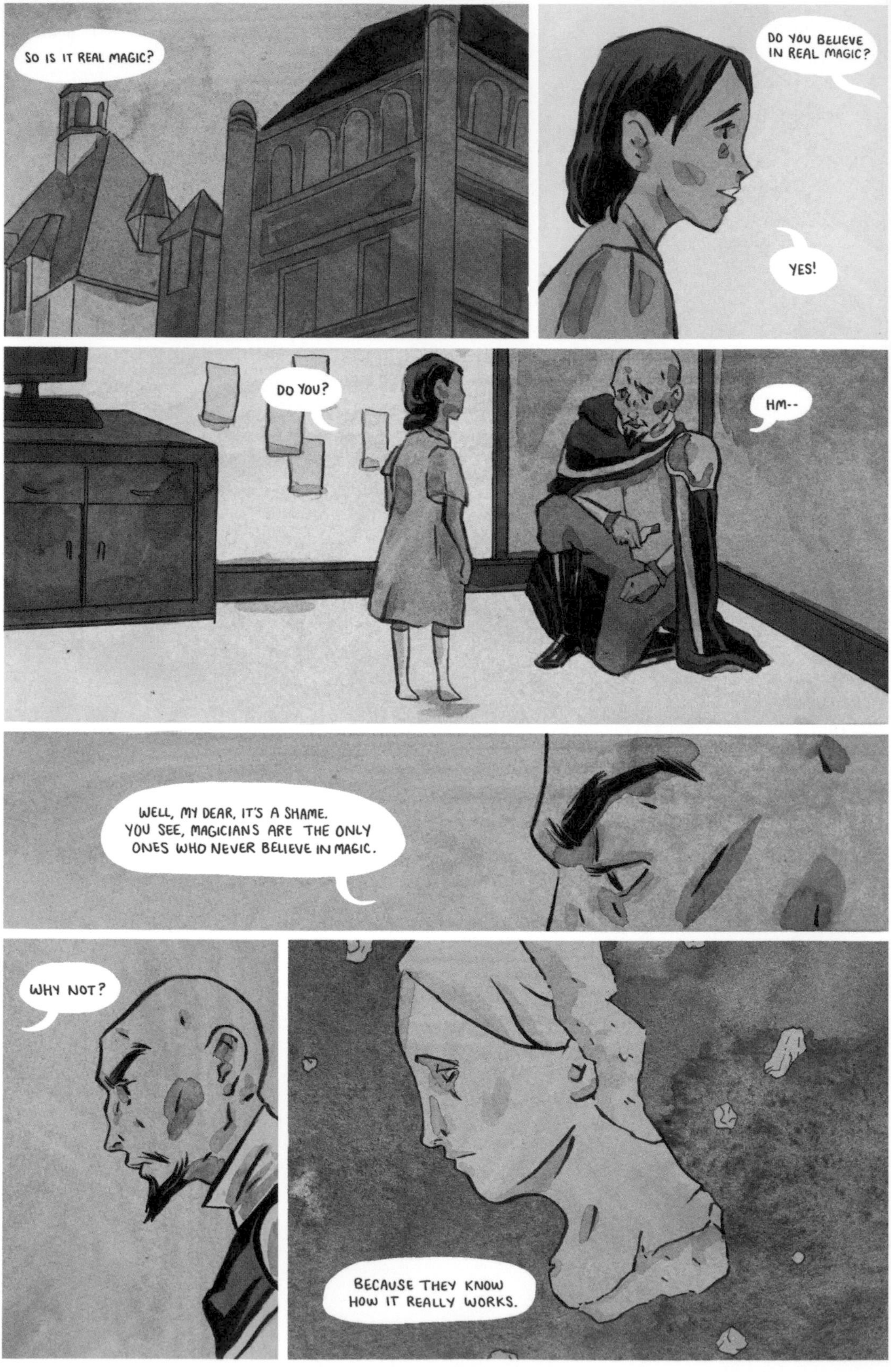
SO IS IT REAL MAGIC?
DO YOU BELIEVE IN REAL MAGIC?
YES!
DO YOU?
HM--
WELL, MY DEAR, IT'S A SHAME. YOU SEE, MAGICIANS ARE THE ONLY ONES WHO NEVER BELIEVE IN MAGIC.
WHY NOT?
BECAUSE THEY KNOW HOW IT REALLY WORKS.

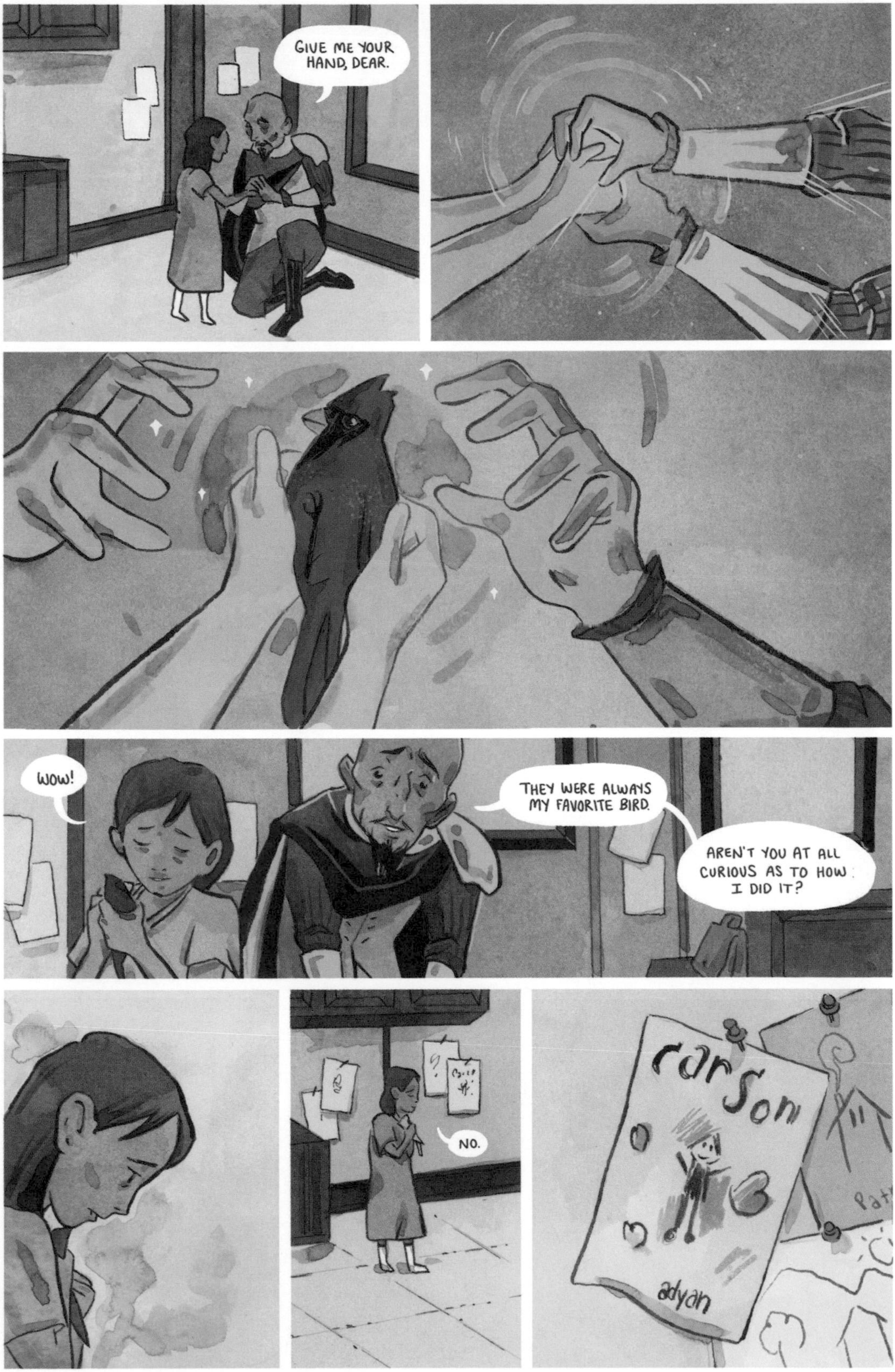
GIVE ME YOUR HAND, DEAR.
WOW!
THEY WERE ALWAYS MY FAVORITE BIRD.
AREN'T YOU AT ALL CURIOUS AS TO HOW I DID IT?
NO.
carson
adyan

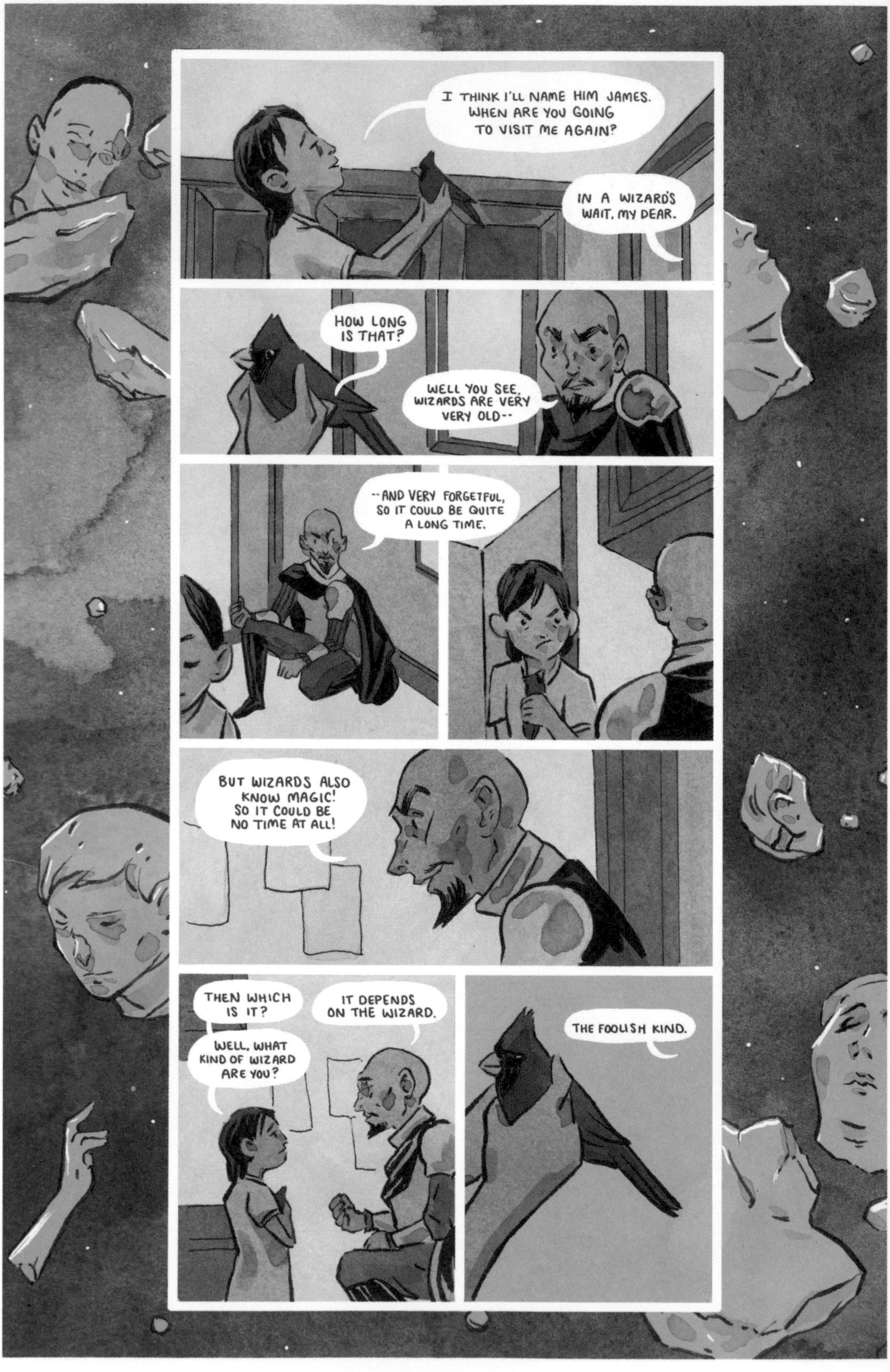
I THINK I'LL NAME HIM JAMES. WHEN ARE YOU GOING TO VISIT ME AGAIN?
IN A WIZARD'S WAIT, MY DEAR.
HOW LONG IS THAT?
WELL YOU SEE, WIZARDS ARE VERY VERY OLD--
--AND VERY FORGETFUL, SO IT COULD BE QUITE A LONG TIME.
BUT WIZARDS ALSO KNOW MAGIC! SO IT COULD BE NO TIME AT ALL!
THEN WHICH IS IT?
IT DEPENDS ON THE WIZARD.
WELL, WHAT KIND OF WIZARD ARE YOU?
THE FOOLISH KIND.

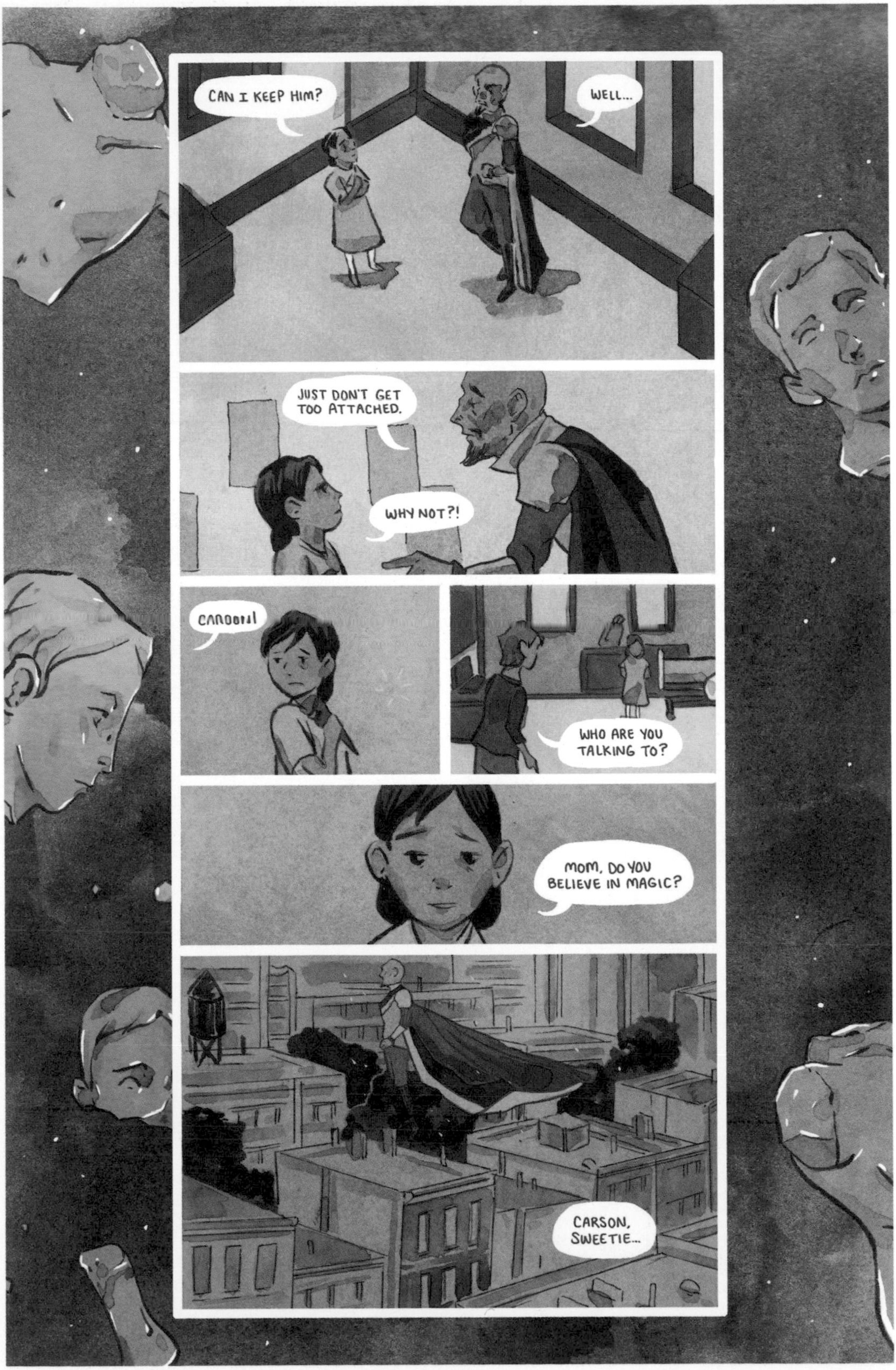
CAN I KEEP HIM?
WELL...
JUST DON'T GET TOO ATTACHED.
WHY NOT?!
CAROON!
WHO ARE YOU TALKING TO?
MOM, DO YOU BELIEVE IN MAGIC?
CARSON, SWEETIE...

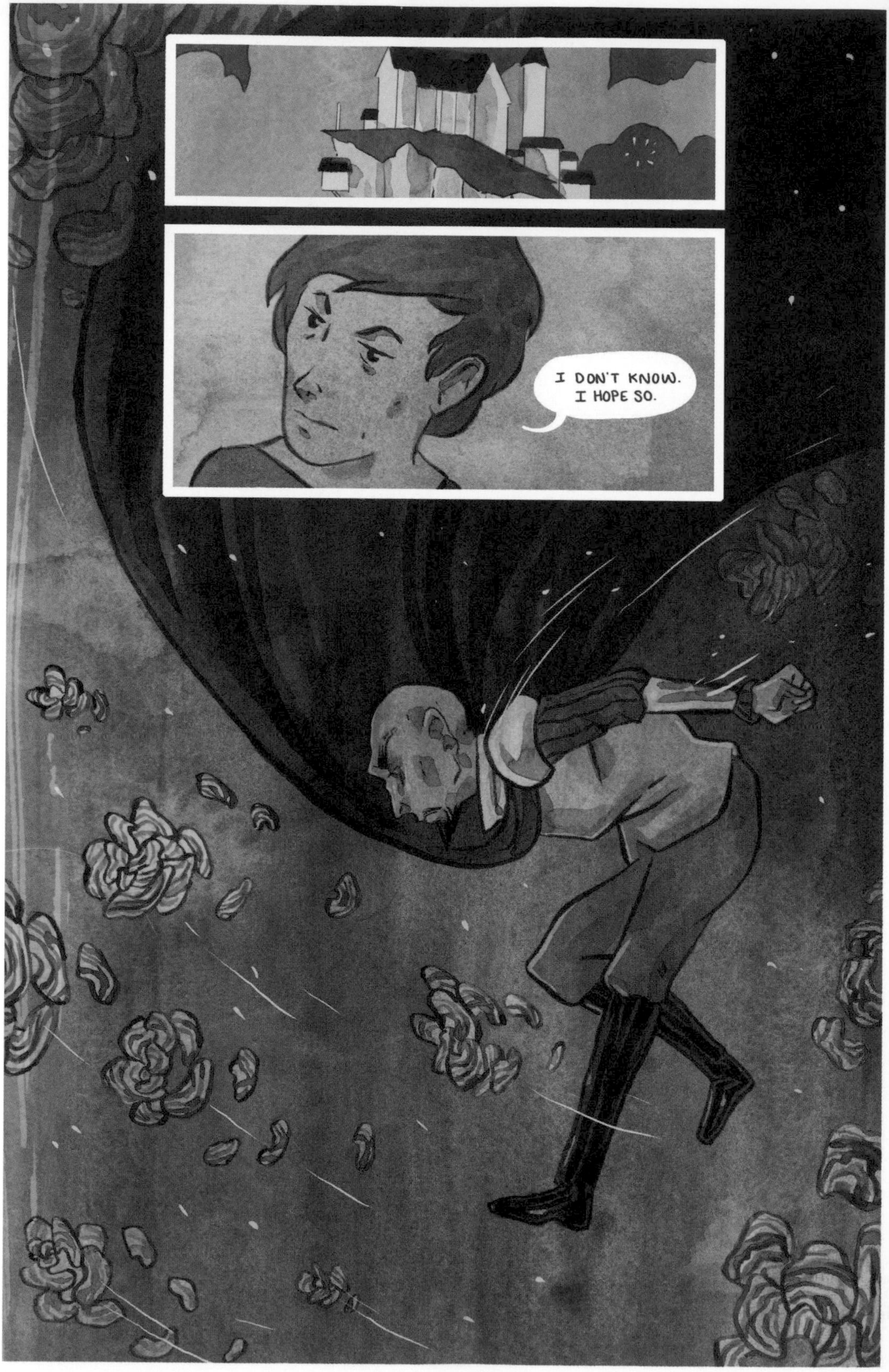
I DON'T KNOW. I HOPE SO.

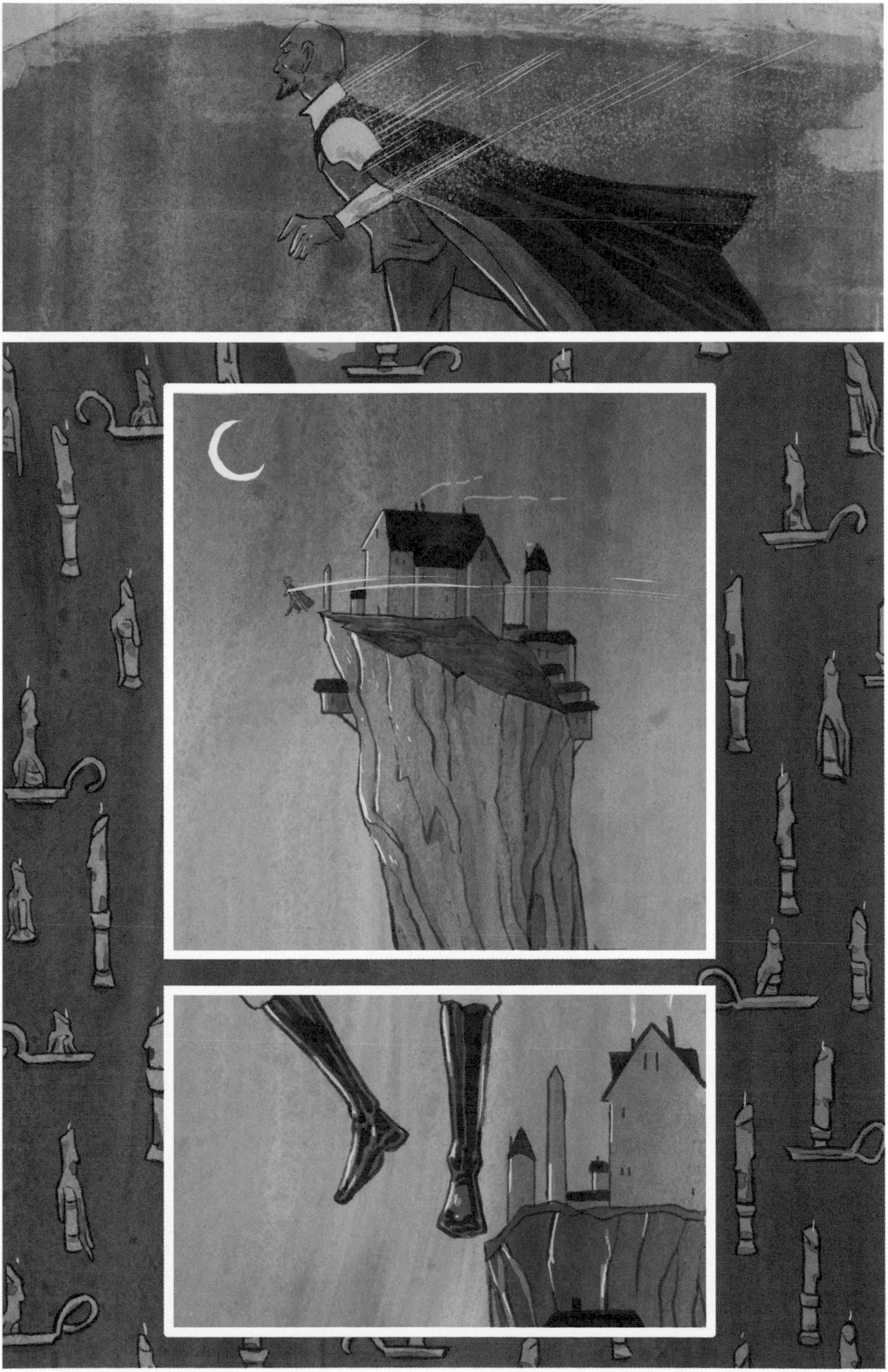

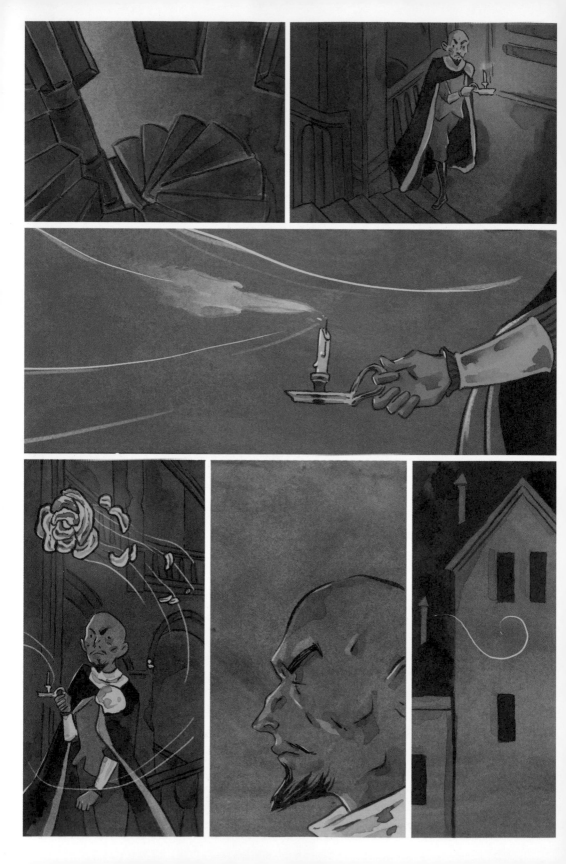

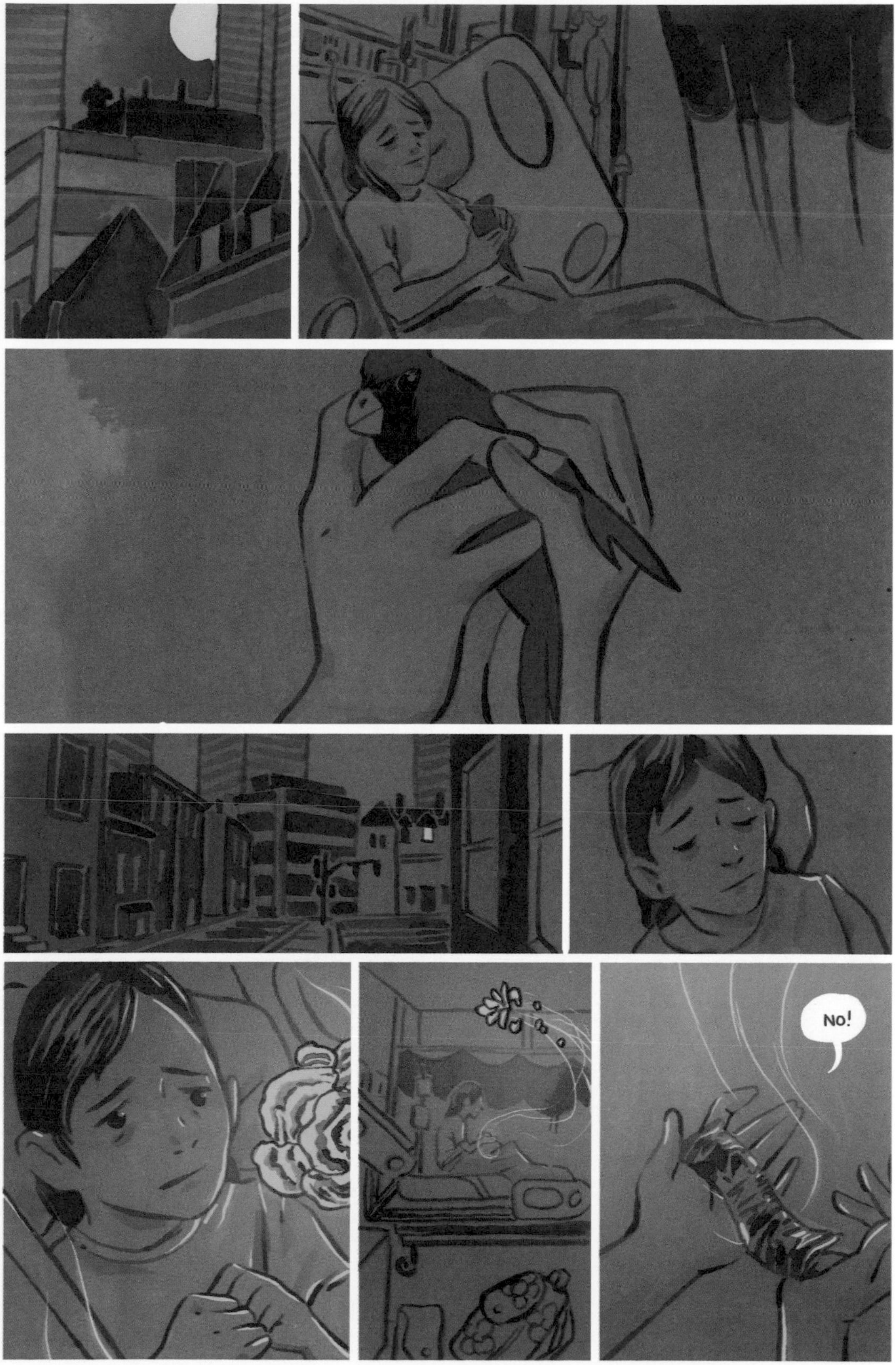
No!

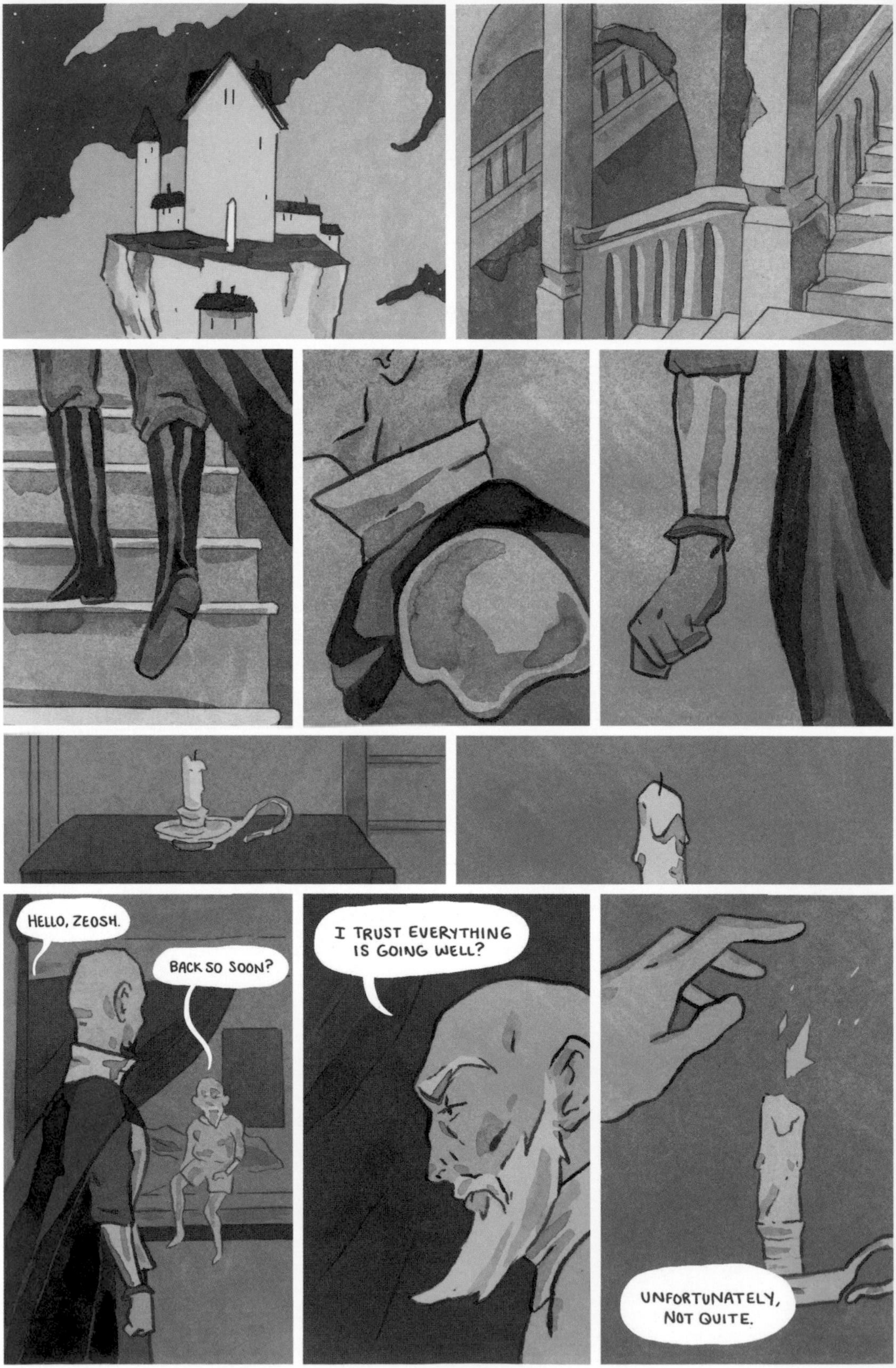
HELLO, ZEOSH.
BACK SO SOON?
I TRUST EVERYTHING IS GOING WELL?
UNFORTUNATELY, NOT QUITE.

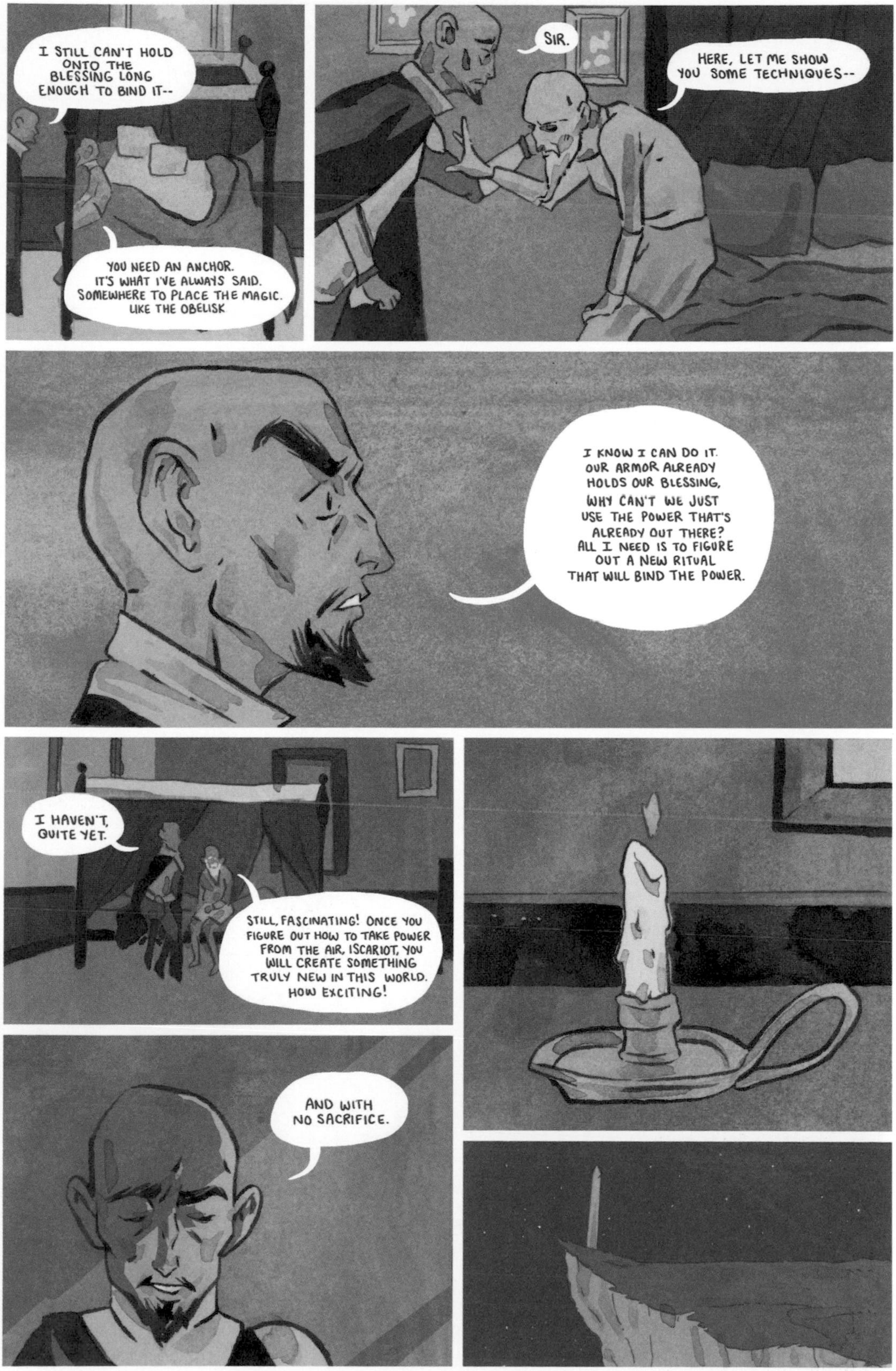
I STILL CAN'T HOLD ONTO THE BLESSING LONG ENOUGH TO BIND IT--
YOU NEED AN ANCHOR. IT'S WHAT I'VE ALWAYS SAID. SOMEWHERE TO PLACE THE MAGIC. LIKE THE OBELISK
SIR.
HERE, LET ME SHOW YOU SOME TECHNIQUES--
I KNOW I CAN DO IT. OUR ARMOR ALREADY HOLDS OUR BLESSING, WHY CAN'T WE JUST USE THE POWER THAT'S ALREADY OUT THERE? ALL I NEED IS TO FIGURE OUT A NEW RITUAL THAT WILL BIND THE POWER.
I HAVEN'T, QUITE YET.
STILL, FASCINATING! ONCE YOU FIGURE OUT HOW TO TAKE POWER FROM THE AIR, ISCARIOT, YOU WILL CREATE SOMETHING TRULY NEW IN THIS WORLD. HOW EXCITING!
AND WITH NO SACRIFICE.

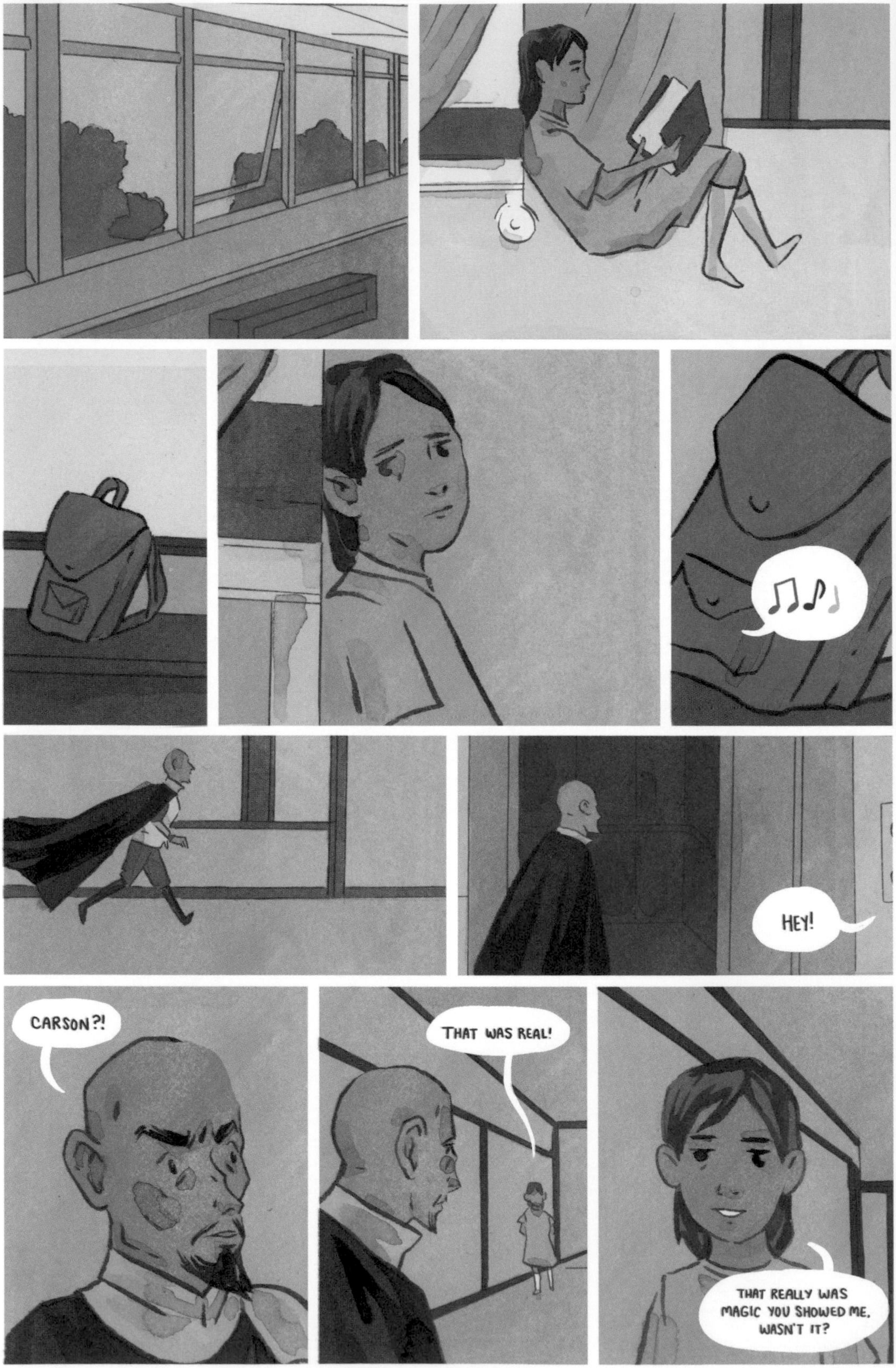
♫♪
HEY!
CARSON?!
THAT WAS REAL!
THAT REALLY WAS MAGIC YOU SHOWED ME, WASN'T IT?

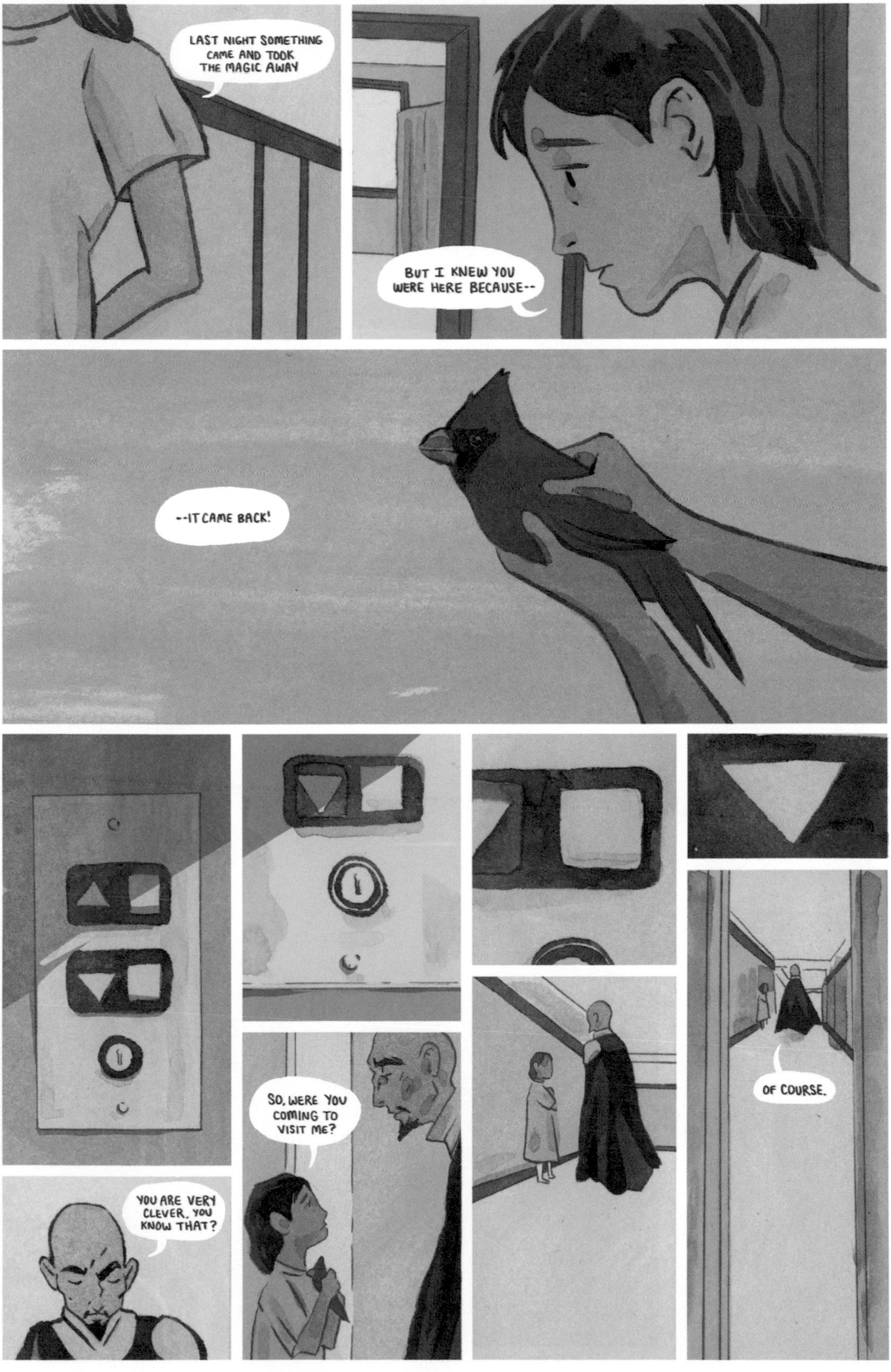
LAST NIGHT SOMETHING CAME AND TOOK THE MAGIC AWAY
BUT I KNEW YOU WERE HERE BECAUSE--
--IT CAME BACK!
SO, WERE YOU COMING TO VISIT ME?
YOU ARE VERY CLEVER, YOU KNOW THAT?
OF COURSE.

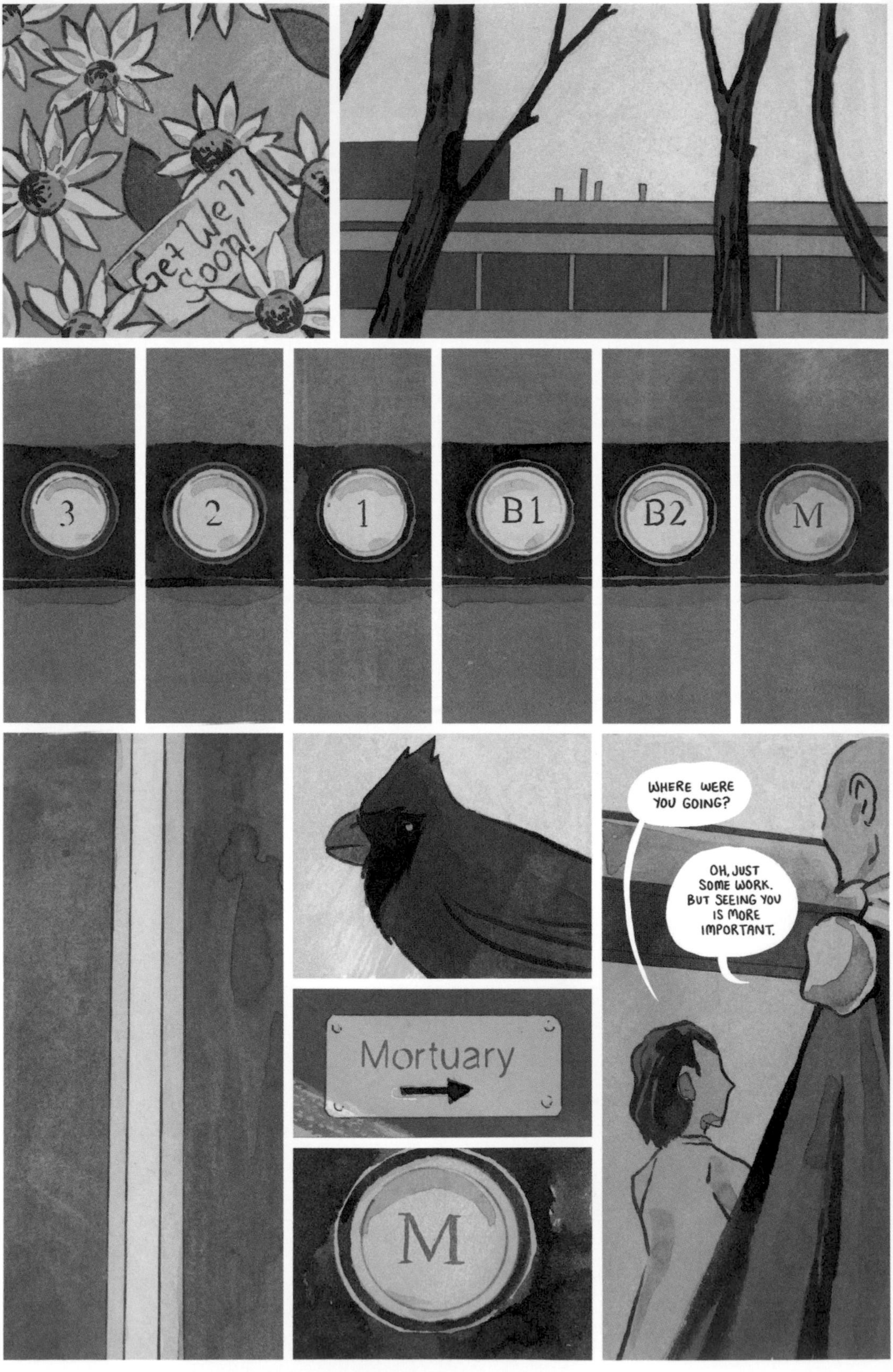
Get Well Soon!
3
2
1
B1
B2
M
WHERE WERE YOU GOING?
OH, JUST SOME WORK. BUT SEEING YOU IS MORE IMPORTANT.
Mortuary
M

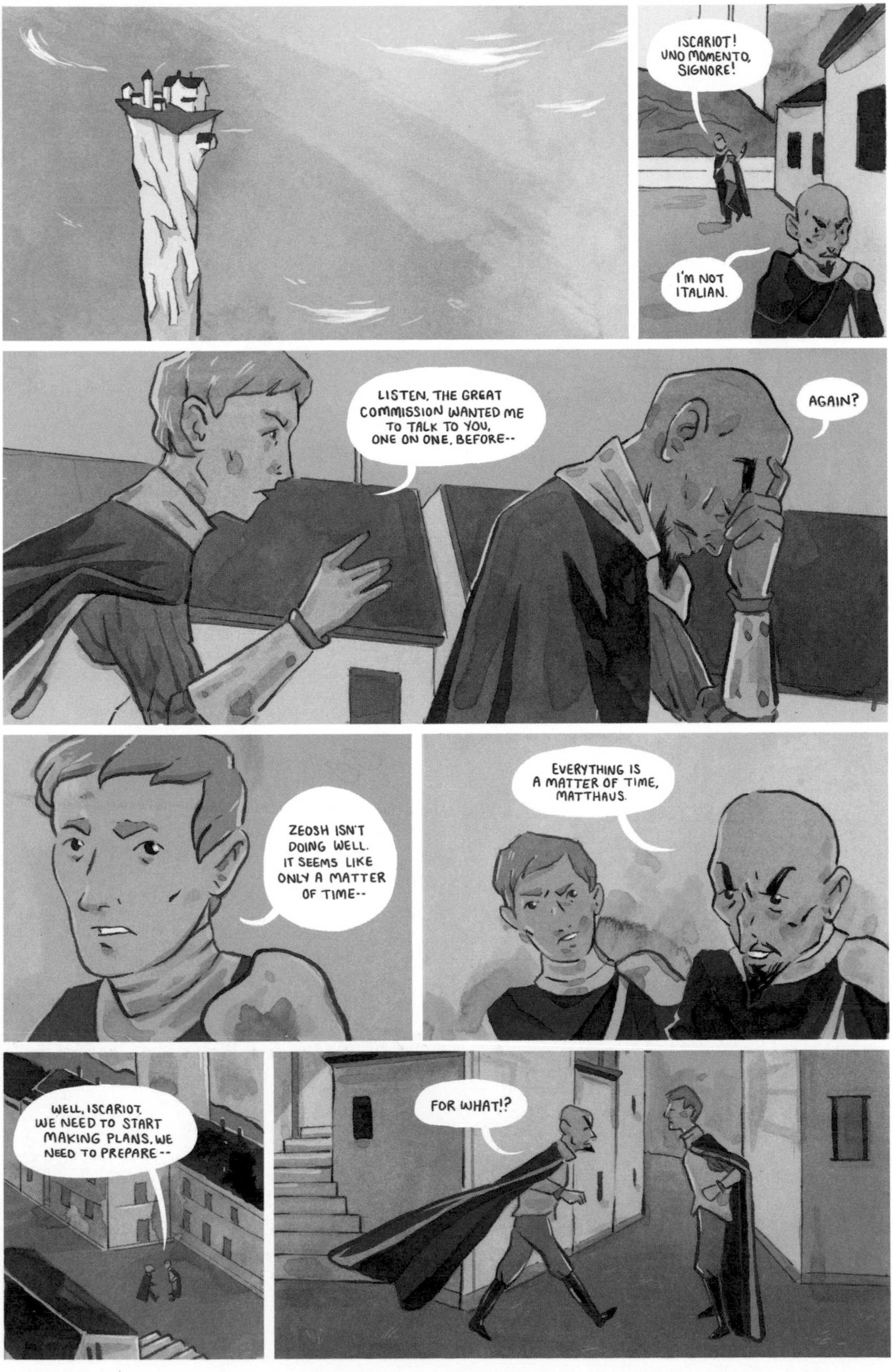
ISCARIOT! UNO MOMENTO, SIGNORE!
I'M NOT ITALIAN.
LISTEN, THE GREAT COMMISSION WANTED ME TO TALK TO YOU, ONE ON ONE, BEFORE--
AGAIN?
ZEOSH ISN'T DOING WELL. IT SEEMS LIKE ONLY A MATTER OF TIME--
EVERYTHING IS A MATTER OF TIME, MATTHAUS.
WELL, ISCARIOT, WE NEED TO START MAKING PLANS. WE NEED TO PREPARE--
FOR WHAT!?

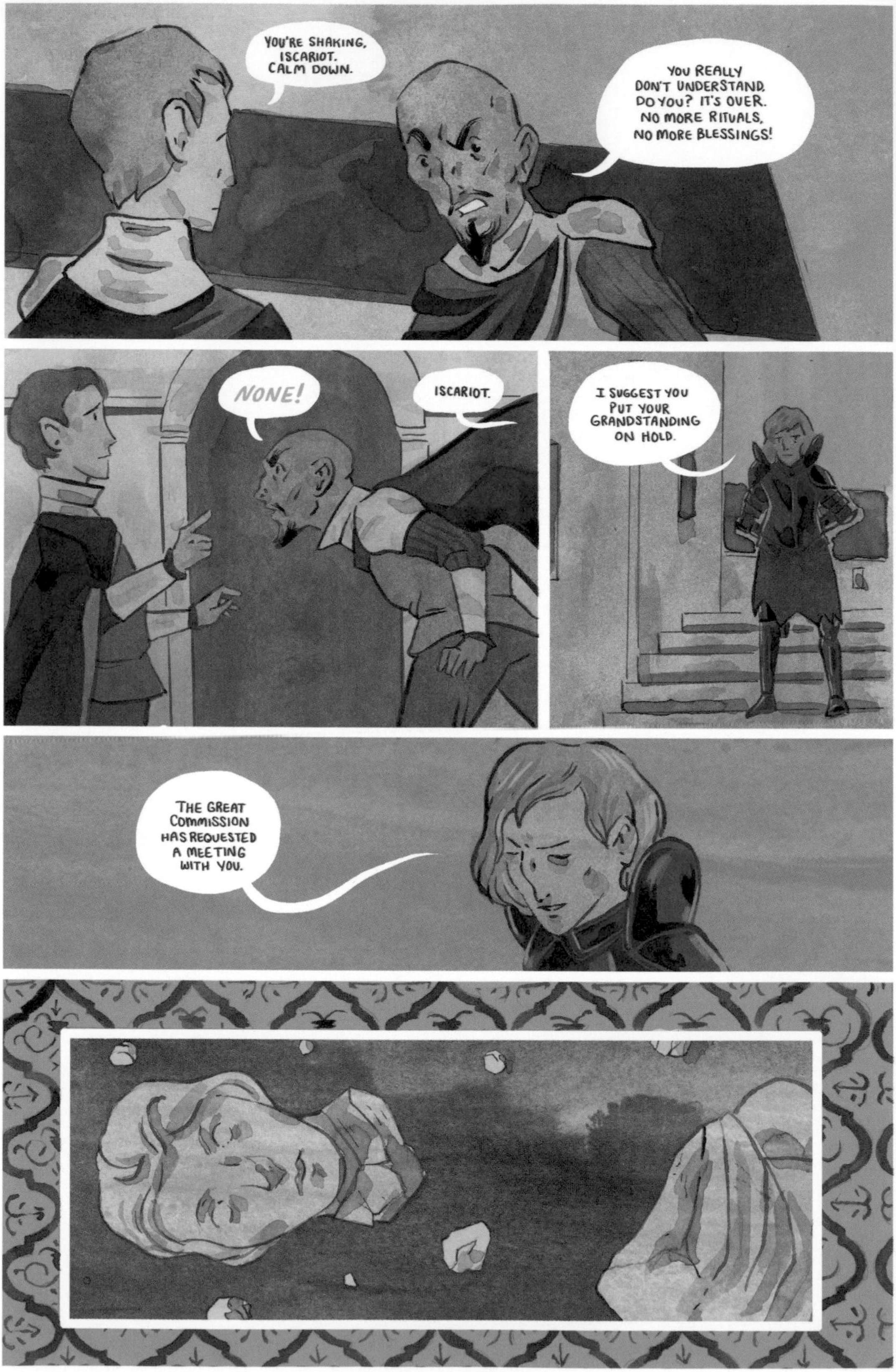
YOU'RE SHAKING, ISCARIOT. CALM DOWN.
YOU REALLY DON'T UNDERSTAND, DO YOU? IT'S OVER. NO MORE RITUALS, NO MORE BLESSINGS!
NONE!
ISCARIOT.
I SUGGEST YOU PUT YOUR GRANDSTANDING ON HOLD.
THE GREAT COMMISSION HAS REQUESTED A MEETING WITH YOU.

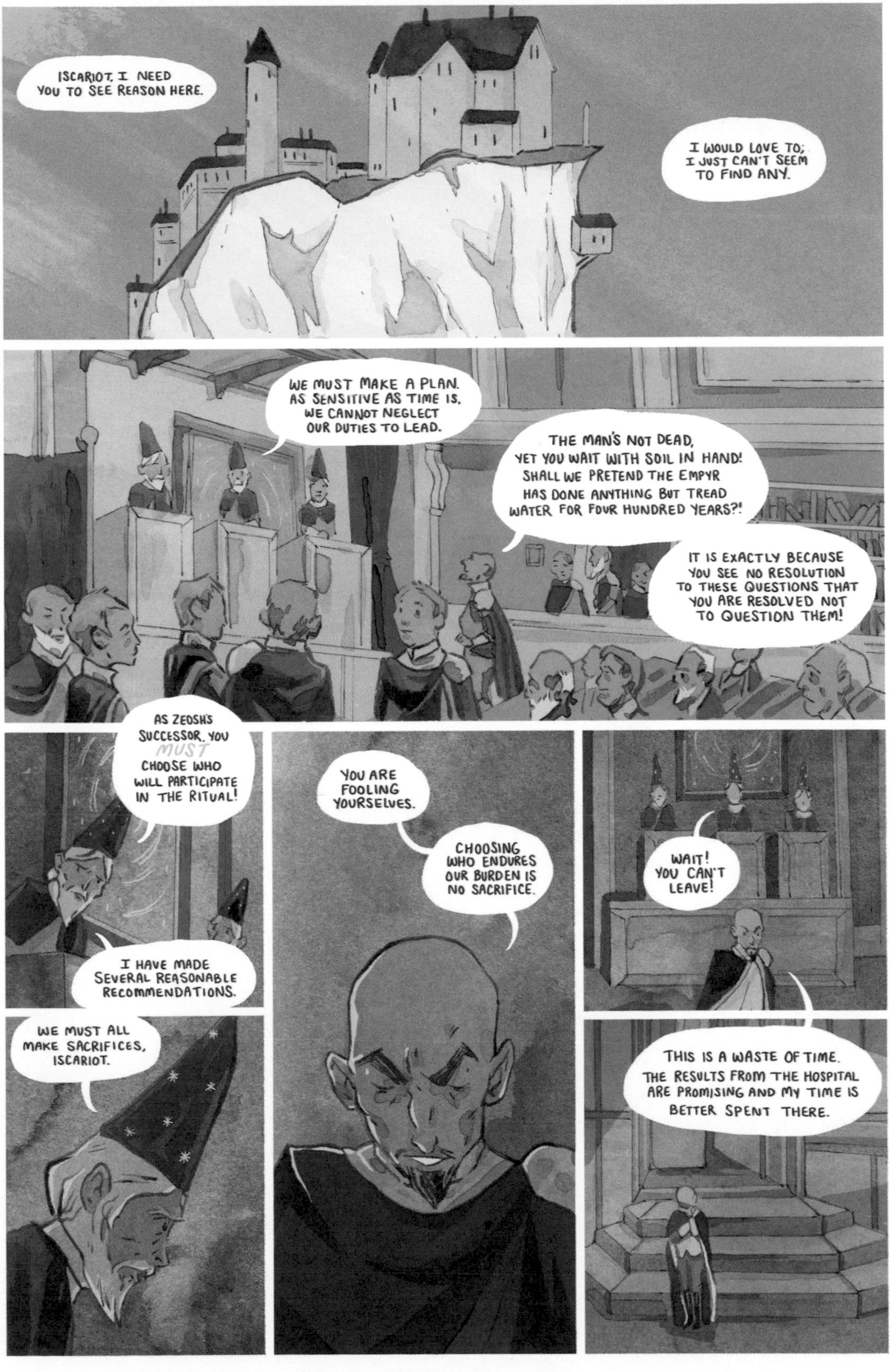
ISCARIOT, I NEED YOU TO SEE REASON HERE.
I WOULD LOVE TO; I JUST CAN'T SEEM TO FIND ANY.
WE MUST MAKE A PLAN. AS SENSITIVE AS TIME IS, WE CANNOT NEGLECT OUR DUTIES TO LEAD.
THE MAN'S NOT DEAD, YET YOU WAIT WITH SOIL IN HAND! SHALL WE PRETEND THE EMPYR HAS DONE ANYTHING BUT TREAD WATER FOR FOUR HUNDRED YEARS?!
IT IS EXACTLY BECAUSE YOU SEE NO RESOLUTION TO THESE QUESTIONS THAT YOU ARE RESOLVED NOT TO QUESTION THEM!
AS ZEOSH'S SUCCESSOR, YOU MUST CHOOSE WHO WILL PARTICIPATE IN THE RITUAL!
I HAVE MADE SEVERAL REASONABLE RECOMMENDATIONS.
WE MUST ALL MAKE SACRIFICES, ISCARIOT.
YOU ARE FOOLING YOURSELVES.
CHOOSING WHO ENDURES OUR BURDEN IS NO SACRIFICE.
WAIT! YOU CAN'T LEAVE!
THIS IS A WASTE OF TIME. THE RESULTS FROM THE HOSPITAL ARE PROMISING AND MY TIME IS BETTER SPENT THERE.

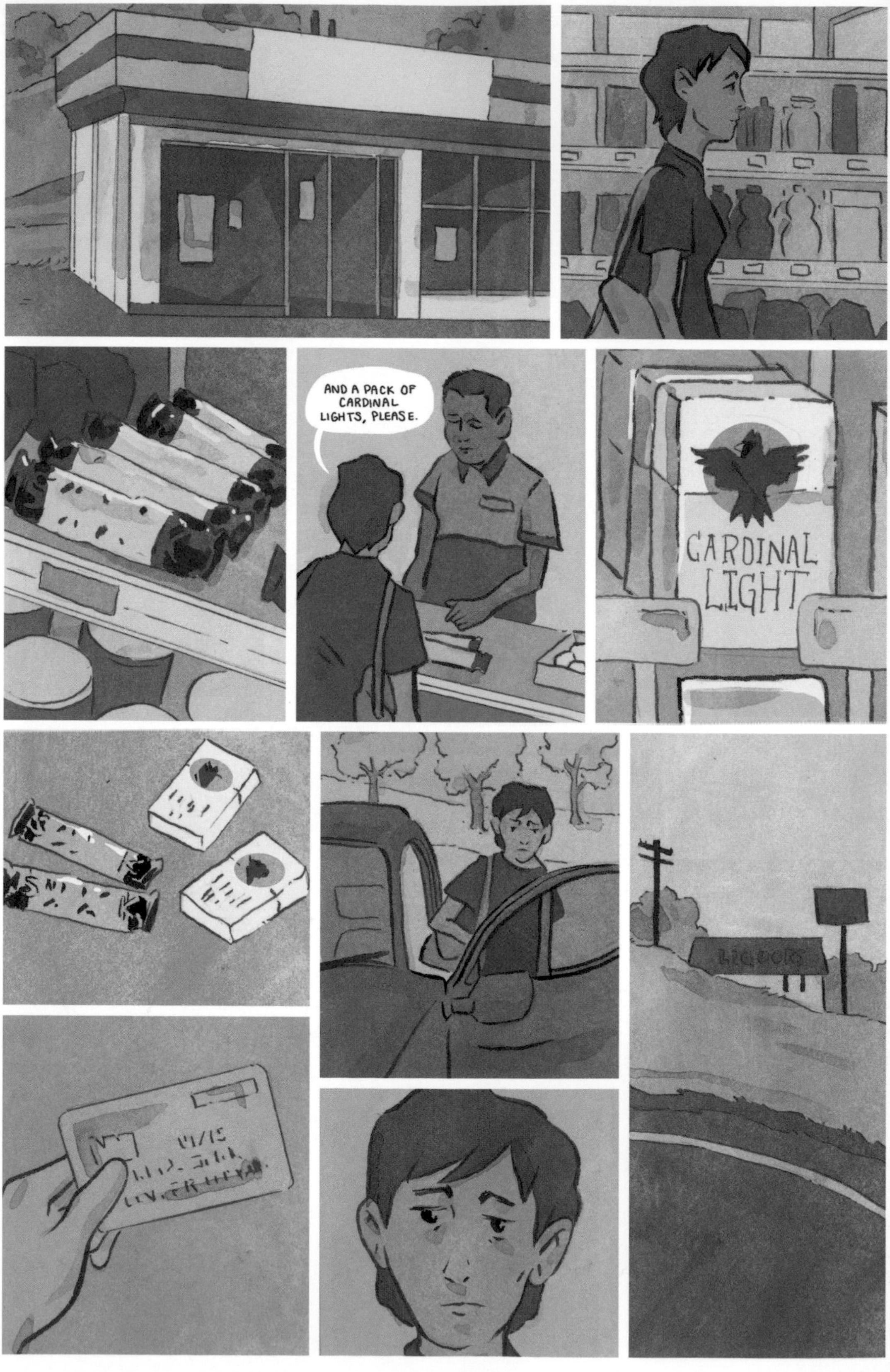
AND A PACK OF CARDINAL LIGHTS, PLEASE.
CARDINAL LIGHT

OH, MISS DEWITT, I WAS HOPING TO RUN INTO YOU.

YEAH, SORRY, I'M RUNNING A BIT LATE TODAY. TRYING TO MAKE IT UP.

WELL, CARSON IS RECOVERING WELL. IT LOOKS LIKE THE SURGERY WAS SUCCESSFUL, BUT WE STILL DON'T KNOW FOR CERTAIN.

OTHERWISE, CARSON IS A HANDFUL. THE STAFF HAVE A HARD TIME KEEPING HER IN BED OR HER ROOM.

HONESTLY, IT'S HARD TO COMMUTE FOR HER TREATMENT. I'D HAVE TO TAKE OFF WORK--

AND I'VE ALREADY TAKEN OFF SO MUCH. AND SHE STILL SEEMS TO BE COMPLAINING ABOUT HEADACHES.

SHE HASN'T BEEN HOME FOR MORE THAN A COUPLE DAYS IN ALMOST FOUR MONTHS.

I'M NOT SURE IF IT'S A GOOD IDEA.

WELL, DECIDE WHAT IS BEST FOR YOU.

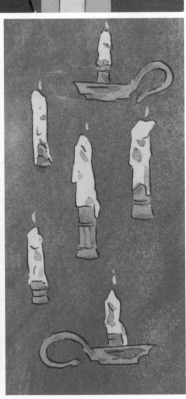

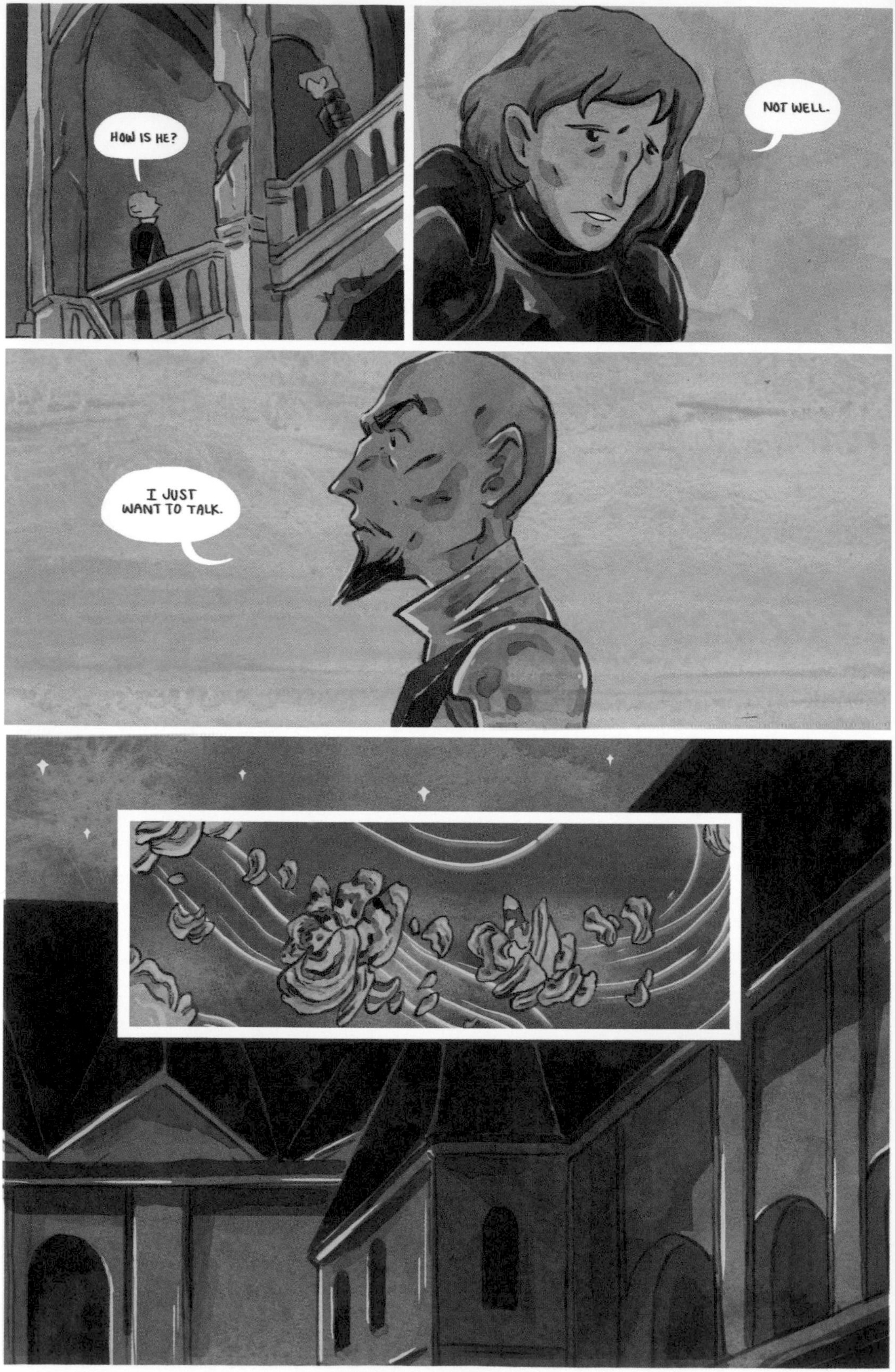
HOW IS HE?
NOT WELL.
I JUST WANT TO TALK.

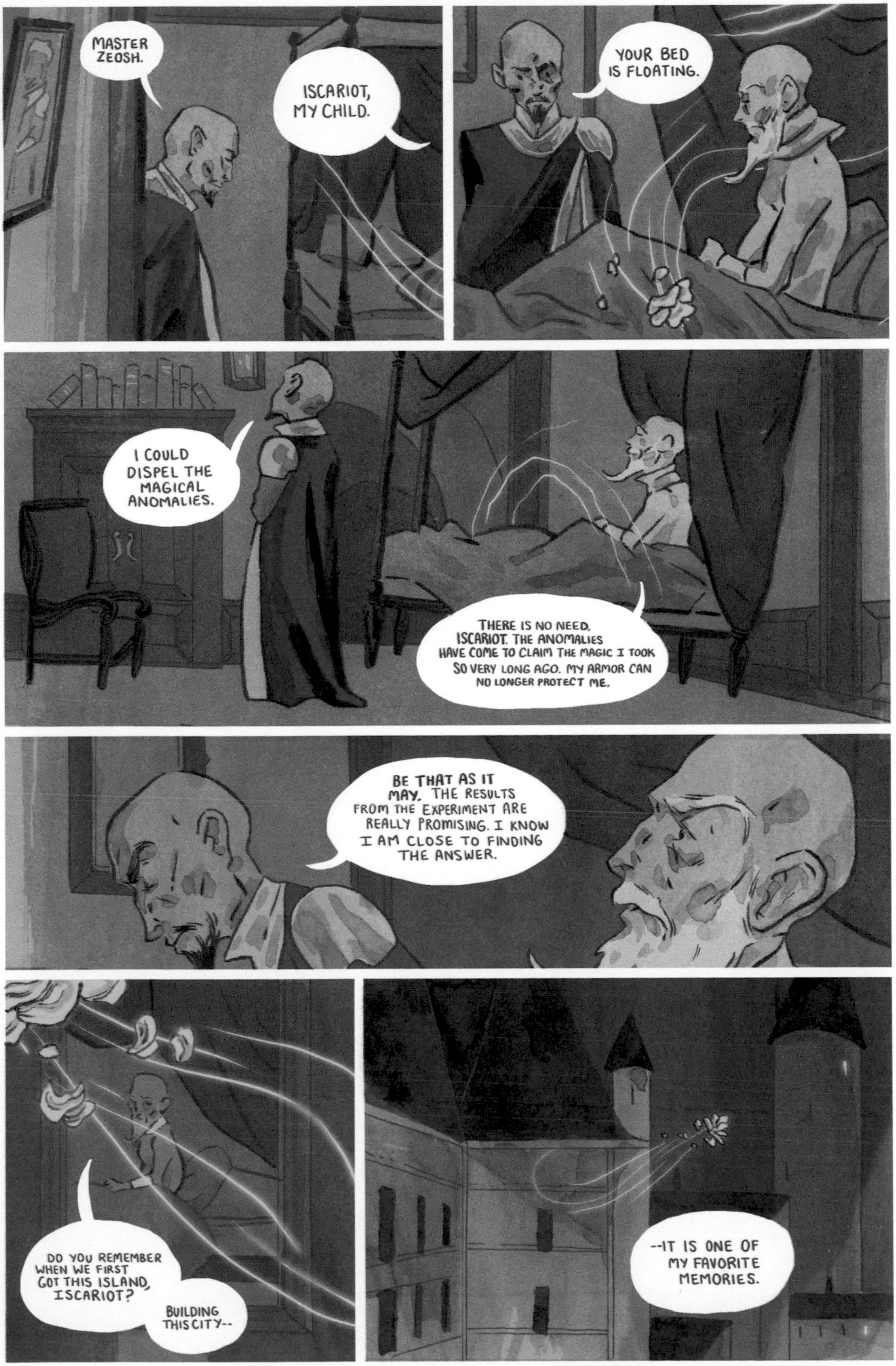
MASTER ZEOSH.
ISCARIOT, MY CHILD.
YOUR BED IS FLOATING.
I COULD DISPEL THE MAGICAL ANOMALIES.
THERE IS NO NEED, ISCARIOT. THE ANOMALIES HAVE COME TO CLAIM THE MAGIC I TOOK SO VERY LONG AGO. MY ARMOR CAN NO LONGER PROTECT ME.
BE THAT AS IT MAY. THE RESULTS FROM THE EXPERIMENT ARE REALLY PROMISING. I KNOW I AM CLOSE TO FINDING THE ANSWER.
DO YOU REMEMBER WHEN WE FIRST GOT THIS ISLAND, ISCARIOT?
BUILDING THIS CITY--
--IT IS ONE OF MY FAVORITE MEMORIES.

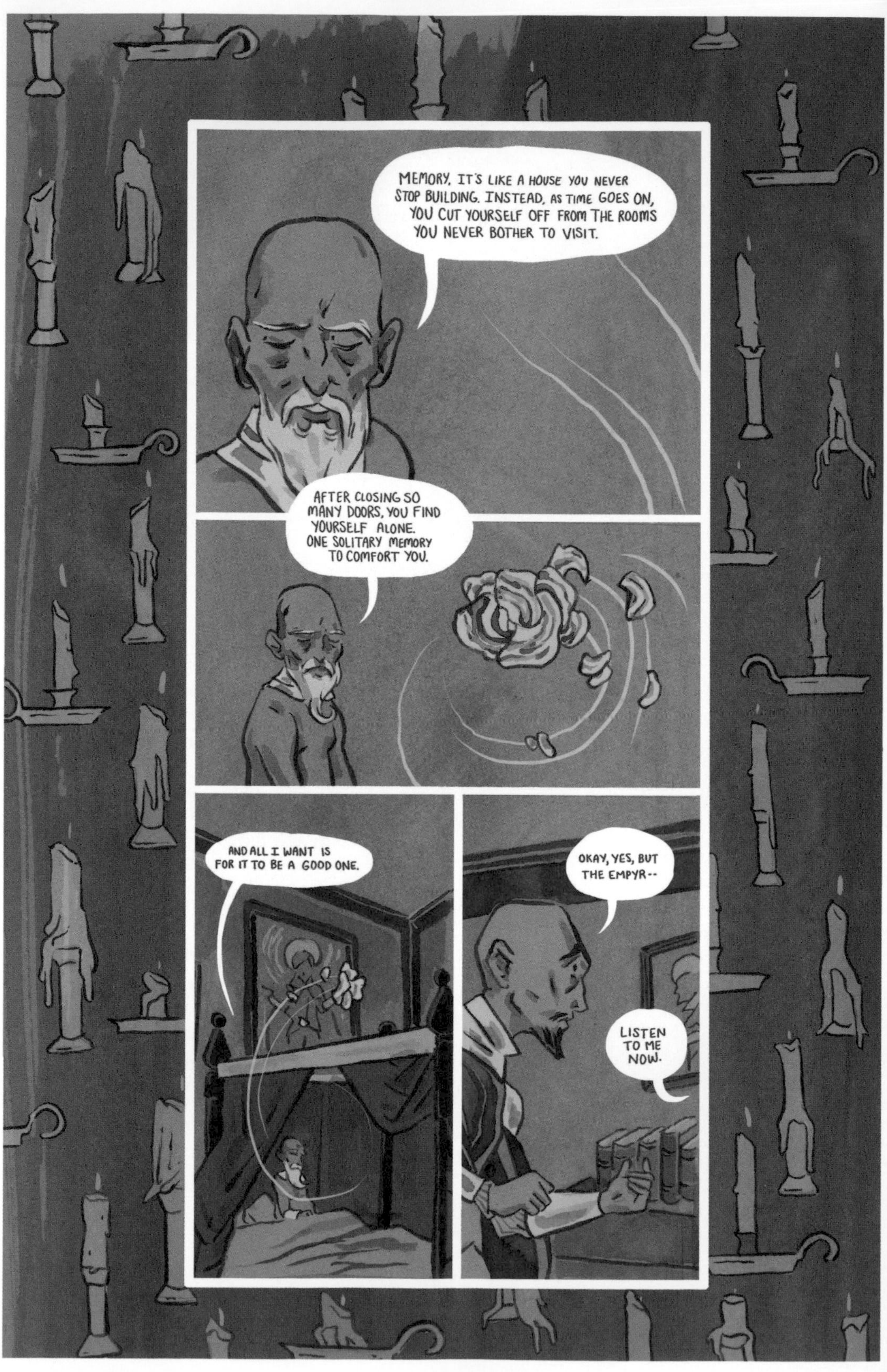
MEMORY, IT'S LIKE A HOUSE YOU NEVER STOP BUILDING. INSTEAD, AS TIME GOES ON, YOU CUT YOURSELF OFF FROM THE ROOMS YOU NEVER BOTHER TO VISIT.
AFTER CLOSING SO MANY DOORS, YOU FIND YOURSELF ALONE. ONE SOLITARY MEMORY TO COMFORT YOU.
AND ALL I WANT IS FOR IT TO BE A GOOD ONE.
OKAY, YES, BUT THE EMPYR--
LISTEN TO ME NOW.

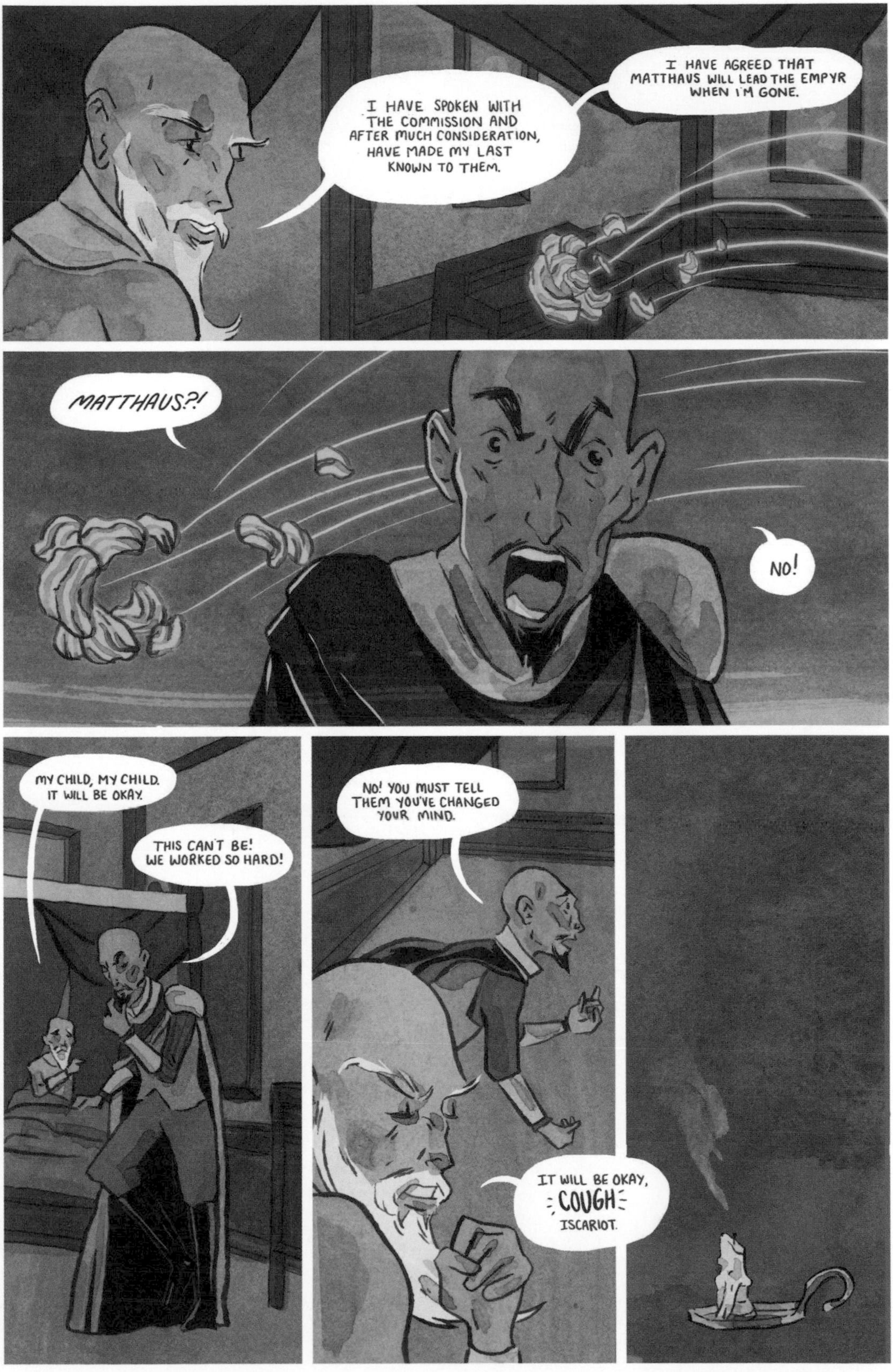
I HAVE SPOKEN WITH THE COMMISSION AND AFTER MUCH CONSIDERATION, HAVE MADE MY LAST KNOWN TO THEM.
I HAVE AGREED THAT MATTHAUS WILL LEAD THE EMPYR WHEN I'M GONE.
MATTHAUS?!
NO!
MY CHILD, MY CHILD. IT WILL BE OKAY.
THIS CAN'T BE! WE WORKED SO HARD!
NO! YOU MUST TELL THEM YOU'VE CHANGED YOUR MIND.
IT WILL BE OKAY,
COUGH
ISCARIOT.

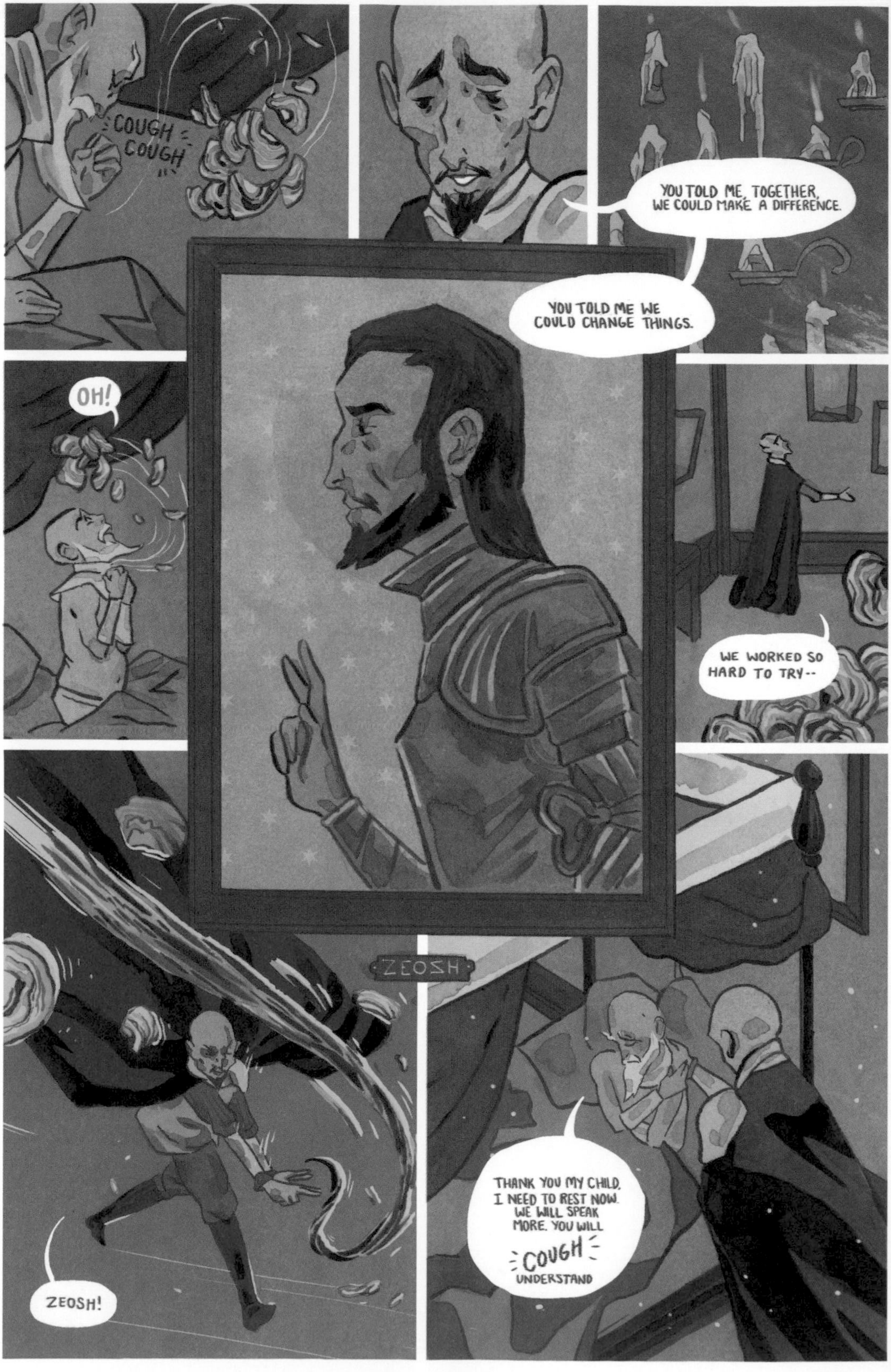
COUGH COUGH
YOU TOLD ME, TOGETHER, WE COULD MAKE A DIFFERENCE.
YOU TOLD ME WE COULD CHANGE THINGS.
OH!
WE WORKED SO HARD TO TRY--
ZEOSH
ZEOSH!
THANK YOU MY CHILD. I NEED TO REST NOW. WE WILL SPEAK MORE. YOU WILL COUGH UNDERSTAND

I'M SORRY, CHILD.

I'M SORRY.

I JUST NEED TO REST.
EVERYTHING IS GOING TO BE OKAY.

I JUST NEED
TO REST.

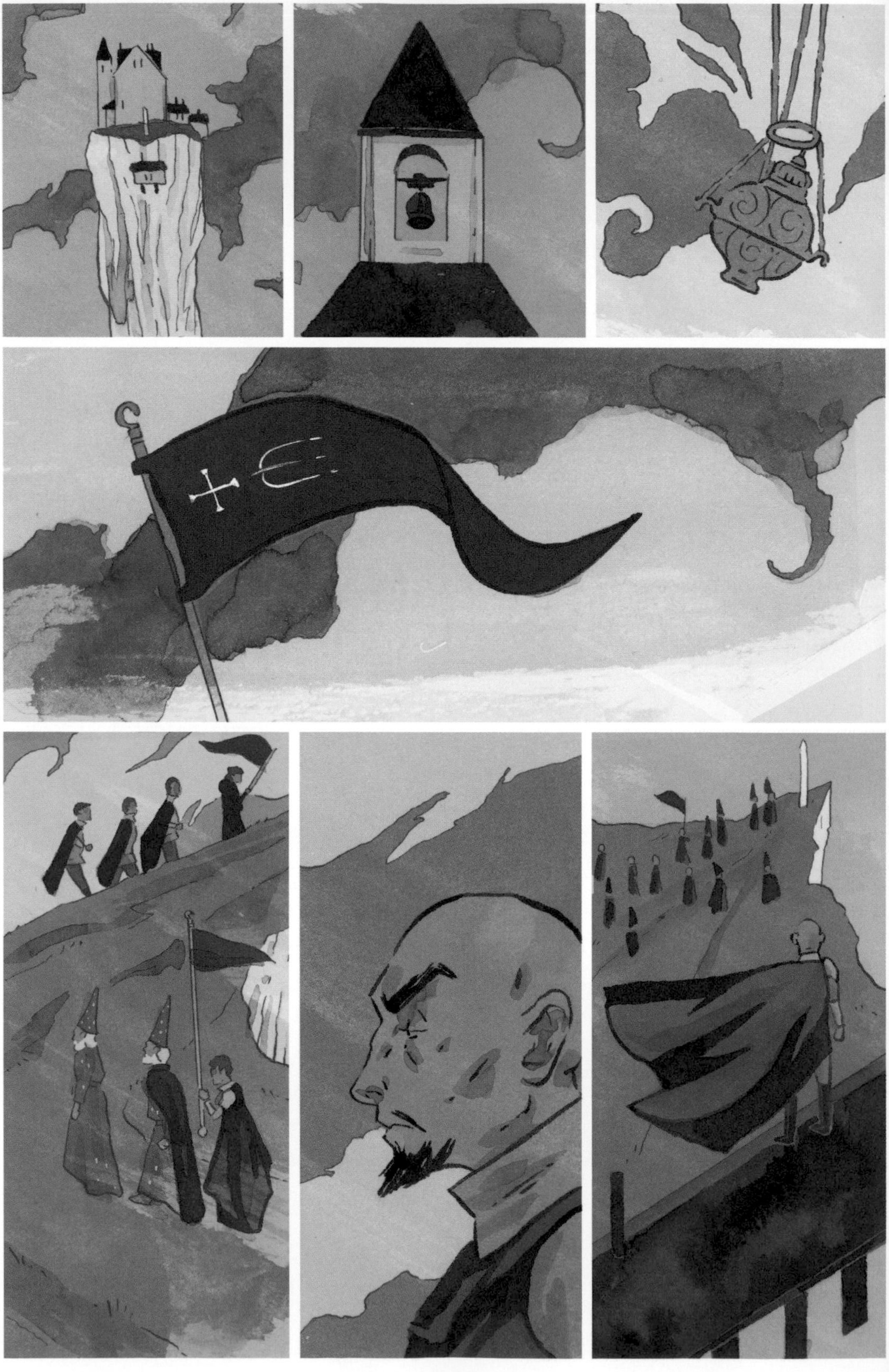

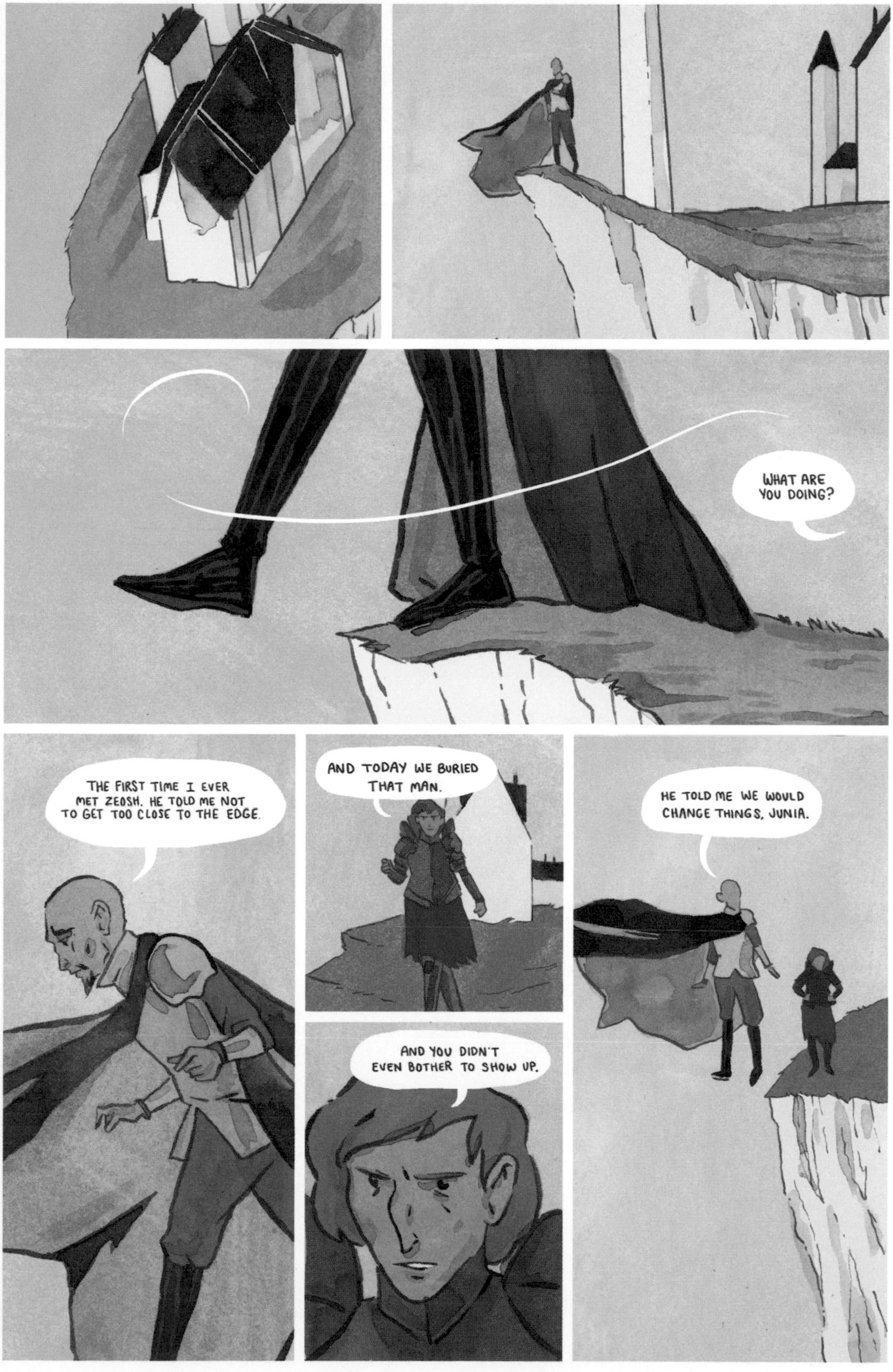
WHAT ARE YOU DOING?
THE FIRST TIME I EVER MET ZEOSH. HE TOLD ME NOT TO GET TOO CLOSE TO THE EDGE.
AND TODAY WE BURIED THAT MAN.
AND YOU DIDN'T EVEN BOTHER TO SHOW UP.
HE TOLD ME WE WOULD CHANGE THINGS, JUNIA.

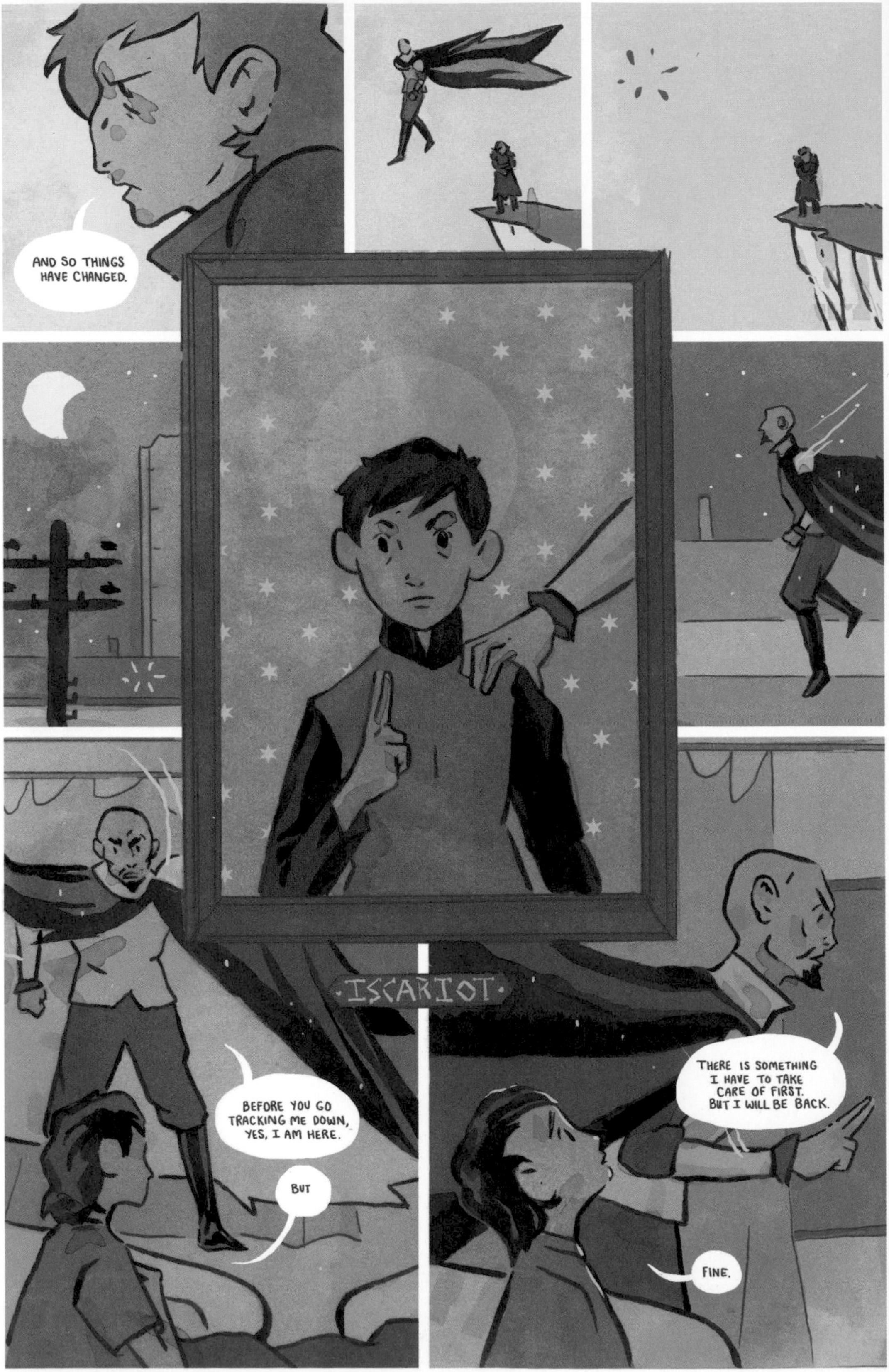
AND SO THINGS HAVE CHANGED.
ISCARIOT
BEFORE YOU GO TRACKING ME DOWN, YES, I AM HERE.
BUT
THERE IS SOMETHING I HAVE TO TAKE CARE OF FIRST. BUT I WILL BE BACK.
FINE.

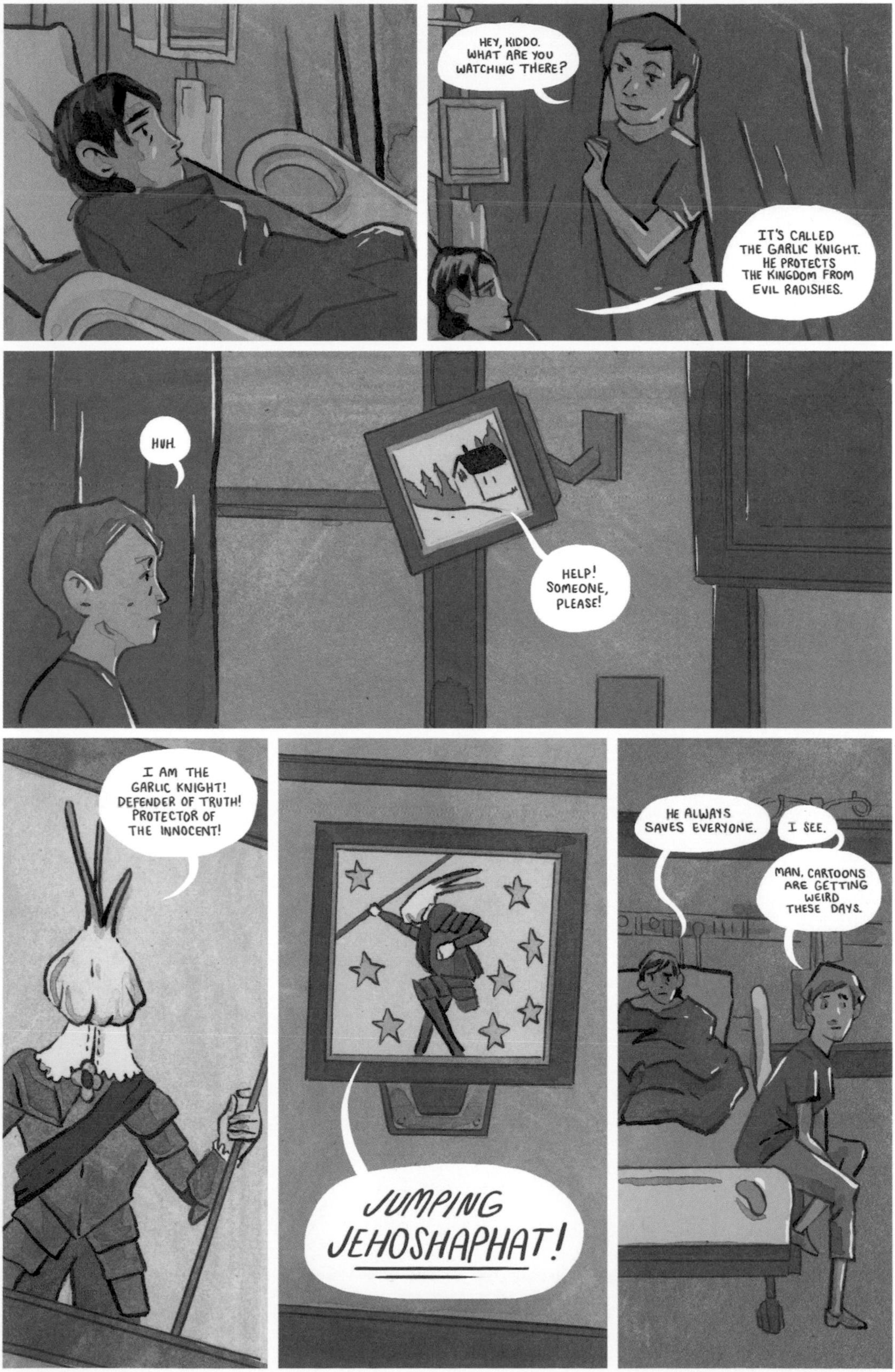
HEY, KIDDO. WHAT ARE YOU WATCHING THERE?
IT'S CALLED THE GARLIC KNIGHT. HE PROTECTS THE KINGDOM FROM EVIL RADISHES.
HUH.
HELP! SOMEONE, PLEASE!
I AM THE GARLIC KNIGHT! DEFENDER OF TRUTH! PROTECTOR OF THE INNOCENT!
JUMPING JEHOSHAPHAT!
HE ALWAYS SAVES EVERYONE.
I SEE.
MAN, CARTOONS ARE GETTING WEIRD THESE DAYS.

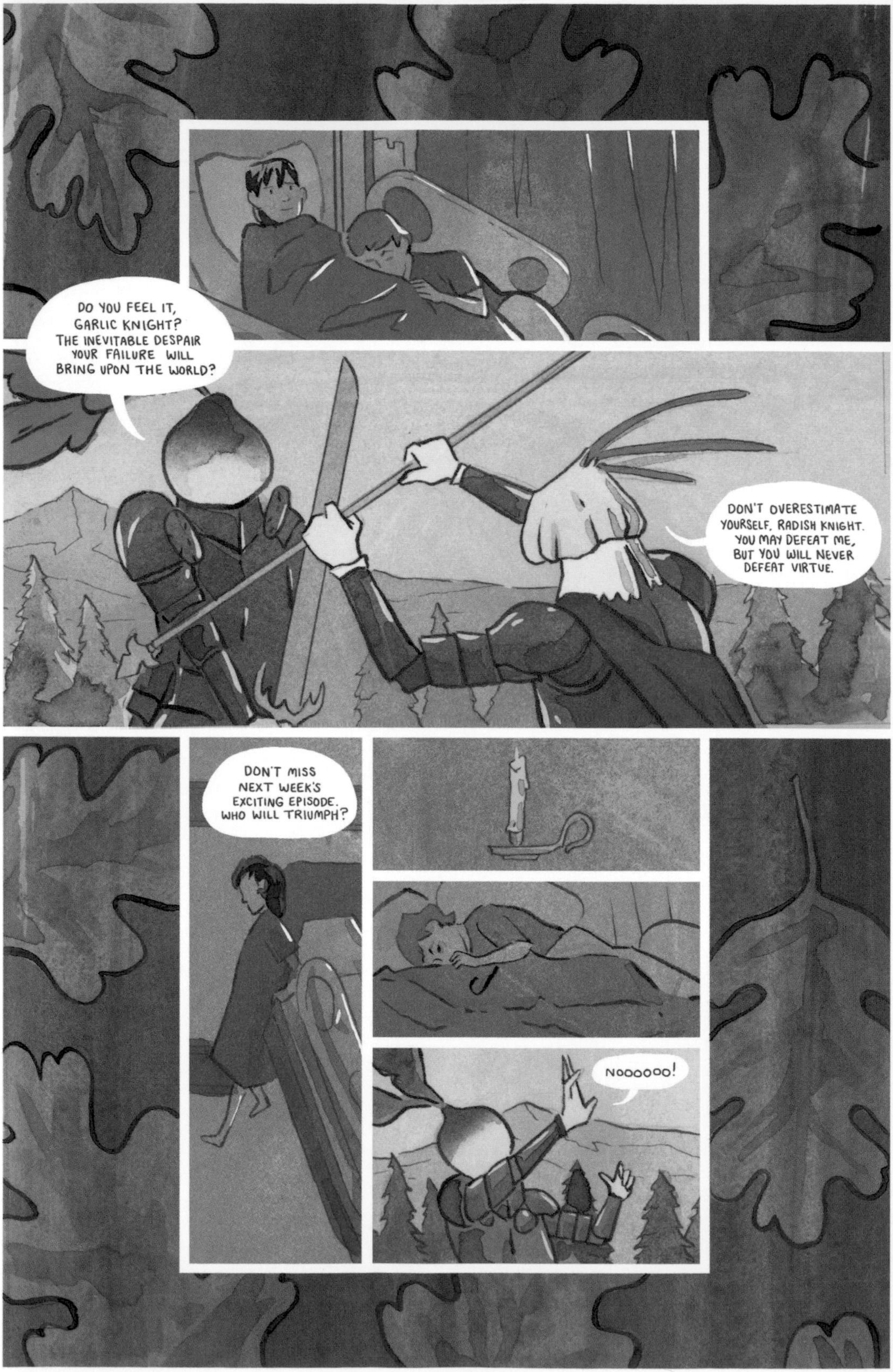
DO YOU FEEL IT, GARLIC KNIGHT? THE INEVITABLE DESPAIR YOUR FAILURE WILL BRING UPON THE WORLD?
DON'T OVERESTIMATE YOURSELF, RADISH KNIGHT. YOU MAY DEFEAT ME, BUT YOU WILL NEVER DEFEAT VIRTUE.
DON'T MISS NEXT WEEK'S EXCITING EPISODE. WHO WILL TRIUMPH?
NOOOOOO!

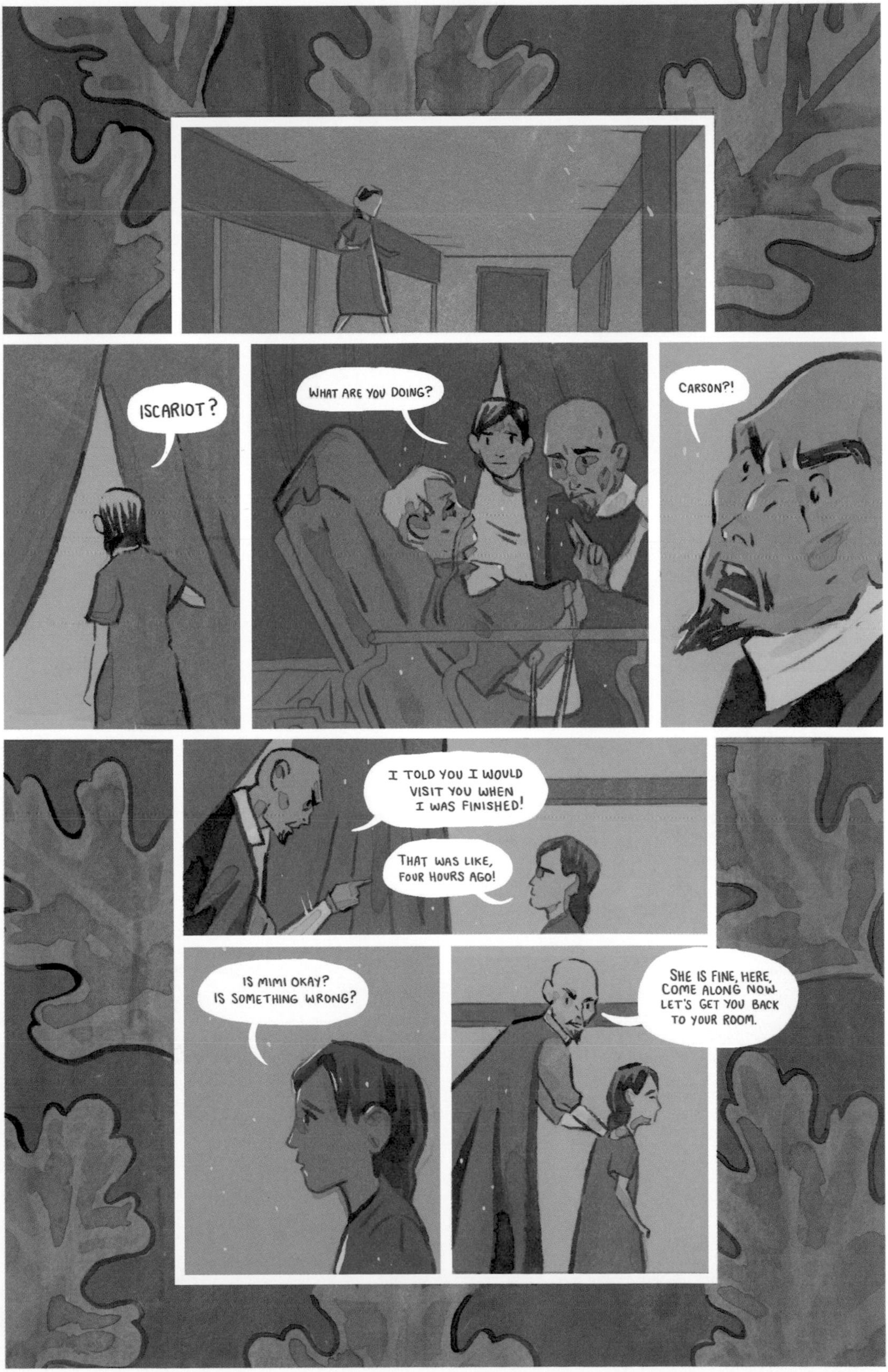
ISCARIOT?
WHAT ARE YOU DOING?
CARSON?!
I TOLD YOU I WOULD VISIT YOU WHEN I WAS FINISHED!
THAT WAS LIKE, FOUR HOURS AGO!
IS MIMI OKAY? IS SOMETHING WRONG?
SHE IS FINE, HERE, COME ALONG NOW. LET'S GET YOU BACK TO YOUR ROOM.

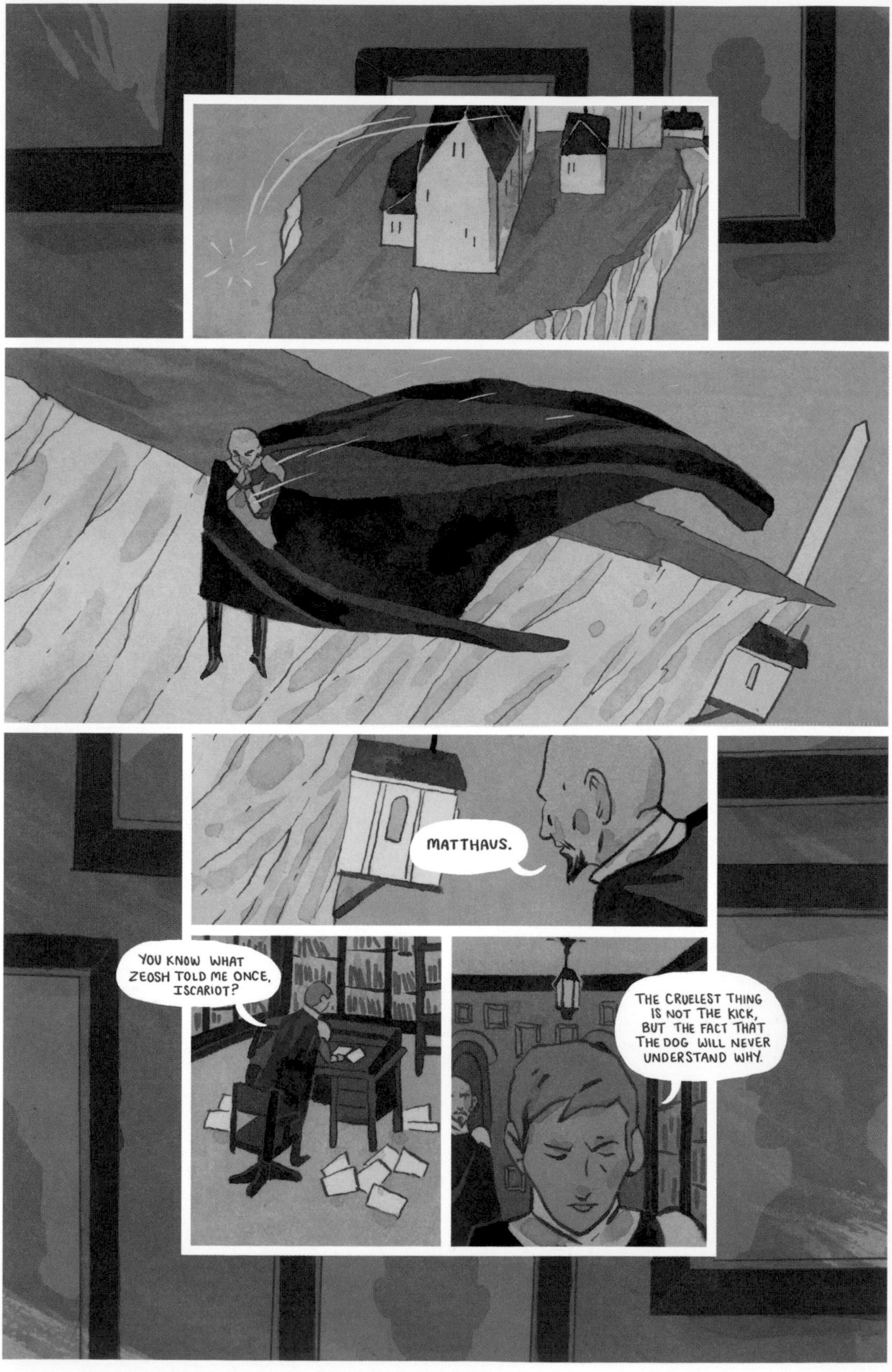
MATTHAUS.
YOU KNOW WHAT ZEOSH TOLD ME ONCE, ISCARIOT?
THE CRUELEST THING IS NOT THE KICK, BUT THE FACT THAT THE DOG WILL NEVER UNDERSTAND WHY.

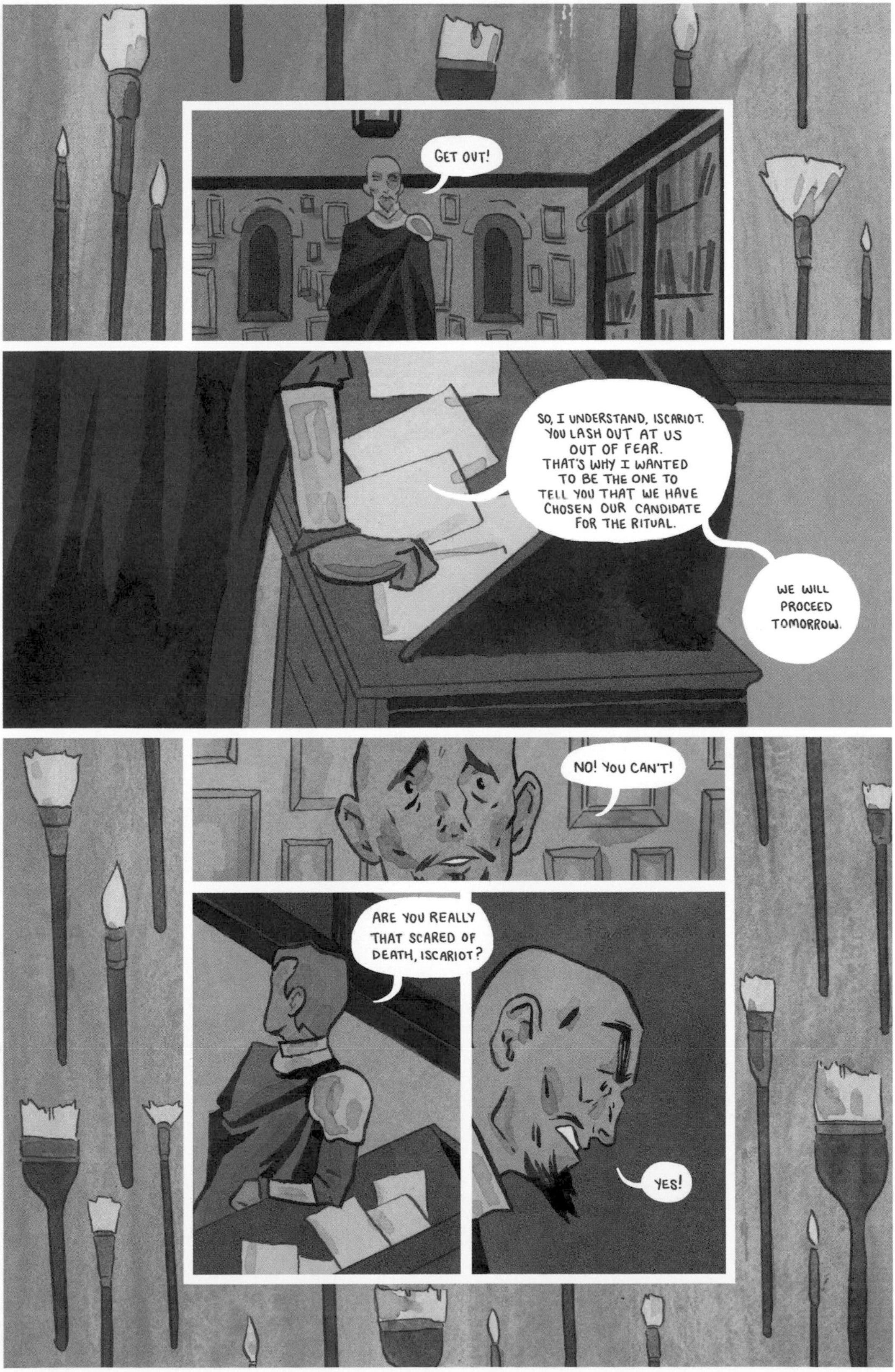
GET OUT!
SO, I UNDERSTAND, ISCARIOT. YOU LASH OUT AT US OUT OF FEAR. THAT'S WHY I WANTED TO BE THE ONE TO TELL YOU THAT WE HAVE CHOSEN OUR CANDIDATE FOR THE RITUAL.
WE WILL PROCEED TOMORROW.
NO! YOU CAN'T!
ARE YOU REALLY THAT SCARED OF DEATH, ISCARIOT?
YES!

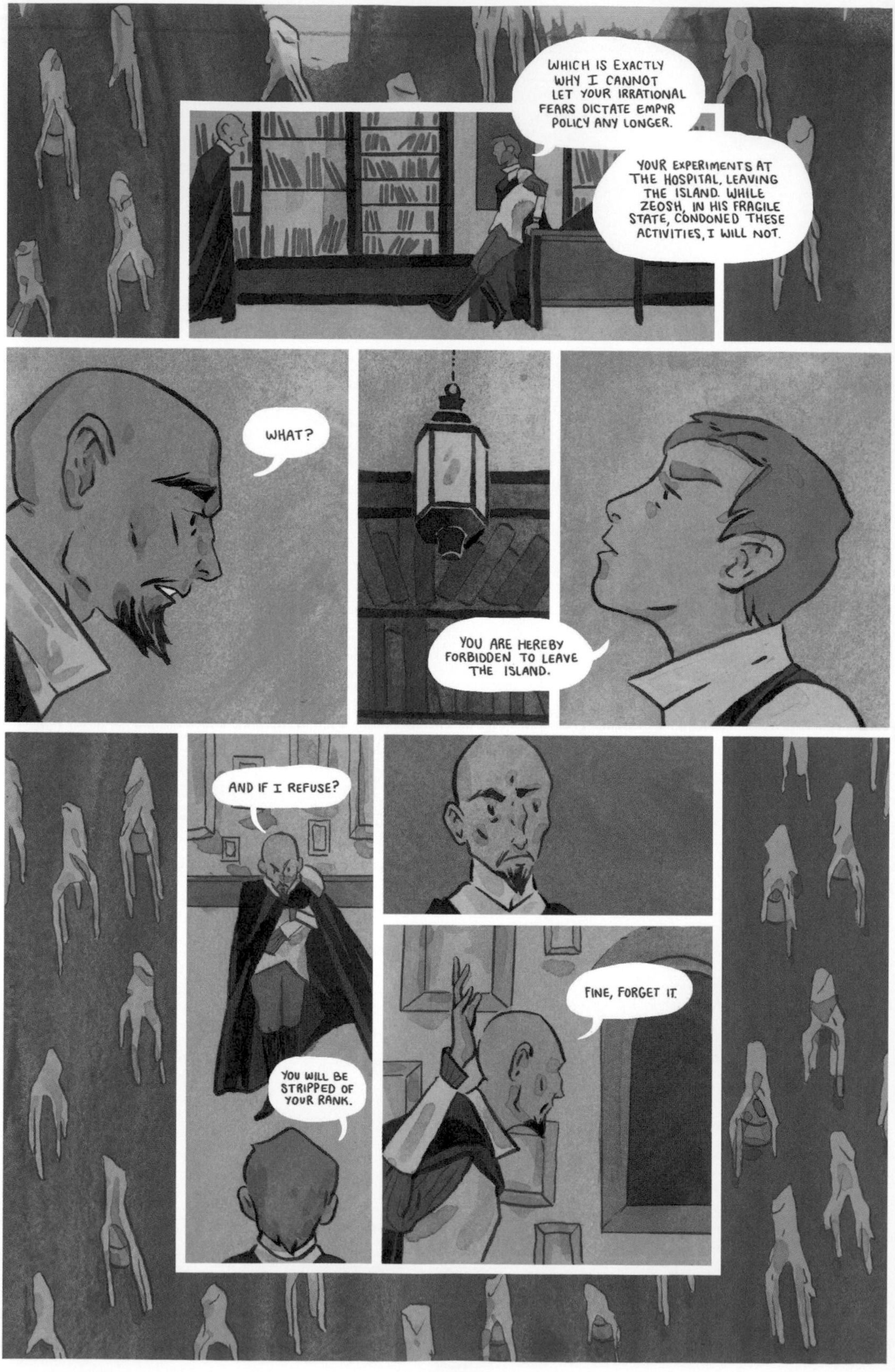
WHICH IS EXACTLY WHY I CANNOT LET YOUR IRRATIONAL FEARS DICTATE EMPYR POLICY ANY LONGER.
YOUR EXPERIMENTS AT THE HOSPITAL, LEAVING THE ISLAND. WHILE ZEOSH, IN HIS FRAGILE STATE, CONDONED THESE ACTIVITIES, I WILL NOT.
WHAT?
YOU ARE HEREBY FORBIDDEN TO LEAVE THE ISLAND.
AND IF I REFUSE?
YOU WILL BE STRIPPED OF YOUR RANK.
FINE, FORGET IT.

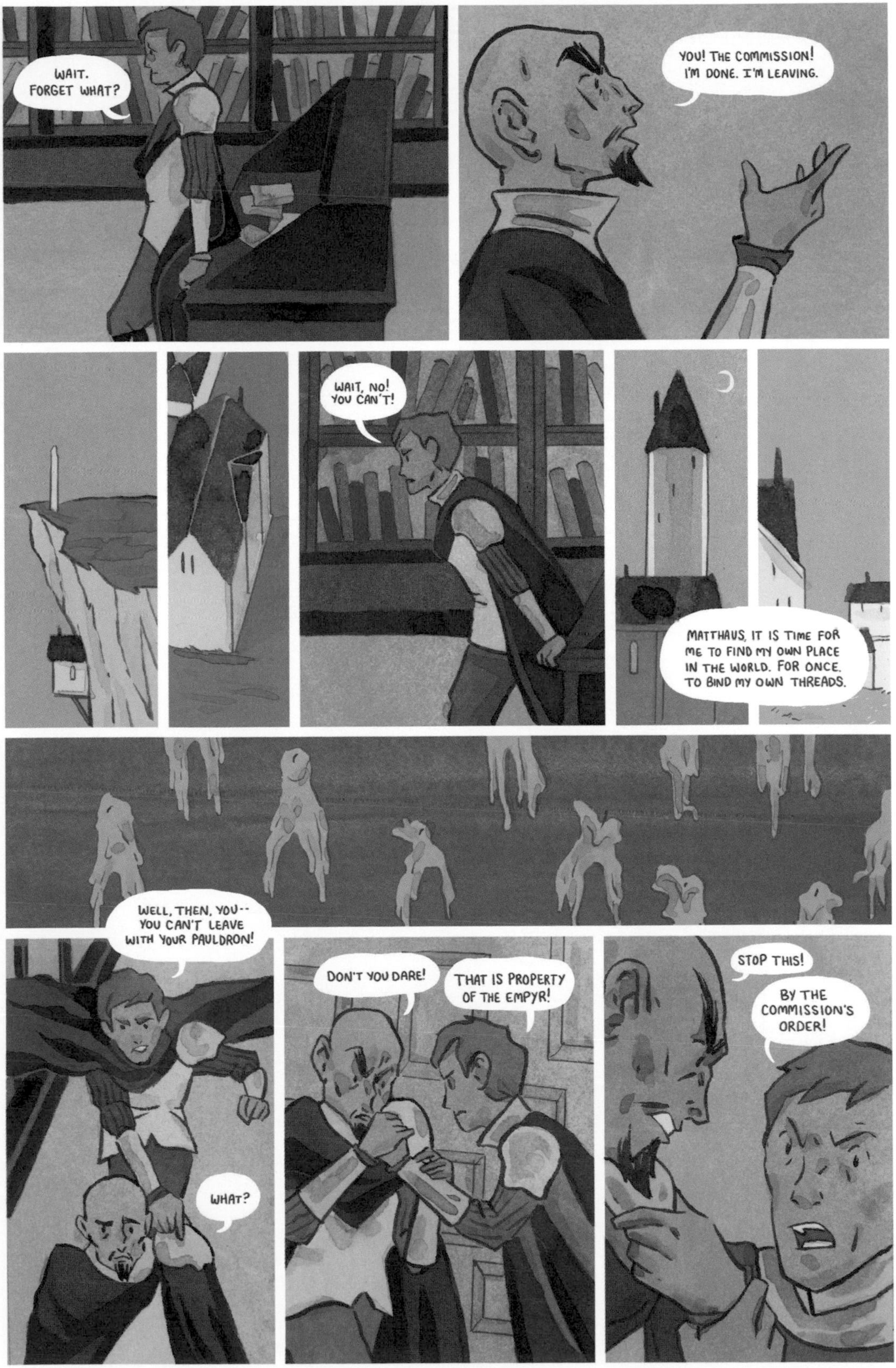
WAIT. FORGET WHAT?
YOU! THE COMMISSION! I'M DONE. I'M LEAVING.
WAIT, NO! YOU CAN'T!
MATTHAUS, IT IS TIME FOR ME TO FIND MY OWN PLACE IN THE WORLD. FOR ONCE, TO BIND MY OWN THREADS.
WELL, THEN, YOU-- YOU CAN'T LEAVE WITH YOUR PAULDRON!
WHAT?
DON'T YOU DARE!
THAT IS PROPERTY OF THE EMPYR!
STOP THIS!
BY THE COMMISSION'S ORDER!

NO! GIVE HIM BACK!

I WARNED YOU.

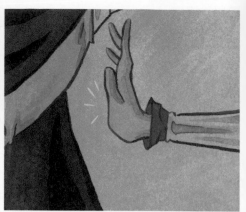

DON'T.

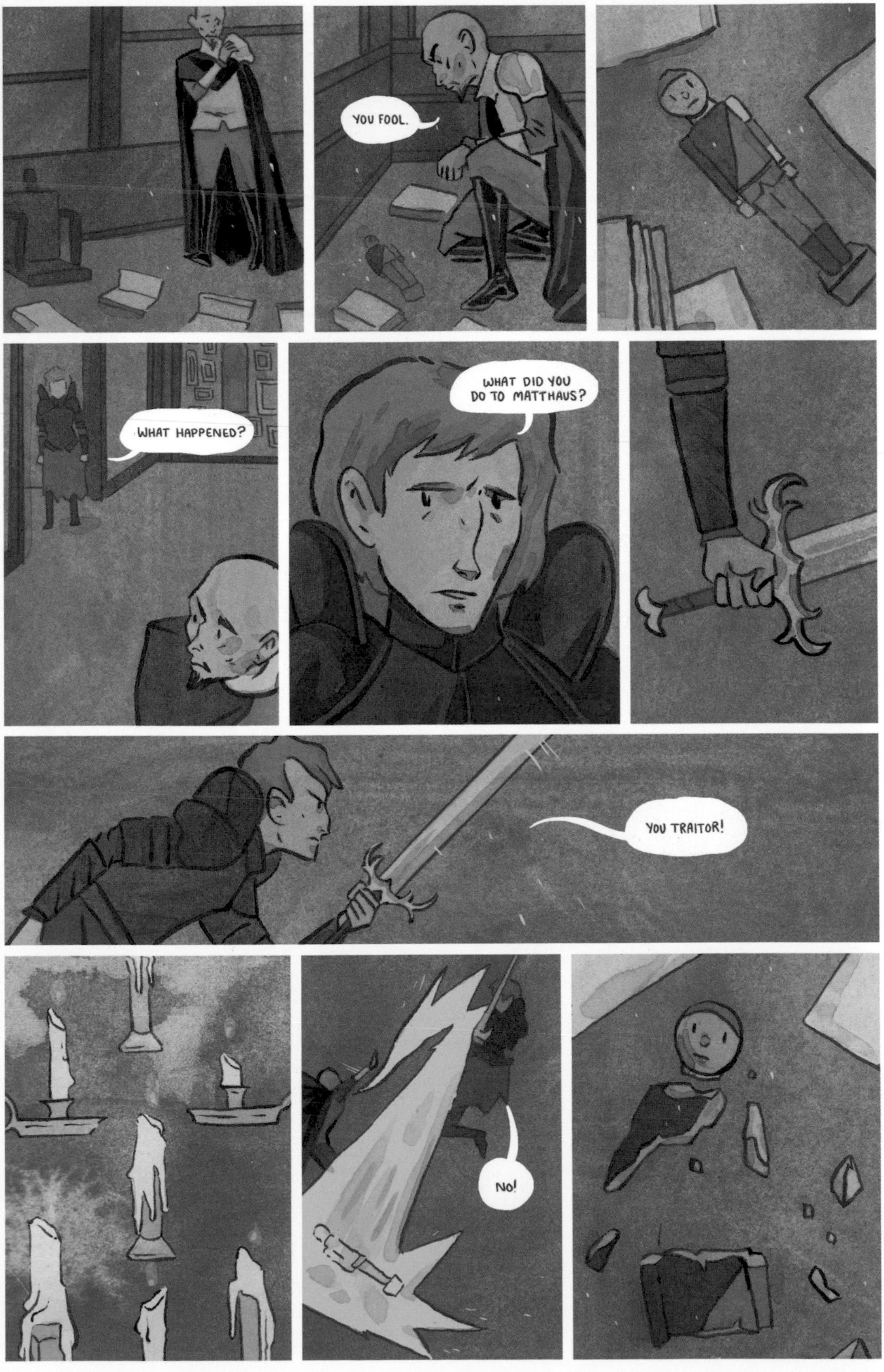
YOU FOOL.
WHAT HAPPENED?
WHAT DID YOU DO TO MATTHAUS?
YOU TRAITOR!
NO!

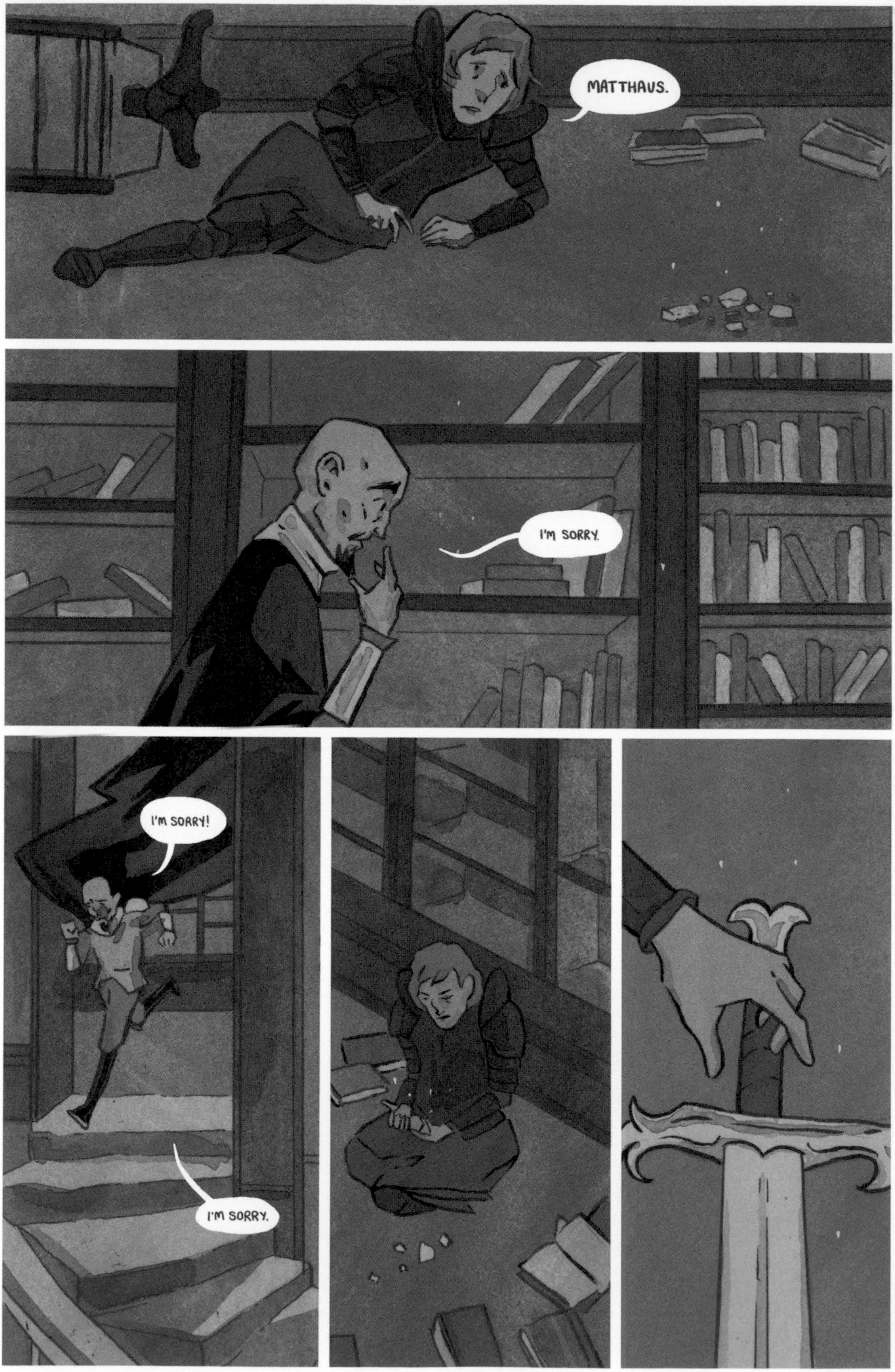
MATTHAUS.
I'M SORRY.
I'M SORRY!
I'M SORRY.

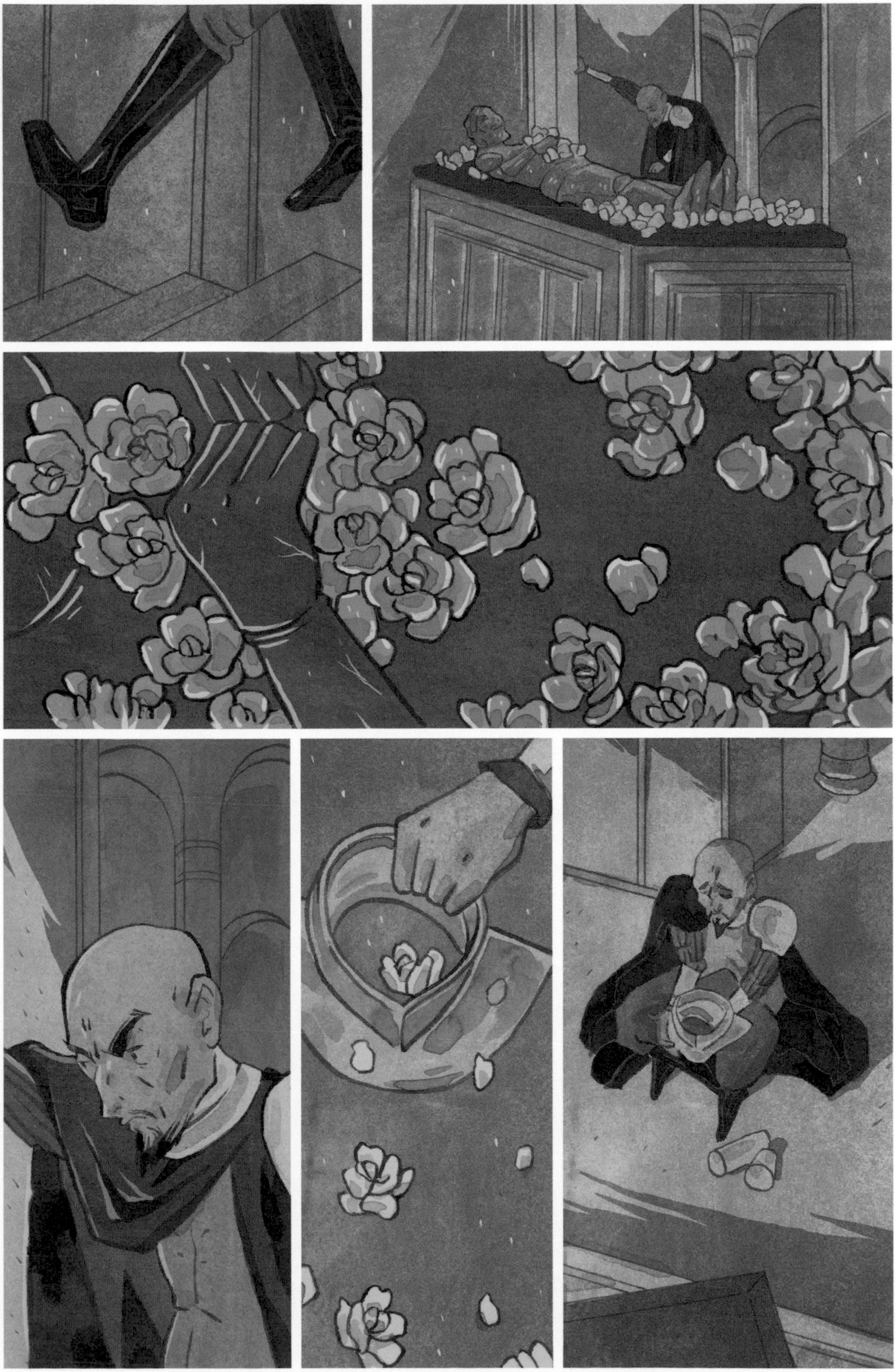

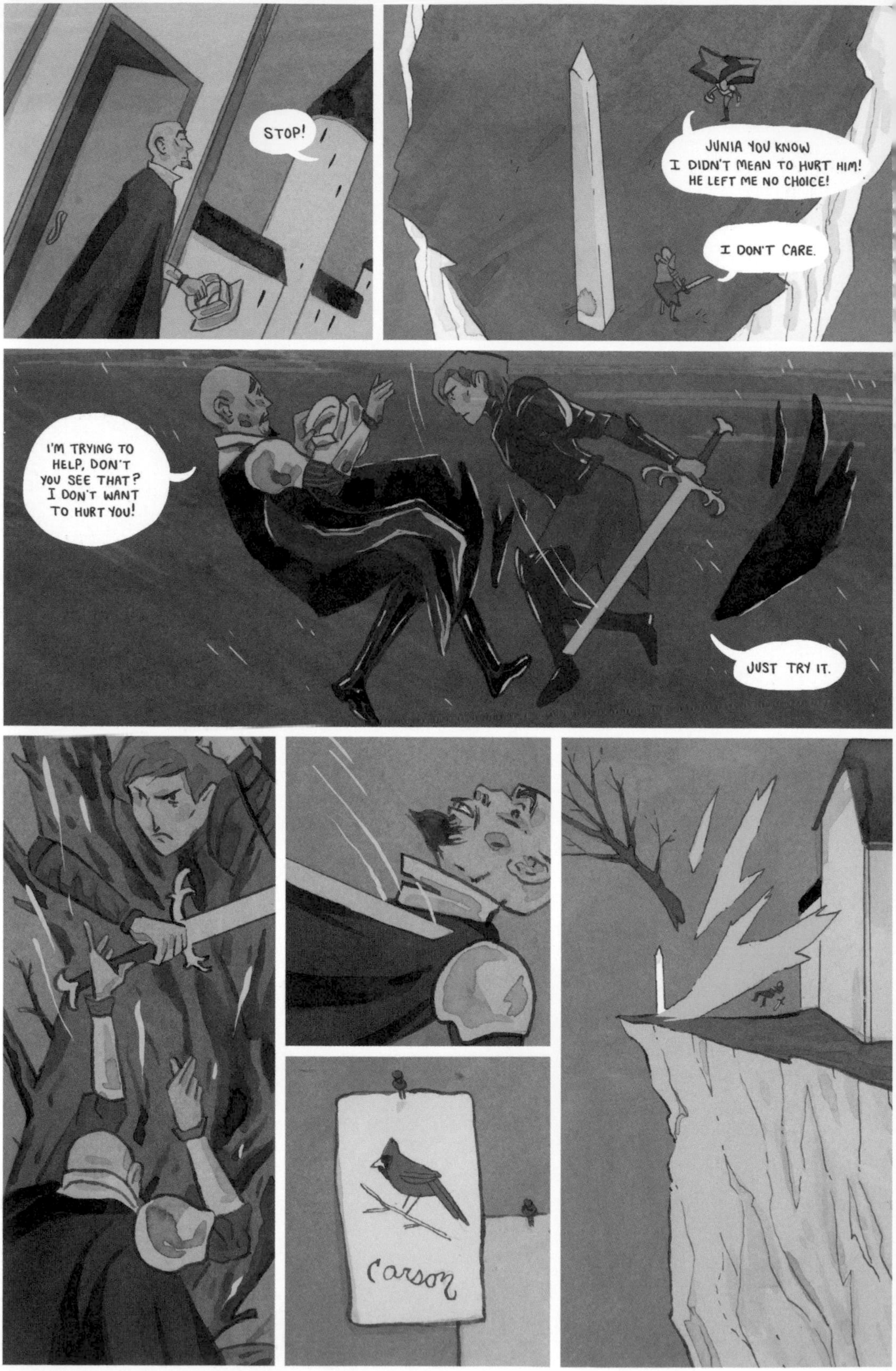
STOP!
JUNIA YOU KNOW I DIDN'T MEAN TO HURT HIM! HE LEFT ME NO CHOICE!
I DON'T CARE.
I'M TRYING TO HELP, DON'T YOU SEE THAT? I DON'T WANT TO HURT YOU!
JUST TRY IT.
Carson

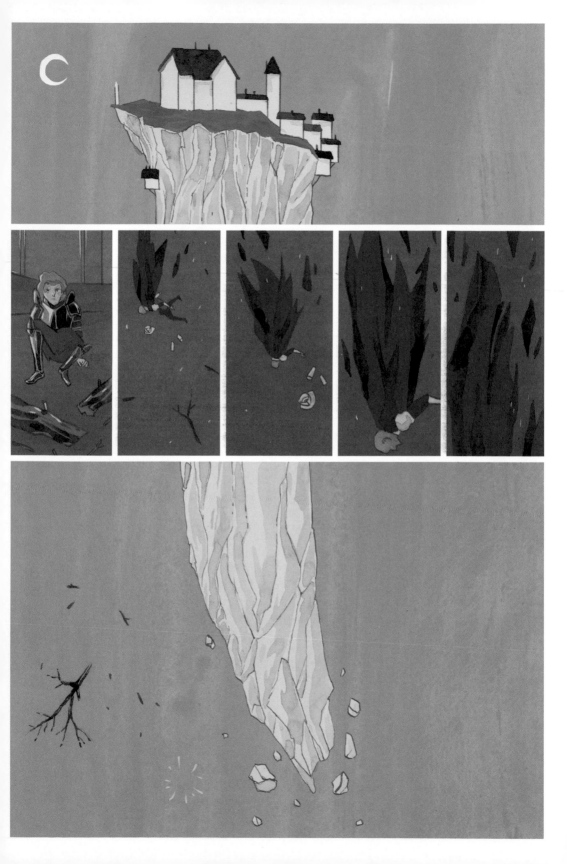

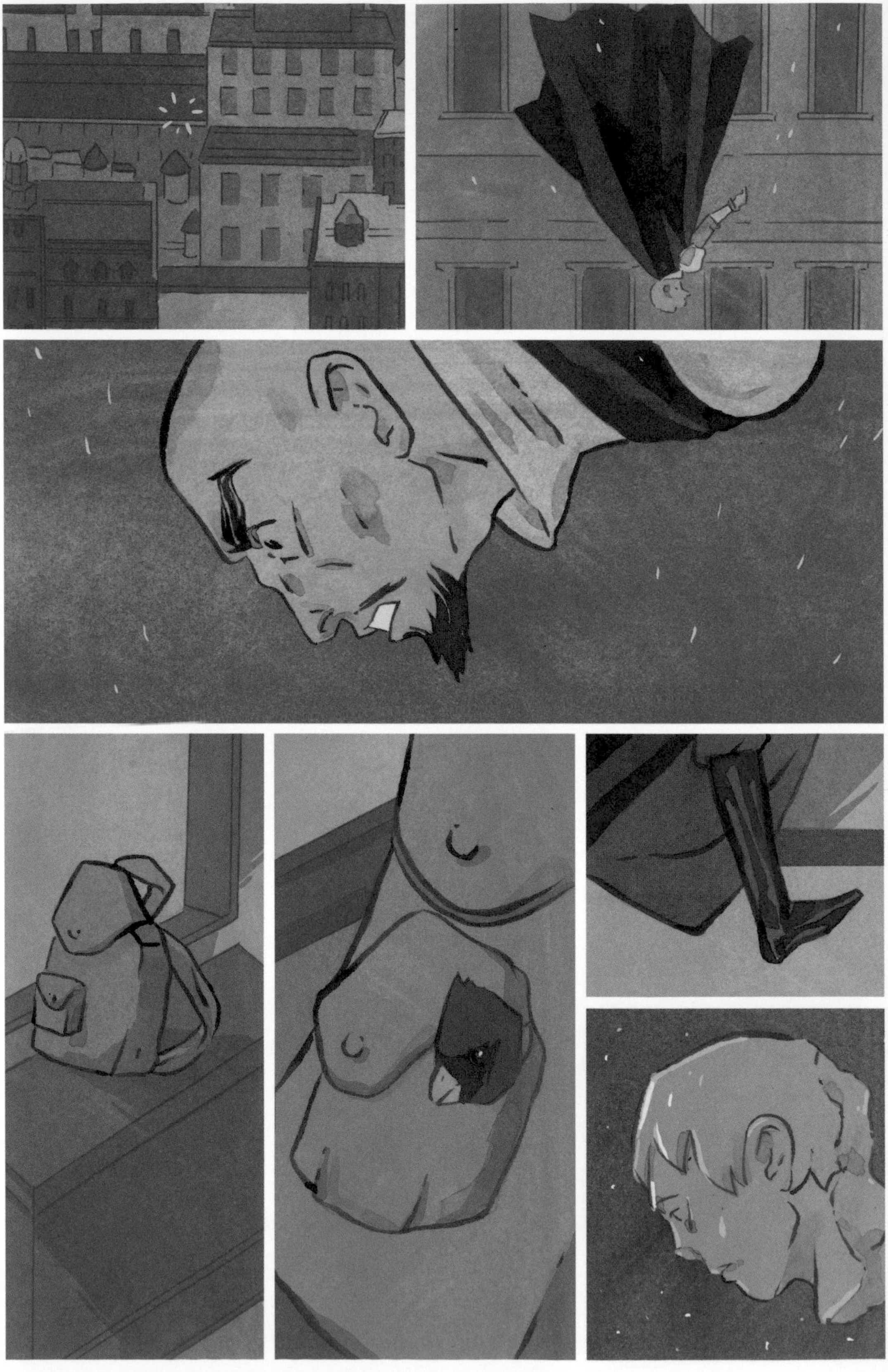

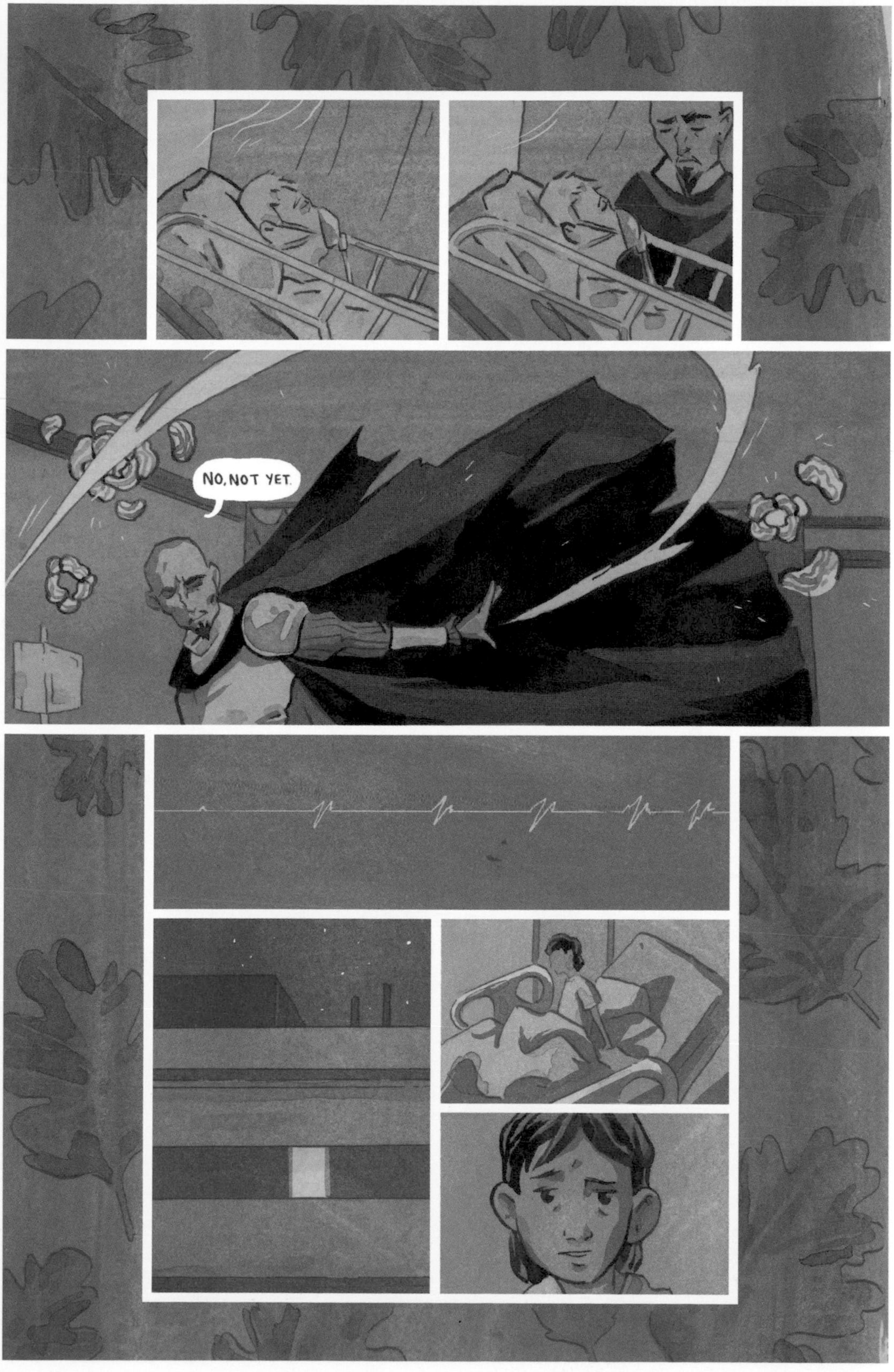
NO, NOT YET.

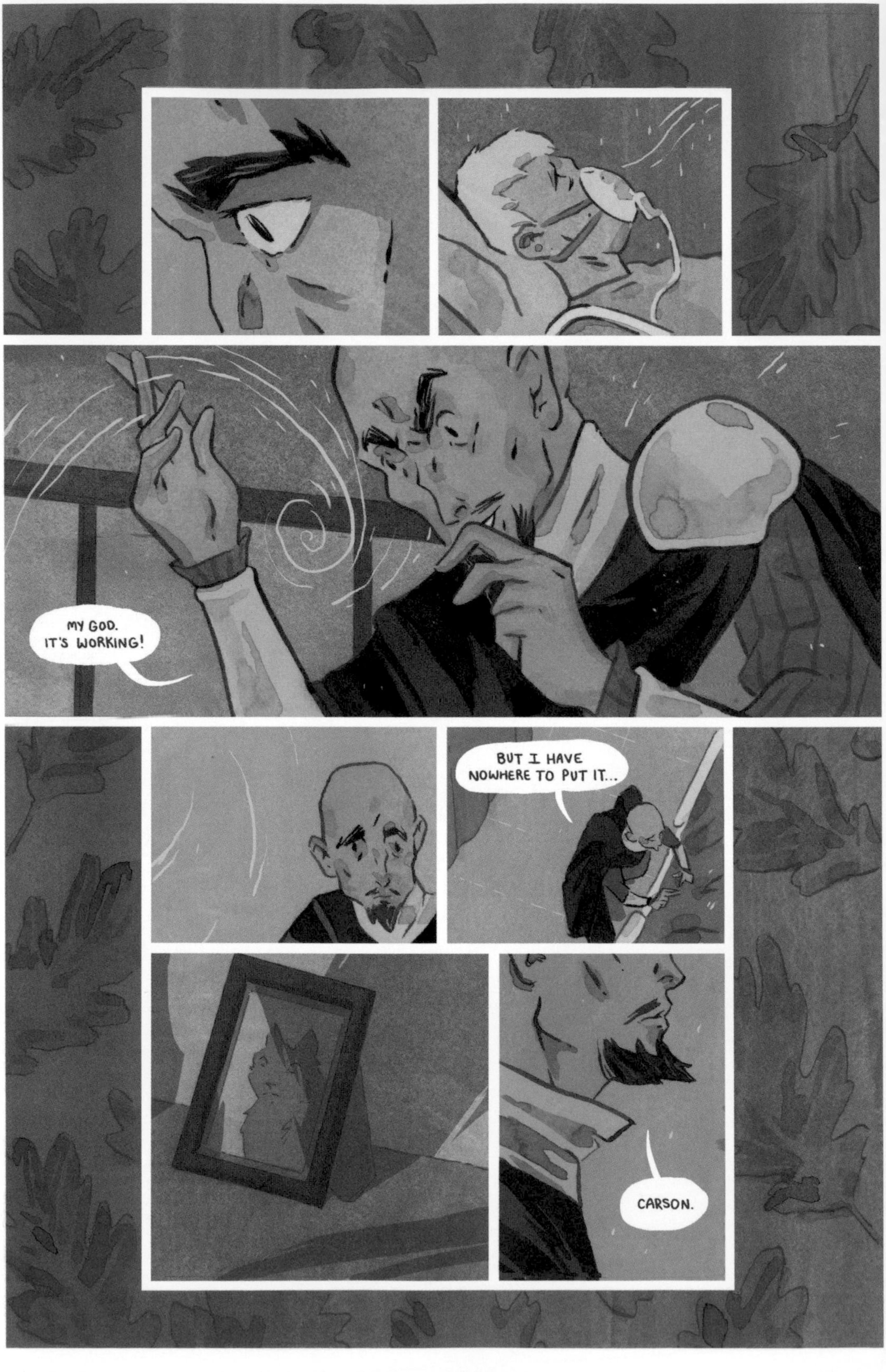
MY GOD. IT'S WORKING!
BUT I HAVE NOWHERE TO PUT IT...
CARSON.

I KNEW YOU WERE HERE!

DO YOU WANT TO LEARN MAGIC, CARSON?

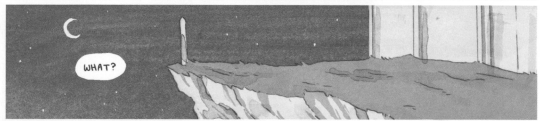

WHAT?

YOU REMIND ME SO MUCH OF MYSELF.

UH. OKAY.

GIVE ME YOUR HAND.

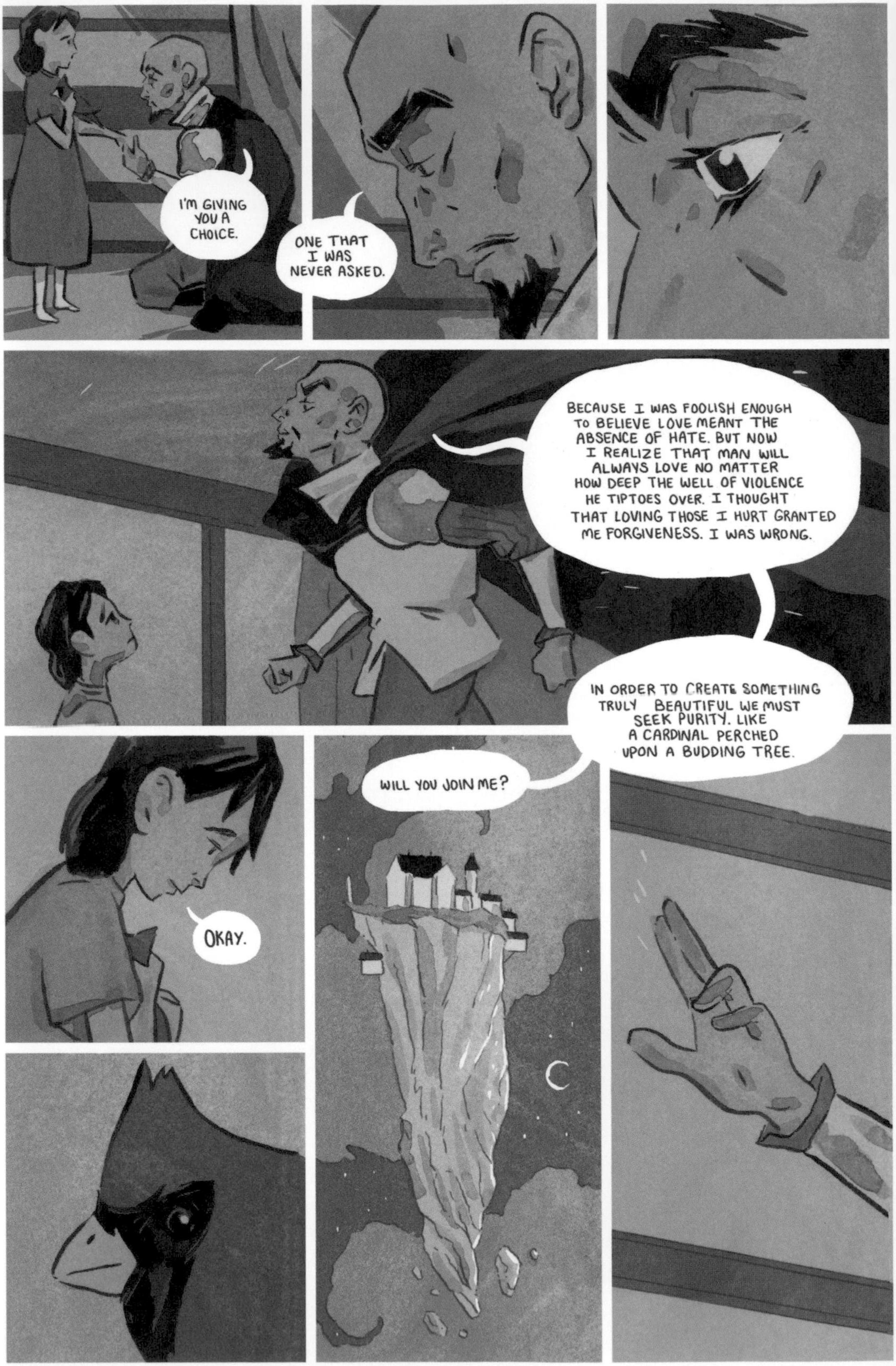
I'M GIVING YOU A CHOICE.
ONE THAT I WAS NEVER ASKED.
BECAUSE I WAS FOOLISH ENOUGH TO BELIEVE LOVE MEANT THE ABSENCE OF HATE. BUT NOW I REALIZE THAT MAN WILL ALWAYS LOVE NO MATTER HOW DEEP THE WELL OF VIOLENCE HE TIPTOES OVER. I THOUGHT THAT LOVING THOSE I HURT GRANTED ME FORGIVENESS. I WAS WRONG.
IN ORDER TO CREATE SOMETHING TRULY BEAUTIFUL WE MUST SEEK PURITY. LIKE A CARDINAL PERCHED UPON A BUDDING TREE.
OKAY.
WILL YOU JOIN ME?

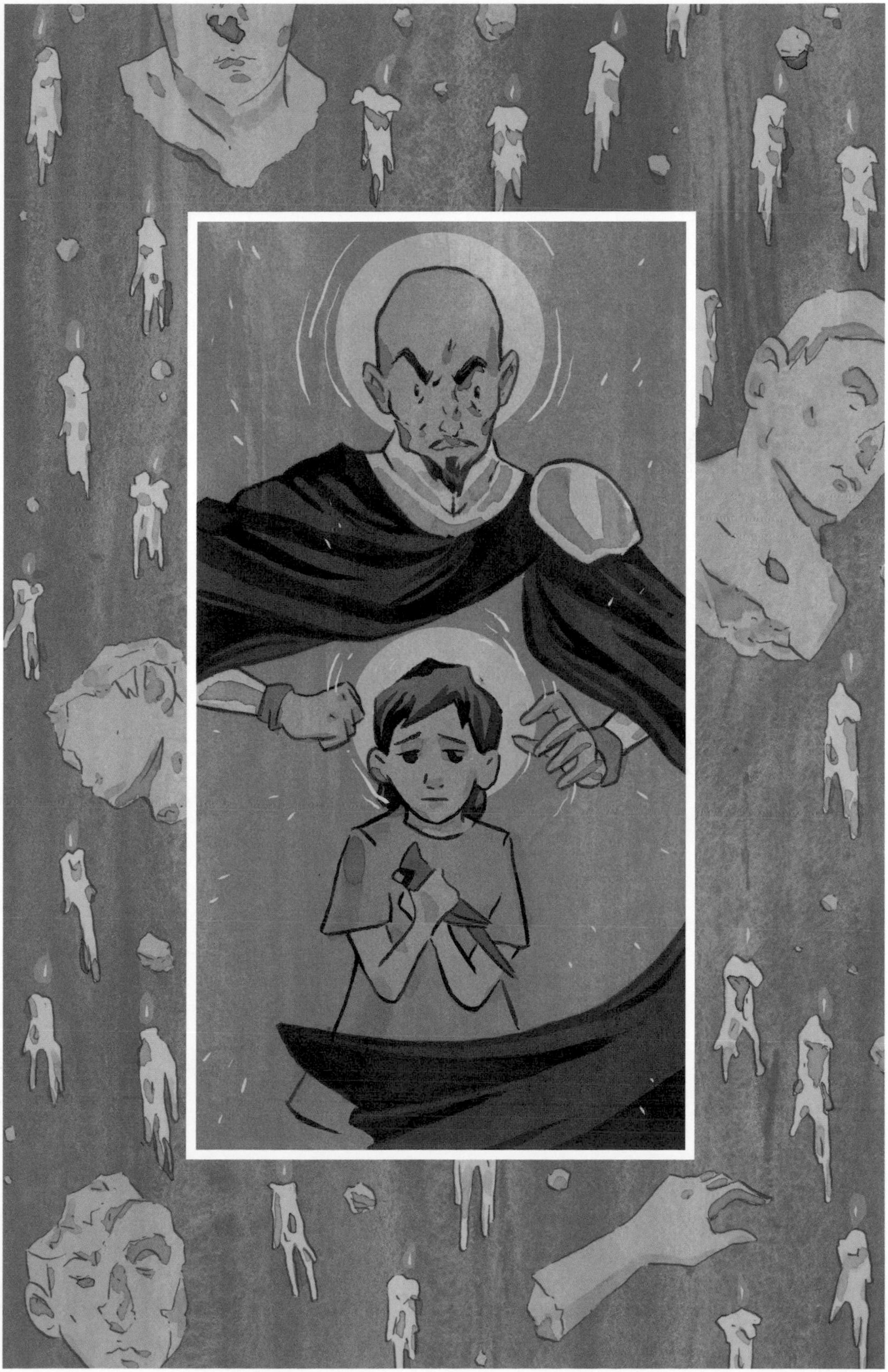

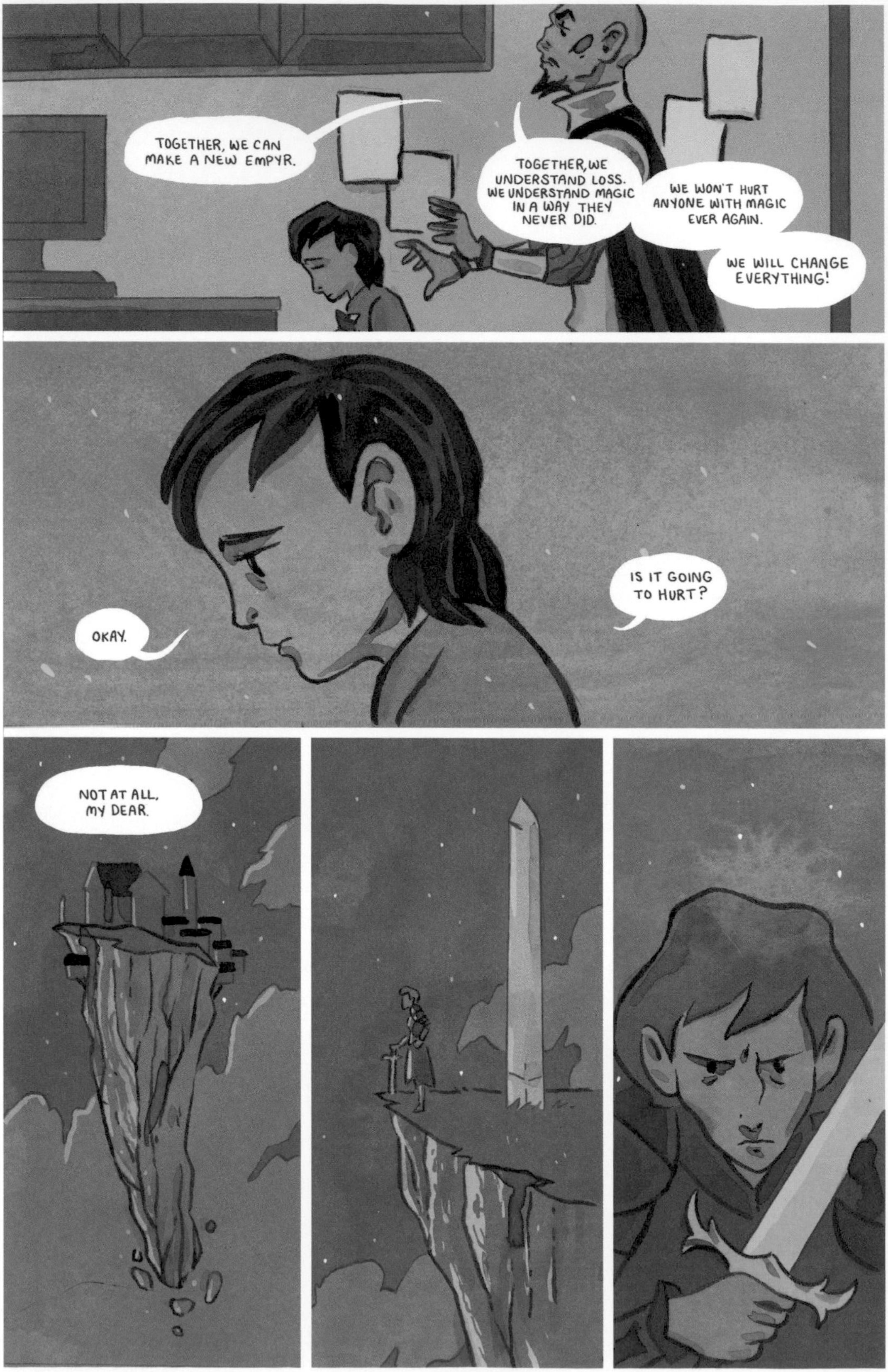
TOGETHER, WE CAN MAKE A NEW EMPYR.
TOGETHER, WE UNDERSTAND LOSS. WE UNDERSTAND MAGIC IN A WAY THEY NEVER DID.
WE WON'T HURT ANYONE WITH MAGIC EVER AGAIN.
WE WILL CHANGE EVERYTHING!
OKAY.
IS IT GOING TO HURT?
NOT AT ALL, MY DEAR.

CHAPTER TWO

Of all the harm done
The worst is the embrace
Clothed in a coat of thorns
That says
Everything will be okay.

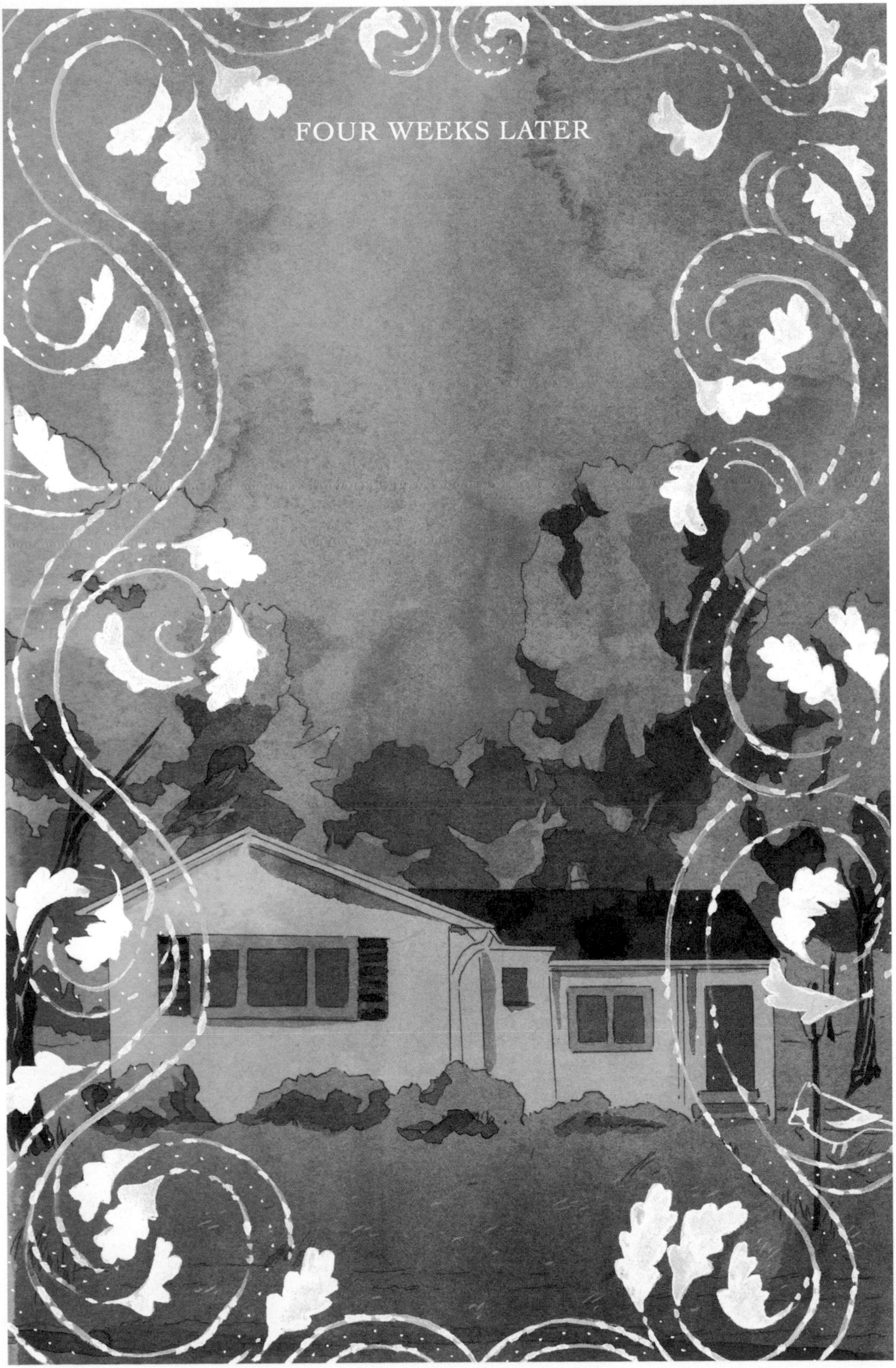
FOUR WEEKS LATER

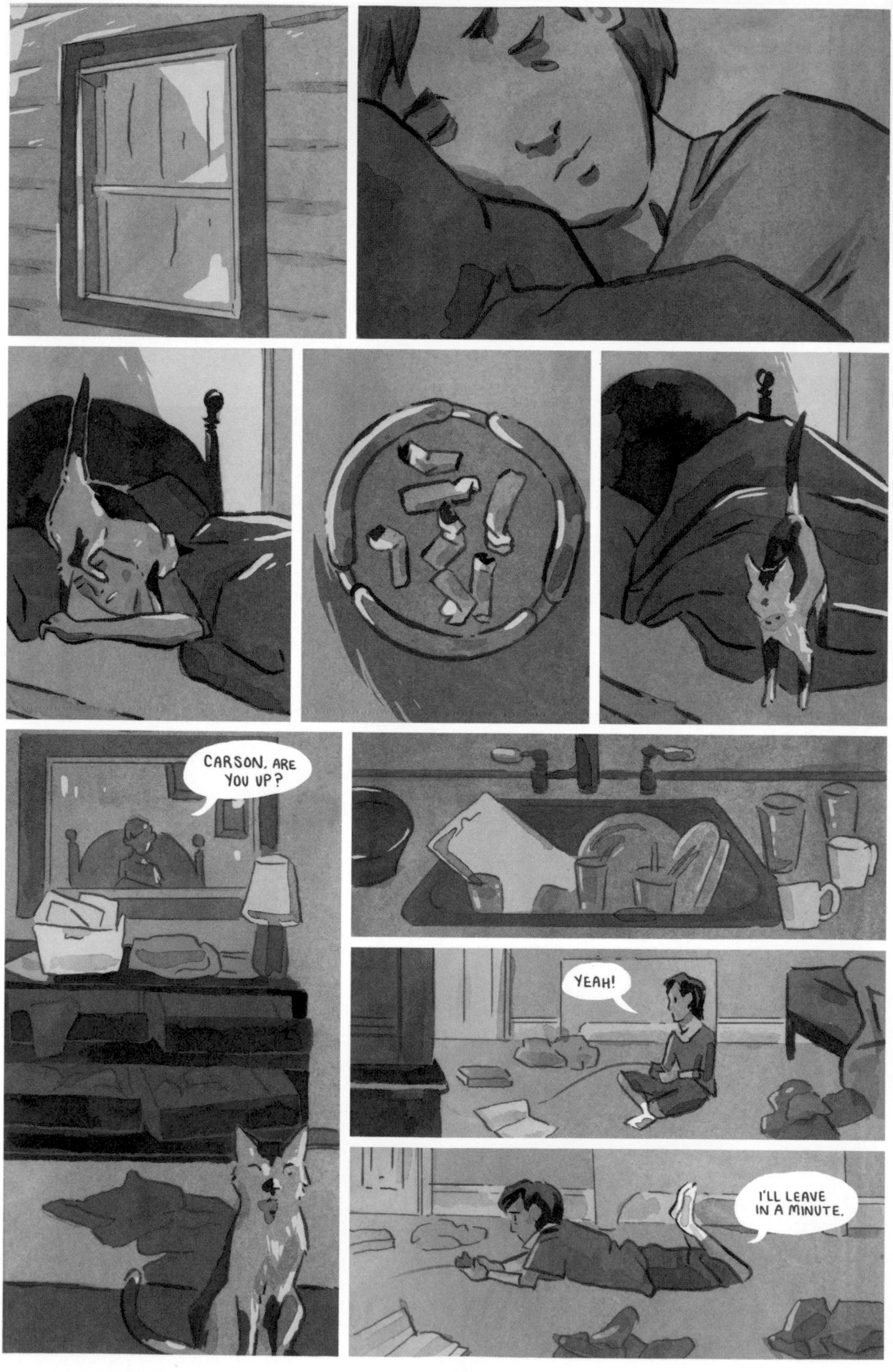
CARSON, ARE YOU UP?
YEAH!
I'LL LEAVE IN A MINUTE.

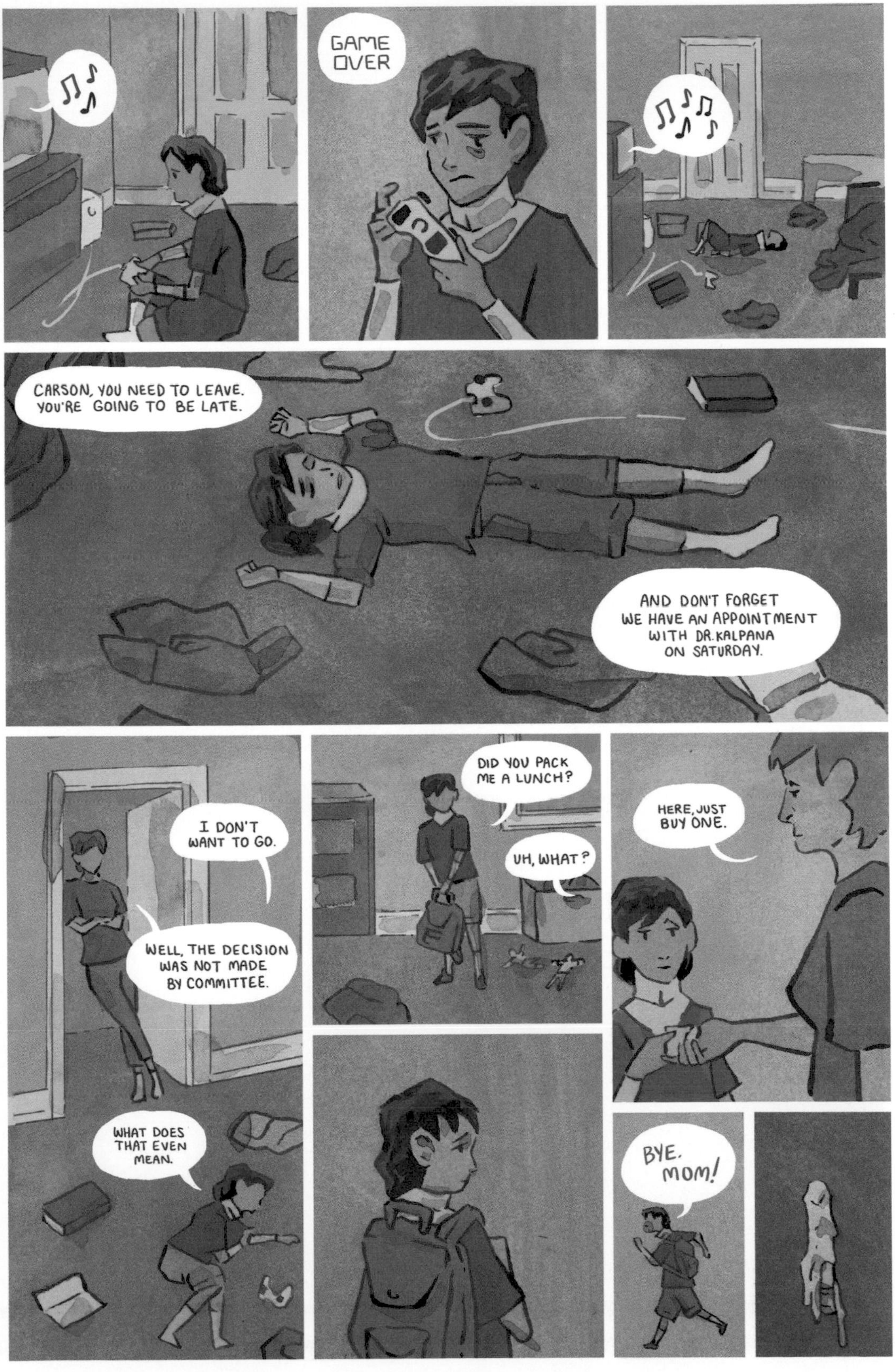
GAME OVER
CARSON, YOU NEED TO LEAVE. YOU'RE GOING TO BE LATE.
AND DON'T FORGET WE HAVE AN APPOINTMENT WITH DR. KALPANA ON SATURDAY.
I DON'T WANT TO GO.
WELL, THE DECISION WAS NOT MADE BY COMMITTEE.
WHAT DOES THAT EVEN MEAN.
DID YOU PACK ME A LUNCH?
UH, WHAT?
HERE, JUST BUY ONE.
BYE. MOM!

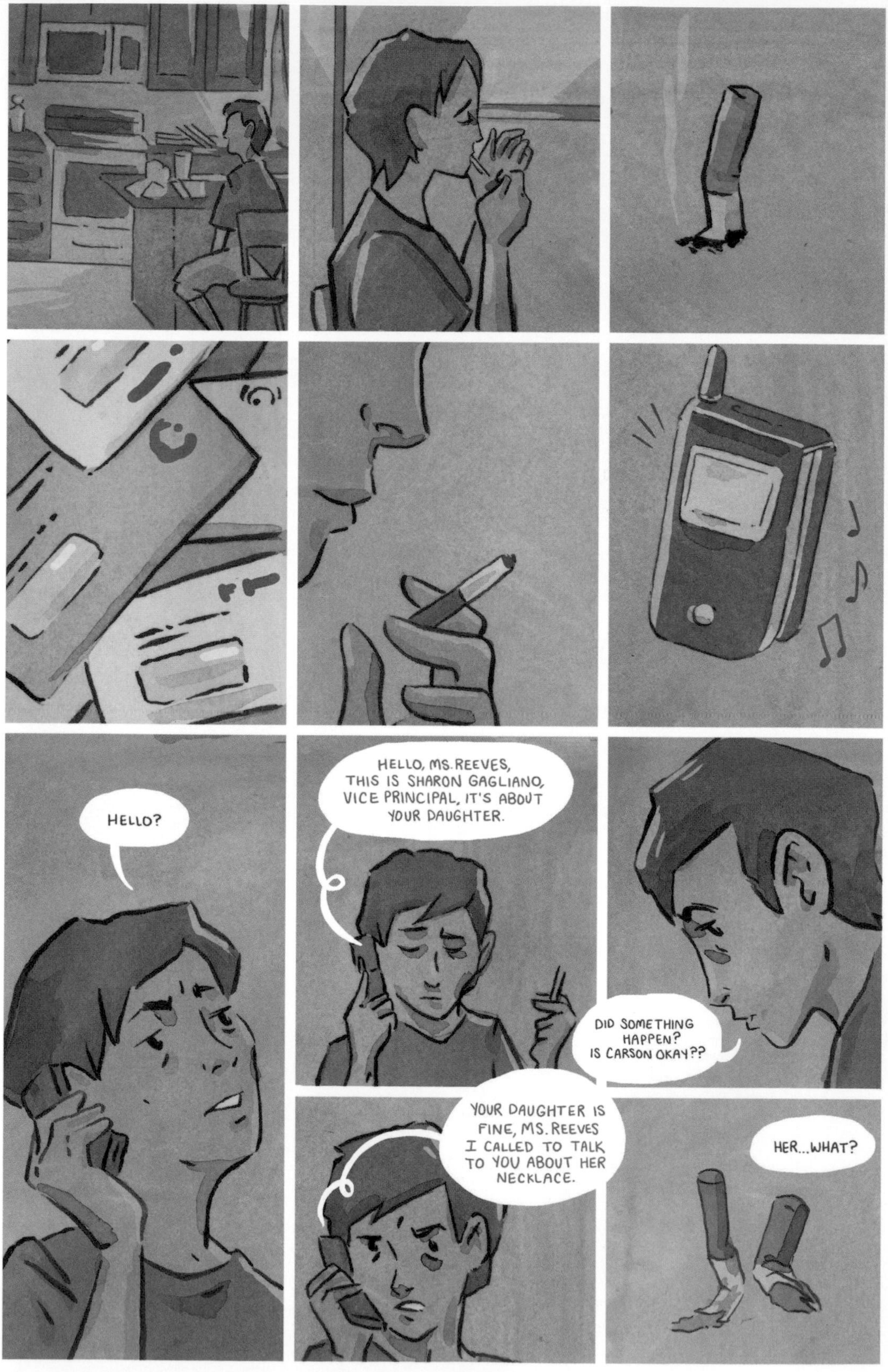
HELLO?
HELLO, MS. REEVES, THIS IS SHARON GAGLIANO, VICE PRINCIPAL, IT'S ABOUT YOUR DAUGHTER.
DID SOMETHING HAPPEN? IS CARSON OKAY??
YOUR DAUGHTER IS FINE, MS. REEVES I CALLED TO TALK TO YOU ABOUT HER NECKLACE.
HER...WHAT?

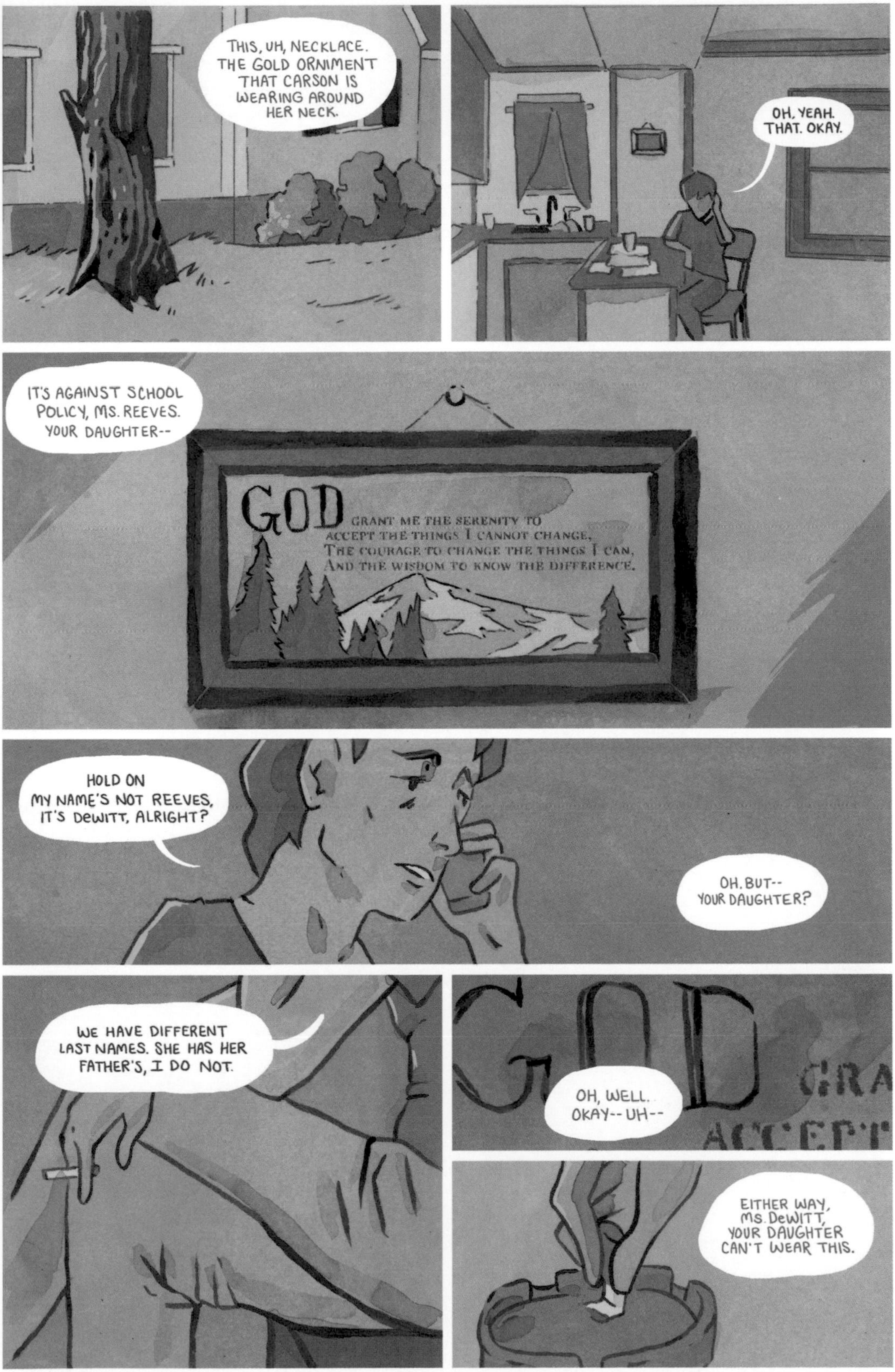

THIS, UH, NECKLACE. THE GOLD ORNIMENT THAT CARSON IS WEARING AROUND HER NECK.
OH, YEAH. THAT. OKAY.
IT'S AGAINST SCHOOL POLICY, MS. REEVES. YOUR DAUGHTER--
GOD GRANT ME THE SERENITY TO ACCEPT THE THINGS I CANNOT CHANGE, THE COURAGE TO CHANGE THE THINGS I CAN, AND THE WISDOM TO KNOW THE DIFFERENCE.
HOLD ON MY NAME'S NOT REEVES, IT'S DeWITT, ALRIGHT?
OH. BUT-- YOUR DAUGHTER?
WE HAVE DIFFERENT LAST NAMES. SHE HAS HER FATHER'S, I DO NOT.
OH, WELL. OKAY-- UH--
EITHER WAY, MS. DeWITT, YOUR DAUGHTER CAN'T WEAR THIS.

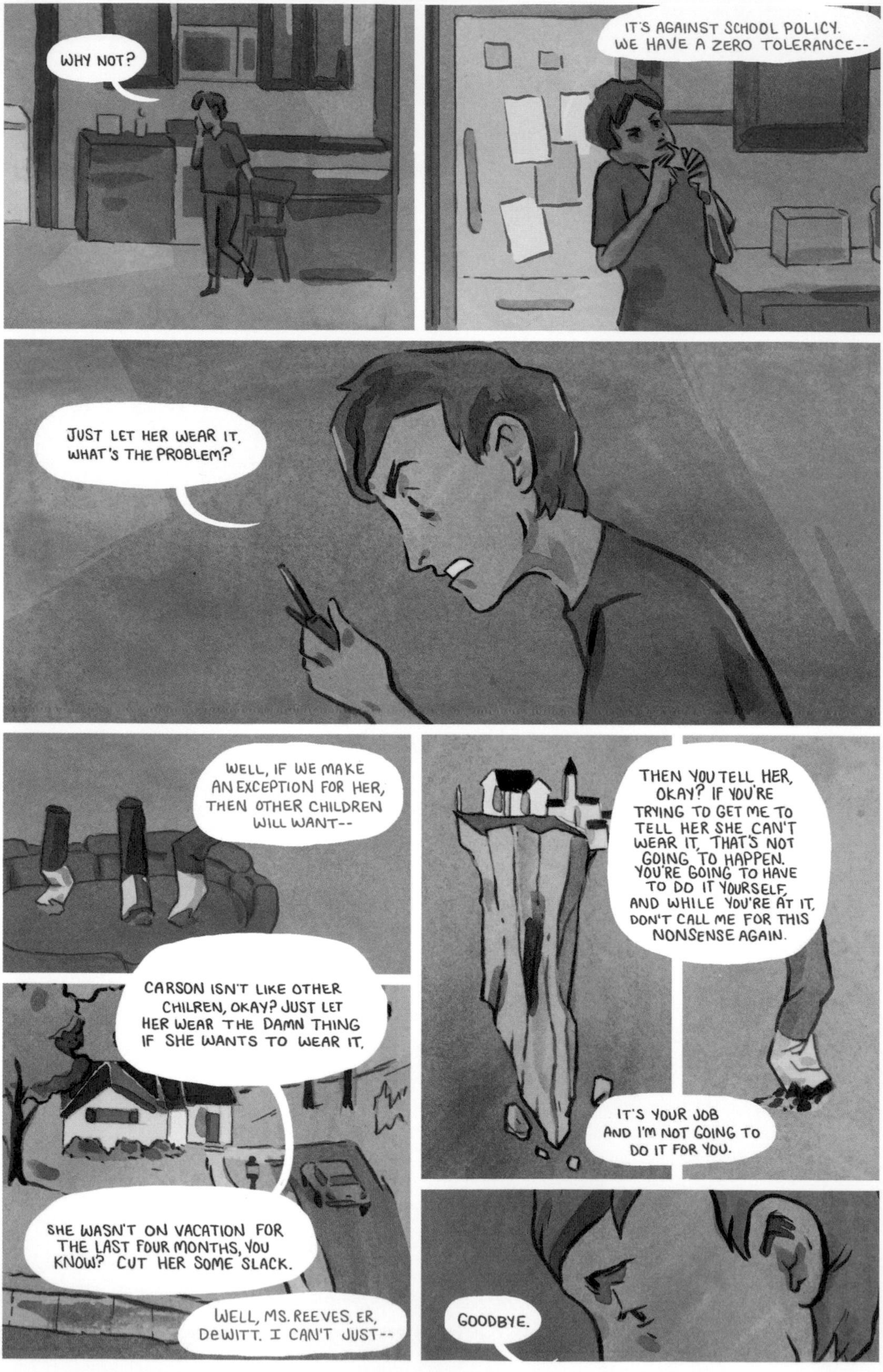
WHY NOT?
IT'S AGAINST SCHOOL POLICY. WE HAVE A ZERO TOLERANCE--
JUST LET HER WEAR IT. WHAT'S THE PROBLEM?
WELL, IF WE MAKE AN EXCEPTION FOR HER, THEN OTHER CHILDREN WILL WANT--
CARSON ISN'T LIKE OTHER CHILREN, OKAY? JUST LET HER WEAR THE DAMN THING IF SHE WANTS TO WEAR IT.
SHE WASN'T ON VACATION FOR THE LAST FOUR MONTHS, YOU KNOW? CUT HER SOME SLACK.
WELL, MS. REEVES, ER, DeWITT. I CAN'T JUST--
THEN YOU TELL HER, OKAY? IF YOU'RE TRYING TO GET ME TO TELL HER SHE CAN'T WEAR IT, THAT'S NOT GOING TO HAPPEN. YOU'RE GOING TO HAVE TO DO IT YOURSELF, AND WHILE YOU'RE AT IT, DON'T CALL ME FOR THIS NONSENSE AGAIN.
IT'S YOUR JOB AND I'M NOT GOING TO DO IT FOR YOU.
GOODBYE.

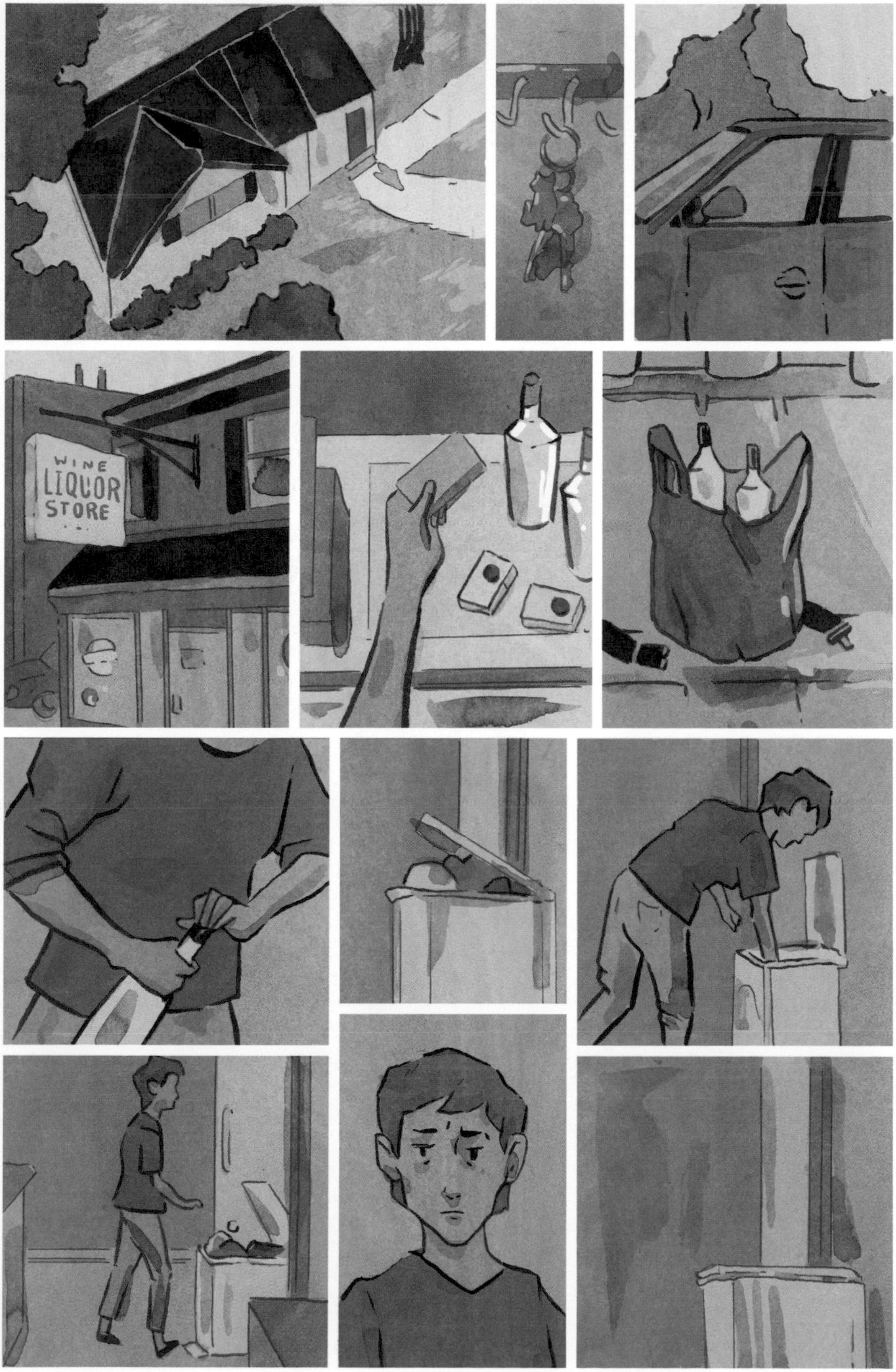
WINE
LIQUOR
STORE

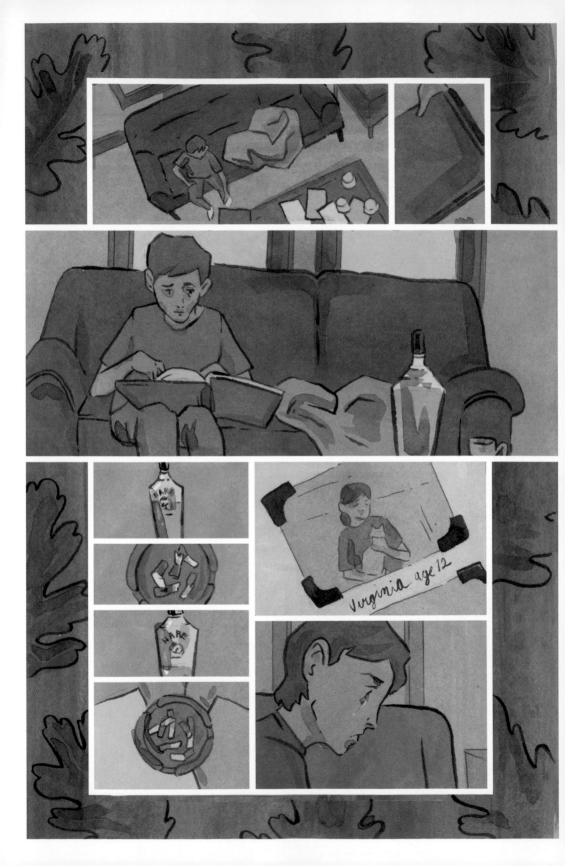

Virginia age 12

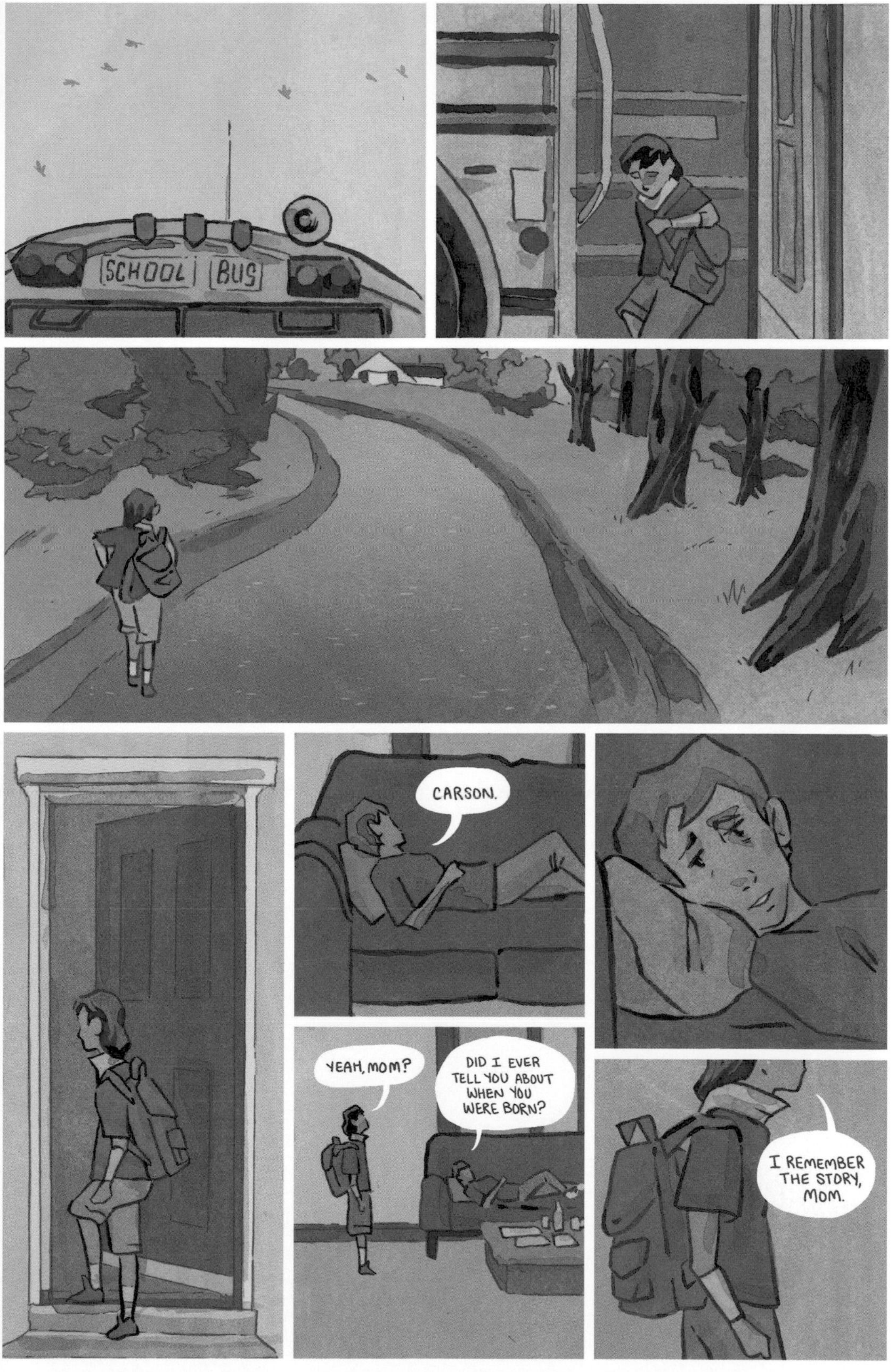

SCHOOL BUS
CARSON.
YEAH, MOM?
DID I EVER TELL YOU ABOUT WHEN YOU WERE BORN?
I REMEMBER THE STORY, MOM.

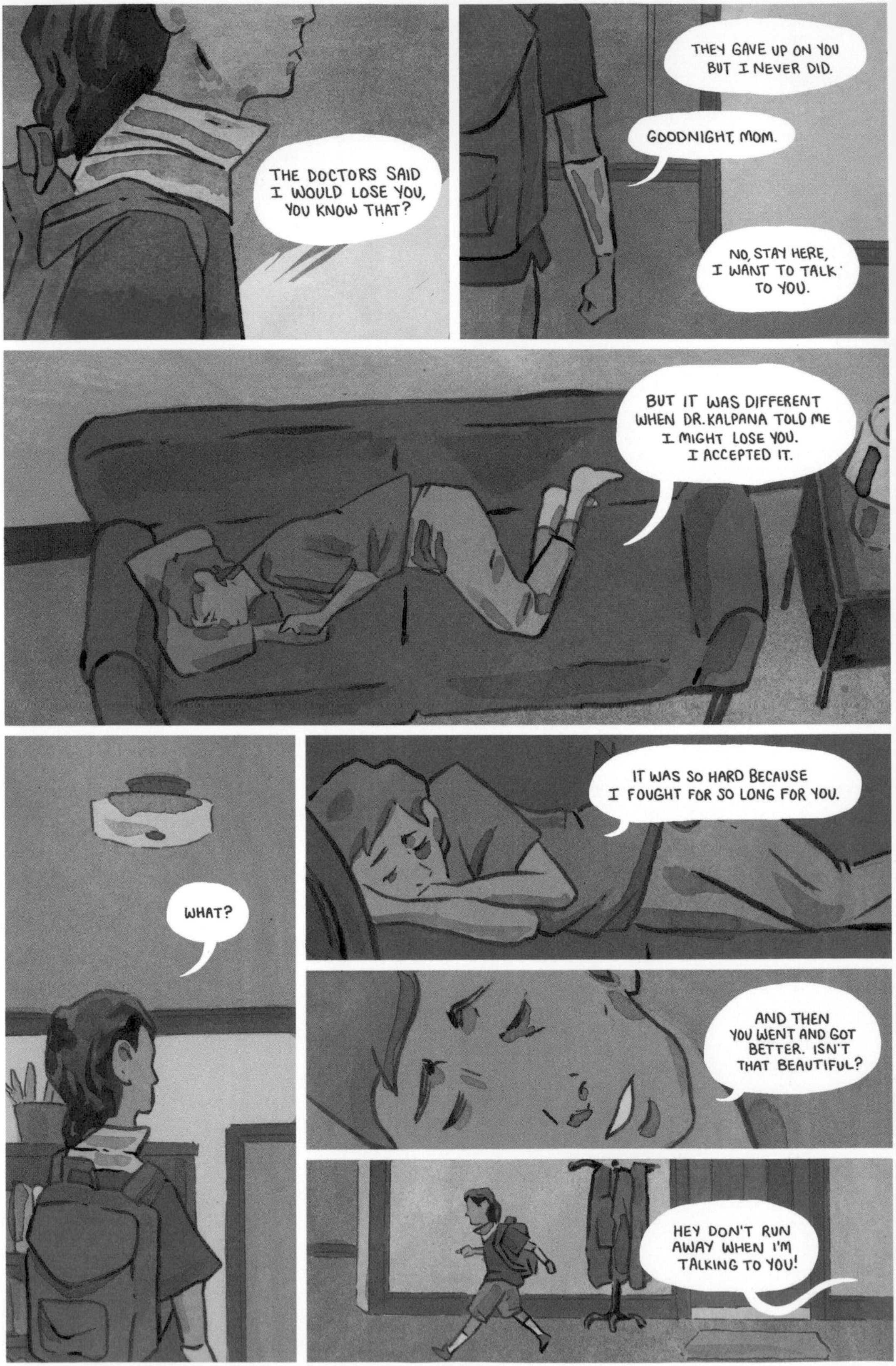
THE DOCTORS SAID I WOULD LOSE YOU, YOU KNOW THAT?
THEY GAVE UP ON YOU BUT I NEVER DID.
GOODNIGHT, MOM.
NO, STAY HERE, I WANT TO TALK TO YOU.
BUT IT WAS DIFFERENT WHEN DR. KALPANA TOLD ME I MIGHT LOSE YOU. I ACCEPTED IT.
WHAT?
IT WAS SO HARD BECAUSE I FOUGHT FOR SO LONG FOR YOU.
AND THEN YOU WENT AND GOT BETTER. ISN'T THAT BEAUTIFUL?
HEY DON'T RUN AWAY WHEN I'M TALKING TO YOU!

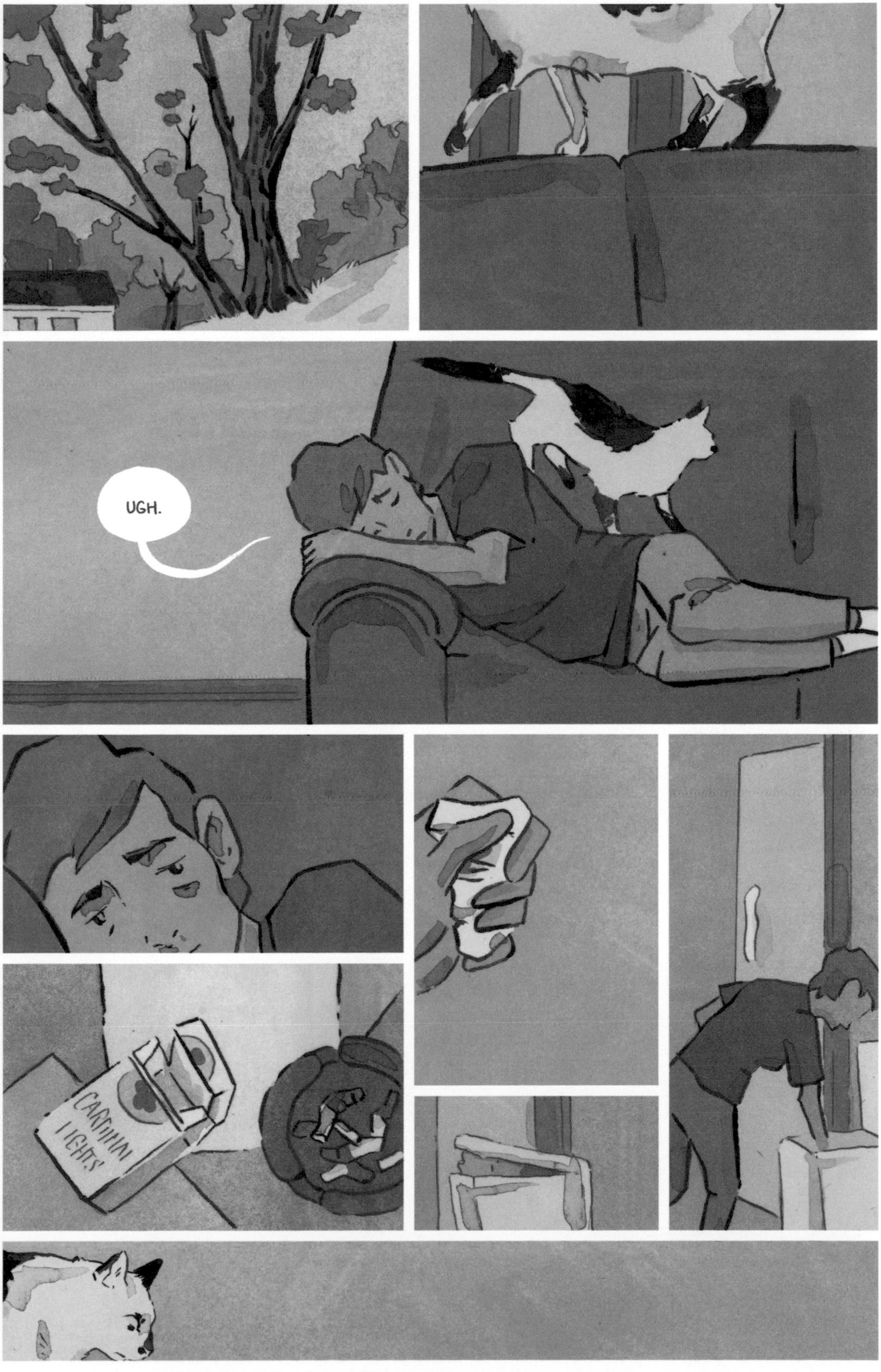
UGH.
CARMINI LIGHTS

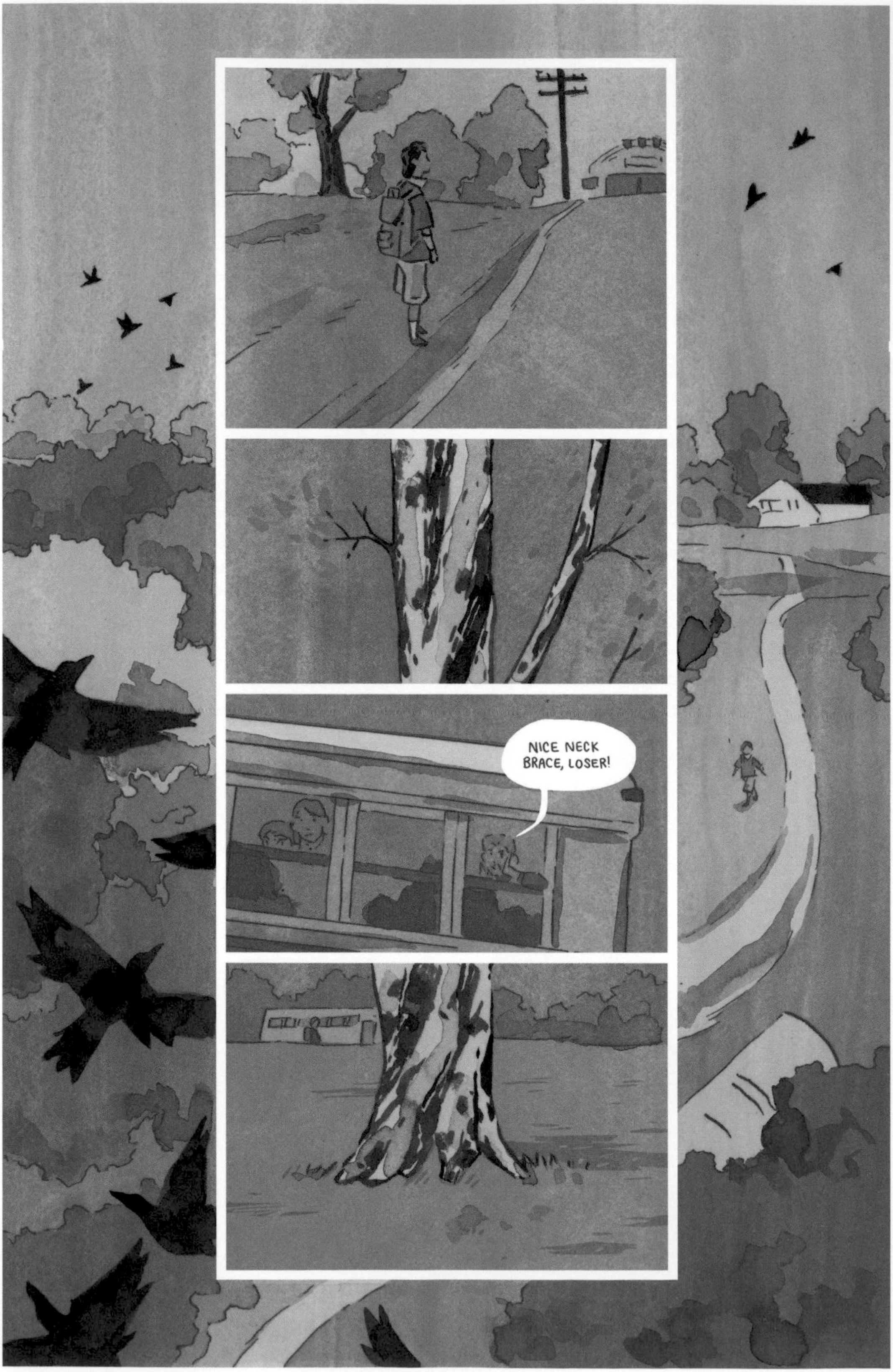
NICE NECK BRACE, LOSER!

Solving Equations
1) 6x = 66
2) 56 = -8x
3) 60 = -12x
4) -16x = 32
Solving Equations
Carson Reeves
1) 6x = 66
2) 56 = -8x
3) 60 = -12x
4) -16x = 32
5) 81 = 9x
EYES FORWARD CLASS.
IF YOU'RE DONE WITH YOUR WORKSHEET, THEN PLEASE PASS IT FORWARD.

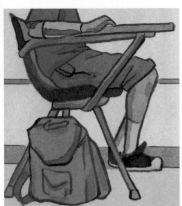

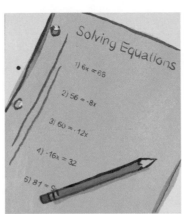

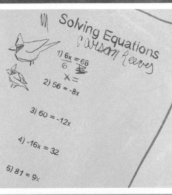

NOW FOR HOMEWORK, I WANT YOU ALL TO DO PAGE FIFTEEN IN THE WORKBOOK.

AND I WANT YOU TO SHOW YOUR WORK. I WON'T COUNT ANSWERS THAT DON'T HAVE WORK.

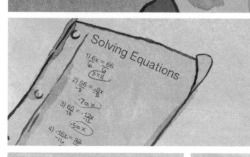

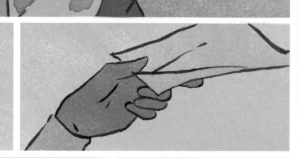

HEY, CARSON.

WHY ARE YOU REALLY WEARING THAT GOLDEN NECK BRACE?

EYES FORWARD!

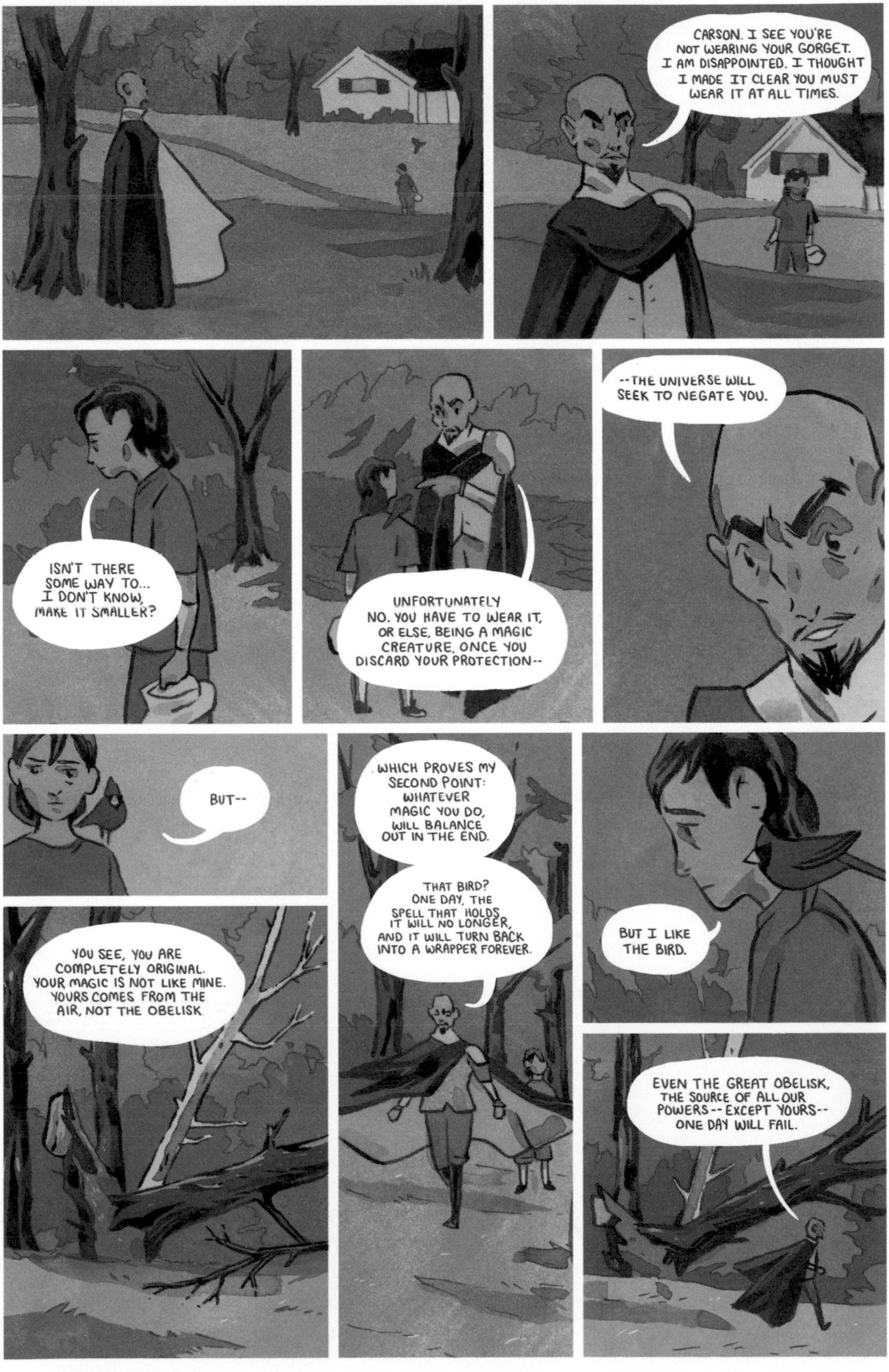
CARSON. I SEE YOU'RE NOT WEARING YOUR GORGET. I AM DISAPPOINTED. I THOUGHT I MADE IT CLEAR YOU MUST WEAR IT AT ALL TIMES.
ISN'T THERE SOME WAY TO... I DON'T KNOW, MAKE IT SMALLER?
UNFORTUNATELY NO. YOU HAVE TO WEAR IT, OR ELSE, BEING A MAGIC CREATURE, ONCE YOU DISCARD YOUR PROTECTION--
--THE UNIVERSE WILL SEEK TO NEGATE YOU.
BUT--
YOU SEE, YOU ARE COMPLETELY ORIGINAL. YOUR MAGIC IS NOT LIKE MINE. YOURS COMES FROM THE AIR, NOT THE OBELISK.
WHICH PROVES MY SECOND POINT: WHATEVER MAGIC YOU DO, WILL BALANCE OUT IN THE END.
THAT BIRD? ONE DAY, THE SPELL THAT HOLDS IT WILL NO LONGER, AND IT WILL TURN BACK INTO A WRAPPER FOREVER.
BUT I LIKE THE BIRD.
EVEN THE GREAT OBELISK, THE SOURCE OF ALL OUR POWERS--EXCEPT YOURS--ONE DAY WILL FAIL.

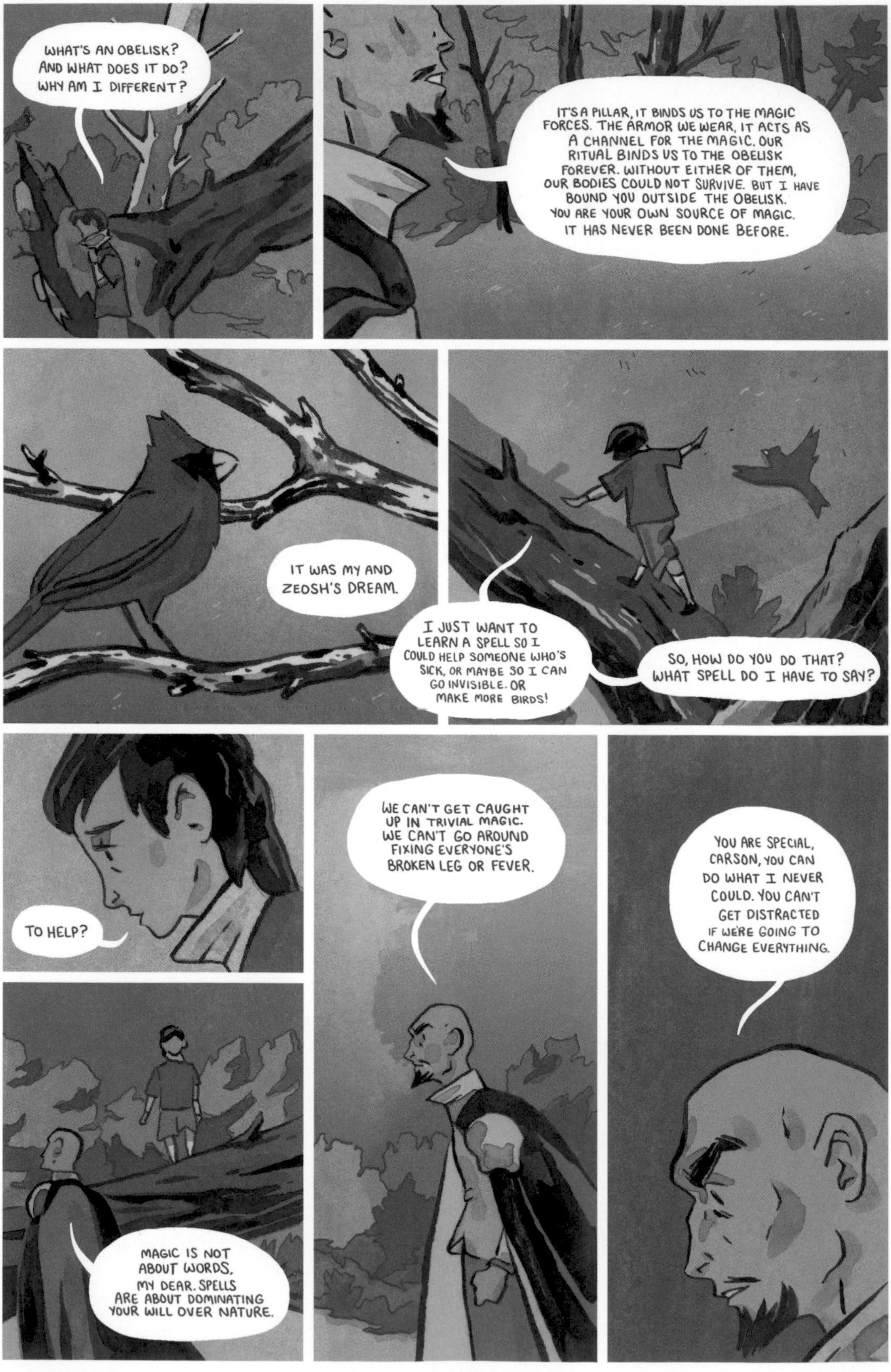
WHAT'S AN OBELISK? AND WHAT DOES IT DO? WHY AM I DIFFERENT?
IT'S A PILLAR, IT BINDS US TO THE MAGIC FORCES. THE ARMOR WE WEAR, IT ACTS AS A CHANNEL FOR THE MAGIC. OUR RITUAL BINDS US TO THE OBELISK FOREVER. WITHOUT EITHER OF THEM, OUR BODIES COULD NOT SURVIVE. BUT I HAVE BOUND YOU OUTSIDE THE OBELISK. YOU ARE YOUR OWN SOURCE OF MAGIC. IT HAS NEVER BEEN DONE BEFORE.
IT WAS MY AND ZEOSH'S DREAM.
I JUST WANT TO LEARN A SPELL SO I COULD HELP SOMEONE WHO'S SICK, OR MAYBE SO I CAN GO INVISIBLE. OR MAKE MORE BIRDS!
SO, HOW DO YOU DO THAT? WHAT SPELL DO I HAVE TO SAY?
TO HELP?
MAGIC IS NOT ABOUT WORDS, MY DEAR. SPELLS ARE ABOUT DOMINATING YOUR WILL OVER NATURE.
WE CAN'T GET CAUGHT UP IN TRIVIAL MAGIC. WE CAN'T GO AROUND FIXING EVERYONE'S BROKEN LEG OR FEVER.
YOU ARE SPECIAL, CARSON, YOU CAN DO WHAT I NEVER COULD. YOU CAN'T GET DISTRACTED IF WE'RE GOING TO CHANGE EVERYTHING.

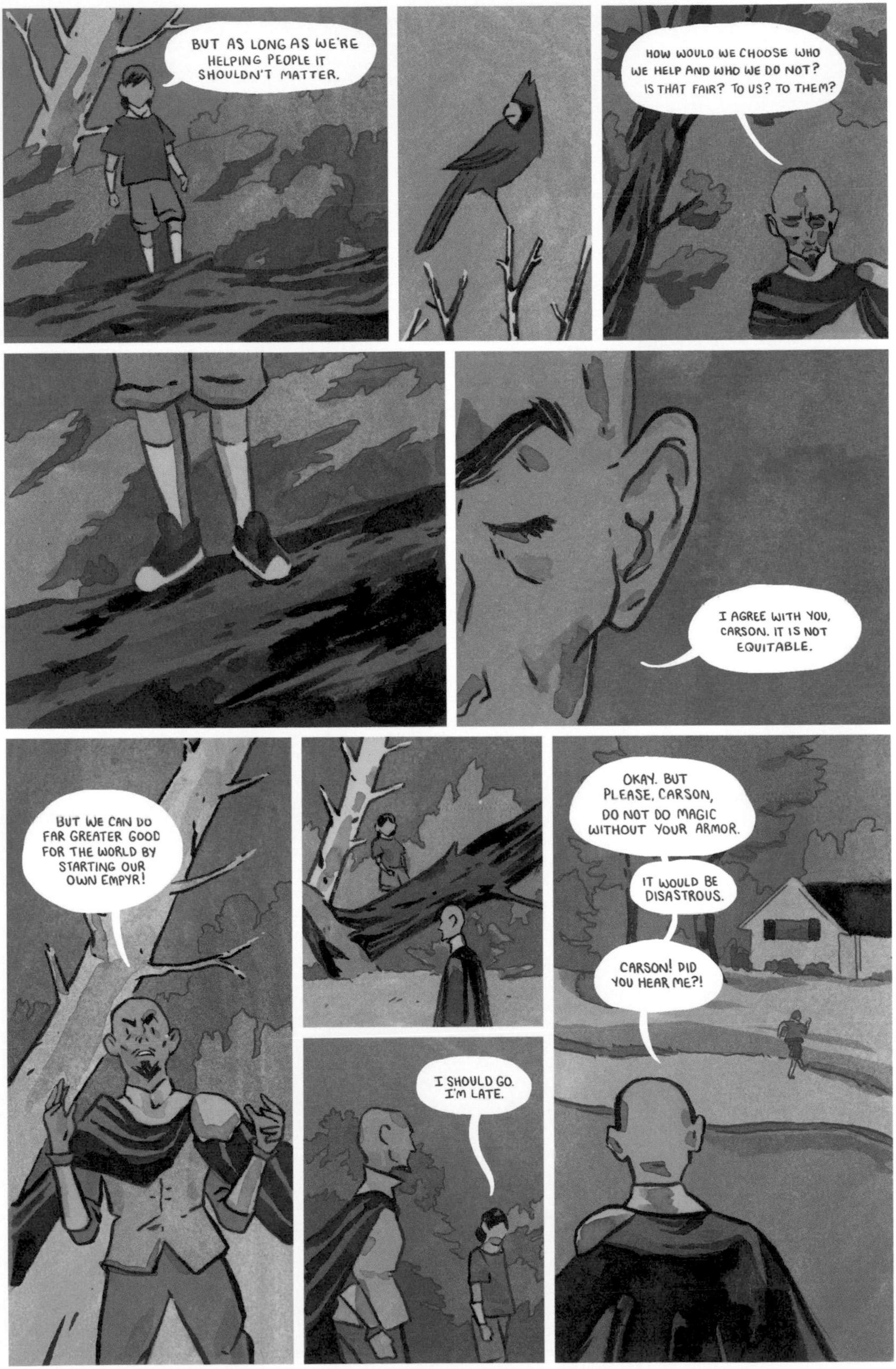
BUT AS LONG AS WE'RE HELPING PEOPLE IT SHOULDN'T MATTER.
HOW WOULD WE CHOOSE WHO WE HELP AND WHO WE DO NOT? IS THAT FAIR? TO US? TO THEM?
I AGREE WITH YOU, CARSON. IT IS NOT EQUITABLE.
BUT WE CAN DO FAR GREATER GOOD FOR THE WORLD BY STARTING OUR OWN EMPYR!
I SHOULD GO. I'M LATE.
OKAY. BUT PLEASE, CARSON, DO NOT DO MAGIC WITHOUT YOUR ARMOR.
IT WOULD BE DISASTROUS.
CARSON! DID YOU HEAR ME?!

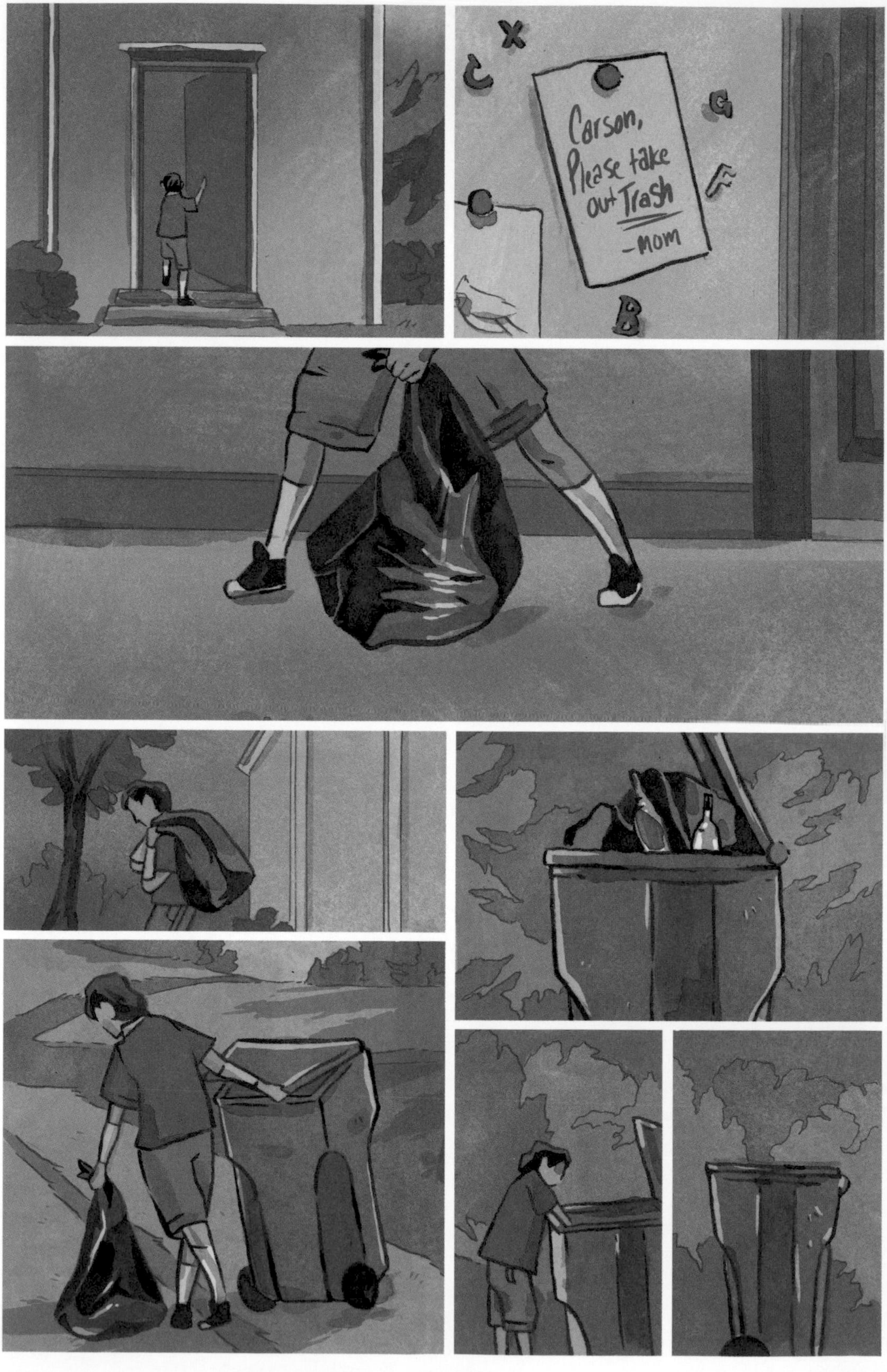

C
X
G
Carson,
Please take
out Trash
-mom
B

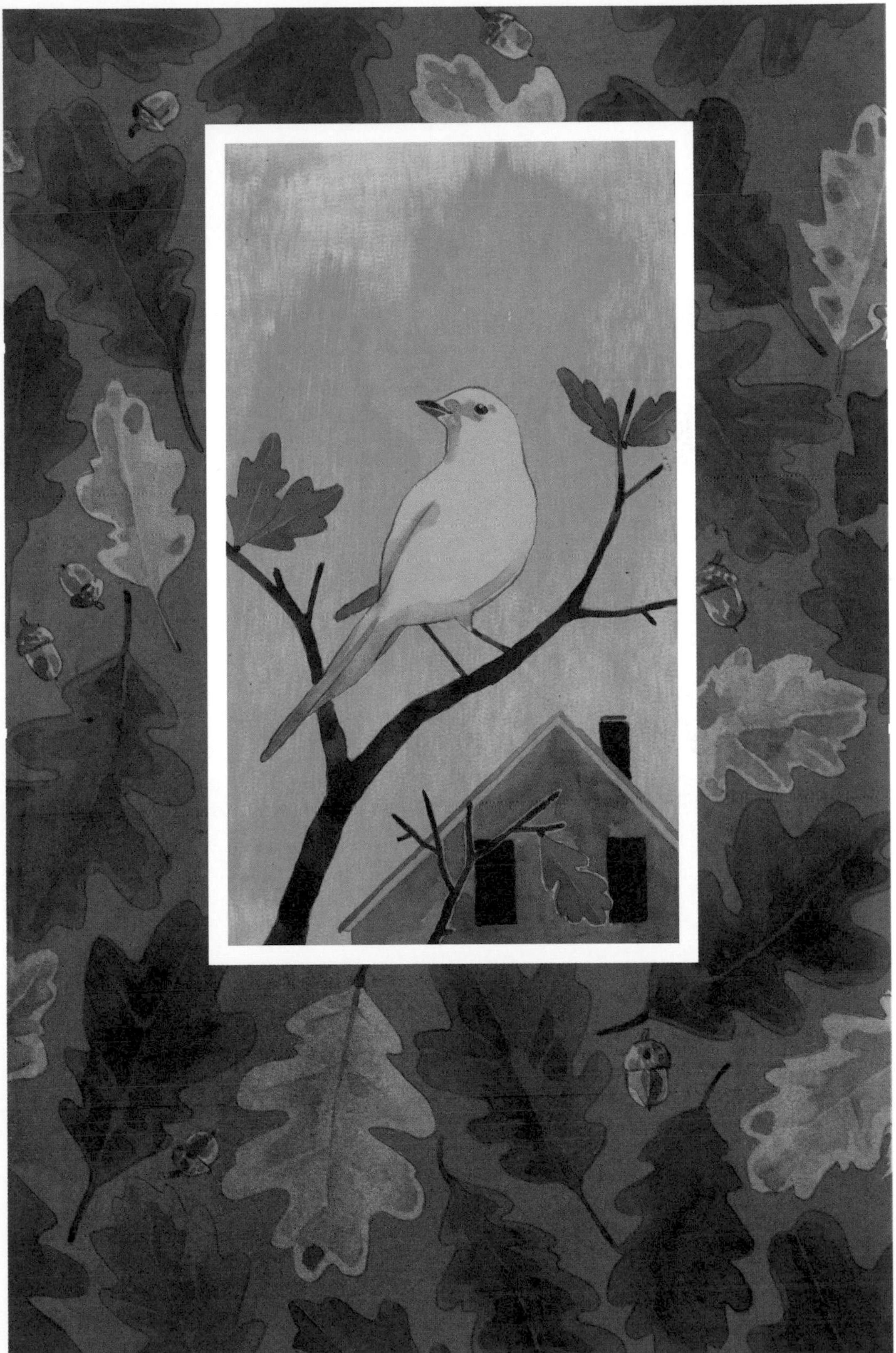

NONE OF YOU SHOULD BE HAVING ANY TROUBLE. THESE ARE ALL FROM LAST WEEK'S VOCAB WORKSHEET.

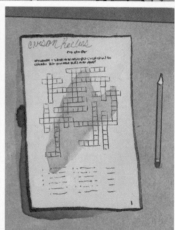

WOAH!

IT WORKED!

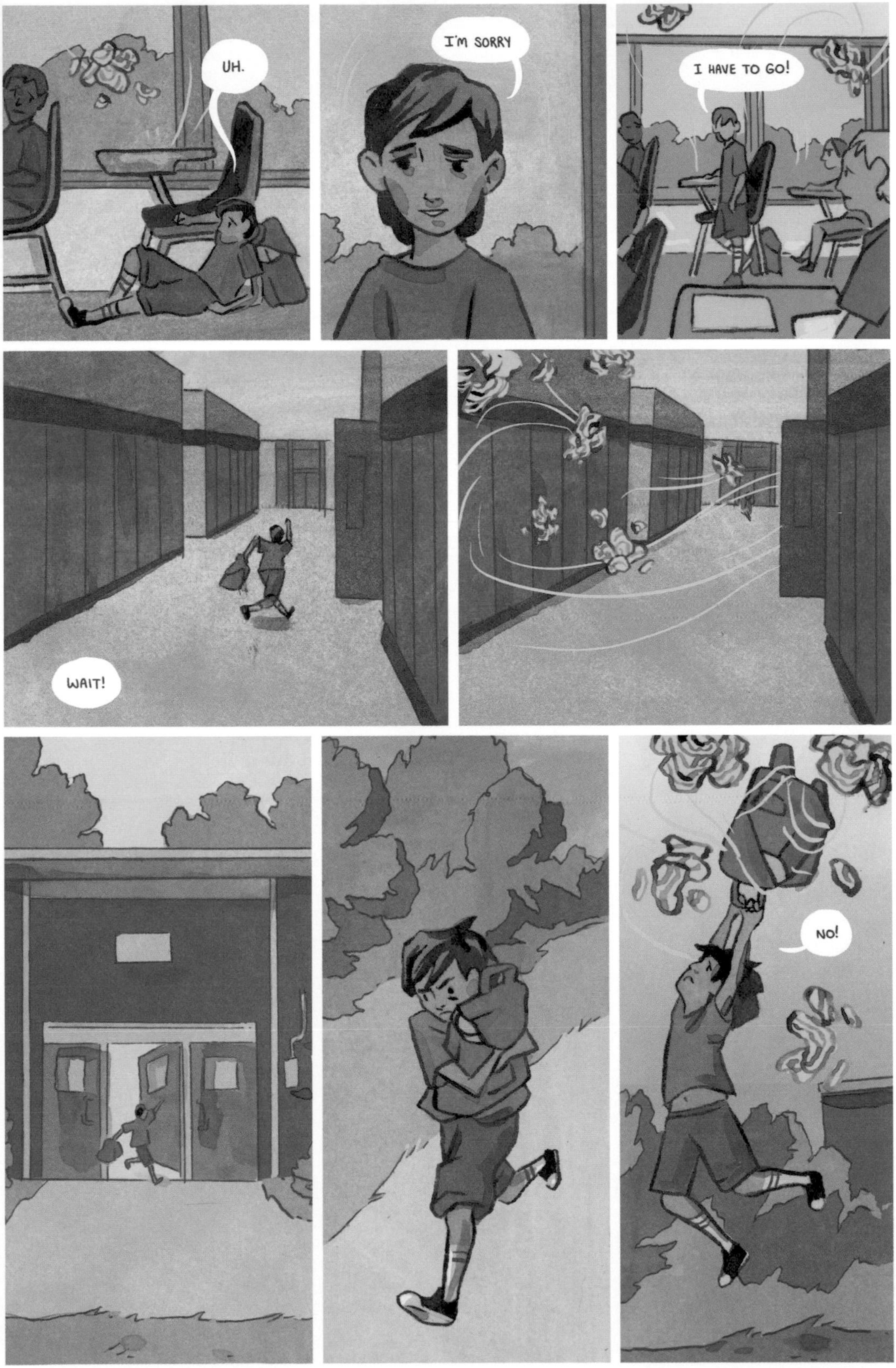
UH.
I'M SORRY
I HAVE TO GO!
WAIT!
NO!

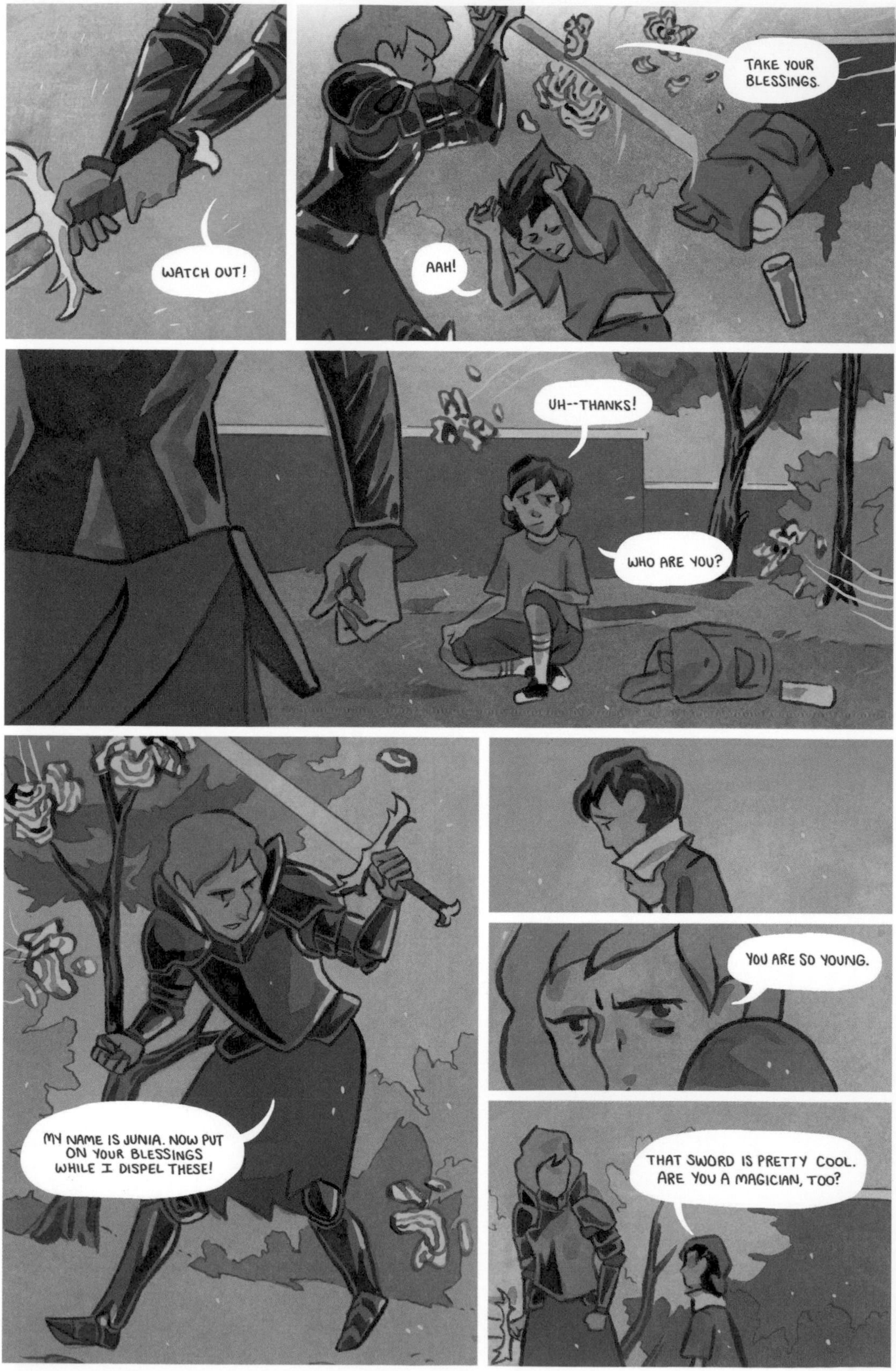
WATCH OUT!
TAKE YOUR BLESSINGS.
AAH!
UH--THANKS!
WHO ARE YOU?
MY NAME IS JUNIA. NOW PUT ON YOUR BLESSINGS WHILE I DISPEL THESE!
YOU ARE SO YOUNG.
THAT SWORD IS PRETTY COOL. ARE YOU A MAGICIAN, TOO?

NO.

I AM A KNIGHT OF THE EMPYR, I AM HERE TO HELP YOU.

DO WHAT?

TAKE AWAY YOUR MAGIC.

ISCARIOT IS USING YOU; HE HASN'T TOLD YOU THE TRUTH.

WHEN YOU'RE READY TO LEAVE-- I'LL FIND YOU.

ABOUT WHAT?

WAIT!

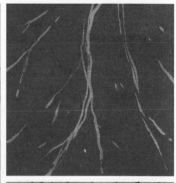

WHAT DID ISCARIOT DO?

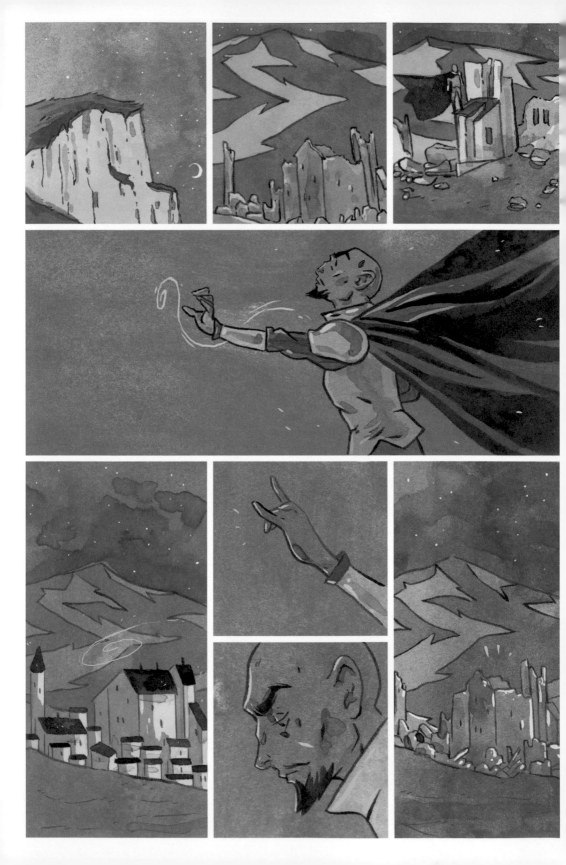

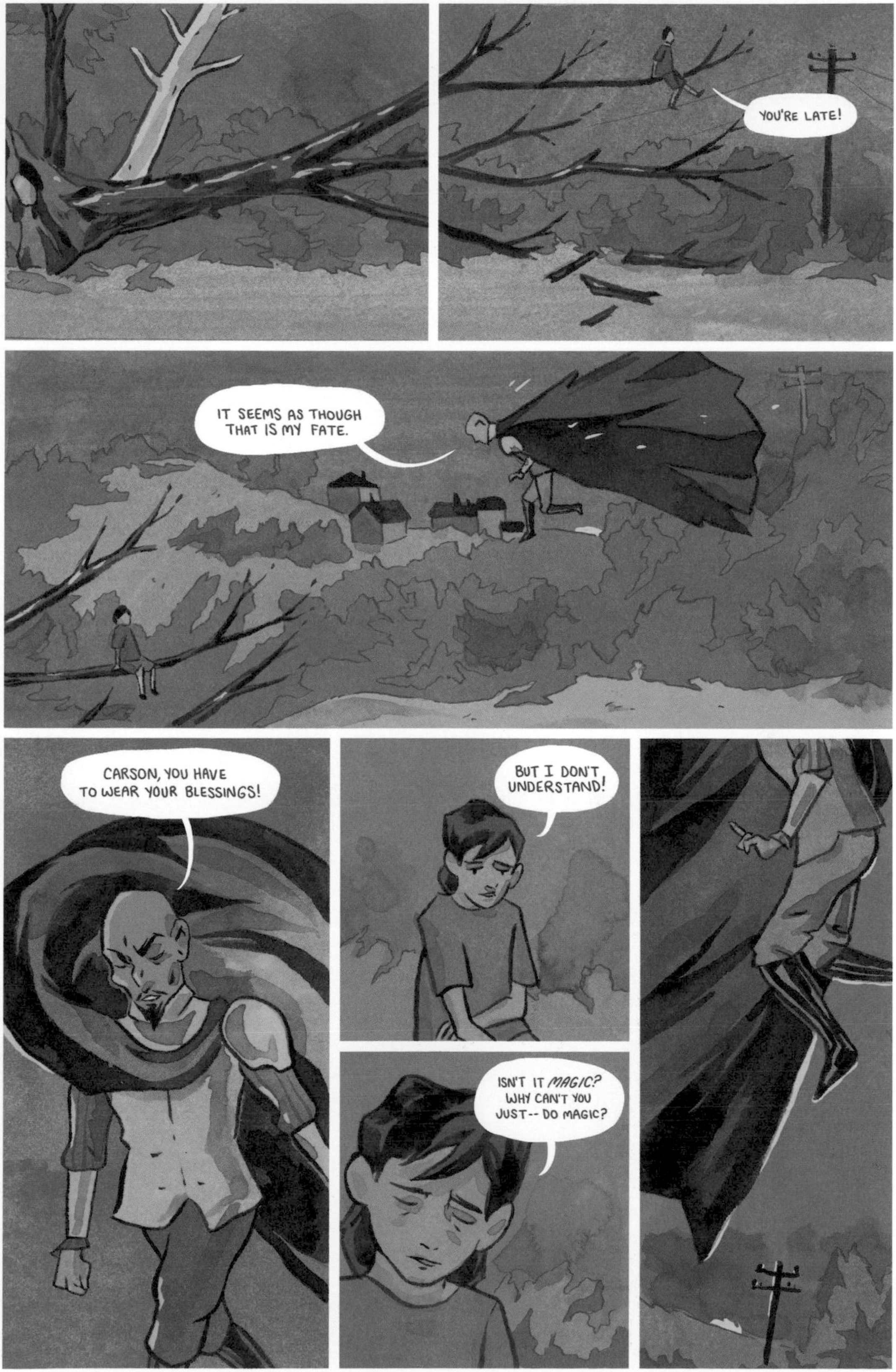
YOU'RE LATE!
IT SEEMS AS THOUGH THAT IS MY FATE.
CARSON, YOU HAVE TO WEAR YOUR BLESSINGS!
BUT I DON'T UNDERSTAND!
ISN'T IT *MAGIC?* WHY CAN'T YOU JUST-- DO MAGIC?

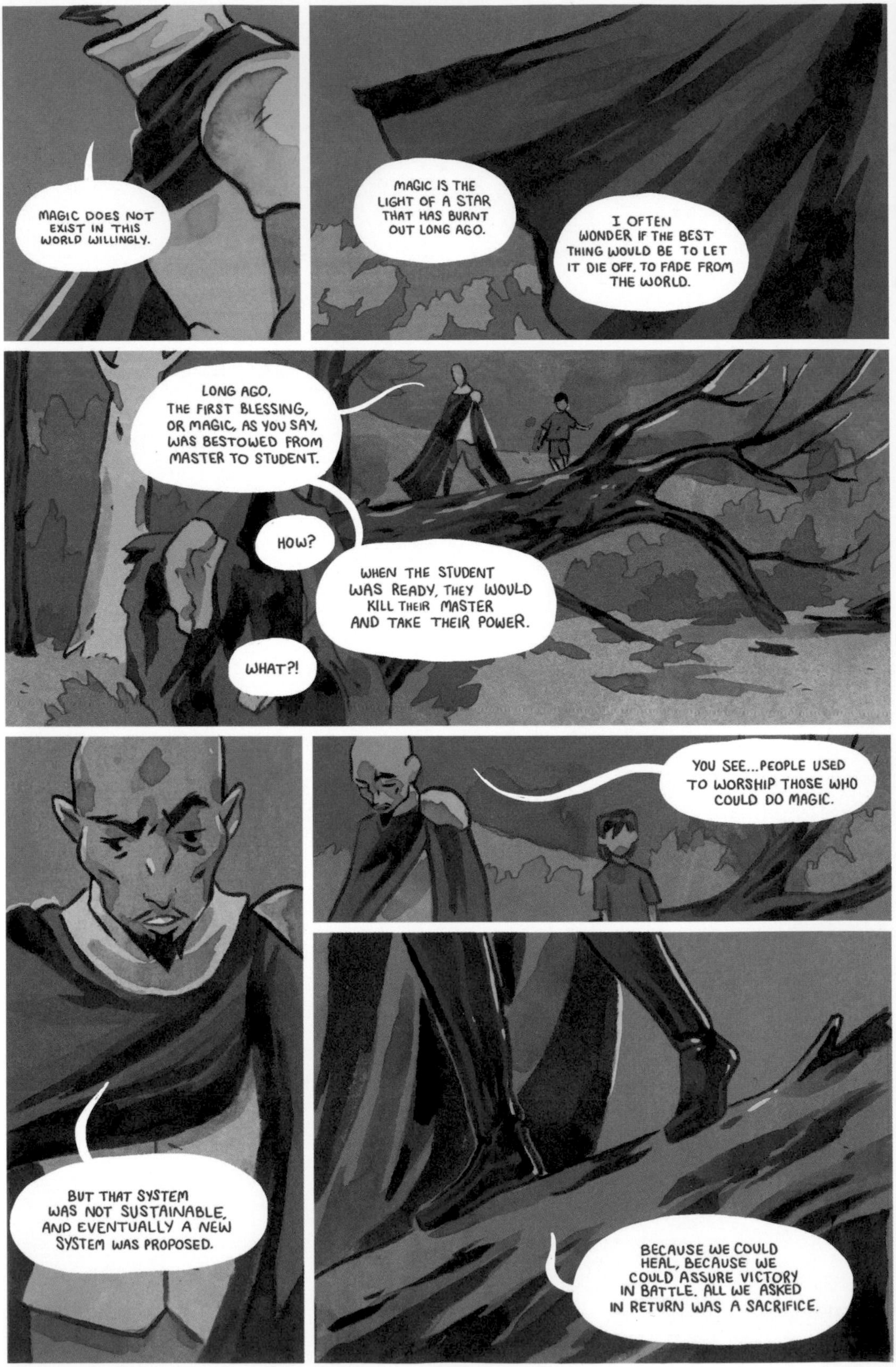
MAGIC DOES NOT EXIST IN THIS WORLD WILLINGLY.
MAGIC IS THE LIGHT OF A STAR THAT HAS BURNT OUT LONG AGO.
I OFTEN WONDER IF THE BEST THING WOULD BE TO LET IT DIE OFF, TO FADE FROM THE WORLD.
LONG AGO, THE FIRST BLESSING, OR MAGIC, AS YOU SAY, WAS BESTOWED FROM MASTER TO STUDENT.
HOW?
WHEN THE STUDENT WAS READY, THEY WOULD KILL THEIR MASTER AND TAKE THEIR POWER.
WHAT?!
BUT THAT SYSTEM WAS NOT SUSTAINABLE, AND EVENTUALLY A NEW SYSTEM WAS PROPOSED.
YOU SEE... PEOPLE USED TO WORSHIP THOSE WHO COULD DO MAGIC.
BECAUSE WE COULD HEAL, BECAUSE WE COULD ASSURE VICTORY IN BATTLE. ALL WE ASKED IN RETURN WAS A SACRIFICE.

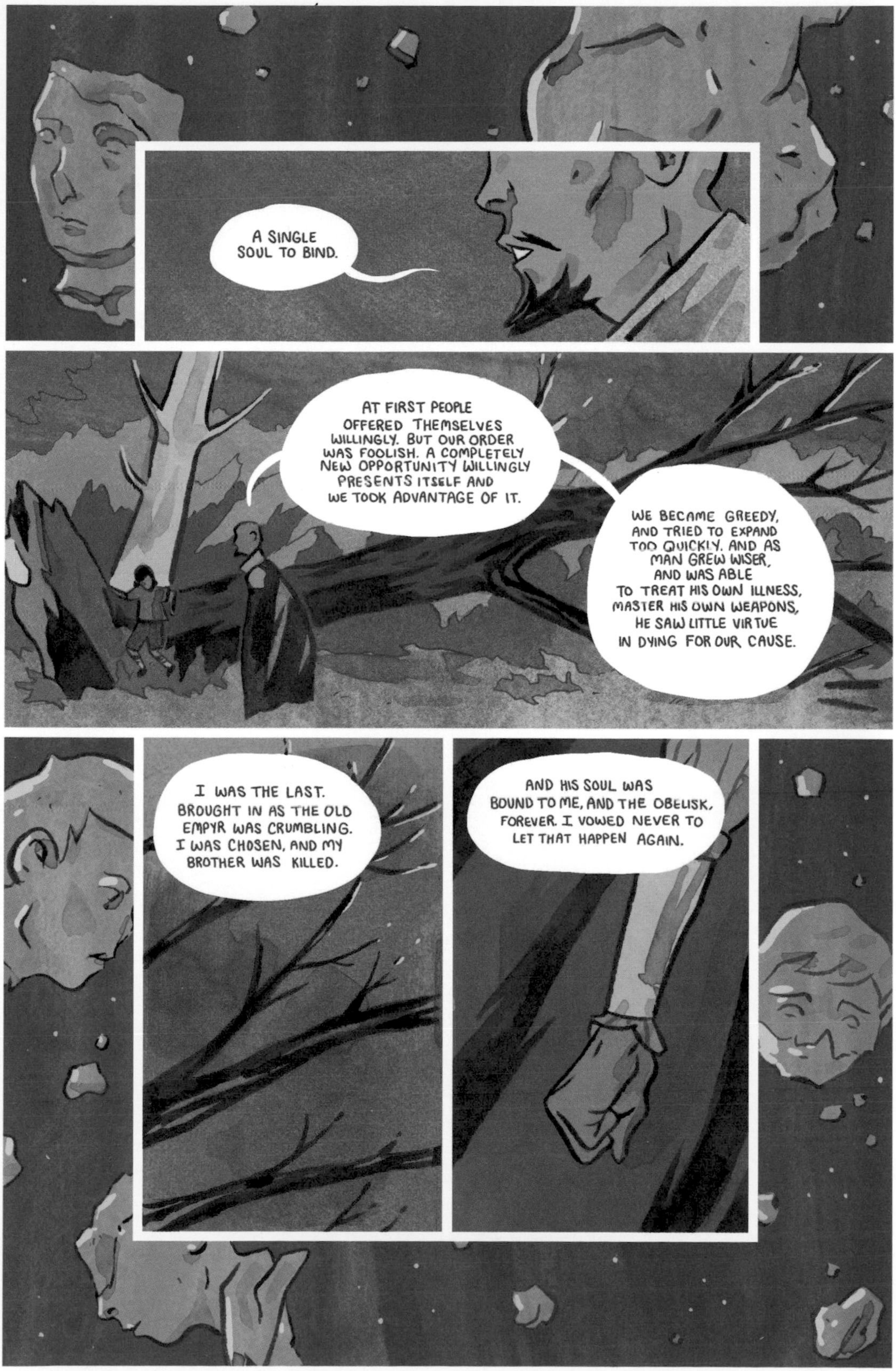
A SINGLE SOUL TO BIND.
AT FIRST PEOPLE OFFERED THEMSELVES WILLINGLY. BUT OUR ORDER WAS FOOLISH. A COMPLETELY NEW OPPORTUNITY WILLINGLY PRESENTS ITSELF AND WE TOOK ADVANTAGE OF IT.
WE BECAME GREEDY, AND TRIED TO EXPAND TOO QUICKLY. AND AS MAN GREW WISER, AND WAS ABLE TO TREAT HIS OWN ILLNESS, MASTER HIS OWN WEAPONS, HE SAW LITTLE VIRTUE IN DYING FOR OUR CAUSE.
I WAS THE LAST. BROUGHT IN AS THE OLD EMPYR WAS CRUMBLING. I WAS CHOSEN, AND MY BROTHER WAS KILLED.
AND HIS SOUL WAS BOUND TO ME, AND THE OBELISK, FOREVER. I VOWED NEVER TO LET THAT HAPPEN AGAIN.

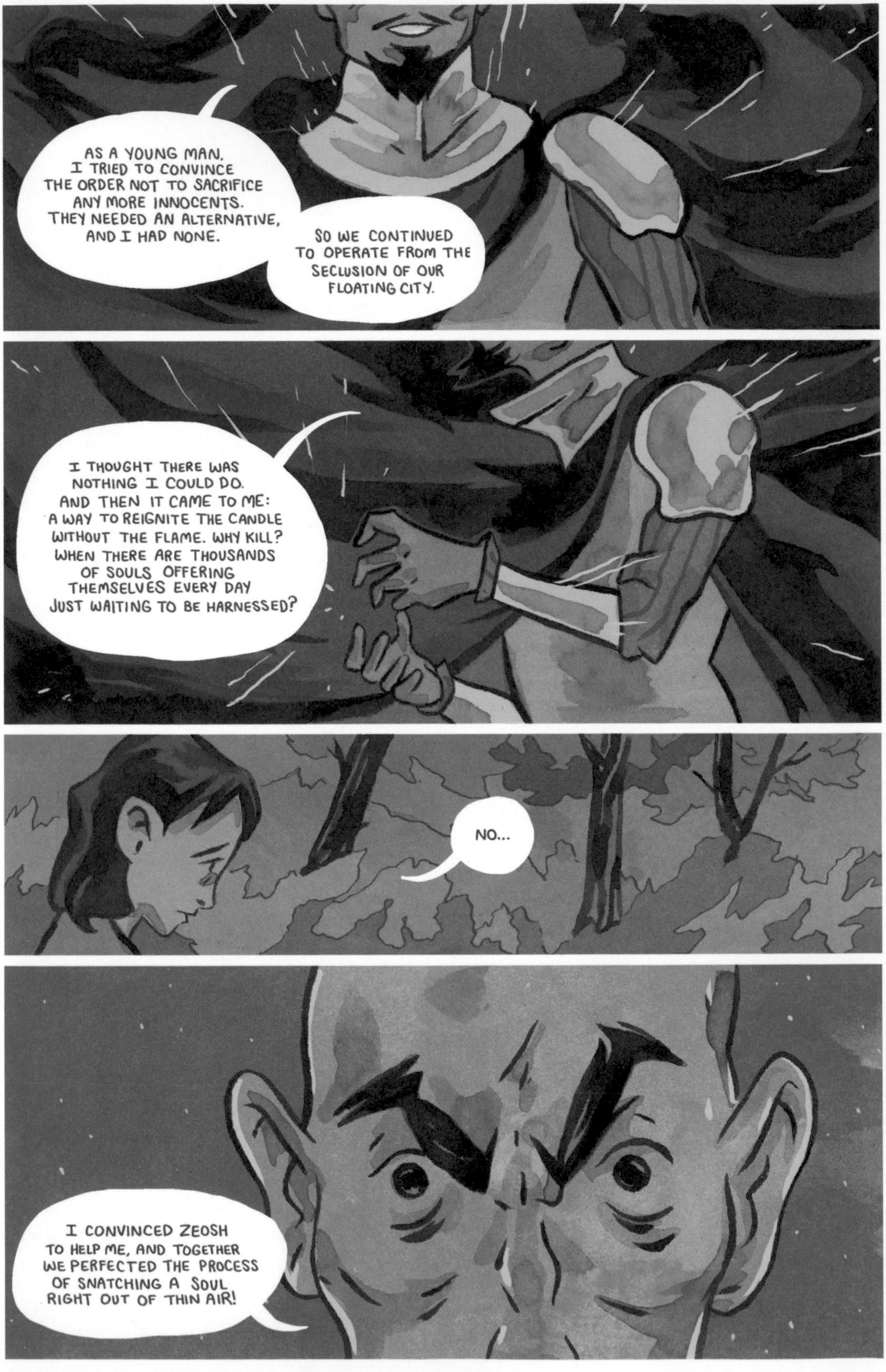
AS A YOUNG MAN, I TRIED TO CONVINCE THE ORDER NOT TO SACRIFICE ANY MORE INNOCENTS. THEY NEEDED AN ALTERNATIVE, AND I HAD NONE.
SO WE CONTINUED TO OPERATE FROM THE SECLUSION OF OUR FLOATING CITY.
I THOUGHT THERE WAS NOTHING I COULD DO. AND THEN IT CAME TO ME: A WAY TO REIGNITE THE CANDLE WITHOUT THE FLAME. WHY KILL? WHEN THERE ARE THOUSANDS OF SOULS OFFERING THEMSELVES EVERY DAY JUST WAITING TO BE HARNESSED?
NO...
I CONVINCED ZEOSH TO HELP ME, AND TOGETHER WE PERFECTED THE PROCESS OF SNATCHING A SOUL RIGHT OUT OF THIN AIR!

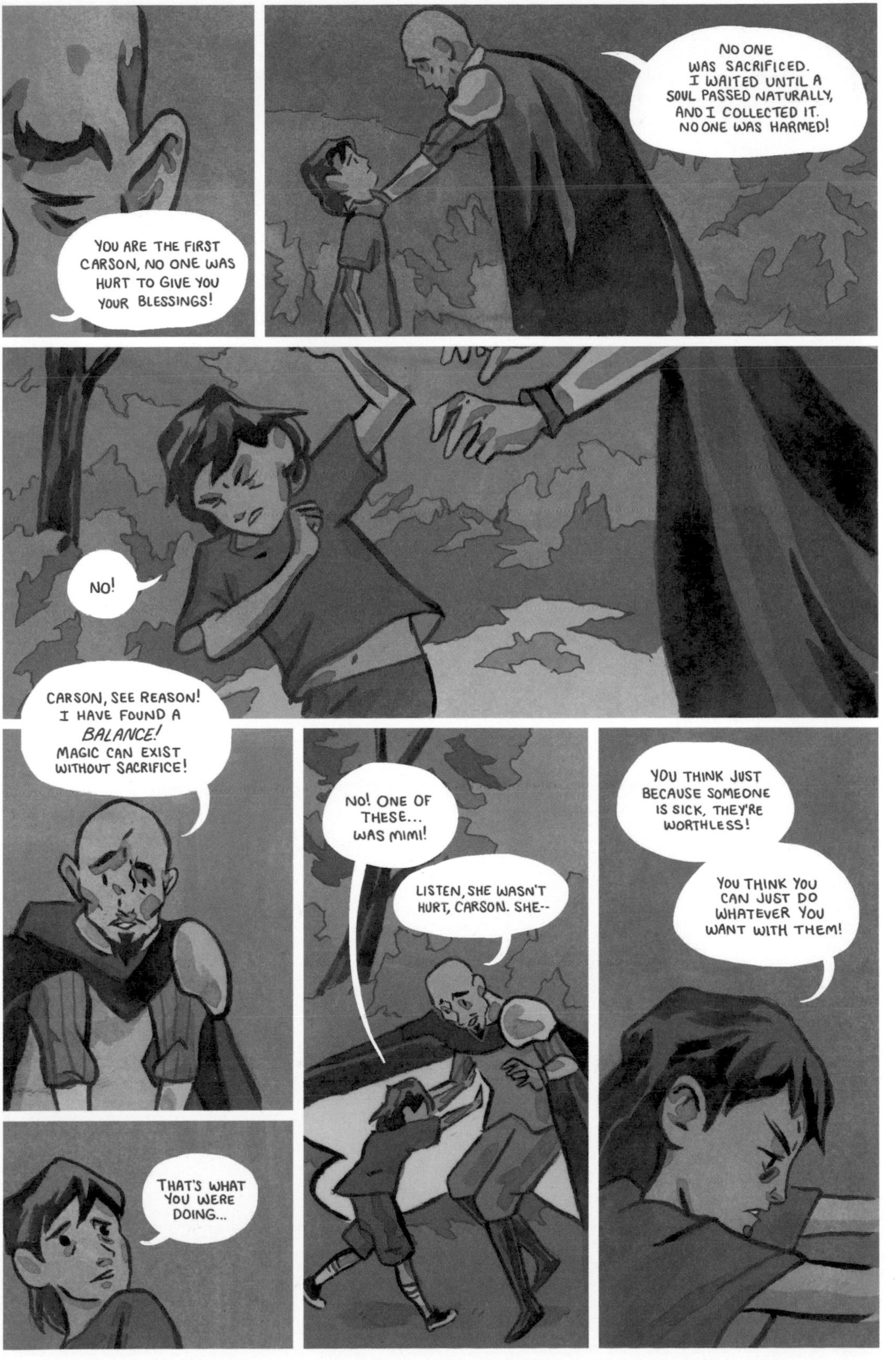
YOU ARE THE FIRST CARSON, NO ONE WAS HURT TO GIVE YOU YOUR BLESSINGS!
NO ONE WAS SACRIFICED. I WAITED UNTIL A SOUL PASSED NATURALLY, AND I COLLECTED IT. NO ONE WAS HARMED!
NO!
CARSON, SEE REASON! I HAVE FOUND A *BALANCE!* MAGIC CAN EXIST WITHOUT SACRIFICE!
THAT'S WHAT YOU WERE DOING...
NO! ONE OF THESE... WAS MIMI!
LISTEN, SHE WASN'T HURT, CARSON. SHE--
YOU THINK JUST BECAUSE SOMEONE IS SICK, THEY'RE WORTHLESS!
YOU THINK YOU CAN JUST DO WHATEVER YOU WANT WITH THEM!

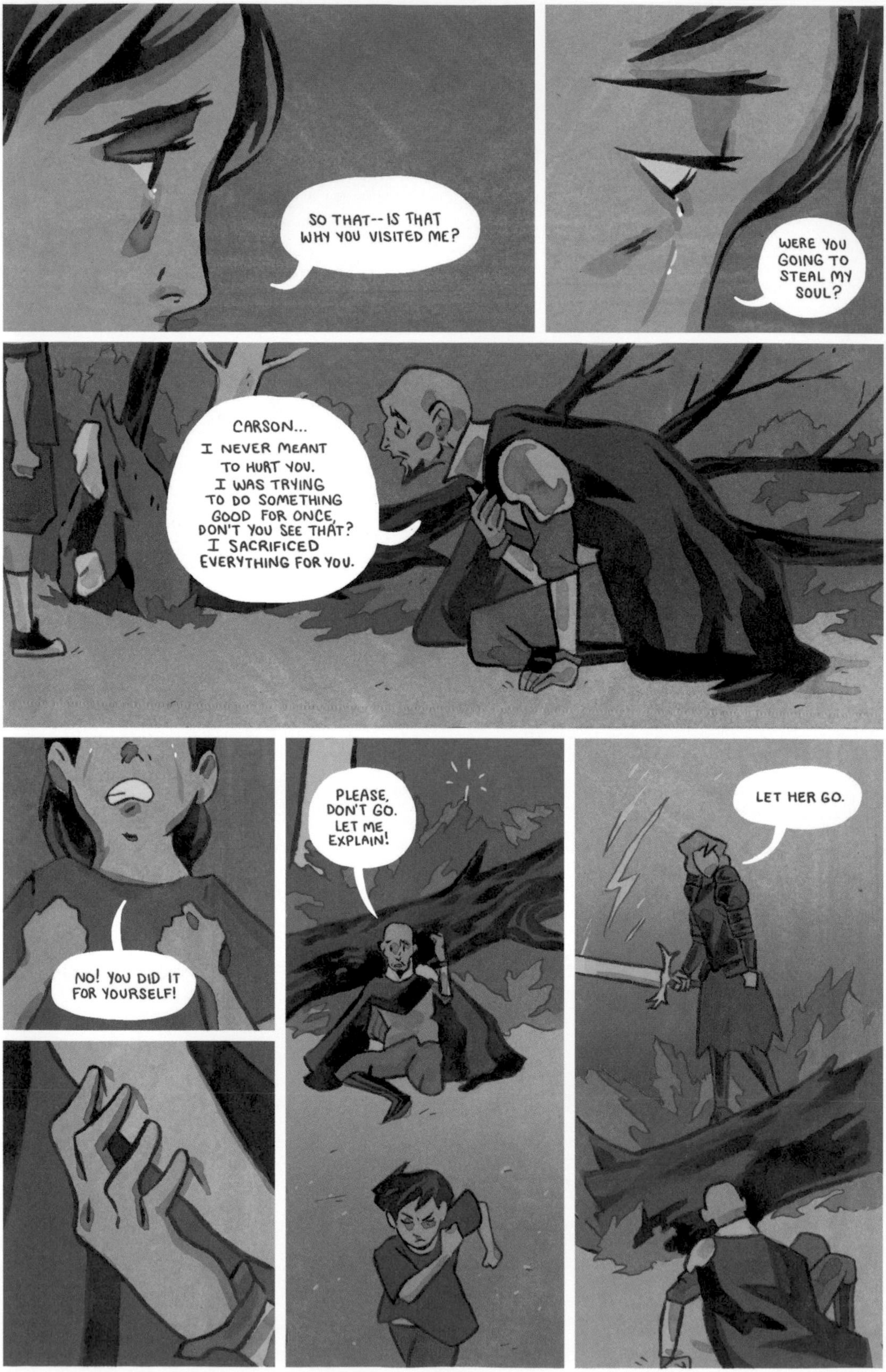
SO THAT-- IS THAT WHY YOU VISITED ME?
WERE YOU GOING TO STEAL MY SOUL?
CARSON... I NEVER MEANT TO HURT YOU. I WAS TRYING TO DO SOMETHING GOOD FOR ONCE, DON'T YOU SEE THAT? I SACRIFICED EVERYTHING FOR YOU.
NO! YOU DID IT FOR YOURSELF!
PLEASE, DON'T GO. LET ME EXPLAIN!
LET HER GO.

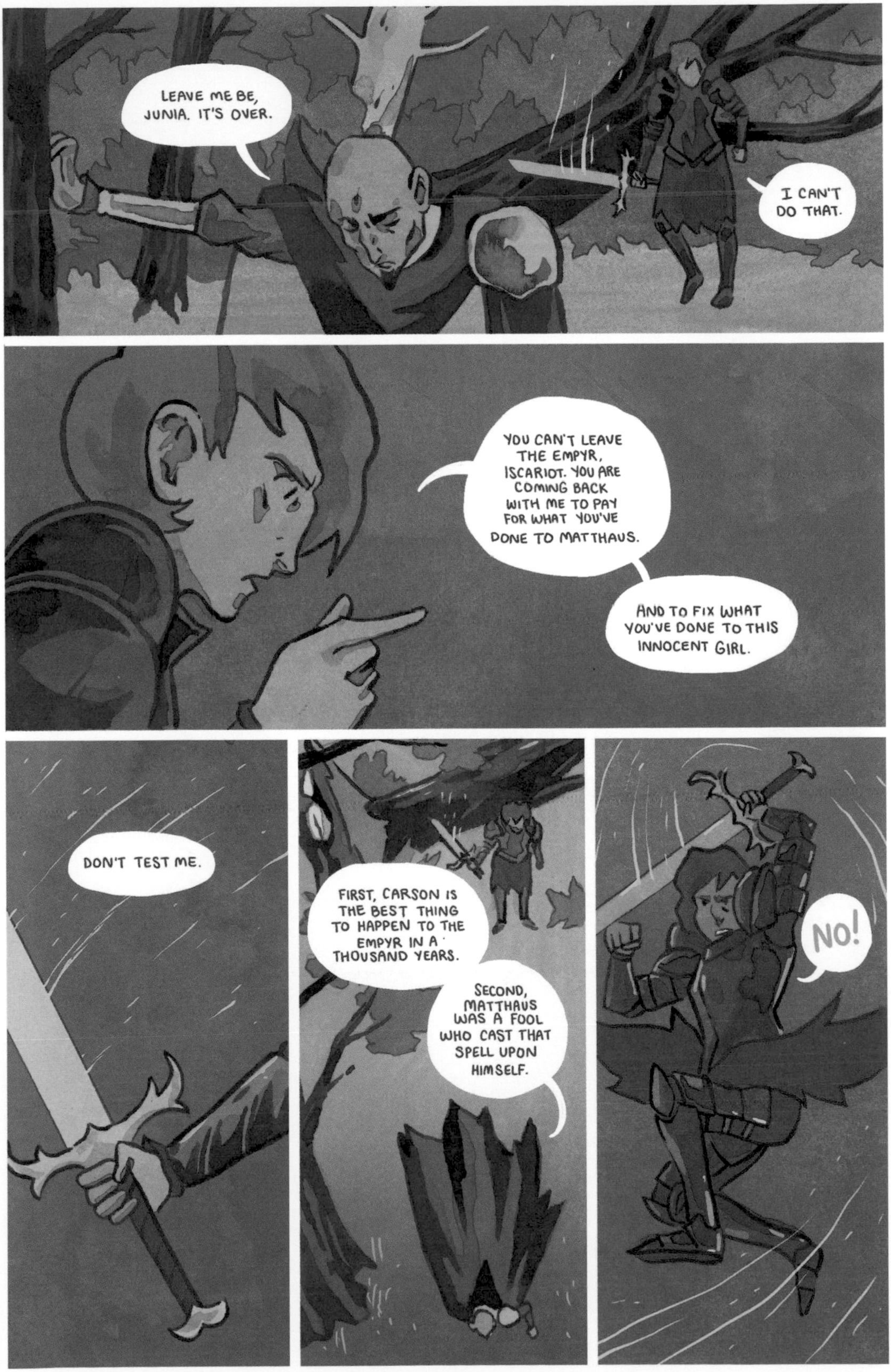
LEAVE ME BE, JUNIA. IT'S OVER.
I CAN'T DO THAT.
YOU CAN'T LEAVE THE EMPYR, ISCARIOT. YOU ARE COMING BACK WITH ME TO PAY FOR WHAT YOU'VE DONE TO MATTHAUS.
AND TO FIX WHAT YOU'VE DONE TO THIS INNOCENT GIRL.
DON'T TEST ME.
FIRST, CARSON IS THE BEST THING TO HAPPEN TO THE EMPYR IN A THOUSAND YEARS.
SECOND, MATTHAUS WAS A FOOL WHO CAST THAT SPELL UPON HIMSELF.
NO!

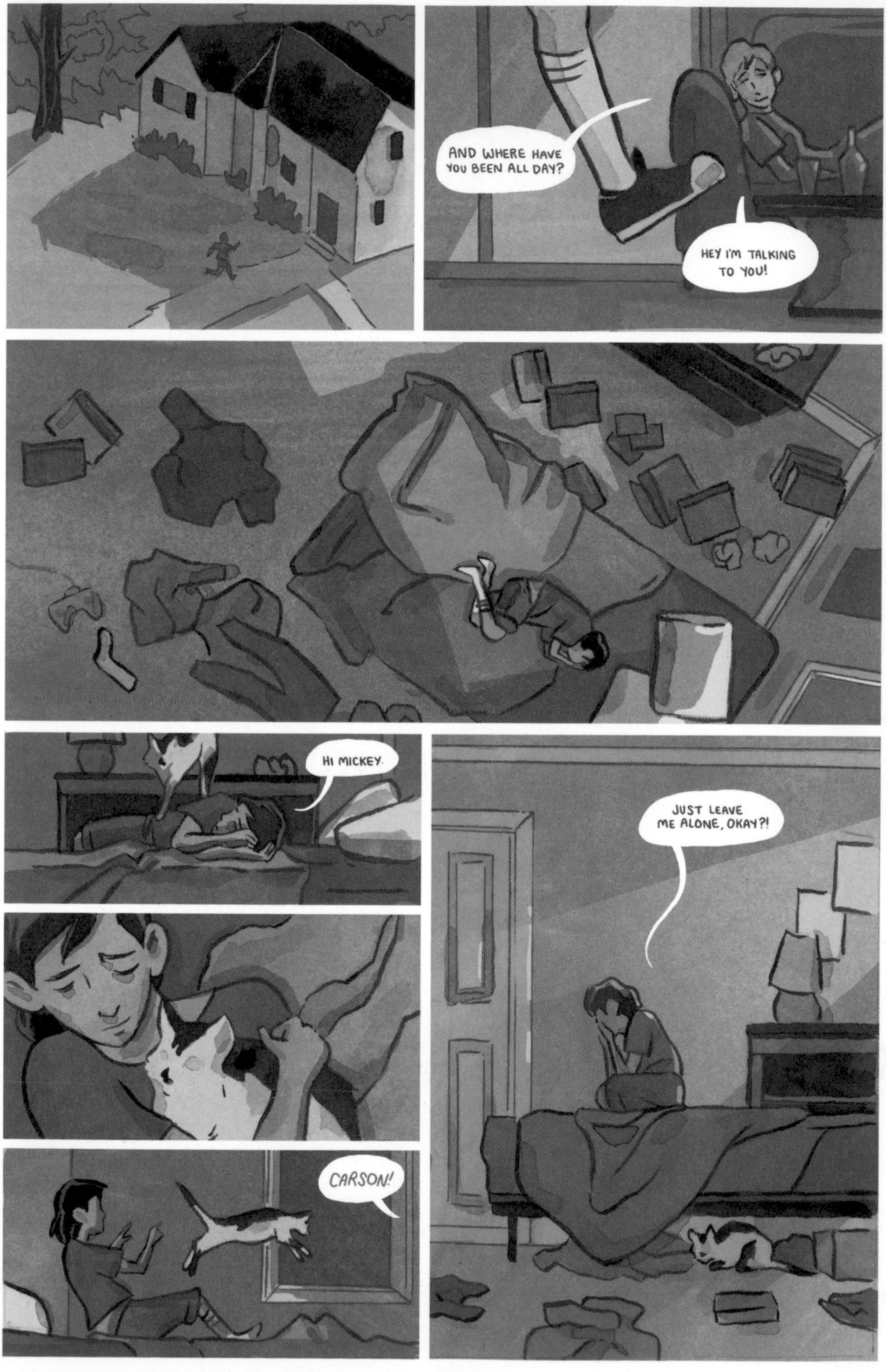

AND WHERE HAVE YOU BEEN ALL DAY?
HEY I'M TALKING TO YOU!
HI MICKEY.
CARSON!
JUST LEAVE ME ALONE, OKAY?!

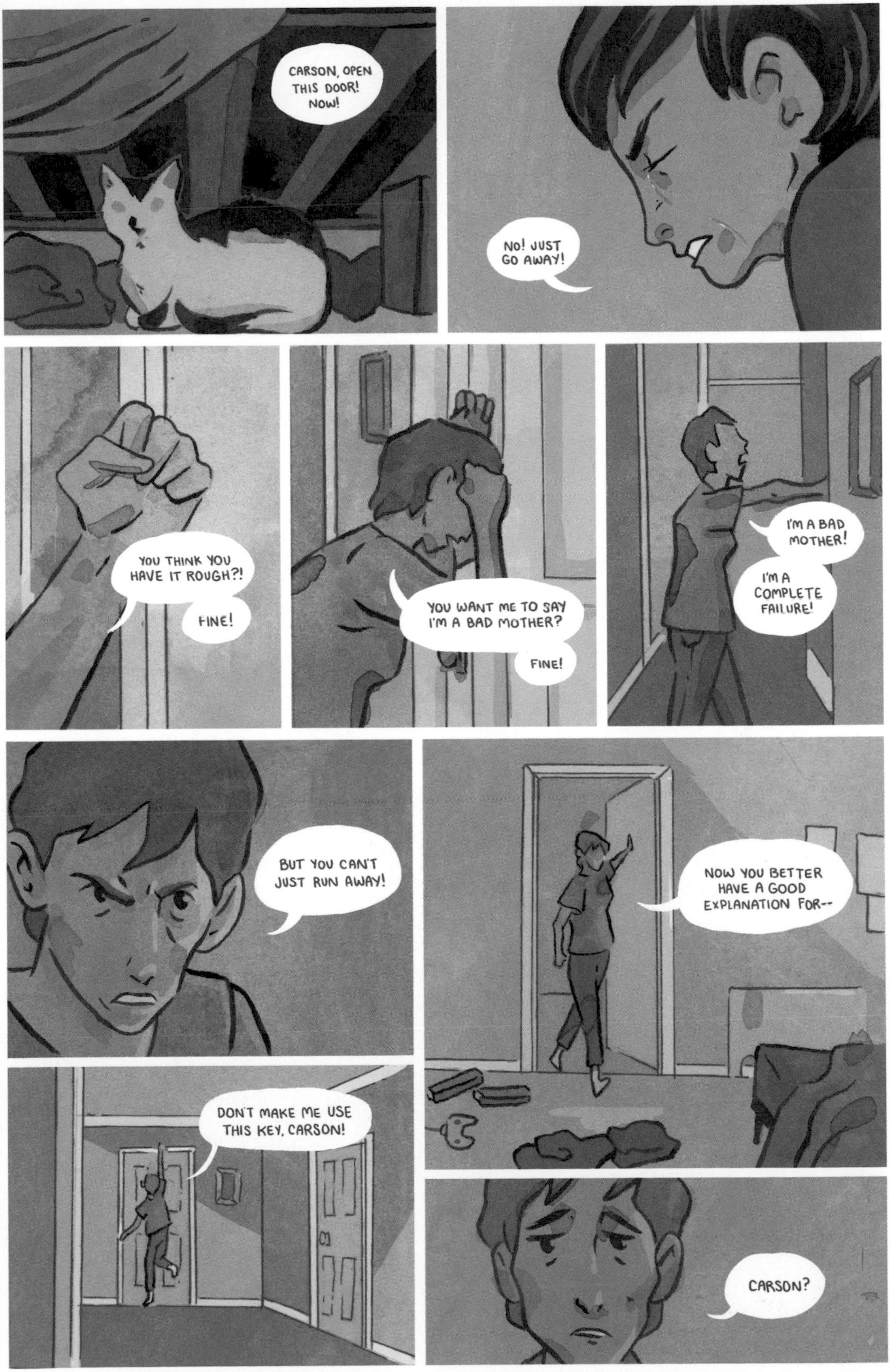
CARSON, OPEN THIS DOOR! NOW!
NO! JUST GO AWAY!
YOU THINK YOU HAVE IT ROUGH?!
FINE!
YOU WANT ME TO SAY I'M A BAD MOTHER?
FINE!
I'M A BAD MOTHER!
I'M A COMPLETE FAILURE!
BUT YOU CAN'T JUST RUN AWAY!
DON'T MAKE ME USE THIS KEY, CARSON!
NOW YOU BETTER HAVE A GOOD EXPLANATION FOR--
CARSON?

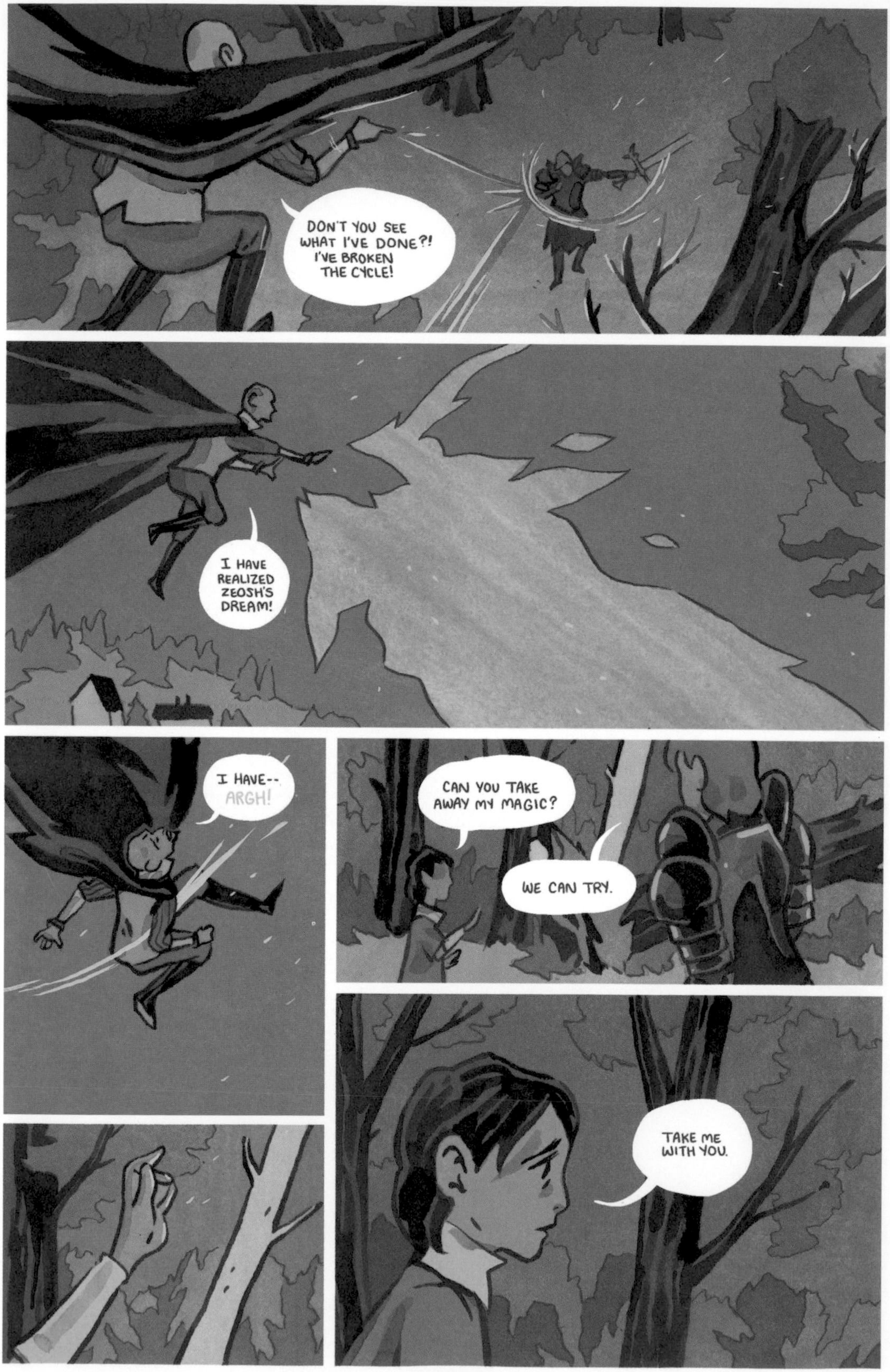
DON'T YOU SEE WHAT I'VE DONE?! I'VE BROKEN THE CYCLE!
I HAVE REALIZED ZEOSH'S DREAM!
I HAVE-- ARGH!
CAN YOU TAKE AWAY MY MAGIC?
WE CAN TRY.
TAKE ME WITH YOU.

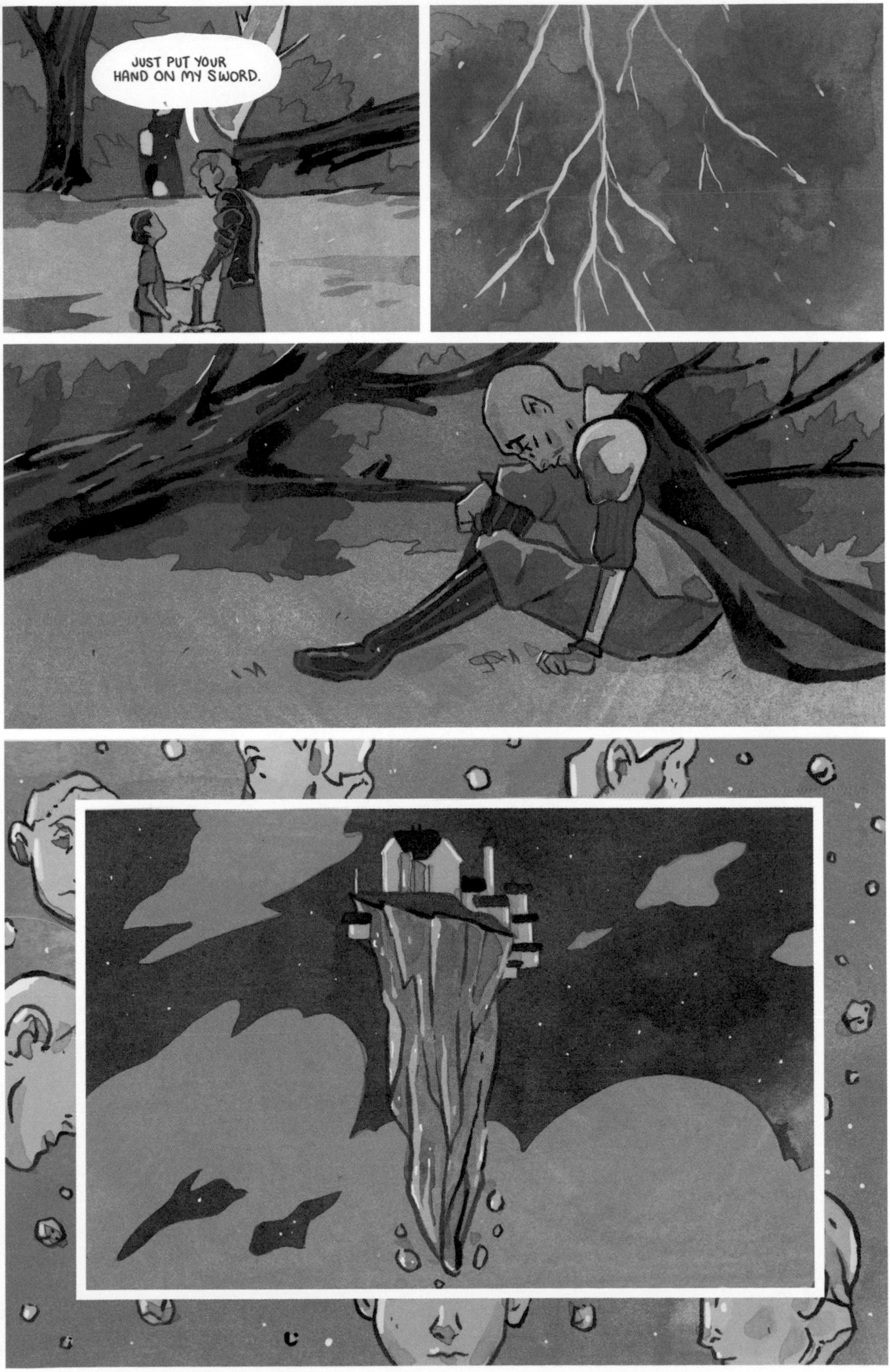
JUST PUT YOUR HAND ON MY SWORD.

CHAPTER THREE

It is not the end
Candle wax can be collected
Shaped and fitted with a new wick
It can burn again
And never remember the flame

But you and I burn red then black
Should we fail to remember
Or if we never knew to begin with.

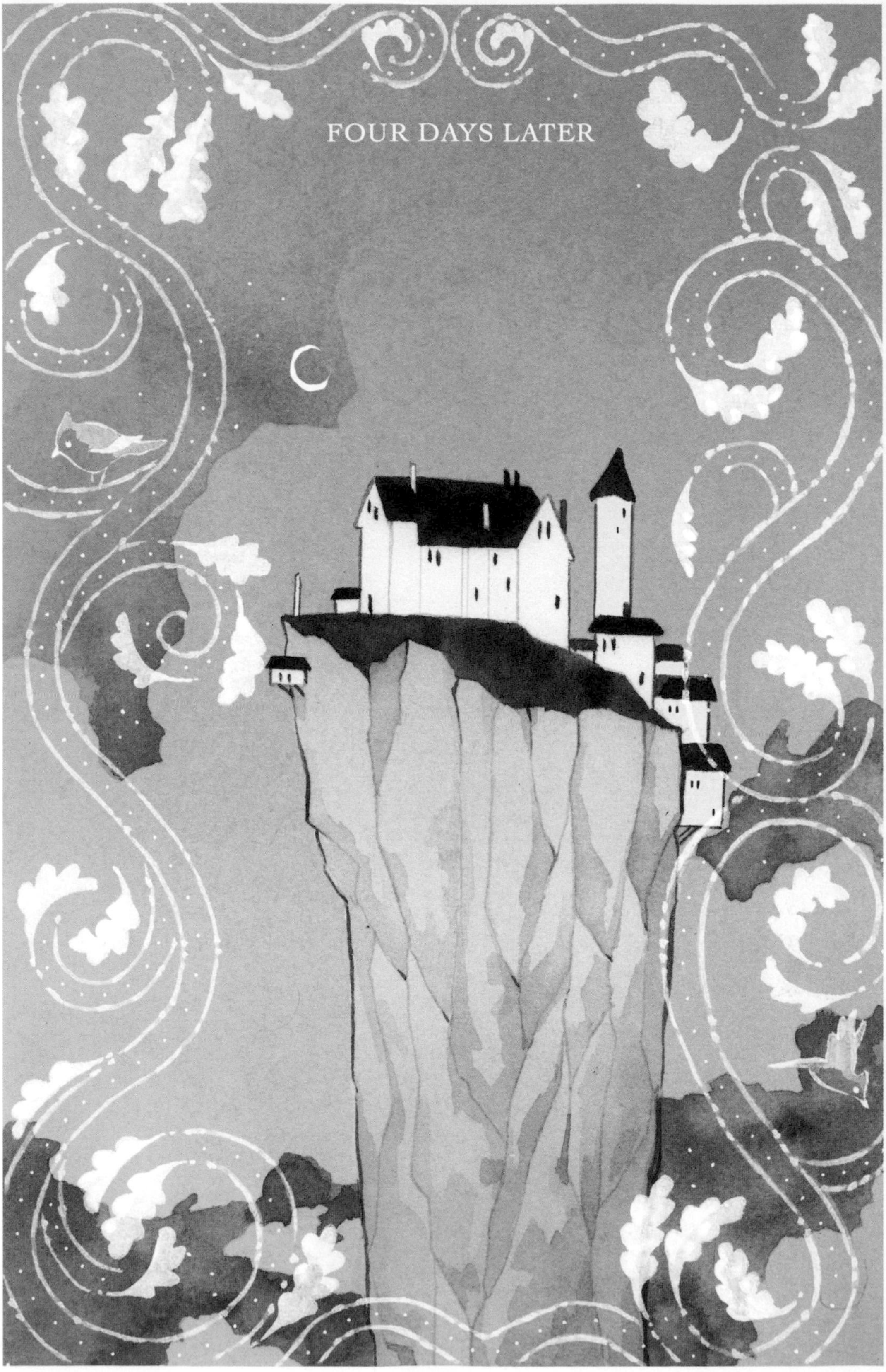
FOUR DAYS LATER

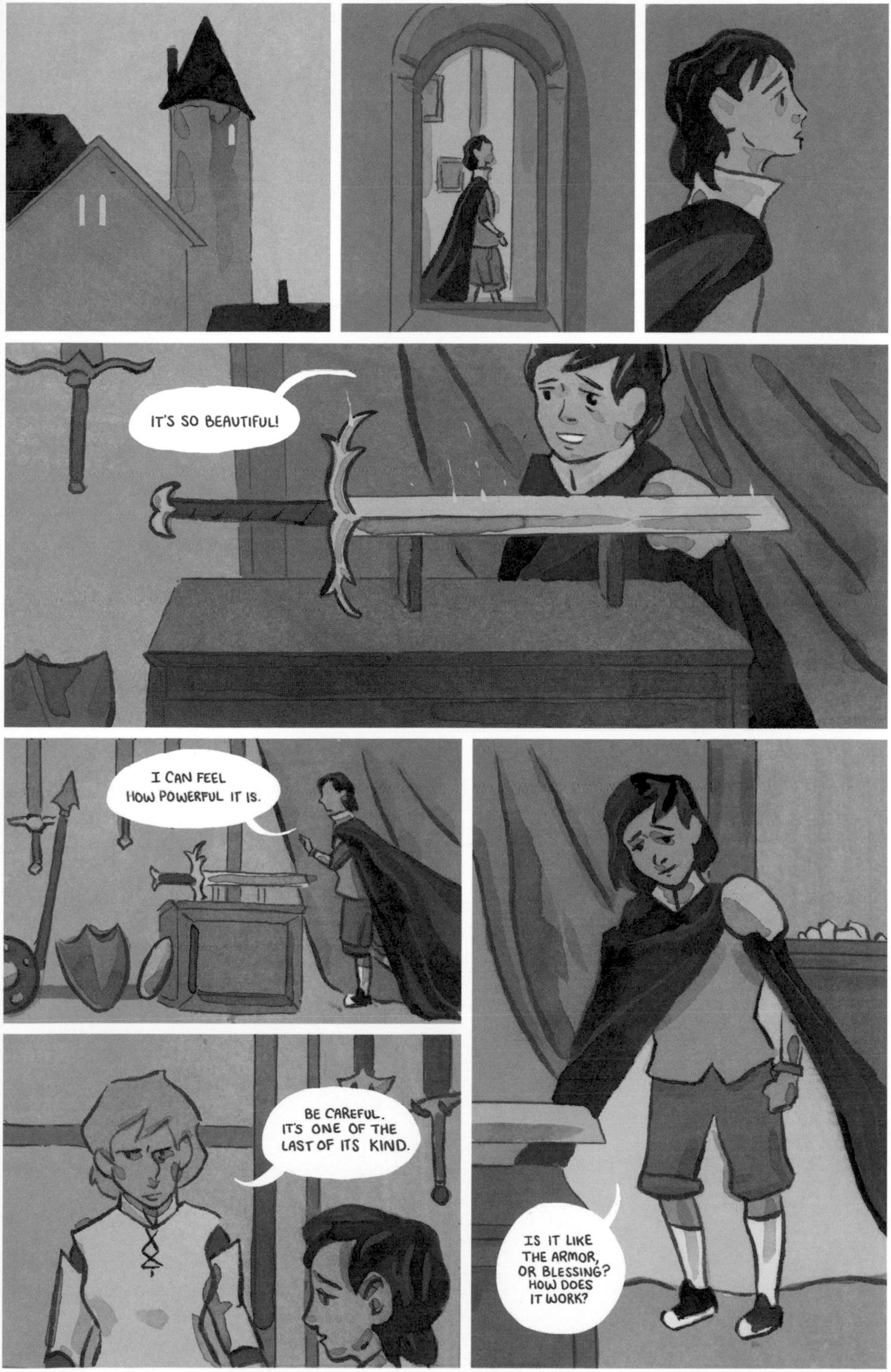
IT'S SO BEAUTIFUL!
I CAN FEEL HOW POWERFUL IT IS.
BE CAREFUL. IT'S ONE OF THE LAST OF ITS KIND.
IS IT LIKE THE ARMOR, OR BLESSING? HOW DOES IT WORK?

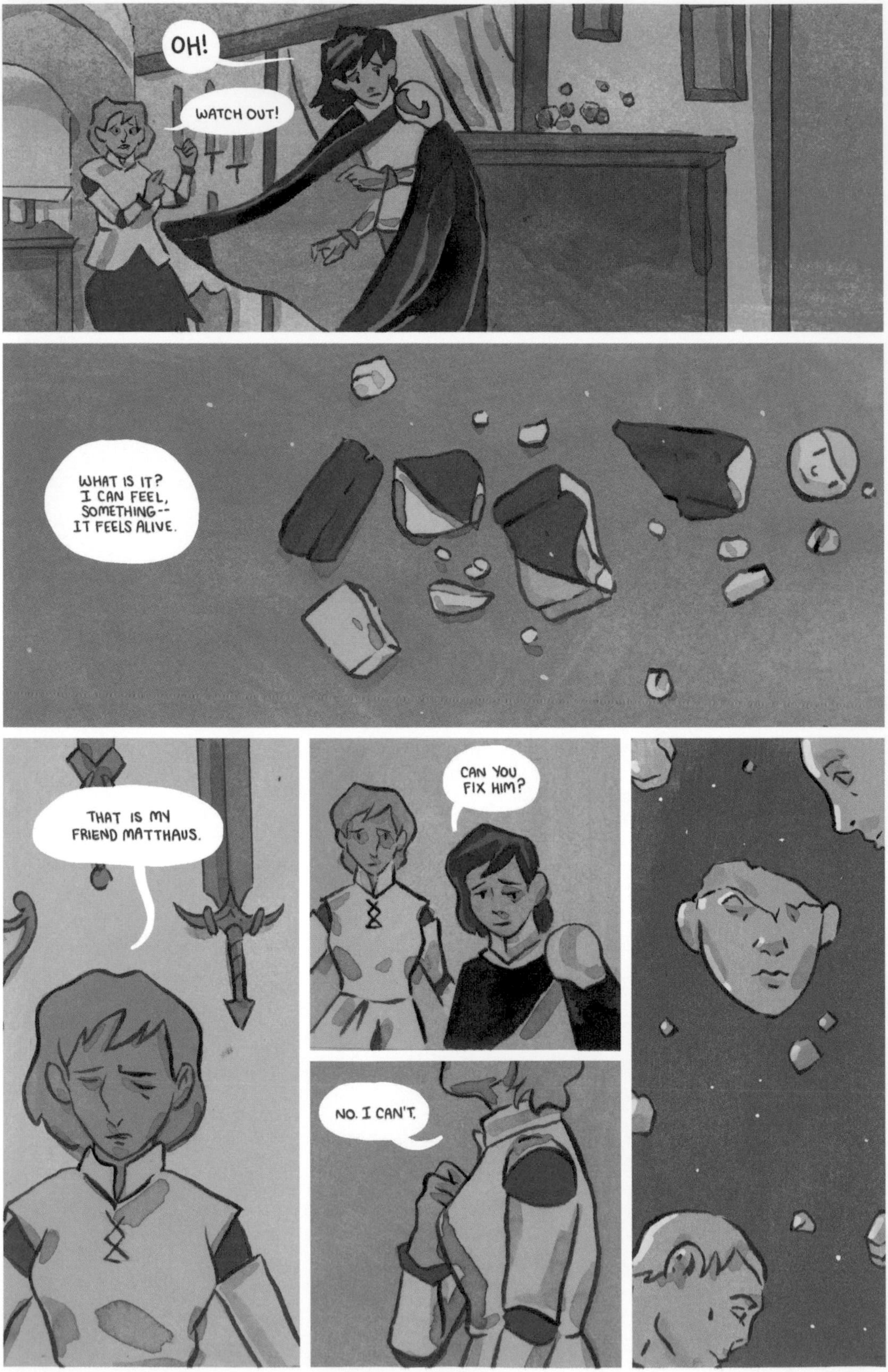
OH!
WATCH OUT!
WHAT IS IT? I CAN FEEL, SOMETHING-- IT FEELS ALIVE.
THAT IS MY FRIEND MATTHAUS.
CAN YOU FIX HIM?
NO. I CAN'T.

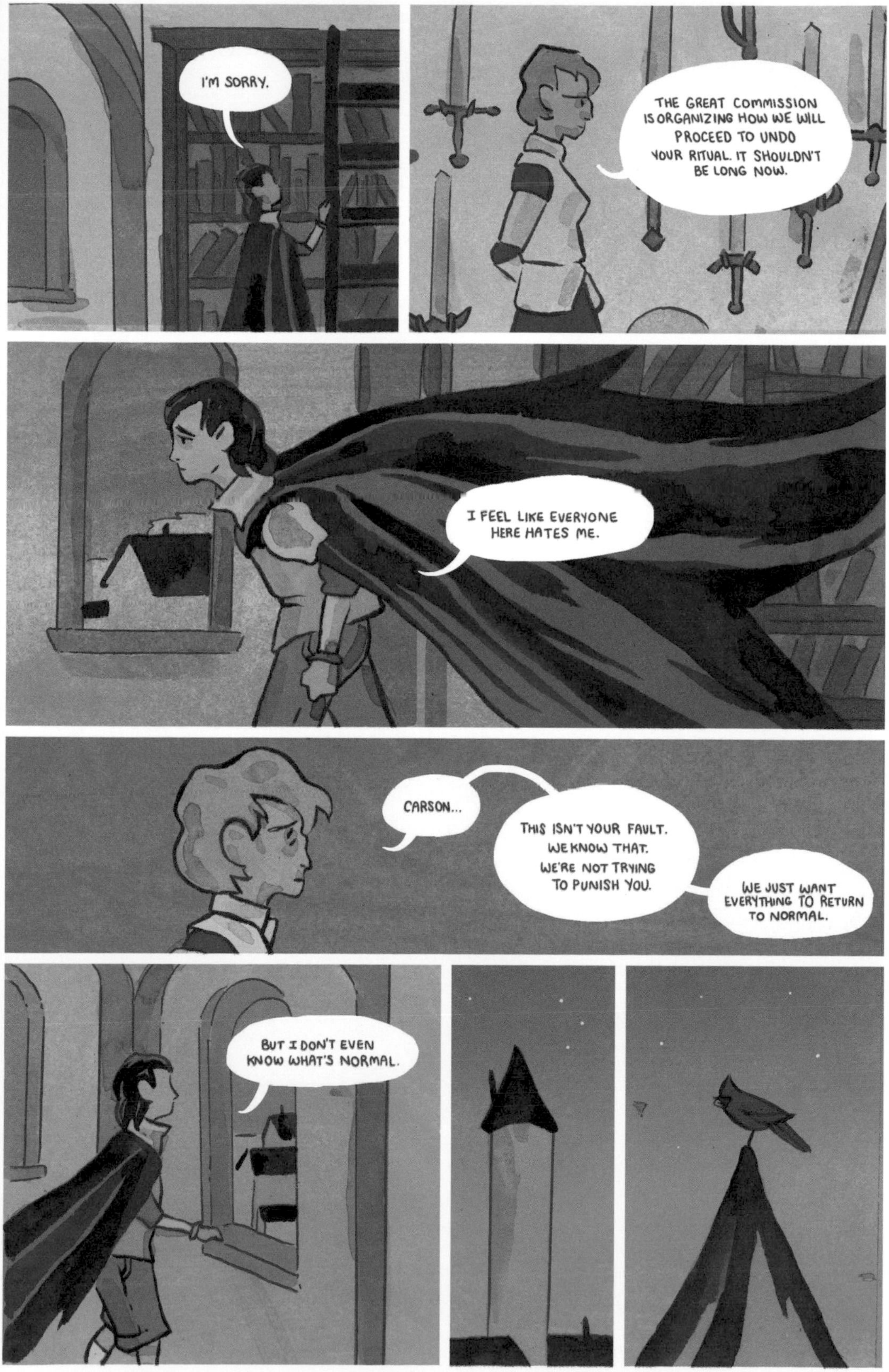
I'M SORRY.
THE GREAT COMMISSION IS ORGANIZING HOW WE WILL PROCEED TO UNDO YOUR RITUAL. IT SHOULDN'T BE LONG NOW.
I FEEL LIKE EVERYONE HERE HATES ME.
CARSON...
THIS ISN'T YOUR FAULT. WE KNOW THAT. WE'RE NOT TRYING TO PUNISH YOU.
WE JUST WANT EVERYTHING TO RETURN TO NORMAL.
BUT I DON'T EVEN KNOW WHAT'S NORMAL.

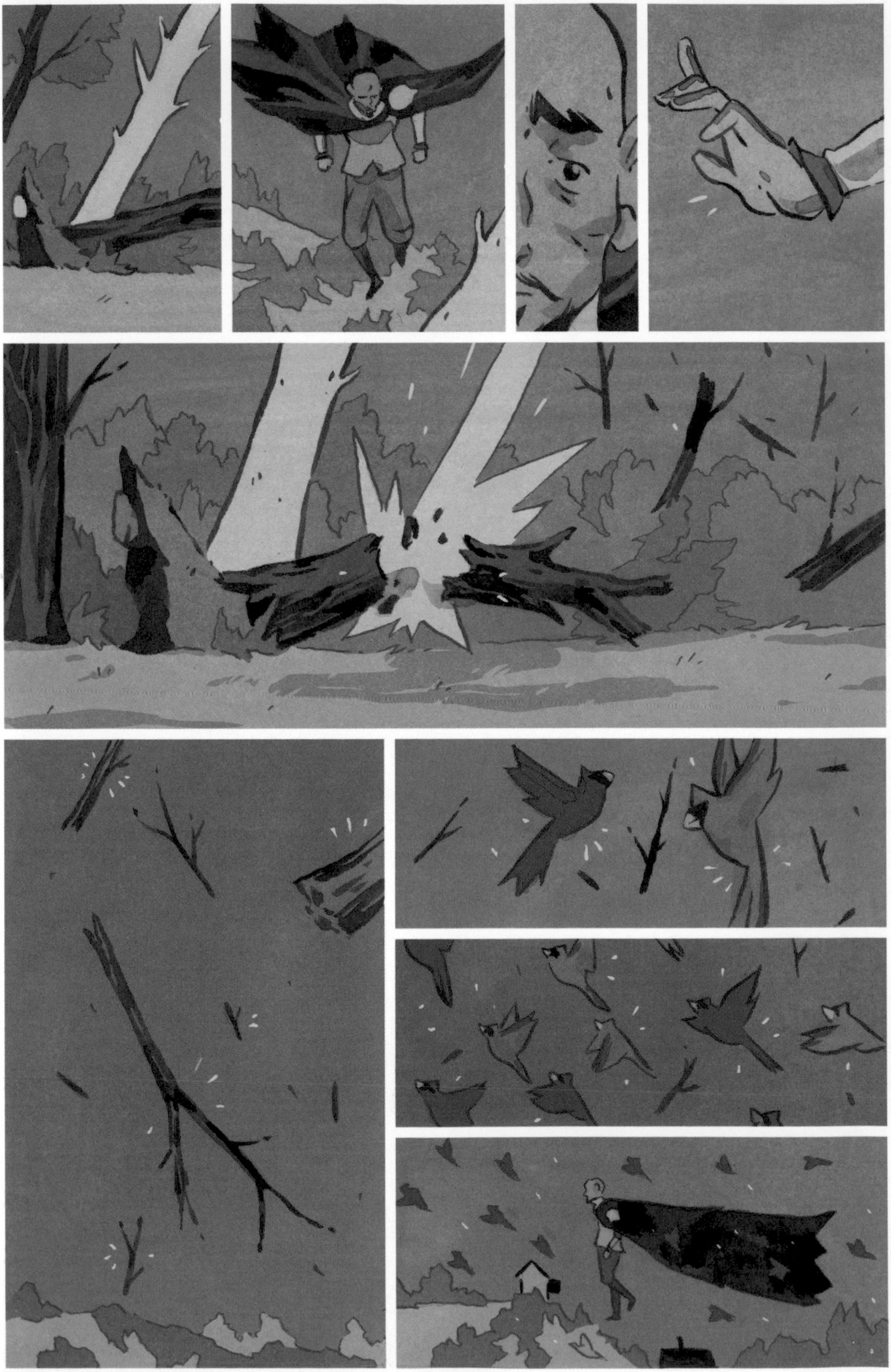

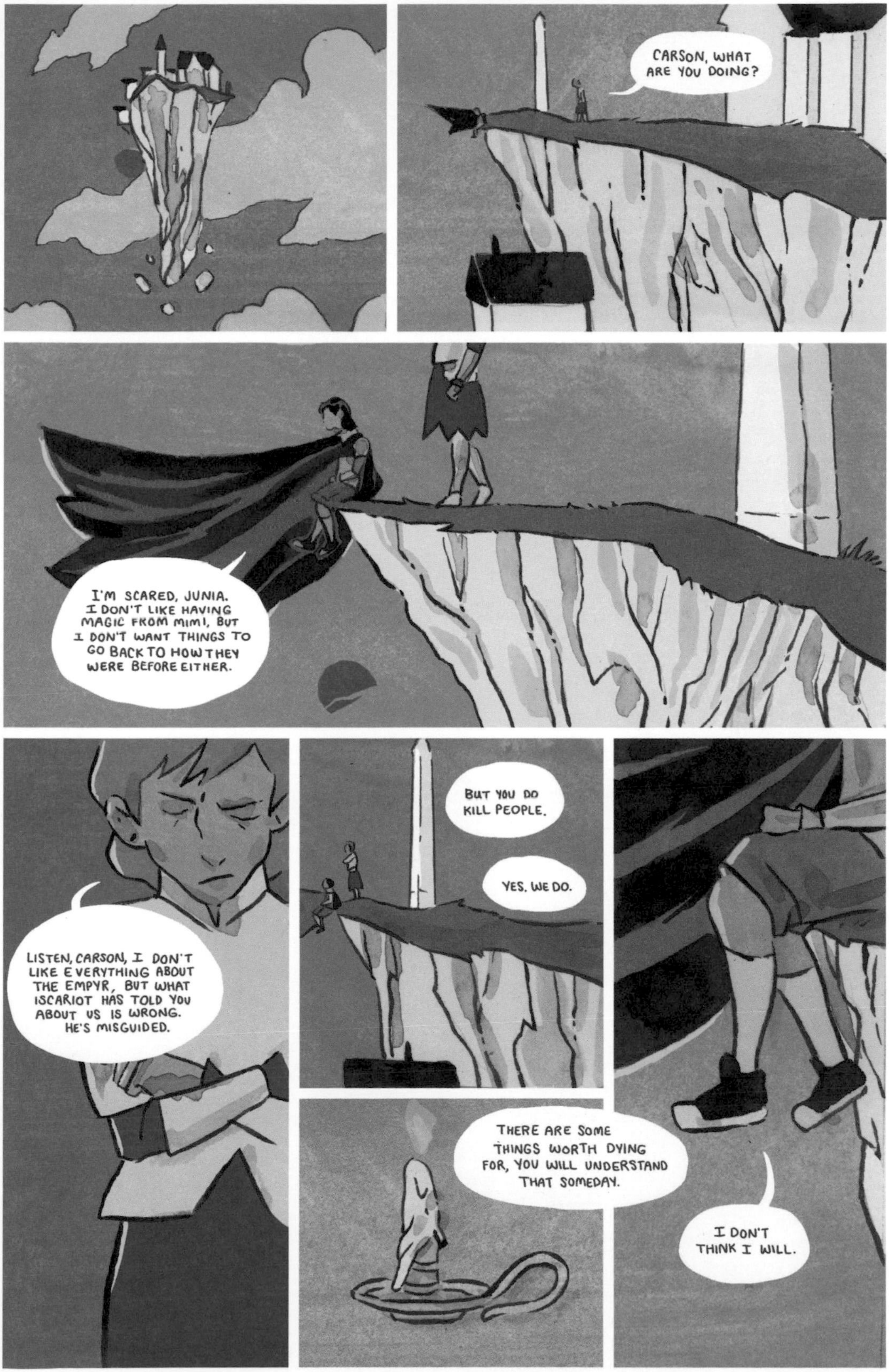
CARSON, WHAT ARE YOU DOING?
I'M SCARED, JUNIA. I DON'T LIKE HAVING MAGIC FROM MIMI, BUT I DON'T WANT THINGS TO GO BACK TO HOW THEY WERE BEFORE EITHER.
LISTEN, CARSON, I DON'T LIKE EVERYTHING ABOUT THE EMPYR, BUT WHAT ISCARIOT HAS TOLD YOU ABOUT US IS WRONG. HE'S MISGUIDED.
BUT YOU DO KILL PEOPLE.
YES. WE DO.
THERE ARE SOME THINGS WORTH DYING FOR, YOU WILL UNDERSTAND THAT SOMEDAY.
I DON'T THINK I WILL.

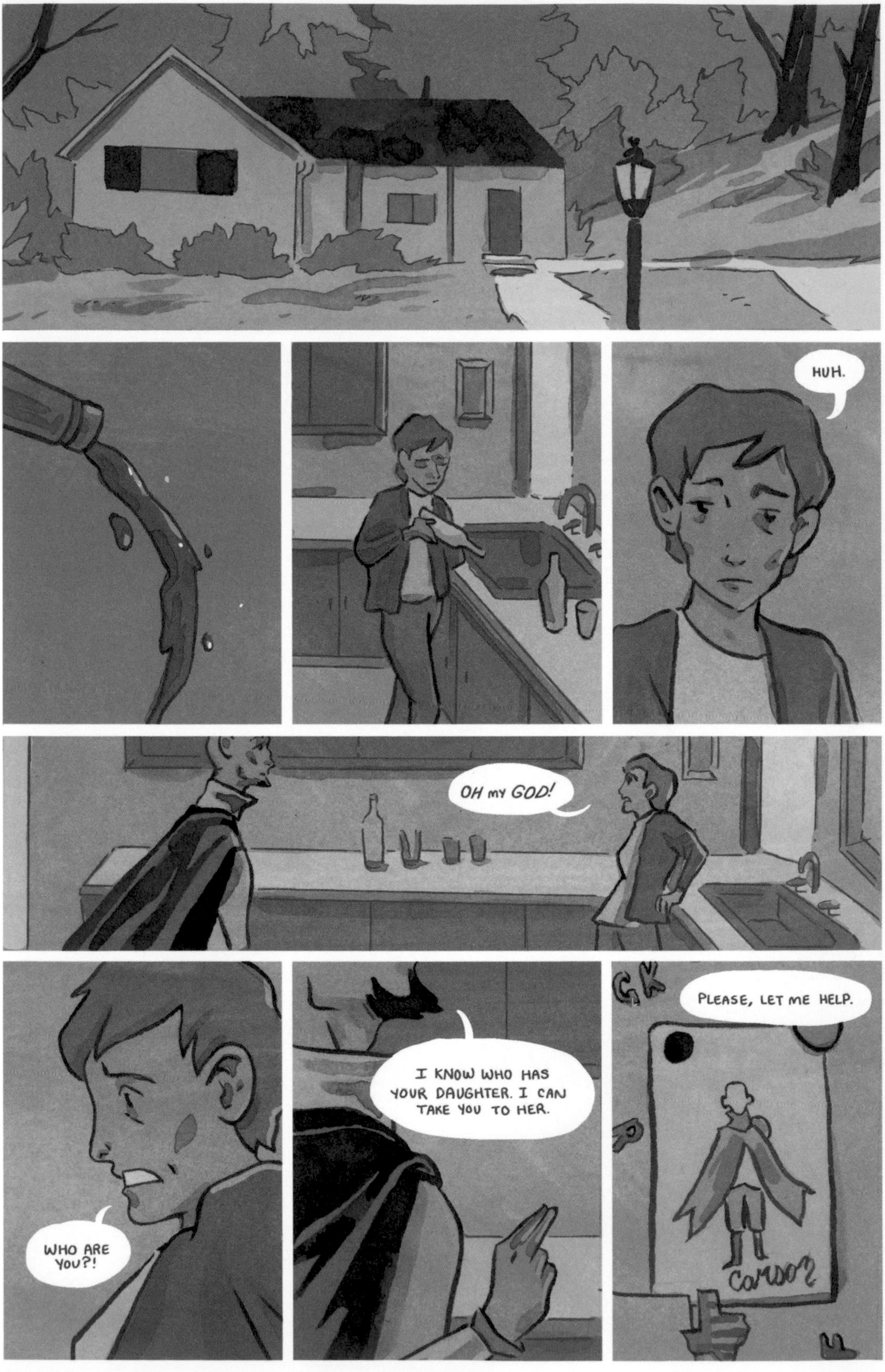
HUH.
OH my GOD!
WHO ARE YOU?!
I KNOW WHO HAS YOUR DAUGHTER. I CAN TAKE YOU TO HER.
PLEASE, LET ME HELP.

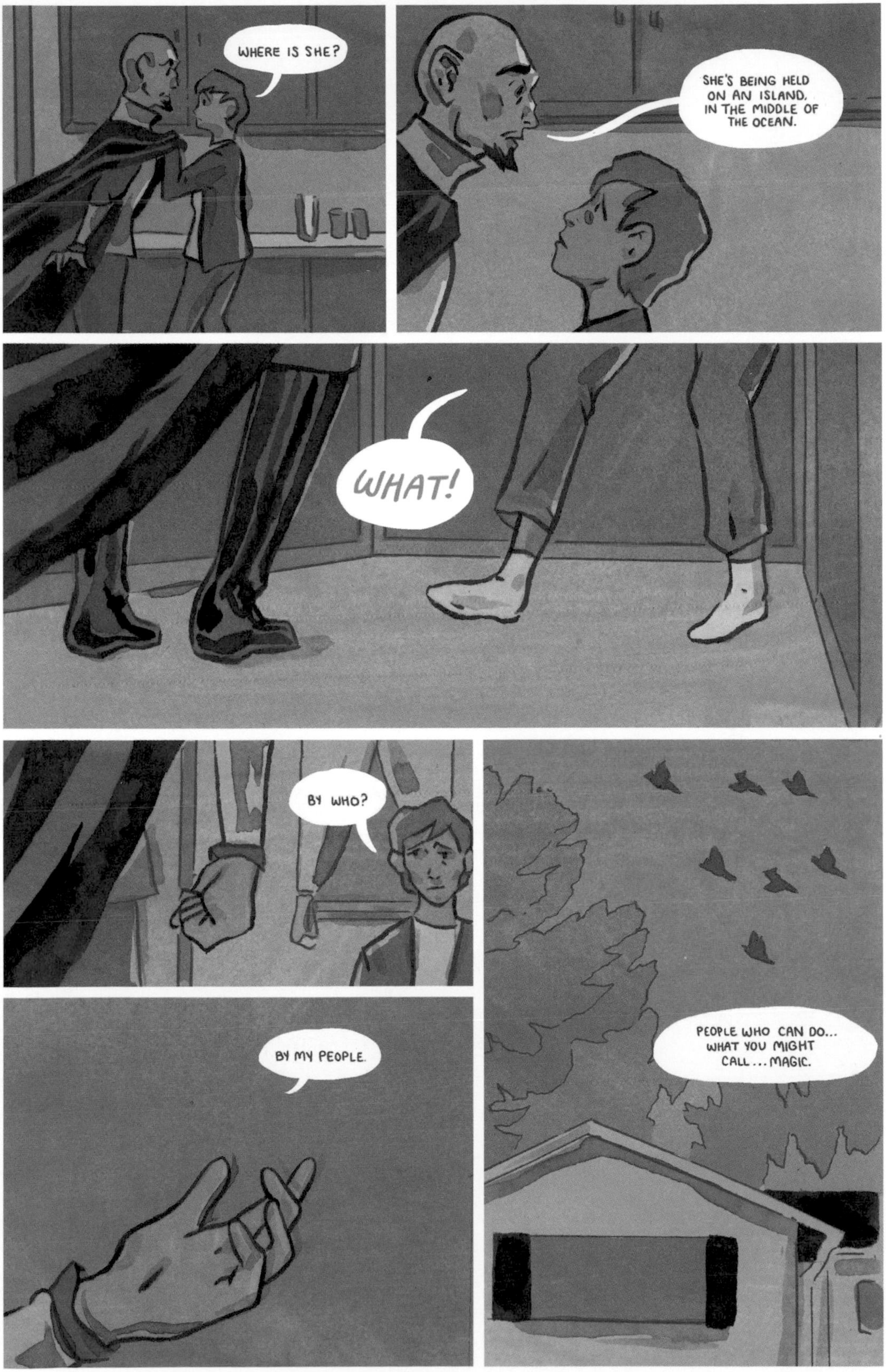
WHERE IS SHE?
SHE'S BEING HELD ON AN ISLAND, IN THE MIDDLE OF THE OCEAN.
WHAT!
BY WHO?
BY MY PEOPLE.
PEOPLE WHO CAN DO... WHAT YOU MIGHT CALL... MAGIC.

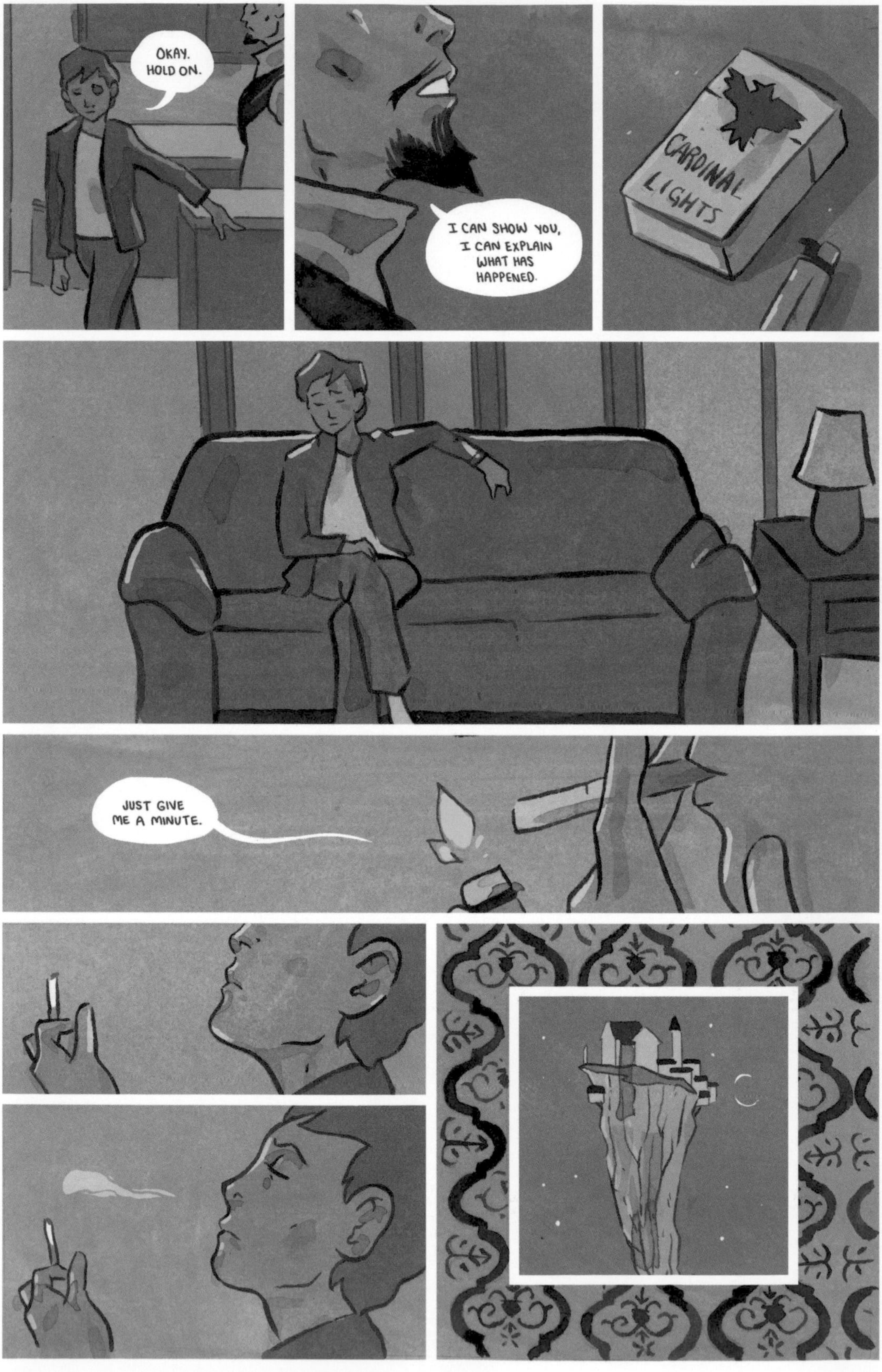
OKAY. HOLD ON.
I CAN SHOW YOU, I CAN EXPLAIN WHAT HAS HAPPENED.
CARDINAL LIGHTS
JUST GIVE ME A MINUTE.

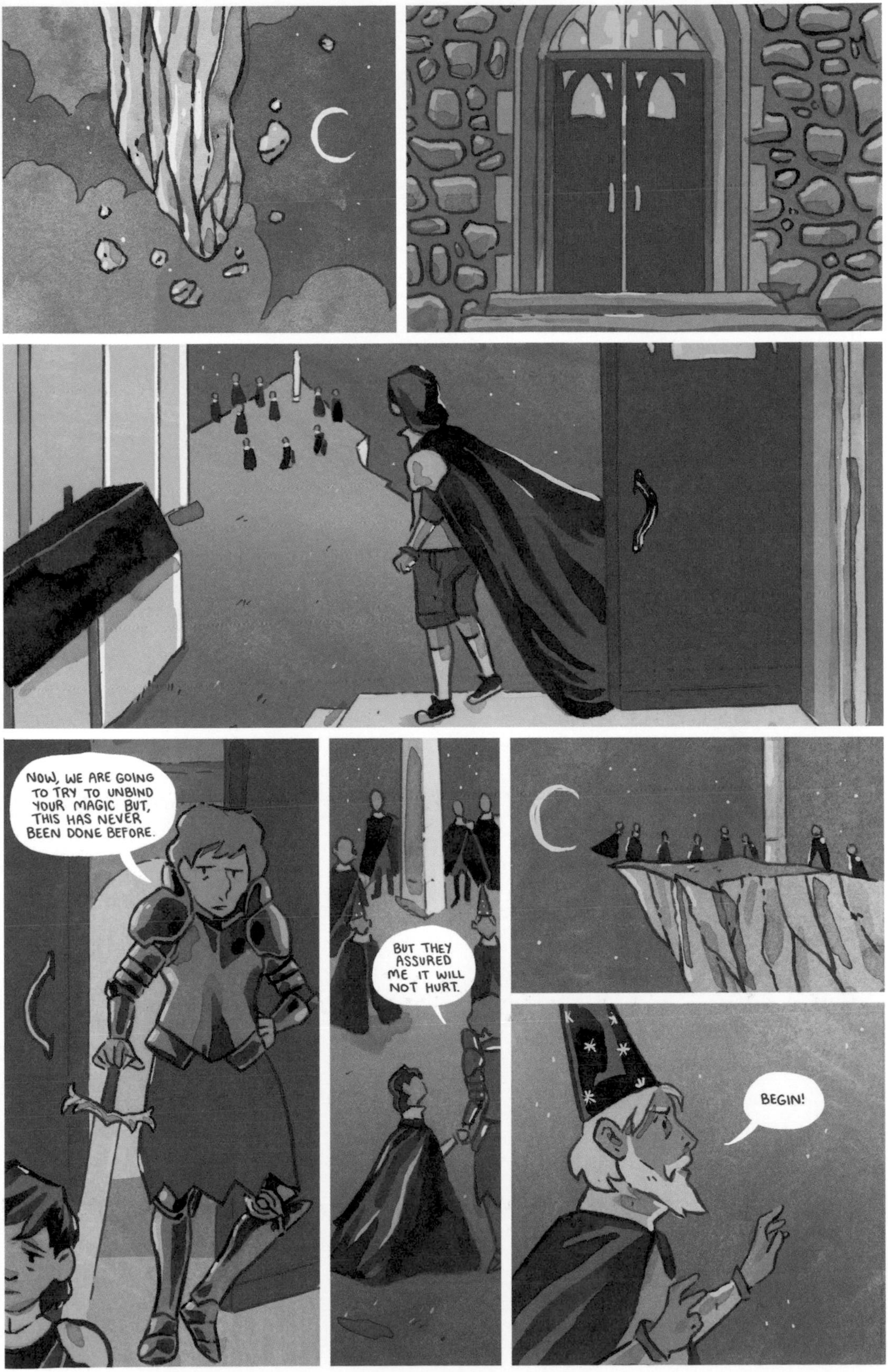
NOW, WE ARE GOING TO TRY TO UNBIND YOUR MAGIC BUT, THIS HAS NEVER BEEN DONE BEFORE.
BUT THEY ASSURED ME IT WILL NOT HURT.
BEGIN!

I'M SORRY, I'M BEING STUPID.

NO, IT'S OKAY, REALLY.

I WAS TAUGHT THAT CRYING MADE ONE WEAK.

AND I BELIEVED IT FOR A VERY LONG TIME.

UNTIL I REALIZED I COULDN'T DO IT ANYMORE.

PERHAPS IT TRULY DOES TAKE STRENGTH TO CUT OFF A PART OF ONESELF.

BUT IN THE END WE ARE UNDENIABLY LESS.

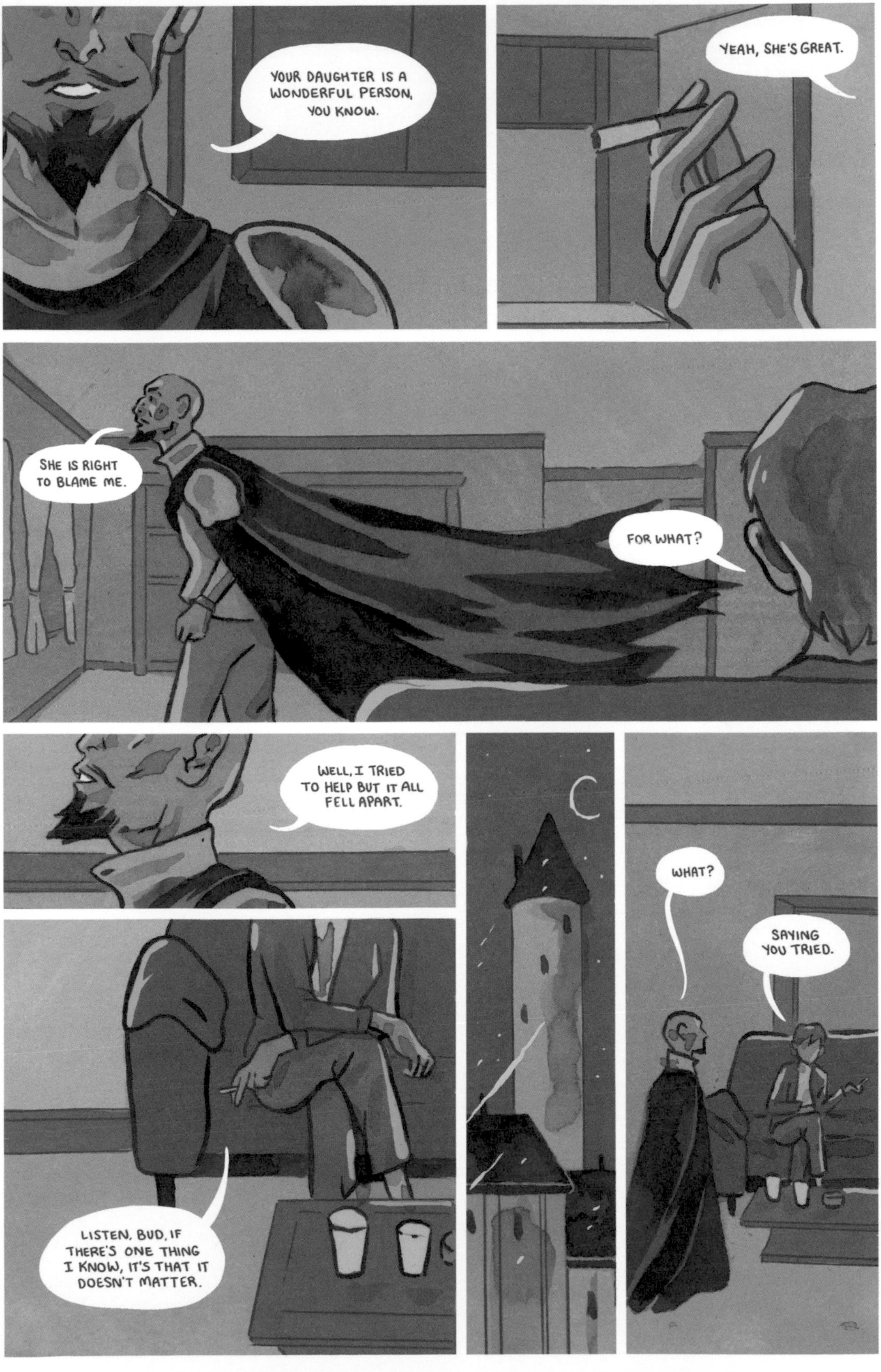
YOUR DAUGHTER IS A WONDERFUL PERSON, YOU KNOW.
YEAH, SHE'S GREAT.
SHE IS RIGHT TO BLAME ME.
FOR WHAT?
WELL, I TRIED TO HELP BUT IT ALL FELL APART.
LISTEN, BUD, IF THERE'S ONE THING I KNOW, IT'S THAT IT DOESN'T MATTER.
WHAT?
SAYING YOU TRIED.

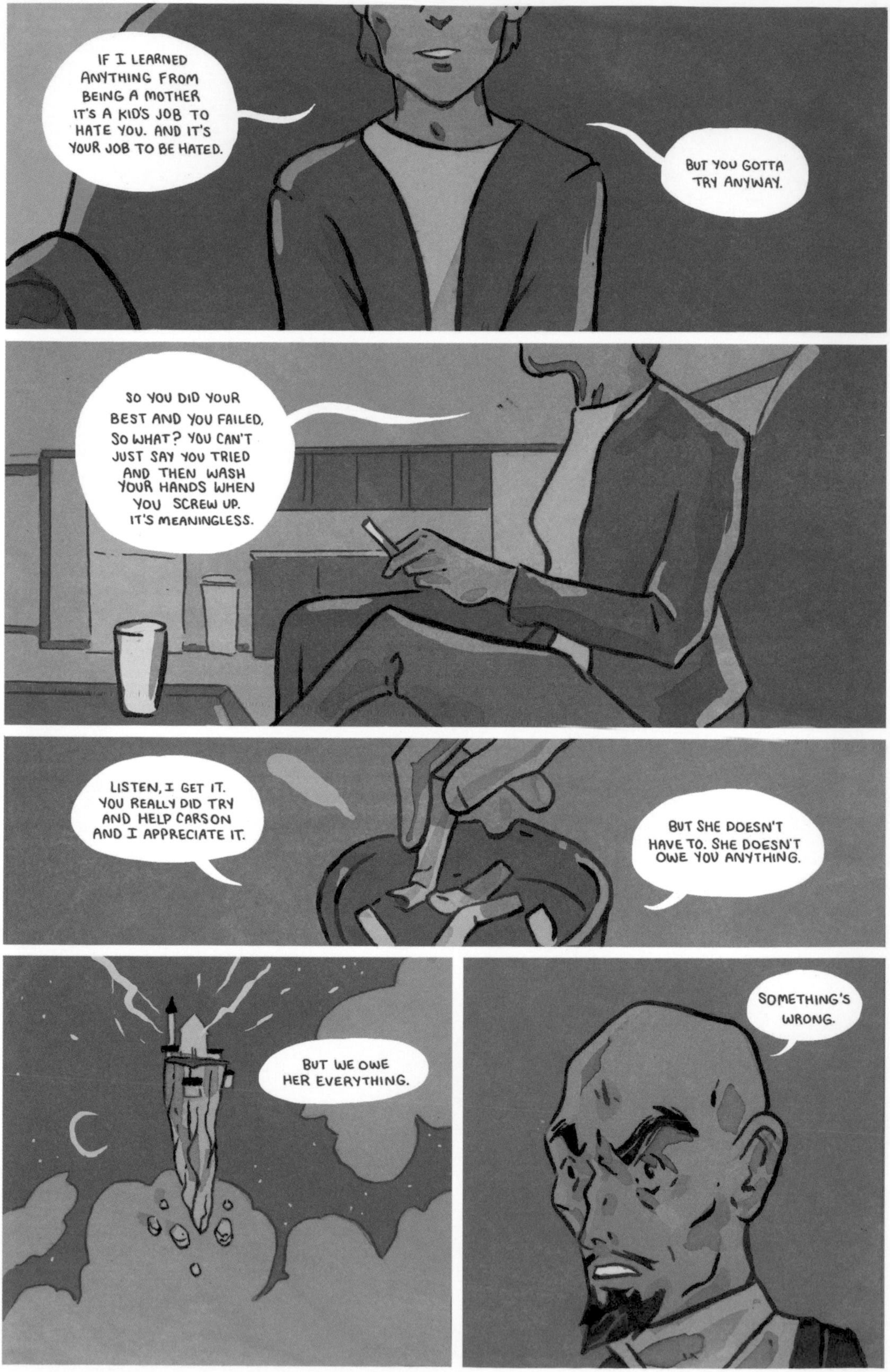
IF I LEARNED ANYTHING FROM BEING A MOTHER IT'S A KID'S JOB TO HATE YOU. AND IT'S YOUR JOB TO BE HATED.
BUT YOU GOTTA TRY ANYWAY.
SO YOU DID YOUR BEST AND YOU FAILED, SO WHAT? YOU CAN'T JUST SAY YOU TRIED AND THEN WASH YOUR HANDS WHEN YOU SCREW UP. IT'S MEANINGLESS.
LISTEN, I GET IT. YOU REALLY DID TRY AND HELP CARSON AND I APPRECIATE IT.
BUT SHE DOESN'T HAVE TO. SHE DOESN'T OWE YOU ANYTHING.
BUT WE OWE HER EVERYTHING.
SOMETHING'S WRONG.

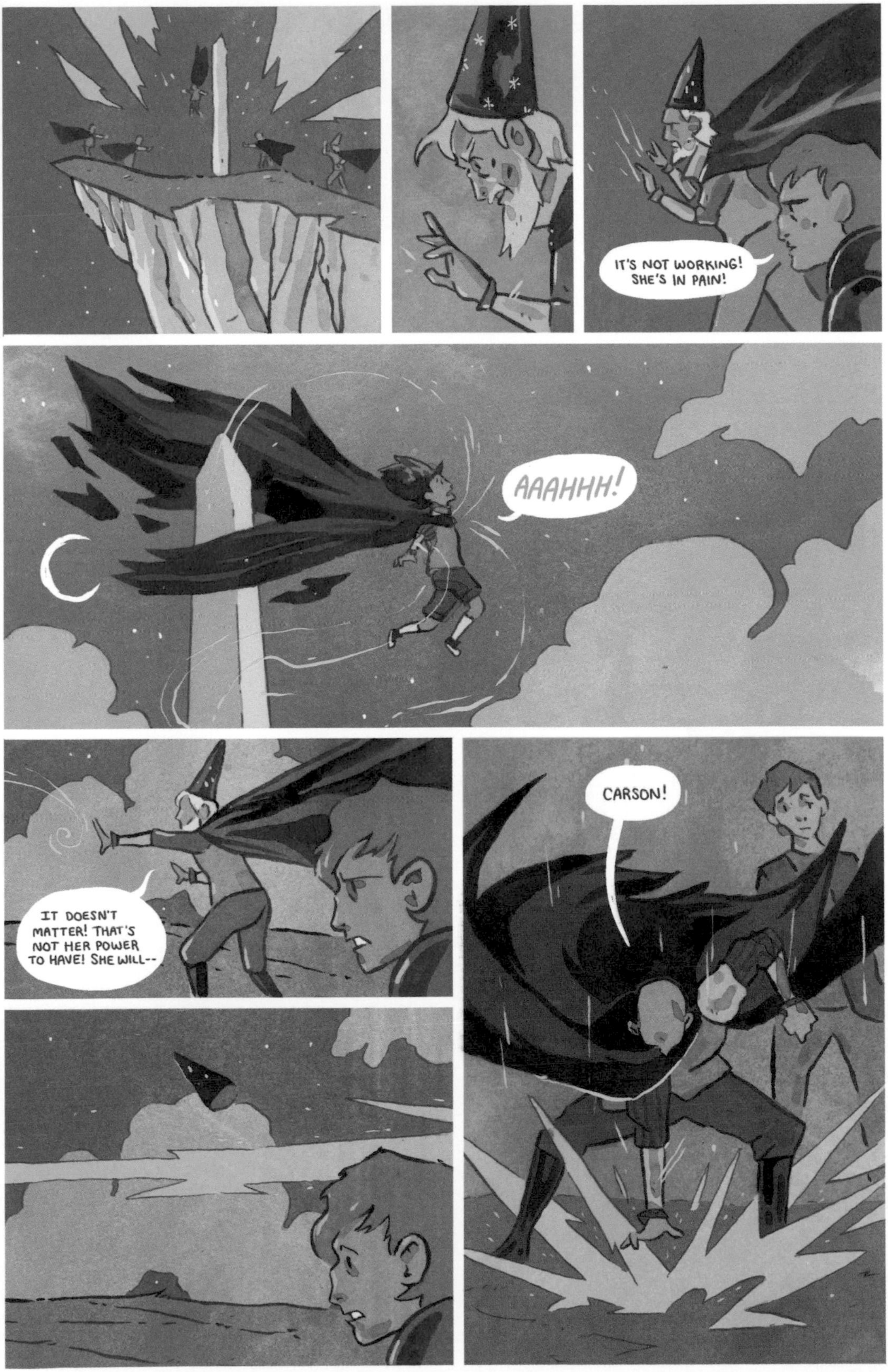
IT'S NOT WORKING! SHE'S IN PAIN!
AAAHHH!
IT DOESN'T MATTER! THAT'S NOT HER POWER TO HAVE! SHE WILL--
CARSON!

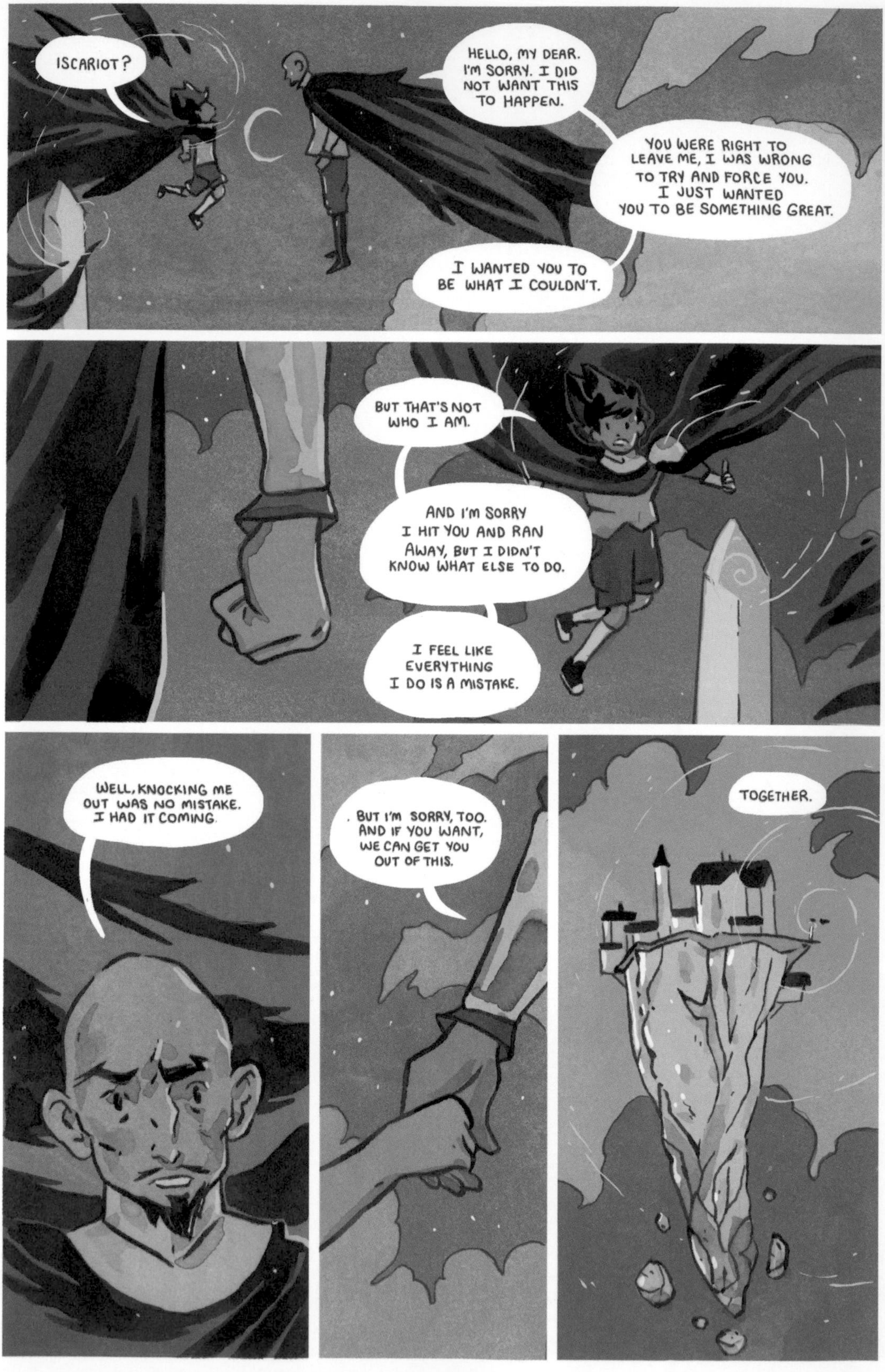
ISCARIOT?
HELLO, MY DEAR. I'M SORRY. I DID NOT WANT THIS TO HAPPEN.
YOU WERE RIGHT TO LEAVE ME, I WAS WRONG TO TRY AND FORCE YOU. I JUST WANTED YOU TO BE SOMETHING GREAT.
I WANTED YOU TO BE WHAT I COULDN'T.
BUT THAT'S NOT WHO I AM.
AND I'M SORRY I HIT YOU AND RAN AWAY, BUT I DIDN'T KNOW WHAT ELSE TO DO.
I FEEL LIKE EVERYTHING I DO IS A MISTAKE.
WELL, KNOCKING ME OUT WAS NO MISTAKE. I HAD IT COMING.
BUT I'M SORRY, TOO. AND IF YOU WANT, WE CAN GET YOU OUT OF THIS.
TOGETHER.

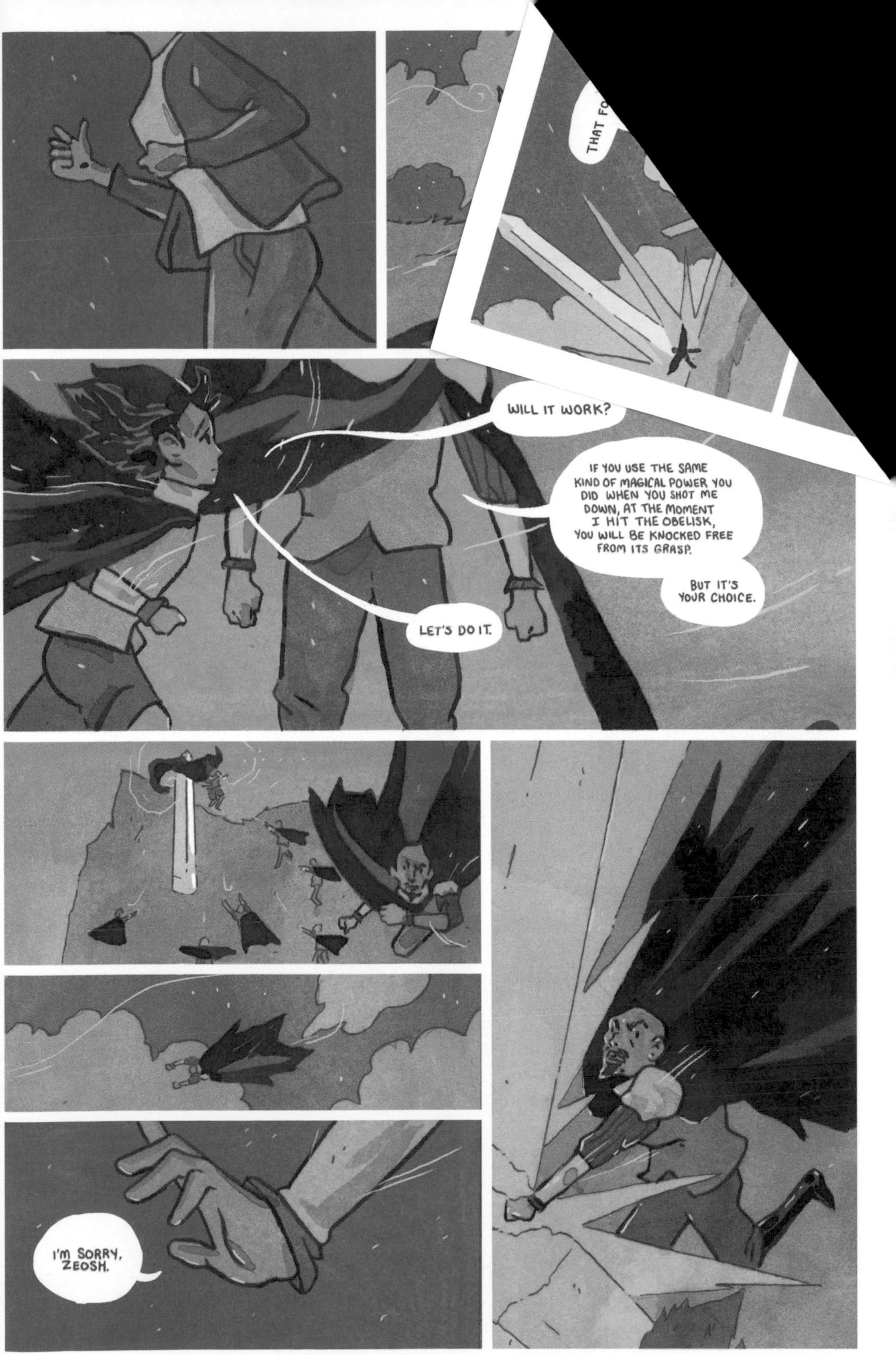
THAT
WILL IT WORK?
IF YOU USE THE SAME KIND OF MAGICAL POWER YOU DID WHEN YOU SHOT ME DOWN, AT THE MOMENT I HIT THE OBELISK, YOU WILL BE KNOCKED FREE FROM ITS GRASP.
BUT IT'S YOUR CHOICE.
LET'S DO IT.
I'M SORRY, ZEOSH.

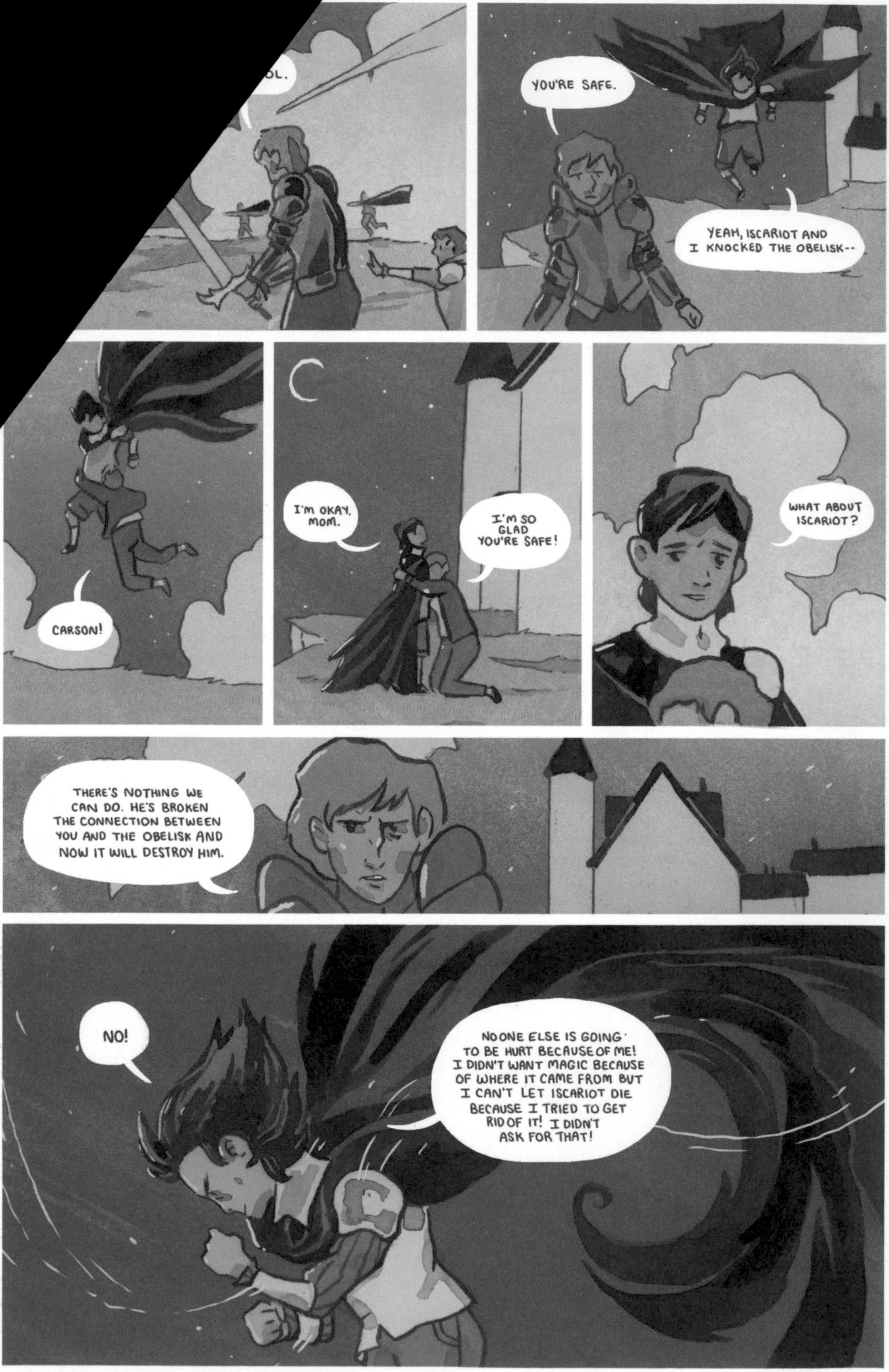
YOU'RE SAFE.
YEAH, ISCARIOT AND I KNOCKED THE OBELISK--
CARSON!
I'M OKAY, MOM.
I'M SO GLAD YOU'RE SAFE!
WHAT ABOUT ISCARIOT?
THERE'S NOTHING WE CAN DO. HE'S BROKEN THE CONNECTION BETWEEN YOU AND THE OBELISK AND NOW IT WILL DESTROY HIM.
NO!
NO ONE ELSE IS GOING TO BE HURT BECAUSE OF ME! I DIDN'T WANT MAGIC BECAUSE OF WHERE IT CAME FROM BUT I CAN'T LET ISCARIOT DIE BECAUSE I TRIED TO GET RID OF IT! I DIDN'T ASK FOR THAT!

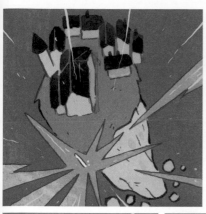

YOU WON'T MAKE IT.

THE OBELISK IS TOO DANGEROUS, THE GREAT COMMISSION AND THEIR MEN ARE FALLING BACK.

IT'S OVERFLOWING WITH UNTEMPERED MAGIC. THERE'S NO WAY TO GET NEAR IT.

WE NEED TO EVACUATE. IT WILL TAKE US DECADES TO REPAIR--

PLEASE PROTECT MOM!

WATCH OUT!

CARSON!

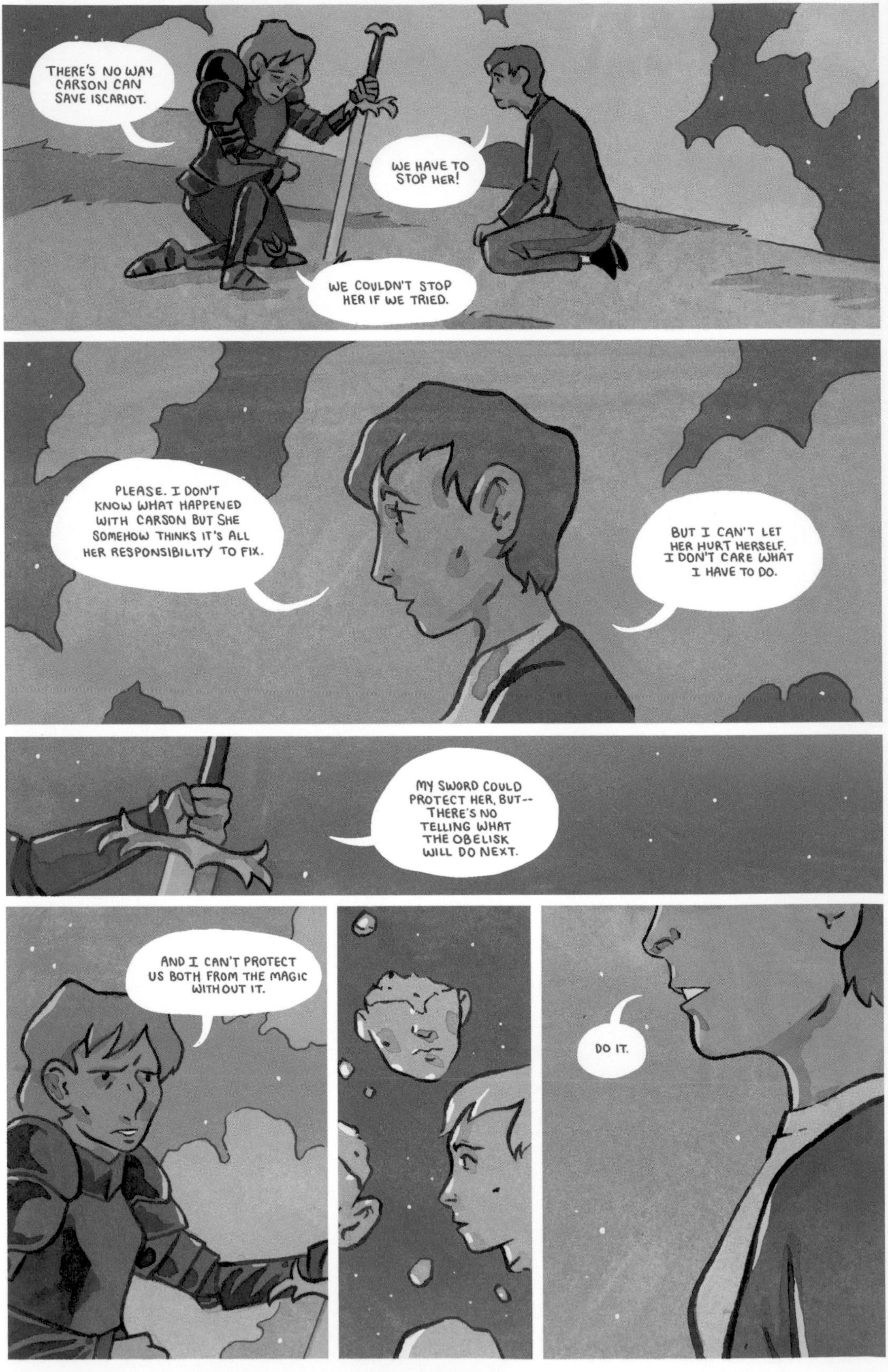
THERE'S NO WAY CARSON CAN SAVE ISCARIOT.
WE HAVE TO STOP HER!
WE COULDN'T STOP HER IF WE TRIED.
PLEASE. I DON'T KNOW WHAT HAPPENED WITH CARSON BUT SHE SOMEHOW THINKS IT'S ALL HER RESPONSIBILITY TO FIX.
BUT I CAN'T LET HER HURT HERSELF. I DON'T CARE WHAT I HAVE TO DO.
MY SWORD COULD PROTECT HER, BUT-- THERE'S NO TELLING WHAT THE OBELISK WILL DO NEXT.
AND I CAN'T PROTECT US BOTH FROM THE MAGIC WITHOUT IT.
DO IT.

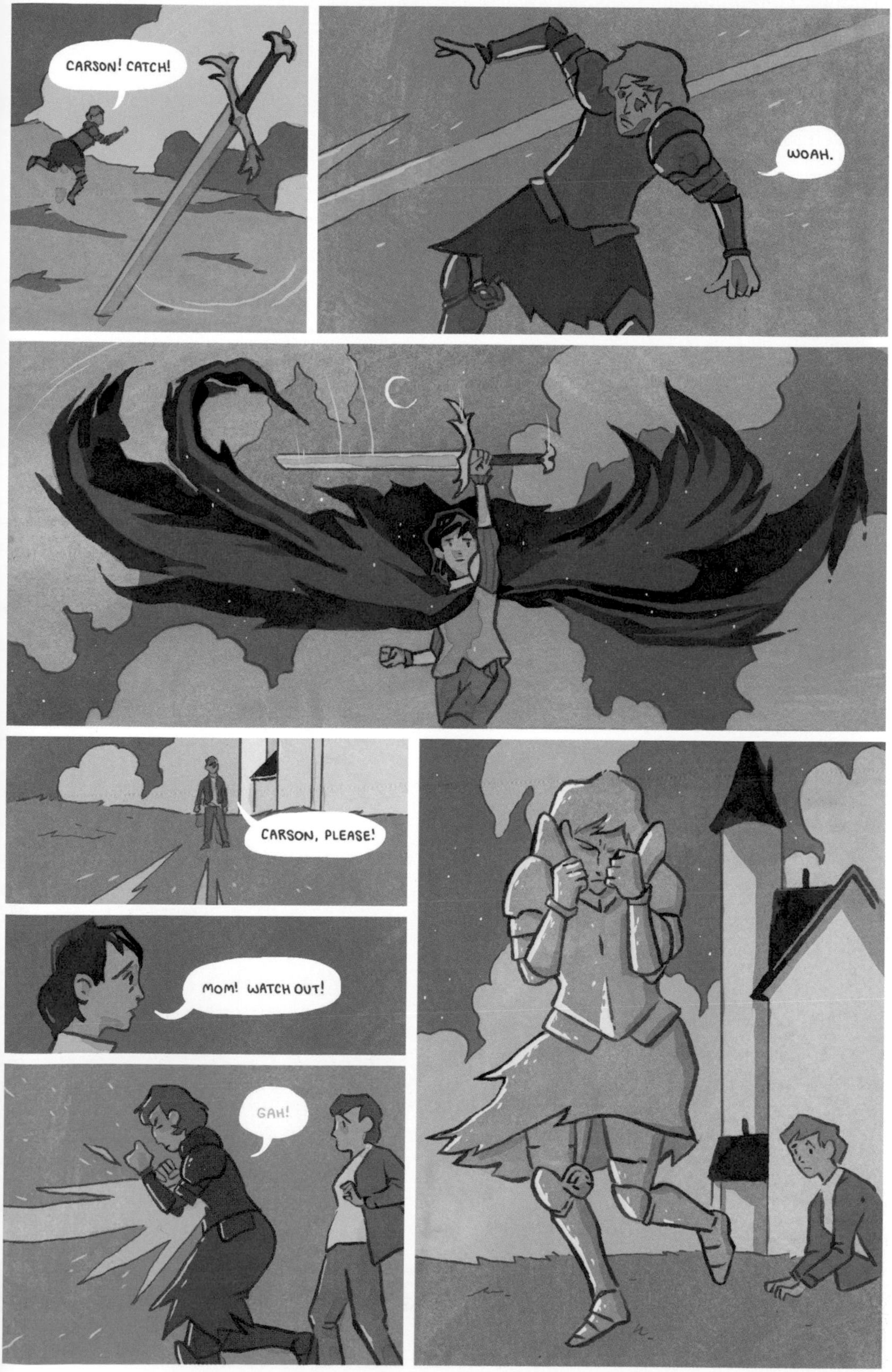
CARSON! CATCH!
WOAH.
CARSON, PLEASE!
MOM! WATCH OUT!
GAH!

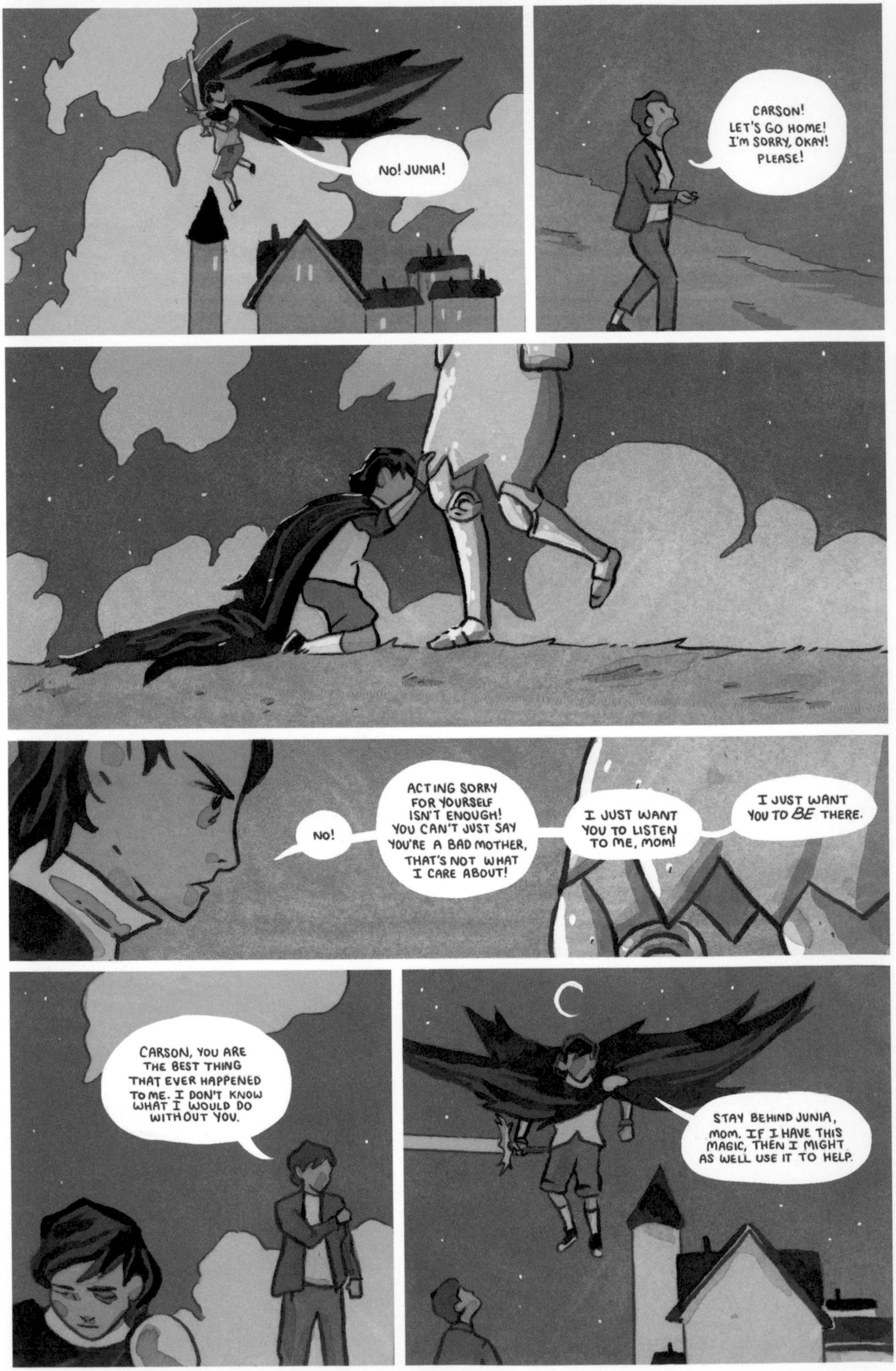
NO! JUNIA!
CARSON! LET'S GO HOME! I'M SORRY, OKAY! PLEASE!
NO!
ACTING SORRY FOR YOURSELF ISN'T ENOUGH! YOU CAN'T JUST SAY YOU'RE A BAD MOTHER, THAT'S NOT WHAT I CARE ABOUT!
I JUST WANT YOU TO LISTEN TO ME, MOM!
I JUST WANT YOU TO BE THERE.
CARSON, YOU ARE THE BEST THING THAT EVER HAPPENED TO ME. I DON'T KNOW WHAT I WOULD DO WITHOUT YOU.
STAY BEHIND JUNIA, MOM. IF I HAVE THIS MAGIC, THEN I MIGHT AS WELL USE IT TO HELP.

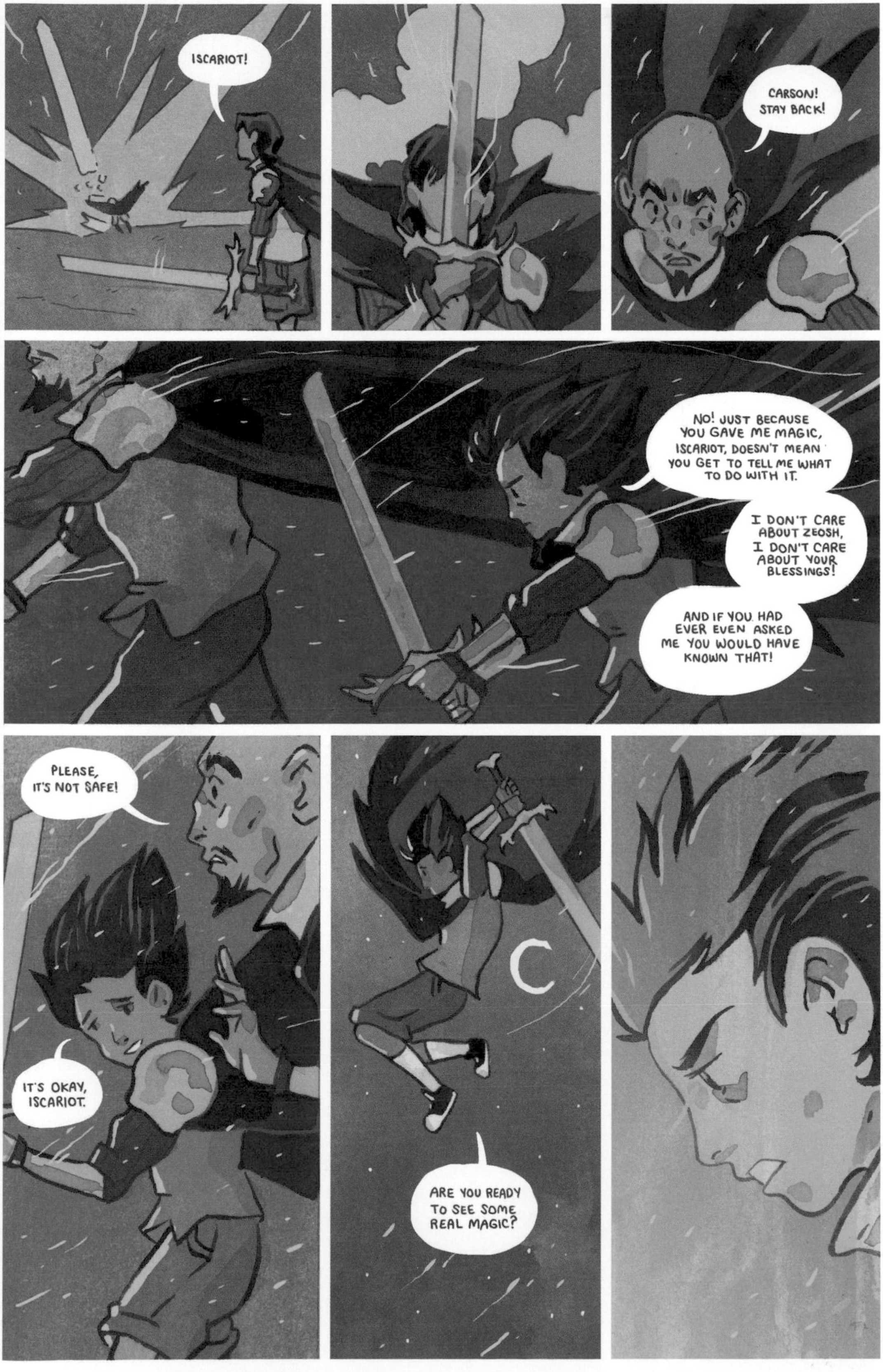
ISCARIOT!
CARSON! STAY BACK!
NO! JUST BECAUSE YOU GAVE ME MAGIC, ISCARIOT, DOESN'T MEAN YOU GET TO TELL ME WHAT TO DO WITH IT.
I DON'T CARE ABOUT ZEOSH, I DON'T CARE ABOUT YOUR BLESSINGS!
AND IF YOU HAD EVER EVEN ASKED ME YOU WOULD HAVE KNOWN THAT!
PLEASE, IT'S NOT SAFE!
IT'S OKAY, ISCARIOT.
ARE YOU READY TO SEE SOME REAL MAGIC?

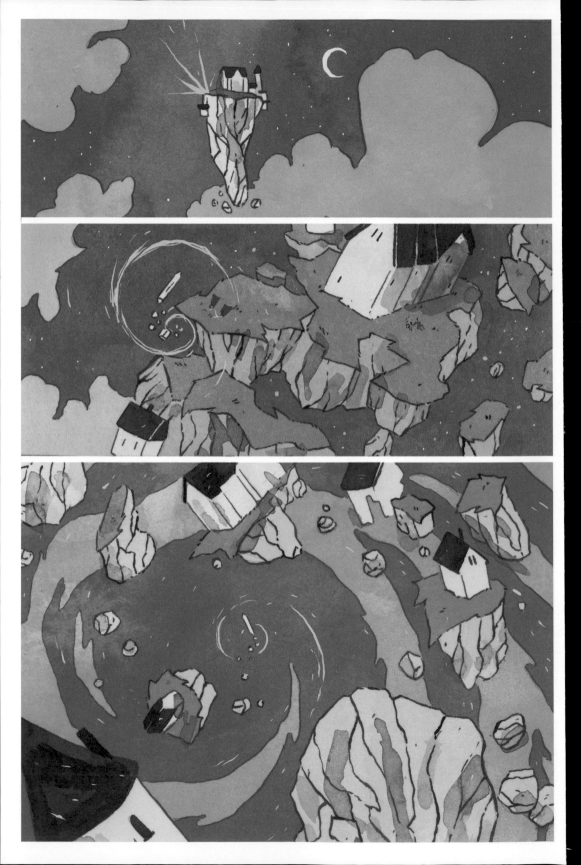

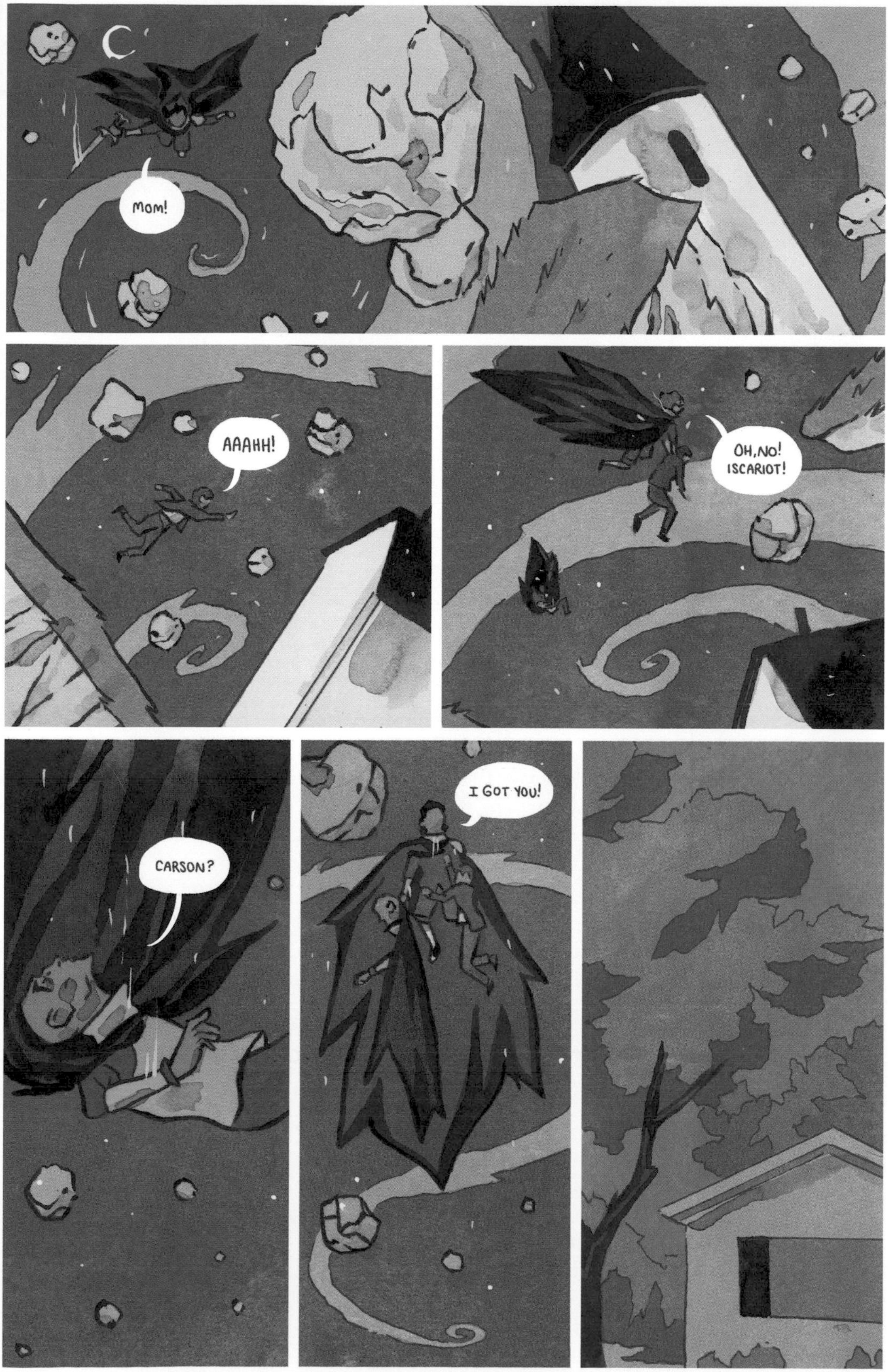
MOM!
AAAHH!
OH, NO! ISCARIOT!
CARSON?
I GOT YOU!

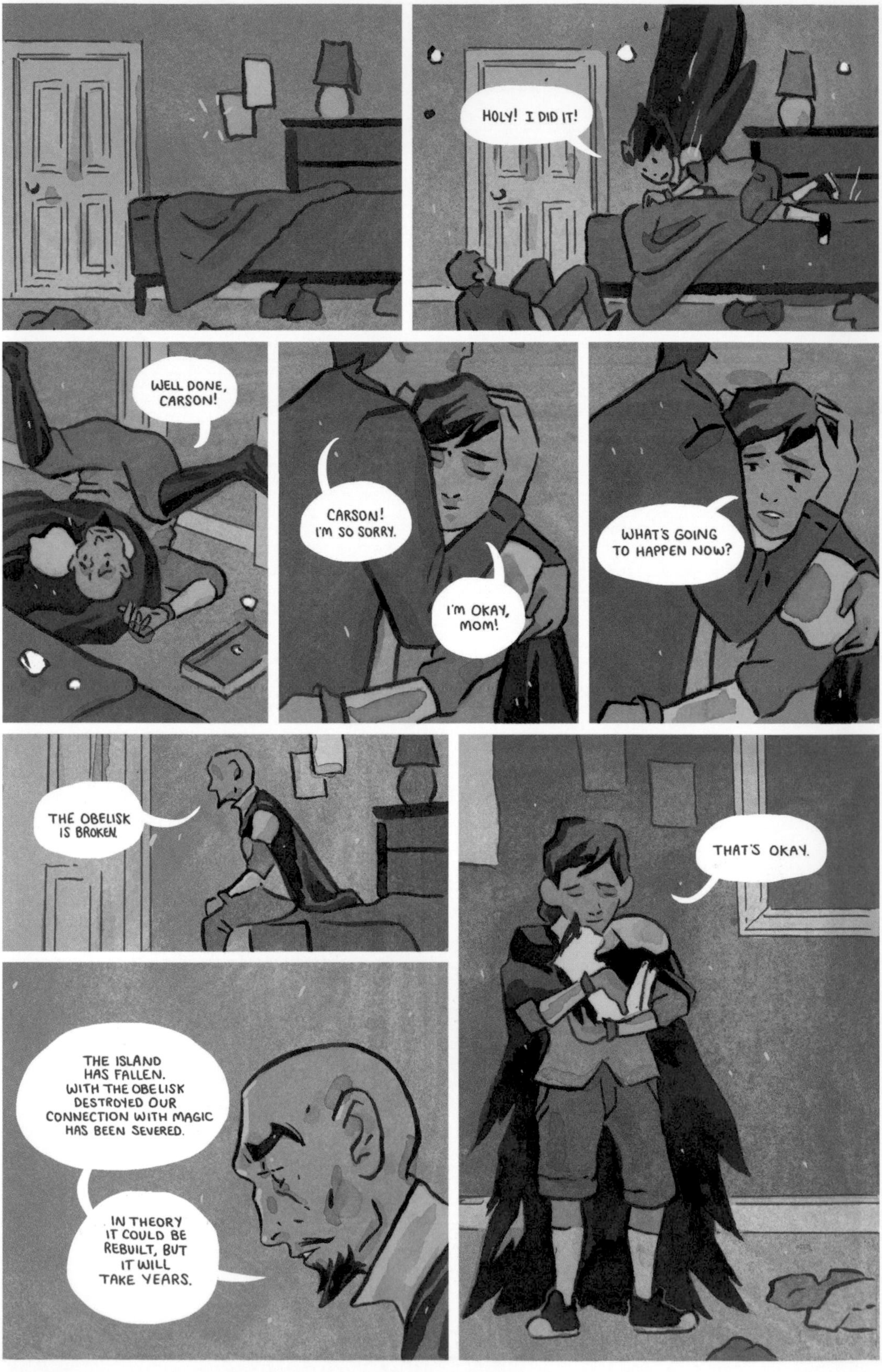
HOLY! I DID IT!
WELL DONE, CARSON!
CARSON! I'M SO SORRY.
I'M OKAY, MOM!
WHAT'S GOING TO HAPPEN NOW?
THE OBELISK IS BROKEN.
THE ISLAND HAS FALLEN. WITH THE OBELISK DESTROYED OUR CONNECTION WITH MAGIC HAS BEEN SEVERED.
IN THEORY IT COULD BE REBUILT, BUT IT WILL TAKE YEARS.
THAT'S OKAY.

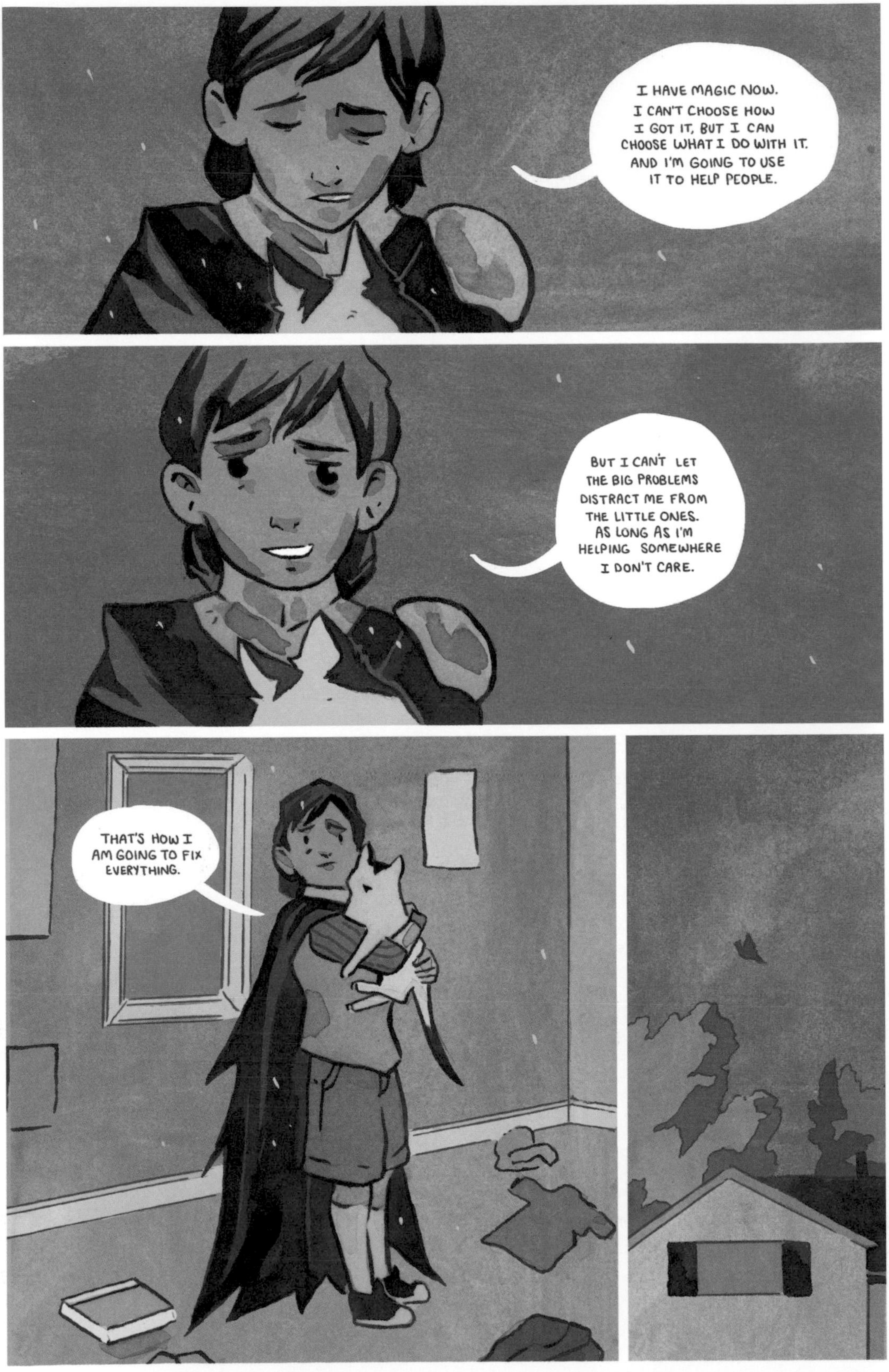
I HAVE MAGIC NOW. I CAN'T CHOOSE HOW I GOT IT, BUT I CAN CHOOSE WHAT I DO WITH IT. AND I'M GOING TO USE IT TO HELP PEOPLE.
BUT I CAN'T LET THE BIG PROBLEMS DISTRACT ME FROM THE LITTLE ONES. AS LONG AS I'M HELPING SOMEWHERE I DON'T CARE.
THAT'S HOW I AM GOING TO FIX EVERYTHING.

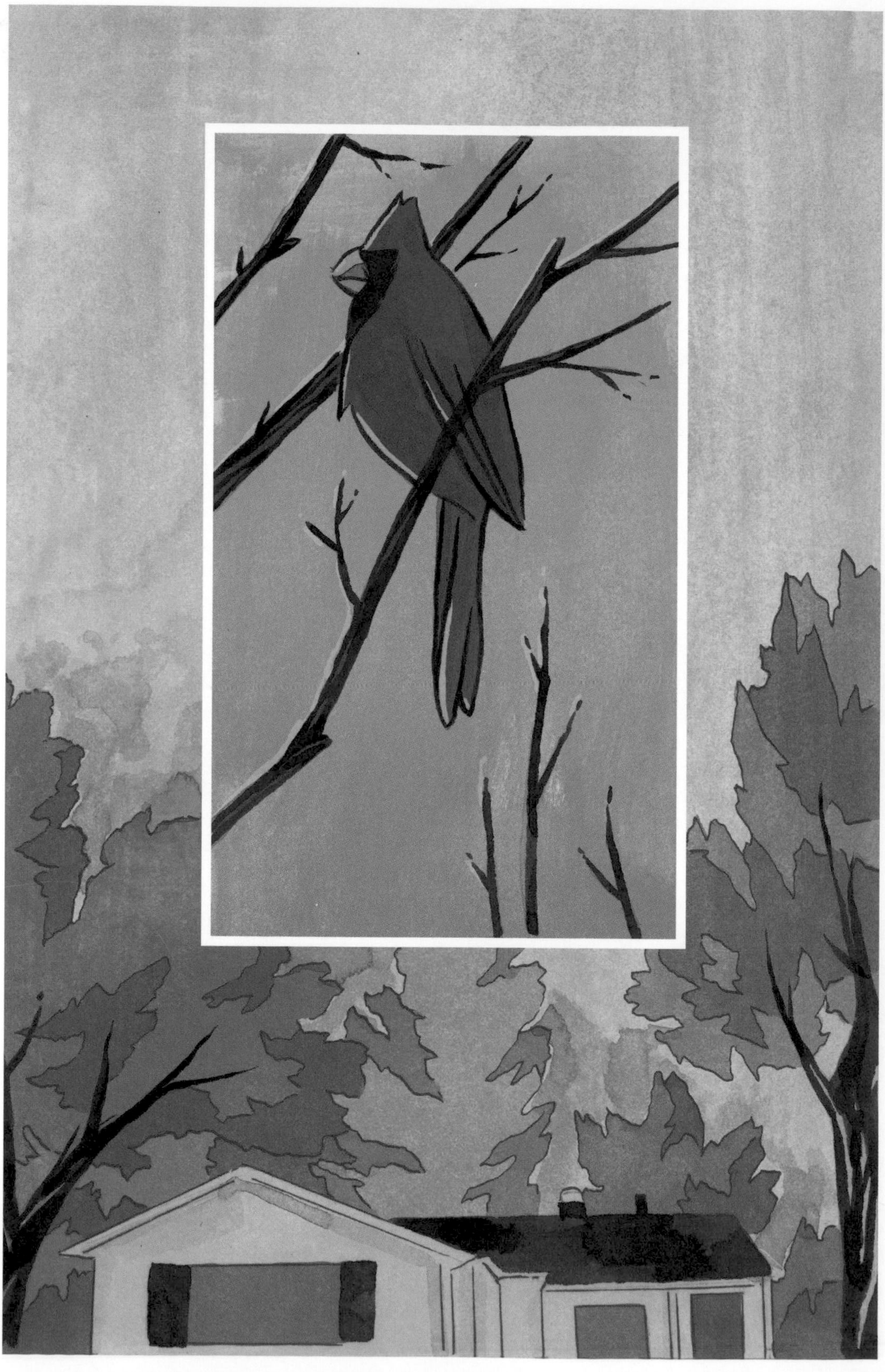

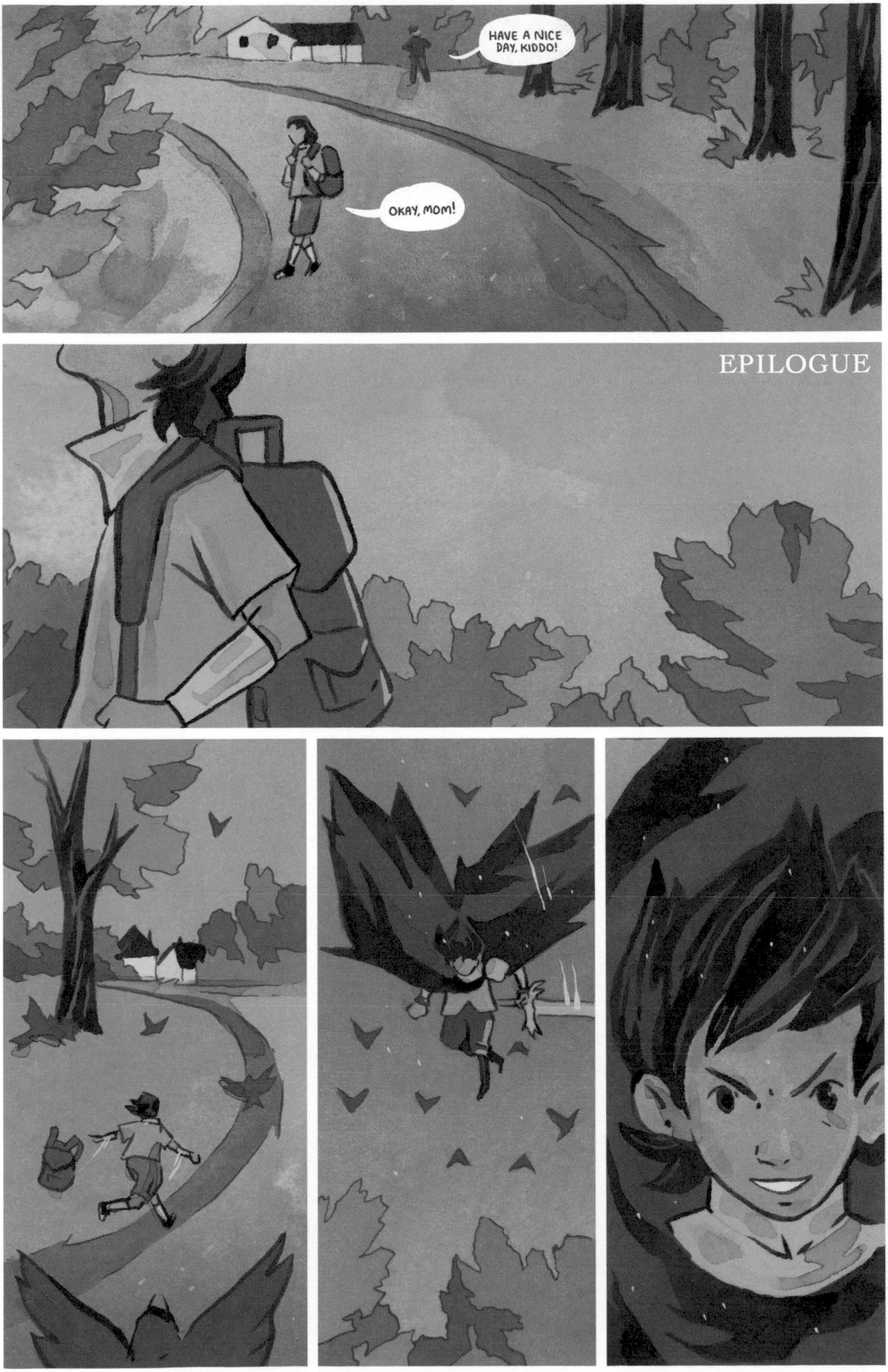
HAVE A NICE DAY, KIDDO!
OKAY, MOM!
EPILOGUE

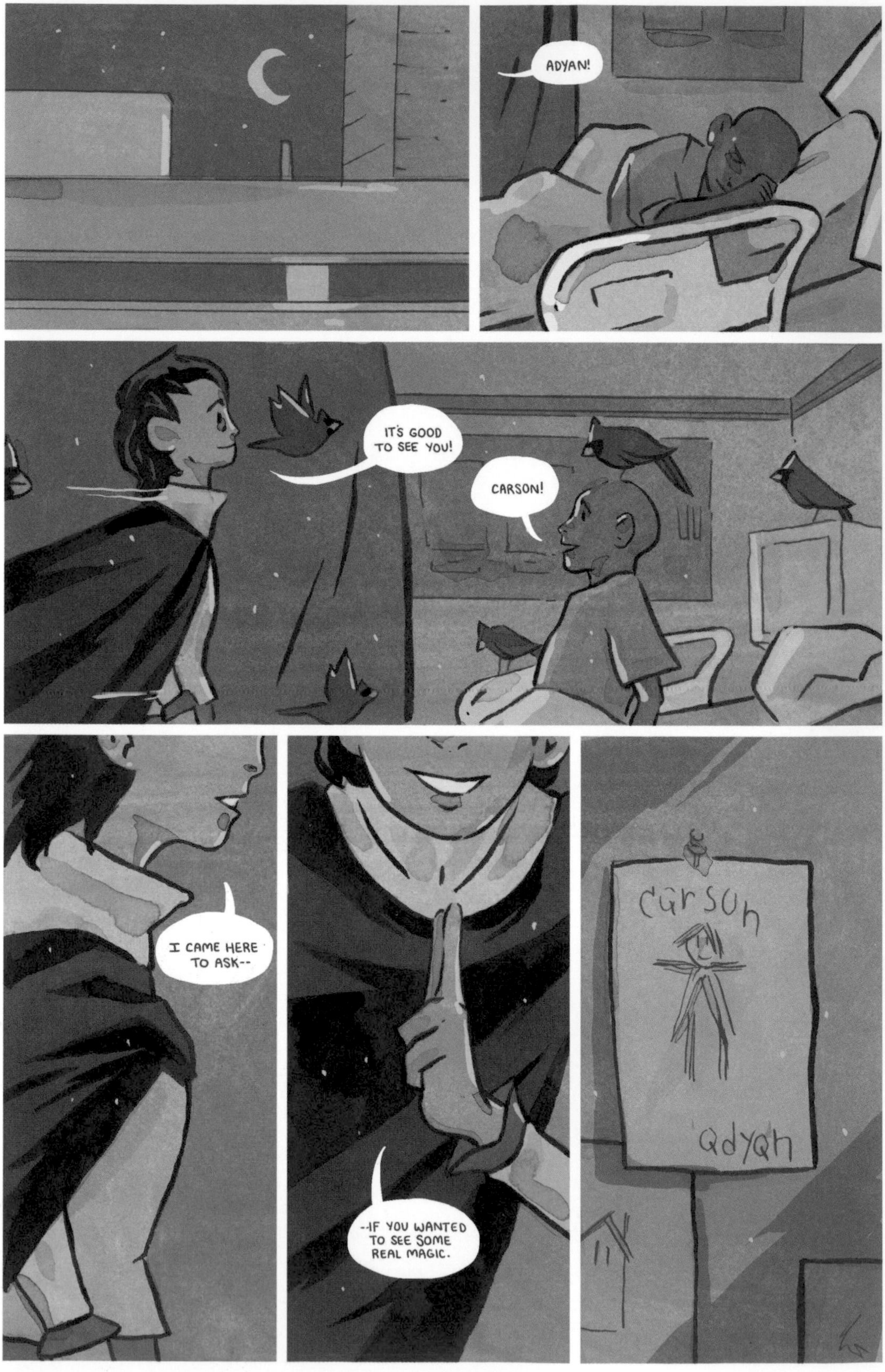
ADYAN!
IT'S GOOD TO SEE YOU!
CARSON!
I CAME HERE TO ASK--
-IF YOU WANTED TO SEE SOME REAL MAGIC.
carson
adyan

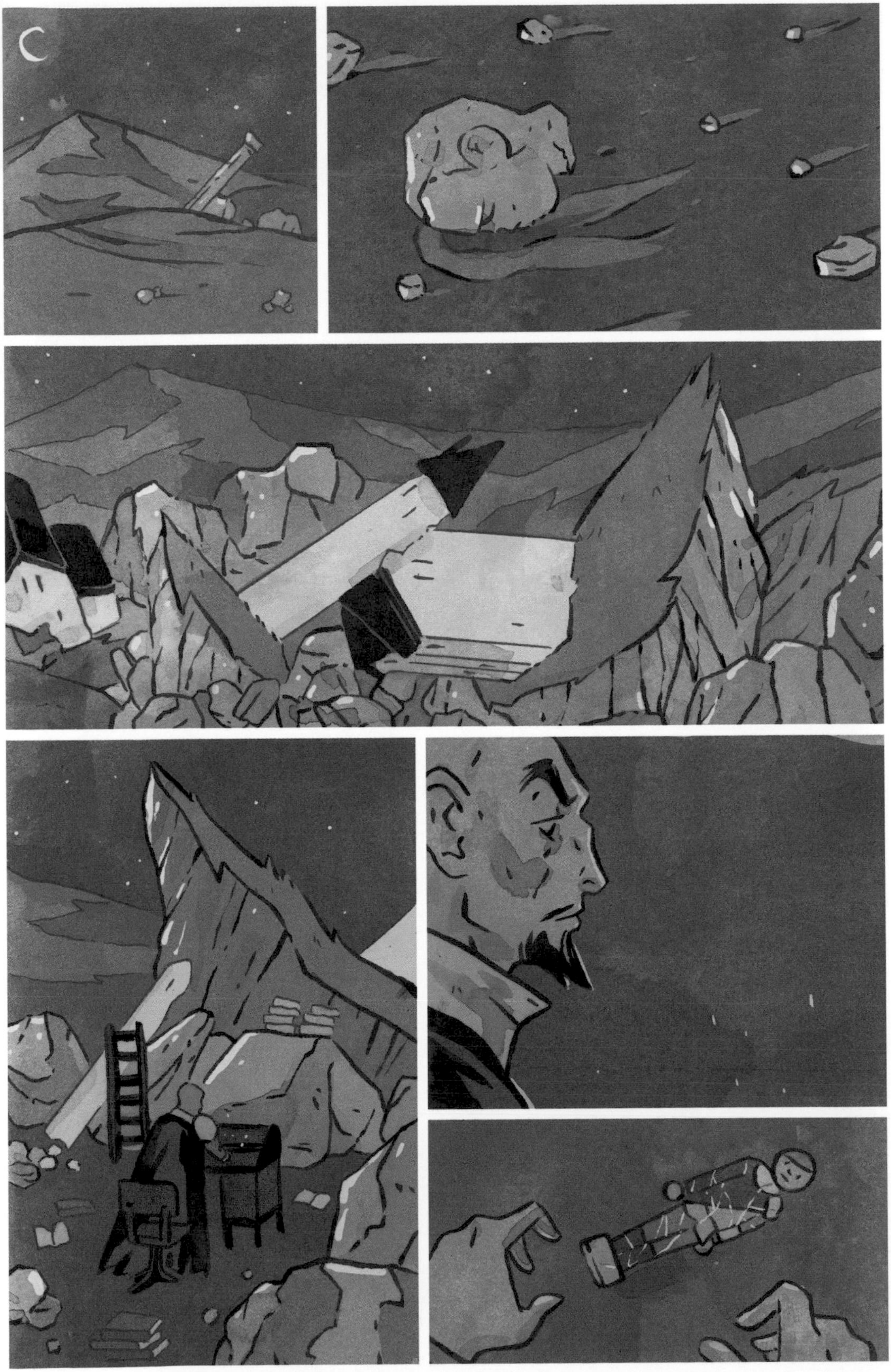

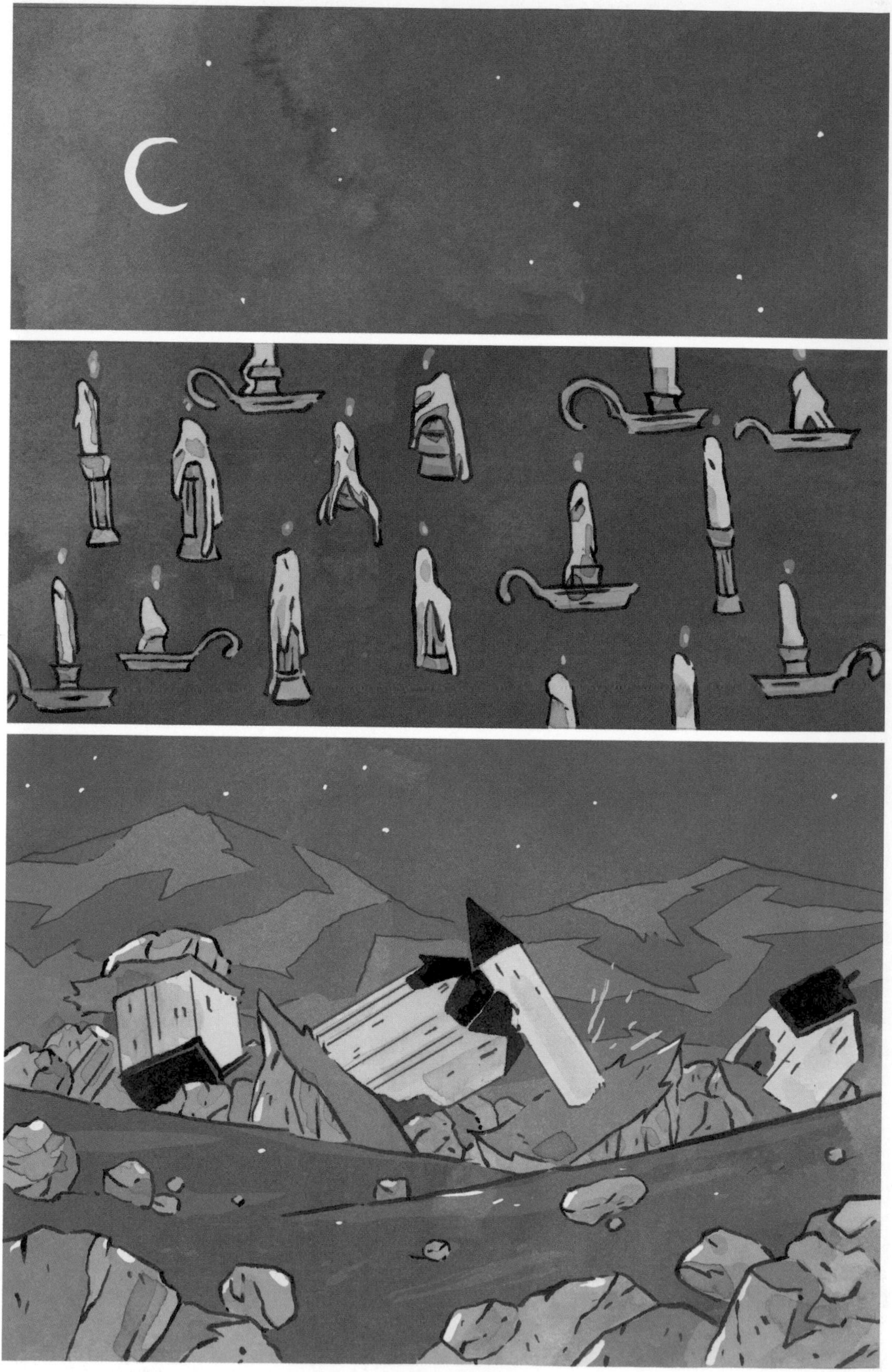

The End

About the Author

S. M. Vidaurri was born and raised in northern New Jersey. He received a BFA in Illustration from the University of the Arts in Philadelphia. His previously published works include *Jim Henson's The Storyteller: Witches,* and the original graphic novel *Iron: Or, the War After.*

www.smvidaurri.com/

Acknowledgements

I had a lot of help making Iscariot and I would like to thank the following:

My mother's support was invaluable and I will always be grateful for it. I am thankful my grandfather tried his best to keep me on task and reminded me that "I better get some pages done!" And I'm always in debt to Tabitha and Chelsea for their understanding. And of course Kat, Strider, Kumquat and Ingrid for all their help.

A big heartfelt thank you to Rebecca Taylor and Cameron Chittock for diving into Iscariot head first with me and helping me navigate my process. Thank you to Shannon Watters, Kelsey Dieterich, and Leigh Luna for all the amazing work they put into the book behind the scenes.

Thank you Godni, Kalpana and everyone at AFreeBird.org for letting me tag along and answering my questions.

Thank you to all my friends who gave their input into Iscariot when I wasn't sure: Thomas & Alec Hanslowe, Brian McDonald, Kevin Farrell, Coleman Engle, Josh Trujillo, Crista Castro, Leia Weathington, Tim Durning and Alex Eckman-Lawn.

Also, for their inspiration: Carson McCullers, Fyodor Dostoevsky, Hayao Miyazaki, and Neil Gaiman.

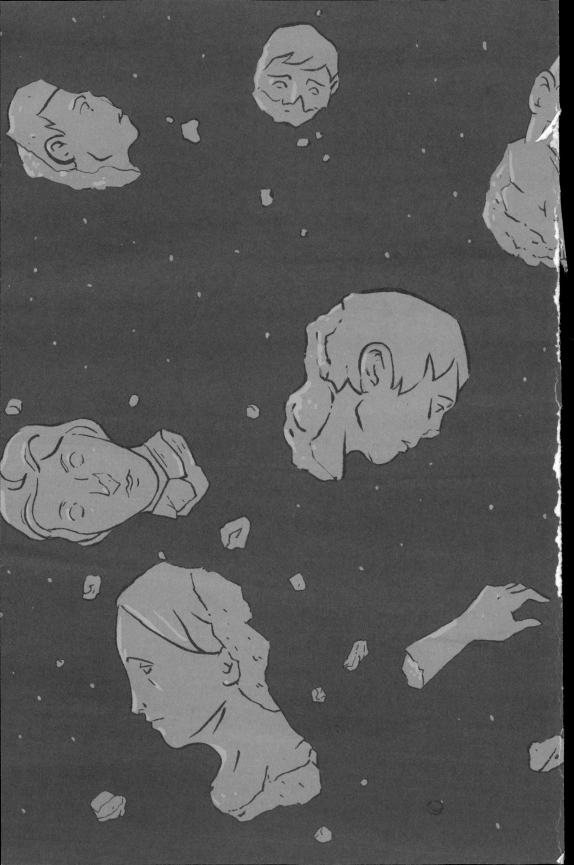